Unmending the Veil

Lisa Heaton

This book is a work of fiction. Names, characters, places, and themes are the product of the author's imagination or are used fictitiously. Any resemblance to actual events or persons, living or dead, is coincidental.

Published by: Lisa Heaton Books
5136 Stewarts Ferry Pike
Mt. Juliet, TN 37122

Copyright © 2012 Lisa Heaton

All rights reserved. No part of this book may be reproduced or transmitted in any form or by any means, electronic or mechanical, including photocopying, recording, or by any information storage and retrieval system, without permission in writing from the publisher.

ISBN: 1-4812-9030-4
ISBN: 13: 9781481290302

Scripture taken from the HOLY BIBLE, NEW INTERNATIONAL VERSION Copyright © 1973, 1978, 1984, by International Bible Society. Used by permission of Zondervan Publishing House. All rights reserved.

The "NIV" and "New International Version" trademarks are registered in the United States Patent and Trademark Office by International Bible Society. Use of either trademark requires the permission of International Bible Society.

King James Version, SLIMLINE™ REFERENCE EDITION. Nashville: Thomas Nelson, Inc., 1989

Dedication

"But by the grace of God I am what I am, and His grace to me was not without effect." 1 Corinthians 15:10

For Jesus ~ The Author and Perfecter of my faith ~ I am no longer a mess because of You.

Teresa, without you this novel would be collecting dust. Thank you for encouraging me, pushing me, believing in me, and singing prayers of faith for me. Always, you show me Jesus. God knew what He was doing when He gave me you. I could have no better bff.

For Kelly and Zack, thanks for your patience as I disappeared for hours on end. Thank you for encouraging me. Thanks for loving me. Kelly, your hard work allows me to do what I love most, writing.

For Adam, as you work on your testimony, know that I love you unconditionally.

For my mom, Nancy, if anyone has ever loved me and believed I could do great things, it's you!

Prologue

~The Dream~

Robin knelt in the thick mud, trembling, listening for Mike, certain he would find her soon enough. Crouching under a row of dense brush, she feared she was still exposed. It was after midnight, a time she should have been hidden by darkness, but the moon was full and cast a telling glow over her. If her white gown against the dark foliage didn't give her away, then the sounds of her raspy breathing surely would. Every labored breath burned deep into her lungs, and a piercing sensation ripped through her right side. Likely, her ribs were broken again. She knew the feeling. Hearing Mike in the not-so-far-off distance, sloshing through the mud, she covered her mouth with her hand hoping to muffle the sound. As he drew nearer, Robin quit breathing altogether. He came to a stop just a few feet from where she hid. Through the openings of the spindly brush, she could see his ankles, and with no escape route open, she watched helplessly as he took those final steps toward her.

"I told you not to run," Mike snarled.

Grabbing Robin by the arms, he lifted her off the ground, her muddy, bare feet dangling in mid-air.

His breath reeked of whiskey, and as it usually did, the smell of it nauseated her. In the past year she had come to equate the smell of alcohol with fear and punishment. As Mike staggered and swayed in his drunkenness, barely able keep himself upright, Robin searched his eyes, hoping for some sign of recognition, something to indicate he even knew who she was. This night, he was a stranger and treated her as if he never loved her at all.

Robin sobbed, pleading with him, "Mike, you love me. Please stop this."

Un-phased by her pleas, he slung her roughly to the ground.

At first sliding through the mud, Robin skidded to an abrupt halt as her face collided with a large protruding tree root. Tasting a peculiar mixture of blood and dirt in her mouth, she grabbed wildly at the ground, at the tree, anything, trying to crawl away from his reach. When she glanced behind her, she could see he was doubled over with his hands on his knees for support, heaving. Often the sickness would be the end of the violence, but unsure this night, she pulled herself up onto her knees and began to crawl away.

When she felt his hands wrap firmly around her ankles, she began to kick, but easily enough Mike flipped her over and reached down to pick her up. He was angry still but crying at this point.

"I won't let you leave me," he sobbed.

Tossing her over his shoulder, he stomped back through the mud the way they had come.

1

Sitting atop the steep stone steps, a painstakingly crafted stairway embedded into the earth over a century before, Robin watched as small fishing boats began to appear out of the mist that often blanketed the lake. In June, while days were warmer and sunny in New Hampshire, early morning at sunrise was still cool and crisp. Crisp enough, in fact, that when she breathed in, the air stung her nose a bit. While refreshing for the most part, there was something about it that took her back, made her remember running and the sting of chilly air burning her nose and lungs. She had run the night before, not in actuality but in her sleep. Running and crying, she sought a place to hide.

The word *dream* wasn't one she used to describe what occurred in her mind at night, as a dream to her brought with it notions of good things, daydreams or dreams of a future and such. Nor would she use the term nightmare, since a nightmare was usually something fictitious or made up. What she experienced some nights, more frequently in the past weeks than had happened in many years, was the reliving of the end of things. It was the night that put an end to who she was and where she belonged. In the wake of it, she became what she had come to call "a misplaced object."

Burning off the mist almost entirely, the sun rose higher still. A boater waved. She waved in return, thankful to see signs of life and summer as Lake Winnipesaukee exploded with color and vacationers flooded the area inns, cabins, and summer homes. It was her favorite time of year. Peering behind her at the charming old mansion – her home year-round, she had long since decided if you must be misplaced, there was no lovelier place to be. While others had to wait for summer vacation to enjoy the scenery, she lived out her life with breathtaking views in her backyard. If there was a possibility of being near to God, it was here.

With regret she stood and took one final look out at the smooth water. It was just after six, and within the hour the grounds and water would come alive as more people began to stir about. The morning and the sunrise had worked its wonder though. Just as it did most mornings, it helped to clear away the shadows from her mind, at least in part. Still, the fog of a fitful night was heavy upon her. Her eyes burned from interrupted sleep and her mouth was dry, but the morning brought with it certainty that the ordeal was hushed at least for another day.

Robin pushed through the swinging door and moved into the large sunny kitchen. She had to grin at the sight before her. Emma, the inn's owner and her best friend, was standing there with a muffin hanging from her mouth, stirring a large bowl of pancake batter. Having known her all of her life, it wasn't often Emma's loveliness struck her as it did at that moment. When someone new to the area saw Emma and was so obviously taken aback by her beauty, Robin was again aware of it, but this morning there was a fresh appreciation. In her early fifties, Emma was more stunning than any woman twenty years her junior, Robin included at only thirty.

Robin sat on a stool and asked, "Do you need any help?"

"Not so much," Emma drawled, her Southern accent even more pronounced than usual, "but you can get the sausage out."

Robin went to the refrigerator, stopping on the way to plant a kiss on Emma's cheek and adjust her hair clip, a little butterfly glued to the end of a brown bobby pin. Emma liked all things winged and colorful, so most days her auburn hair was adorned with some sort of flying creature.

Attempting to sound more chipper than she felt, Robin asked, "How'd you sleep?"

"Like a log. How 'bout you?" Emma knew before asking but hoped to discreetly open the door for Robin to talk to her.

"I've had better nights," Robin admitted.

"Are you okay?"

She had heard Robin calling out in her sleep but had learned years ago that it had to run its course.

"I will be once you get breakfast ready. I'm starving this morning."

Not surprisingly, Robin changed the subject. Emma had come to expect it. Rarely did she discuss her past life, and in truth, Emma could hardly blame her.

"Give me a few minutes, and I'll have something ready for you."

Emma watched Robin as she moved toward the large picture window facing lakeside. With such a faraway expression on her face, Robin looked eerily like her father. Many things about her reminded Emma of him. Robin's hair was long with just a bit of wave to it, and just as his was, a rich, dark brown, reminding Emma of a strong cup of coffee. No taller than five foot four, she had a determined, unwavering presence about her. Though Robin took on a quiet, distant air from time to time, she was always kind to everyone. Her father's nature was very similar. Before her life took such an abrupt turn, Robin laughed often and easily, just as he did. Sadly, that part of her was shrouded now, the real her hidden. As if blanketed by a funeral pall for years on end, Robin was no longer among the living. How familiar that trait was to a woman who had responded precisely the same to death and loss. *Two peas in empty pods — that was them*, Emma thought.

"Are you sure you're all right?"

"Yes," then Robin added with a bit more honesty, "it shakes me up for a while, but by midday it usually goes away." That wasn't exactly true. It never completely went away.

What she needed was time alone to reel in her emotions, so Robin told Emma, "I should go down and check on the Willow. I know Becky cleaned it yesterday, but I want to look the cabin over for myself. That's the one reserved for the summer, for the teacher."

As she glanced at the clock, Emma noted she was running behind schedule. Feeding an army took more stirring and flipping and much less talking. She asked, "Is anyone else up?"

"I haven't seen anyone else stirring about yet."

Emma wanted to say more, something that might help to ease Robin's pain, but she found nothing came to mind, so she settled for, "Okay, I'll see you for breakfast."

Pushing through the screen door, Robin stepped out onto the covered porch. Standing for a moment, she inhaled deeply, beginning to feel more like herself again. The higher the sun rose, the more her spirits lifted along with it. The haze was subsiding. As many times as she tried to convince herself it was over and done, there was that small part of her that wondered if it would ever be finished. She lived her life as if something large and looming teetered overhead, especially over the past few weeks. Somehow she sensed a storm was brewing, one she could never face and survive.

With every blink of the morning, she saw Mike's face, not his angry face but the one of shock, disbelief, and finally fear. Rubbing her eyes, she tried to force the scene from her mind, but her stomach began to churn at the unsettling recollection. Heaving slightly, she covered her mouth with her hand and moved the other to her stomach.

In order to tackle the day ahead, she had to clear her mind and begin again. No matter how haunting her night terrors were, she simply had to choose to step away from them, if only for today. Taking another deep breath, she scanned the scenery before her, hoping the serenity her eyes absorbed could somehow be drawn into her chest and fill her with peace. Something familiar touched her deep inside, not true peace, not the kind she had known as a girl, but more of a stillness that would at least carry her through another day without crumbling.

The inn was nestled into a massive hillside with spectacular views of the lake. Stone steps led to a level lakeshore area of about fifty feet, then to a boat dock with a boathouse attached to the left of it. Emma owned two of the boats moored there, but the others belonged to guests at the inn. The inn had ten guest quarters: four rooms on the second level of the main house and six cabins overlooking the lake. Cabins were usually rented weekly, whereas the rooms in the main house were used for shorter getaways. So at most, there were ten families to care for during peak season, which was manageable.

Her first summer working at the inn, Robin put in fifteen hours a day and still barely kept up. Now, though, she had it down to a science. During the spring and summer months, they brought in extra help, so it wasn't quite as bad as that first year. The busy season was the best by far, as it kept her tangled mind occupied and focused on things other than the reliving and rehashing of history. Unable yet to look forward, at least there was relief in not looking behind.

Climbing the three wooden steps leading to the porch of the Willow, Robin turned back toward the water. As she watched the morning sun dance along the water, she knew she would never tire of such a sight. This was her favorite cabin, as it had the finest view at the inn. As a young girl, she stayed in that very cabin with her parents when they visited Emma during the summer. While Emma pled for them to stay in the main house, her father insisted he felt more comfortable having his own space. He liked the nearness to the lake. There were plenty of shade trees surrounding the small cabin, yet there was a nice clearing leading directly to the lakeshore, the ideal setting.

Once inside, she scrutinized the kitchen before walking into each of the two small bedrooms. She didn't doubt Becky's cleaning ability, but Robin had always made it a point to check the cabins and rooms prior to each guest's arrival. As she was leaving the second bedroom, the front door of the cabin abruptly swung open, and a man tossed a duffle bag through the doorway.

Quickly, the man stopped, stammering, "Oh, I'm sorry. I must have the wrong cabin." He reached for the bag.

"No, wait." Moving to the door, Robin assured him, "You have the right cabin. I work here. I was just checking things out to make sure it was ready for you."

Stepping out onto the porch, she got a clearer look at him. For some reason, maybe familiarity with her own teachers, her expectation was that of a conservatively dressed, tie-wearing bald man with horn-rimmed glasses. This man was like no teacher she had in school. He was tall and lean, probably six feet or more. With thick sandy hair and striking blue eyes, she found him surprisingly handsome. He wore tattered jeans, an old t-shirt, and oddly, no shoes.

When she realized she was staring at him, Robin laughed softly. "Well, everything's fine here. I'll be going. Enjoy your stay."

"Chris Wheeler," he said as he dropped the bag again and held out his hand.

Robin took his hand and nodded. "I know. I spoke with you on the phone."

Completely out of character, Chris was at a loss for words and bewildered as to why. He stood there for what eventually became an awkward moment, until he finally stammered, "Well, I'll run back to the car and get the rest of my gear."

Finding the silent moment amusing, Robin thought she caught a trace of embarrassment on his face. In an effort to lessen the awkwardness of the moment, she offered, "Do you need any help?"

"Sure, thanks."

He walked behind her as they moved toward the back of the cabin where he had parked his car. Realizing she never mentioned her name, he wondered if it was intentional. It seemed to be. She was kind, yet somehow impersonal. Her voice was sweet, though, and with her subtle accent, he supposed she wasn't originally from the region. Though he couldn't see them at the moment, what he first noticed were her eyes—they were dark, velvety brown and obviously had some power to cause a chemical meltdown in his brain. Soft and fluttery as she blinked slowly and quite innocently, there was something about them that disturbed him. They seemed distant somehow; hollow maybe, as if she were looking through him and not at him.

Leaning into his trunk, he grabbed the lightest of his bags and handed it to her, saying, "I appreciate your help."

She grabbed another of the heavier bags. "No problem."

"Hey, that's pretty heavy." Then he watched as she picked the bag up effortlessly.

"I've got it."

"Wow, a real mountain woman."

Robin actually laughed out loud. Having always considered herself slightly on the girly side, she saw great humor in him calling her that. If he knew her better, he would take it back.

As she walked back to the cabin alongside him, she decided she liked him. He didn't seem to take himself too seriously. While some guests could be quite difficult, this man would be an easy one. On the heels of that thought, an unsettling tightness gripped her chest. As she approached the porch, she felt unusually inspired to make a dash for it, to run off to the main house and pretend she never met him. It was something about the look in his eyes or the way he looked at her. Or maybe even, it was the dimples that formed when he smiled at her. He was unnervingly handsome, and she found herself flustered.

When she dropped the bags inside the doorway, Chris noticed she intentionally didn't enter the cabin again. Instead, she turned to go back to the car, so he called behind her, "Hey, I can get the rest of that stuff later."

Robin stopped at the end of the porch and shrugged. "If you'd like," and with that she turned to go, saying over her shoulder, "See you around."

Standing on the porch, Chris watched her move toward the main house. Finally, he figured it out, what had bothered him before. When she smiled, there was some disconnect, as if it never really reached her eyes. There was something lifeless about them, kind but somehow indifferent. Still

Unmending the Veil

a bit baffled by the awkwardness of their encounter, he grabbed his bags from the porch and headed into the cabin.

Once inside, he wasn't at all disappointed. The photos online didn't do the place justice. The main living area was quite large with a stone fireplace directly across from the front door. A sofa faced the fireplace and two oversized armchairs flanked it. To the right was a small kitchen and on both sides of the fireplace was a bedroom, each with its own bathroom. All was in good order and recently updated.

Chris threw a bag onto the bed and sat, feeling tired already. It was early still, but he hadn't slept more than three hours the night before in anticipation of the trip. Lately, even when he did sleep well, tiredness seemed to plague him more and more. The lack of energy he was experiencing was new for him, so it was taking some getting used to. A slower pace was not a lifestyle he knew how to navigate.

Listening to the sound of utter quietness, a nonexistent luxury in his condo back in Boston, his mind began to jump around from thought to thought. Mostly, he thought of Vanessa. She was supposed to come with him for the first week of the trip but at the last minute decided she wasn't exactly camping material. Though he had been angry about it earlier, he now felt relieved. Stretching out on the bed, he replayed their last conversation over in his head.

In hopes of getting an early start, Chris arrived at Vanessa's place just before daylight. When he knocked on the door and she answered in her pajamas, he was immediately irritated.

"You said you would be dressed."

"Chris, I don't think this is a good idea after all."

"Why are you waiting until now to tell me? You couldn't have mentioned this yesterday?"

Frustrated by her lack of consideration, yet not wanting to say something he would later regret, Chris became silent. It was her idea to tag along, even though he all but said he wanted time alone. Exasperating him even further, had she not insisted, he would have never reserved a two-bedroom cabin.

Her eyes filled with tears as she said, "I've wanted to tell you, but then I decided I should go and be with you. I realize now I just can't. Things are so hectic at work. Maybe I can come out in a few weeks and we can..."

He interrupted her, saying, "Just say what you really mean."

For a moment he saw her hesitate, and in that moment, looking into her eyes, he found nothing more than pity there. In his heart he knew she was torn, and watching her struggle with her dilemma, he felt a wave of compassion for her. His tone softened considerably as he said, "It's okay. Tell me what you're feeling."

At his urging, Vanessa broke down. "This is just too much for me. I can't handle it. Believe me, I know how shallow this will sound, but I'm not up for ten days of self-analysis and life introspection."

"Where did you come up with that? Life introspection? That sounds like something you learned on a talk show." He sighed heavily. "Is that what you think I'm going for? I just want to spend time at the lake, away from the city."

He found himself feeling sorry for her. For quite some time he had known things weren't right between them, but it had been easier to stay with her than to get out. Now, he realized he wasn't being fair to her. How could he expect her to stand beside him through what he was facing?

"I really do care about you, but..." She started to cry again. "I'm just not strong enough to be with you through this." Kissing him softly on the cheek, she whispered. "I'm so sorry."

Chris put his arms around her and reassured her, "It really is okay. I understand."

As he looked around the small cabin, Chris had a feeling this was exactly where he needed to be. If Vanessa had come, he would have spent his time catering to her emotions rather than doing what he felt most led to do, spending the time he had left with God.

While Robin washed up at the kitchen sink, Emma moved in close behind her, asking, "Did you see him?"

She knew exactly who Emma was talking about, but playing innocent she asked, "See who?"

"Willow."

"His name is Chris Wheeler, and yes, I saw him."

"He was too early for check in, but who am I to turn him away?" Emma whistled and waved her dishtowel. "If I were a few years younger, why, he'd be in trouble."

"Oh, right! Listen to you. If he paid you any attention at all, you'd run and jump in the lake."

Robin laughed at the thought of Emma pursuing any man. She rarely dated. With sultry brown eyes and an hourglass figure, every unattached man in the surrounding county had made a play for her at one time or another. The only man she could remember Emma showing any interest in was Stan Cooper, the vet in a nearby town, but even he had never won Emma's heart. Robin had to believe no man ever would.

Emma laughed along with Robin, finding the idea just as funny. "I wouldn't go so far as to jump in the lake, but you're right, I'd run."

She popped Robin with her dishtowel. "Breakfast is on the sideboard. Go eat, sassy girl."

The buffet was loaded with every breakfast food imaginable. From hearty, Southern cooking to delicate pastries and waffles, each was displayed on extravagant serving dishes and platters. Breakfast was the only meal provided at the inn, so Emma insisted on doing it properly. The guests who stayed in the cabins were invited as well, so on any given morning during the summer months, the dining room was full of chatter and excitement over the day to come.

Sitting alone at a table near the window, Robin watched as Chris walked toward the inn. Though she had forgotten to mention breakfast to him, obviously Emma had remembered. He disappeared from sight for just a few seconds before he walked into the dining room. Crossing over to the buffet, he picked up a plate. It was then she noticed he still wore no shoes. She had a sense he was a man who drifted with the wind and envied him that.

As she watched him piling his plate high, she wondered if he had a girlfriend. Surely he did. When he turned to look at her, Robin was embarrassed that he found her staring at him as he had on the porch before. Smiling slightly, she turned her attention back to her food. Stabbing a piece of sausage with her fork, she twirled it around in her syrup. Just as she poked it into her mouth, and a dribble of syrup ran down her chin, he walked up to her table.

"Is this seat taken?"

Wiping her face, she scanned the room. There were at least ten empty chairs. What made him decide to sit there?

Hesitantly, she said, "Uh, no."

"May I sit with you?"

"Sure. I'm just about done, though."

He pulled out a chair and sat across from her. Pointing to her plate, he commented, "You've barely touched your food."

She chuckled, admitting, "This is my second plate."

"Wow, good job. You are a mountain woman."

He noticed how she tended to avoid making eye contact. *Skittish* was the term that came to mind, like a pup you might get from a shelter.

Robin stood and picked up her plate, saying, "Well, I hope you enjoy your breakfast. I'm going to get at it."

Without waiting for his response and determined to keep as much distance from this man as she could, she moved quickly away from the table.

He watched her walk away, and as she disappeared through the swinging door into the kitchen, Chris wondered what made her so distant. Maybe it was just her personality. Shrugging, he took his first bite.

As he scanned the dining room, he was again reassured of his decision to come. The room was large and ornate, almost overly so. Most impressive was that the entire back wall was made of glass and overlooked the covered porch, which in turn looked out toward the lake. The inn was situated on a narrow point of the lake, so from where he sat he could see clear across the water to the other side. It was a magnificent view, and he could hardly wait to paint it.

After finishing his first plate, and without reservation, he went back to the buffet and piled another high. What did he have to lose? Would it not be right for any dying man to eat bacon and plenty of it?

Robin sat her plate in the sink. Hanging her head, she closed her eyes and drew in a deep breath. Chris was so handsome, and she was so lonely. A man like that frightened her. Never once, in all the years she had worked at the inn, had she been attracted to a guest. Most disturbing for her, it wasn't just a weekend ahead to try to avoid him; it was the entire summer. She would, though.

"What's wrong with you?"

Becky had walked up behind her so quietly, it caused her to jump. Robin laughed, saying, "Nothing."

Pushing thoughts of the teacher out of her mind, Robin asked, "Where've you been? Emma's looking for you."

"I went to the station with Tommy. He wanted to gas up the boat and get bait to take a group out fishing."

"I came up to your room, assuming you were still asleep. But then I guess I forgot how much you like going to get gas and bait," Robin teased.

It was no secret why she had gone with Tommy. Becky was looking for Brad Parker. Having met Brad the summer before, her first year working at the inn, Becky went out with him for several weeks, but then he suddenly began avoiding her. Robin suspected things went further than Becky intended, which would explain her meltdown when Brad dropped her the way he did. The remainder of her summer was spent heartbroken, and this summer could easily shape up to be the same. It was obvious that, even though the guy had really hurt her, Becky still had some glimmer of hope of running into him again. While it made her sad to see Becky so hopeful, what seemed apparent to Robin was something the girl would have to learn the hard way. No matter what Robin said, Becky was determined.

Noting the change in her appearance, Robin suspected that if Becky did run into Brad, he would certainly regret letting her go. She had dropped a few pounds over the winter and highlighted her already blond hair. Even before the changes, though, she was beautiful, inside and out. This year, however, there was something a bit more sophisticated about her; she seemed less a girl and more of a woman. Though she was only nineteen, Becky was a very mature and bright girl, other than her choice in men.

"Have you seen the guy from the Willow?" Emma asked Becky as she stepped in from the dining room, her eyes sparkling with mischief.

Becky's face lit up. "No. Who is it?"

"While you two old hens gossip, I'm going to work. Is Tommy outside?" Robin asked.

"Yes. He's out on the dock and in a *mood*."

After Robin left, Emma filled Becky in on Chris, and of course Becky had to see for herself. Peeking through the swinging door into the dining room, she turned back to Emma and whispered, "Wow, he's gorgeous. How old do you think he is?"

Emma chuckled softly as she peeked in just over Becky's head.

"Too old for you, little girl."

"I'm nineteen."

"I imagine he's at least thirty five."

"That's ancient." Becky giggled, knowing her comment would get a rise out of Emma.

"Hush. That's young, very, very young."

Emma walked back to the sink, saying, "You know, he would be perfect for Robin."

"Yeah!" Becky snorted sarcastically.

Opening the refrigerator, Becky removed a large bowl of grapes and took them to the work island as she asked, "Are these clean?"

Nodding, Emma continued, "He would."

Becky busied herself filling a crystal dish with the grapes. Plucking one from the stem, she popped it into her mouth as she said, "Robin won't get close enough to notice how good looking he is."

"Oh, she's noticed. I can tell."

Turning rather solemn, Becky asked, "Did you hear her last night?"

Becky's room was on the other side of Emma's, away from Robin's, but still she had heard her screaming. It was bone-chilling screams that made her want to cry. Trapped in her nightmare, Robin pled and begged. Shaking her head, Becky tried to clear the memory of the horrible noise. It happened only once the year before, and it was just as unnerving now as it was then.

"Yes, I heard it."

Emma looked out through the back window. Holding her coffee cup, she watched thoughtfully as Robin moved quickly down the stairway and toward the dock. Her heart ached for her, and she wondered if her sorrow would ever fade. It had been five years since Robin came to live with her, and every moment of it was a joy, but for Robin the time had been spent emotionally on the run from her past. A life that used to be filled with such happiness turned tragic beyond repair. Grieving for her, Emma hoped that someday healing would come.

When Robin reached the dock, she found Tommy in the boathouse working on an inboard motor.

"Is something wrong?" The last thing she needed was for one of the boats to be out of commission.

He glanced up at her and then back at his task. "No. I'm just replacing the spark plugs. I filled her up this morning and got some bait. Does the old couple still want to go out?"

"Yes. I told them you would be ready at eight."

Noticing he seemed annoyed, she asked, "Are you okay?"

Shaking his head, he sighed and asked, "Who's the guy Becky is looking for?"

Robin hid a grin, suspecting he had a crush on Becky. The way he stammered when she talked to him was almost comical, yet very sweet.

"Just a guy from last year." It wasn't her place to tell him any more than that.

"When she said she wanted to go this morning..."

Looking out across the water, Tommy felt foolish. He thought Becky wanted to be with him, but when she started talking about that guy, pointing out his house, he realized she had no interest in him.

"If it makes you feel any better, she's passing up a great thing."

Robin really liked Tommy. He had answered an ad for the job, and though he was only twenty, he had all the necessary experience. His family had owned boats all of his life and he certainly knew much more than she did about them. After meeting him in person, the decision was an easy one. In his junior year at a business school in Boston, he was sharp and mature for his age. Tall and somewhat lanky, he had a kind, handsome face, and his manner was, though quiet at times, still witty and amusing. She had to guess he would surely make something of himself someday. Impressed by his work ethic, something not always proven when they hired young people, not once had Robin regretted hiring him.

As Robin walked back up to the main house, she passed Chris on the way down. The sight of him made her feel peculiar in some way. It was obvious he was trying to be friendly, but she still couldn't bring herself to talk to him comfortably. He made her nervous or uneasy, she wasn't exactly sure which, but it was unpleasant.

"Hey, there." He smiled at her.

"Hi." Robin had to force herself to stop and seem casual.

Pointing to the dock, Chris asked, "Do those boats belong to the inn?"

"Two of them. As a matter of fact, Tommy is about to take the larger one out fishing if you're interested."

"No. I'm not much on fishing. I just wanted to go out and do some painting."

"Painting?"

"Yes. That's the main reason I'm here."

She asked, "Do you know enough about boats to take one out alone?"

"My dad was a fisherman. I ought to."

"But you don't like fishing?"

"No, never did."

Chris liked the way the wind picked up tendrils of Robin's hair and whipped them around her face and the way she was constantly pulling at them and tucking them behind her ears. As if hearing his thoughts, she removed a band from her wrist and pulled her hair back into a ponytail.

When she said nothing more, he asked, "So, is there another boat I can take?"

"Sure, see Tommy. He should have the keys."

"Thanks." Before she turned to leave, he asked, "You're Robin, right?" He had heard Emma call her by name.

"Yes."

"Well, nice to formally meet you, Robin."

"You, too."

Chris observed how she looked past him as she replied, not directly at him. Cheeks flushing, she seemed almost nervous. When she continued on up the stairway, he watched her for a moment. She was intriguing to be sure, but timing was never his strong suit.

As Robin reached the porch, she turned and gazed back at the dock. The wind was blowing briskly, and she could see it ruffle Chris' hair. He really did seem like a nice guy, but there was no room for that in her life. Her only goal was to live quietly at the inn. Just as Emma had managed for so many years, her intention was to stay as far away from men as she could.

2

Unable to sleep, Chris made his way out to the water's edge and sat on the bank watching as the moonlight reflected off the water. Having been there a week, this was the brightest night he had seen so far. The moon was full, and there were millions of stars twinkling overhead, reminding him of his smallness and the infinitesimal space he took up in the grand scheme of things. It was a magnificent evening, one much too beautiful to miss. Slowing down and appreciating such moments was his latest preoccupation. How many wonders had he missed due to busyness, or if not that, out of a sheer lack of comprehension that he was living in a world so extraordinary?

Occasionally, he would see the slight ripple of a fish popping to the surface, but soon the water would again become still. It reminded him of his dad, the fisherman. As a boy, for hours on end they would sit, staring at the water, just waiting for something to grab on to the line and cause a ripple. Some days nothing ever bit; some days they caught more than they meant to. Always, though, he hated that silent waiting. If given the opportunity again to sit and fish with his dad, would he not value such a moment even more than the vastness of the stars and the endlessness of the heavens?

Supposing it was close to midnight, he stood and turned to go, but when he noticed someone running toward the water, he froze and watched as the female figure touched her first foot onto the wooden planks of the dock. Running still, she continued on until she reached the end of the structure and there stopped abruptly. As she was standing directly under the glow of the moonlight, he realized he was watching Robin. Surprised to see her there alone so late at night, he remained silent and observed her as she stood perfectly still, gazing out into the dark water. Standing on the bank just to her left, he could see her as clearly as if it were daylight, but he was certain she was unable to see him in the shadows. Though he should have turned to go, he found he was too fascinated by her presence, there under the warm blanket of moonlight.

A brisk wind swept in from the water, blowing her nightgown, silhouetting her small frame. Her hair was blowing lightly behind her. In the splendor of the moment, all things had gone silent. The sounds of the night were quieted; even the whistle of the wind was hushed. Chris was captivated by her. It was like watching a scene from a movie, the haunting kind that stays with you for days on end, and he stood paralyzed in anticipation of what she might do next. Then unexpectedly, as if snapping out of a trance, she lifted her arms overhead and dove gracefully into the air, entering the water with barely a sound. Running toward the dock, Chris was preparing to jump in after her. All he could think of was what a foolish thing to do. Alone in the dark, she could drown. When he reached the end of the pier, he stood helpless, watching her swim farther from the shore. She swam hard and strong, as if she were pushing herself to the utmost limits. Knowing he couldn't catch her if he tried, he simply watched as she stroked arm over arm. What would possess her to do such a thing?

As he walked back to his cabin, he was relieved he fought the urge to call out to her. If he had, he was quite certain it would have been an invasion of some private moment that was hers alone. Each time he studied her, he found a distinct sadness in her eyes that spoke of distant pain. This night he wondered if he had caught a glimpse of her therapy. People were known to do stranger things when running from sorrow. It was in that moment the Lord revealed to him that the vacant look in her eyes was deep and debilitating sorrow. Robin was broken.

Emma sat on the porch watching as Robin jumped into the dark water. Hearing the horrific screams, then the sound of Robin's bedroom door creaking as it opened, she knew where she would go. Since Robin's arrival, Emma always watched as she swam alone in the darkness. Early on, she feared that Robin might swim out and never return. It was a fear that haunted her. At first, when the dreams came, Emma was unable to sleep soundly, always fearing Robin would go to the lake and she wouldn't hear her. Emma quickly learned, however, the sounds of screaming and pleading alerted her without fail.

When Emma saw the tall figure run out onto the dock, she stood, prepared to go out there until she realized it was Chris. He probably thought Robin was crazy for diving into the dark and chilly water. Maybe she was, but it was the only way she could shake the dreams when they came for her, her only place to run.

Tears sprang to Emma's eyes. Covering her face, she tried to shake the horrible image from her mind. It was the memory of Robin's appearance after surviving such a brutal attack five years before. Barely recognizable, her face was so swollen and battered it had taken over a month for the swelling and deep purple bruising to fade completely. Even still, her wounds inside were far from mended. Emma's own heartbreak of some thirty years before paled in comparison to Robin's. Often, she wondered how Robin continued on under such a heavy burden.

Seeing that Robin had gotten back to the dock safely, Emma stood and quietly made her way back into the house. At the top of the stairway, she met Becky coming out of the restroom.

"Is she okay?"

"She will be." Emma patted Becky on the cheek, wishing that were true. "Go back to bed, sweetie. I'm rolling your tail out early in the morning."

Alone in her room, she waited for Robin's footsteps. Then, hearing the familiar squeak of Robin's door, Emma switched off her light and began to cry.

Hours later, still sitting in the dim light of his cabin, Chris worked in front of his easel. With his eyes closed, he pictured Robin standing there in the moonlight. Her image was burned vividly into his mind, even down to the whipping of the wind against her gown and hair. He was easily able to draw the dock and the water and even the moonlight, but he could never capture the delicate silhouette he saw when he closed his eyes. Chris studied his canvas and realized, the portrait was everything he had seen, everything but her.

Behind the counter in the lobby, Robin braced herself for a confrontation as Mr. Jenkins stormed toward her. The look on his face was already a declaration of war. He and his wife had checked in just a week before, and so far he had complained about everything from the soap to the fishing.

Smiling, she offered, "Good morning, Mr. Jenkins. What can I do for you?"

He only scowled in return as he insisted, "I would like to be moved to another room."

Patiently, she asked, "Is there a problem with the room you're in now?"

"Yes, I'd say. Last night, in the middle of the night, someone began screaming at the top of their lungs. Even when it stopped, I lay awake for hours. It was the worst sound I've ever heard."

Feeling the blood drain from her face, deeply embarrassed, Robin was prepared to apologize. "I'm sorry, that…"

"It was either someone playing a horrible joke or…well, I'm not sure what, but I refuse to go through that again. I mean, waking from a dead sleep like that could give an old man a heart attack."

For the first time she saw what seemed to be a trace of vulnerability in the crotchety old man.

"Mr. Jenkins, I apologize, but that was…"

Emma rounded the corner in time to hear much of Robin's exchange with Mr. Jenkins.

"Robin, can you see to Mr. Wheeler?" she interrupted. "He's on the back porch and has a question about the shore tour. I told him you would be right out."

Emma turned to Mr. Jenkins and gave him her best smile. Looping her arm through his, she bragged, "Why, Mr. Jenkins, you're looking quite dapper this morning."

Embarrassed and about to cry, Robin slammed through the door and stepped out onto the back porch looking for Chris. He wasn't there. She quickly looked back inside before starting toward the steps, trying to figure out where he might have gone.

"I just wanted to get you away from Mr. Jenkins."

Emma walked through the screen door and immediately grabbed Robin into her arms. "I'm so sorry, sweetie."

"I'm the one who's sorry. I don't know why it's happening again or what to do to make it stop."

Emma was rubbing the back of her head softly. When Robin first came there to live, the dreams happened most nights, but eventually they seemed to taper off.

As much as she hated to bring it up, Emma said, "I know you must realize, it's been almost five years and…"

She knew where the conversation would lead, so Robin pulled away from Emma's embrace and cut her off. "Look, I was thinking maybe I should move to the Birchwood. Since the Taylors canceled, I can stay there until someone else needs it."

Robin turned, walked to the edge of the porch, and crossed her arms over her chest. Bowing her head, she admitted, "I think I could use the time alone anyway."

"Hummingbird, I've always told you, you are welcome to stay in one of the cabins, for good if you want."

Emma's heart broke at the sight before her. Robin's shoulders slumped under the weight of the load she carried. She reached out and moved Robin's hair from her shoulder and smoothed it down her back, saying, "I don't want to see you turn out like me. There's so much more to life. I hate to see you live like this. Maybe you should talk to someone who would know how to help you."

Emma had tried over the years to get her to open up, but Robin refused to talk about that dreadful night or even the things that happened before.

Robin glanced up at Emma. "Turning out like you wouldn't be all that bad."

"You know what I mean. Don't stop living, Robin. Look at the years I've wasted because of a broken heart."

"I don't think you can call what I have a broken heart."

She looked down, wanting to believe her own words. Her case was truly different. Emma was hanging on to lost love, but Robin was trying to escape it.

"I know. You have a broken spirit, and I think maybe that's worse." Emma reached out and rubbed her cheek. "We're damaged goods, you and me. I just want more for you. You know how much I love you. You're all I have in this world, you and your mom."

Robin put her arms around Emma, deliberating her words, *damaged goods*. Though Emma had used the term for herself, this was the first time she had ever included her in that, but it was true. Robin was damaged goods, and she had no doubt she would never be whole again.

Chris was standing at the water's edge. From his line of vision, he could see Robin and Emma on the porch, embracing. He wasn't sure what their relationship was, but it was evident they were especially close. Based on how comfortable they seemed together, he wondered if they might be related. Determined to ask the next chance he got, he began to walk toward the inn. When the two women noticed his approach, they disappeared quickly inside. He was beginning to take it personally.

Having slept but a few hours, Chris was tired, but no matter how hard he had tried to drift off, the image of Robin jumping into the water kept floating through his mind. Something was wrong with her, no doubt. She was troubled, which was likely what caused her to keep her distance. He would almost rather think it was a distant personality. Instead, he now knew she was seriously wounded. That made him sad for her, and as usual, eager to help.

While in Robin's room packing her things, Emma felt terribly sad knowing Robin wouldn't be as close, but more than anything, Emma wanted her to be where she felt most comfortable.

What had been troubling Emma and what she was about to say before Robin changed the subject earlier, was that Mike would likely be getting out of prison soon. With good behavior he may serve as little as five years. Surely that possibility was at the forefront of Robin's mind, which likely brought on the dreams again. Would he come for revenge? It was something they both wondered but never dared to discuss.

Robin and Tommy each had a handful of clothes and personal items from her room as they passed by Chris. She noticed he was looking at her, but he never spoke. Deeply regretting how she had treated him, Robin decided she could hardly blame him if he never spoke to her again. Nearly every time she saw him over the past week, she made it a point to go the opposite direction. Having dodged him in every way possible, it must have become obvious to him.

"Hi, Chris." She smiled apologetically.

"Hi. Do you need any help with that?"

Chris was surprised by her acknowledgement, as she had clearly avoided any contact with him. Time after time he recounted their earliest conversations trying to determine if he had said something offensive or insulting. Having come up with nothing, he resigned himself to the fact that maybe she simply didn't like him, or maybe maintaining distance from people was her way of dealing with her sorrows.

"There are some things on the back porch. If you want to grab a load, that would be great."

"Sure."

Chris headed for the house with a smile on his face. Maybe she was finally warming up to him. It wasn't as if he was trying to hit on her or anything. The last thing he wanted was to get involved with someone at this stage of his life. While his only motive was to simply be friends with her, Chris struggled to understand why she shied away from him. Maybe that was changing now. He grabbed an armload and headed back toward the cabins, then realized he had no idea where he was taking his load.

Meeting her on her return trip, he asked, "So, where exactly am I taking this stuff?"

Purposefully trying to be friendly, she smiled as she said, "The Birchwood, just down from you."

Her smile knocked him off balance and just as she passed by, he stumbled over a large rock. Embarrassed, he joked, "I meant to do that."

Shaking her head, she kept moving. "Oh, obviously."

Chris took his load into the cabin and looked around, wondering who was going to be staying there and why nothing was in suitcases. Setting the clothes on the bed, he turned and walked back out onto the small porch. When Robin returned, he went to her and took one of the boxes she was carrying.

"Who's going to be staying here? Is it a family?"

"No, me."

"You?"

"Yes. I've decided to stay down here for a while, maybe for good."

Since it was none of his business, he refrained from asking any more questions. Whatever distance she maintained was possibly closing, so he certainly wasn't going to push his luck. Relieved that she was even talking to him after a week of silence, he would take it slowly. After observing her the night before, Chris realized she was much more fragile than she appeared. His mountain woman was not at all what she seemed to be.

3

As he sat alone in the dining room, inhaling his second plate of food, Chris noticed Robin and Emma walk into the room. Since that first day, in the week since he had been there, he hadn't seen Robin eat in the dining room again. He assumed she ate her meals in the kitchen, probably to avoid him. So after she filled her plate, he was truly surprised when she approached his table.

"Do you mind if we sit here?" she asked softly.

Chris smiled and stammered, "No, not at all."

Robin sat across from him and quietly began to eat. She regretted how rude she must seem to him and wanted to try to make up for it. Finally, she admitted, "Look, I know I haven't been exactly friendly, and I just wanted to say that I'm very sorry about that. It's not you."

"No, that's quite all right. You were fine."

Grinning, she accused, "Liar."

"Okay, maybe a little."

He laughed this laugh that made her feel better instantly. He was as lighthearted as she first presumed him to be, and there was something distinctly different about him. On more than one occasion, she had seen him by the water's edge, reading what appeared to be a Bible. It didn't surprise her in the least, as it fit his gentle disposition.

When Emma joined them at the table, she was glad to see the two were hitting it off. Though unable to pinpoint exactly why, she had a good feeling about Chris. Somehow, she knew he might be exactly what Robin needed. The conversation was cheerful and easy, and sensing Robin's comfort with him, Emma quickly made an excuse to leave them alone. Her hope was that Robin would find some kind of happiness, even if it was in the form of a summer romance. She had to start somewhere.

After breakfast and throughout the remainder of the day, Robin pondered her conversation with Chris. She decided he was truly a nice guy, and what made her feel most relaxed was that she never sensed he was hitting on her. He simply talked about various things, asked questions, and surprisingly, really listened to her answers. The nervousness she felt around him early on was gone. Relieved by this new impression of him, she saw her summer as something more than maintaining a strategy to avoid him. It had become tiring, and honestly, she didn't have the energy to keep it up.

As she did every morning, Robin sat on the stone steps awaiting the sun's next appearance. In five years, other than the miserable cold season, rarely had she missed a morning. There was something about the sun rising from behind the trees across the expanse of water. It made her feel almost alive to witness the beginning of another day. Other times, mostly later in the day, she felt as if she merely existed and longed for the feeling of renewal and possibility the sun brought with it.

While the sun had not yet come up, there was enough light already to make out a form walking toward the stairs. It was Chris. In the two weeks since his arrival, this was the first morning she saw him out so early. Smiling to herself, she could tell he hadn't been awake for long. His hair was practically standing on end, and as he drew nearer, she saw that his eyes still had that puffy, half-asleep look about them. Without a word he took a seat next to her.

"What are you doing up this time of morning?" she asked.

Yawning, he explained, "I got up early yesterday to paint the sunrise and realized what I've been missing all my life. After all these years, I figured out what God does first thing each morning. It's worth losing sleep over, so I set my clock for this morning, too."

He intentionally left out the part where he had seen her sitting on the steps the day before, and this morning he had hoped he would find her here again.

Robin admitted, "I think this may be where God lives. He's most real to me when I'm here."

There was something about the combination of the sun and water; the two in unison unlocked a door within her that had been closed off for nearly six years. It was only the early morning hours when she experienced such a thing. All other times, even when looking at the very same sight from the very same step, her heart was securely fastened shut against Him.

Watching Robin as the sun rose was quite remarkable. Her expression went from all but lifeless to glowing as brightly as the sun itself; something about it transformed her from the inside out. She smiled brighter and more fully than he had yet to see.

Robin found Chris' presence surprisingly uplifting. He had this wild, unkempt look about him, like a little boy up early to watch Saturday morning cartoons. Lifting her coffee cup, she offered it to him, and surprisingly, he took it.

"Are you officially a morning person now?"

Chris rolled his eyes. "Maybe not officially."

While his head ached less than the evening before, it hurt still. It was opposite of the usual pattern. Typically, he felt worse in the mornings, but this morning he was able to fend off the throbbing in his head.

Sipping the cool, strong coffee, he asked, "So, how long have you been here."

"About half an hour, I guess."

He chuckled as he clarified, "I mean at the inn."

"Oh." She laughed with him.

Taking her coffee cup back, she told him, "Almost five years now."

"For some reason I thought you may have grown up here."

Her Southern drawl was so much less pronounced than Emma's that he considered she might have lived local since childhood.

"No, I was raised in North Carolina, but I did spend many of my summers here."

"Really? I did too when I was a kid." Grinning, he stated the obvious, "Not here at this inn but at the lake."

"How old were you?" she asked.

"We were here every summer until I was twelve."

The recollection of how happy his family had been then made him feel warm inside. That was what he had come back for, to find that feeling again.

"My dad died just a month after we got home that last year. Things were never the same after that."

The change in his expression moved her. She understood the difficulty of loss and the fact that life is somehow supposed to go on in spite of it. The problem is – no one can tell you how to do that.

"I'm sorry. That must have been hard, losing your dad at such a young age."

"It was tough, but I guess we survived."

He thought about his mom after his father's death. Two weeks after his father drowned Chris saw her drunk for the first time, and by no means was it the last. Every year she got a little worse, until finally he went to live with his aunt at the age of fifteen. That was when he started school at Lincoln, the year his life changed for the better – the year he found God.

Chris glanced often at Robin but tried not to stare. She was wearing shorts and a light sweatshirt, and her long hair was pulled pack into a loose ponytail, which disappointed him. He really liked the way her hair flew this way and that with the winds that blew in off the water. Many times, he felt the urge to reach out and move a strand of hair from her face, but good sense told him it would be a mistake on his part. Somehow, he knew better than to touch her.

"So I've been wondering, are you and Emma related?"

"Not really, but as close as you can get, I suppose. Emma and my mom grew up together in Raleigh. That's near where I grew up."

"How did you two end up here?"

"Emma moved here right before I was born."

Robin slid the band from her ponytail and let her hair tumble over her shoulders as she continued, "Her great aunt owned the inn for over fifty years, so when she died, she left the place to Emma."

"What made you decide to move here? I mean, I guess it's pretty understandable. This place is amazing."

"I was in kind of a bad place in my life. I really only came here to get away for a while," she sighed, remembering how lost she felt, "but then I just never went back. My parents moved out West, so there was really nothing to draw me back to North Carolina. This is just kind of where I landed, with Emma."

"She seems like a wonderful lady."

He was sincere. Emma reminded him of Sophia Loren or Ann Margret, one of those legendary stars. Her presence in the room charged the air, and everything about her was bigger than life. She dressed far above what the day as an innkeeper would require and lent a glamorous, 1940s atmosphere to the place.

"I think the world of her," Robin said. "She's had a rough way to go. Back in her twenties she was a nurse in the Army and engaged to another soldier. Right before they were supposed to be married, he was killed in an accident."

"So, she never married?"

"No, never. She barely even dated. She just kind of shut down."

Understanding how such a thing could happen, Robin easily related to Emma's story. Feeling a bit uncomfortable at how personal the conversation had become, she reached for her coffee cup and said, "Well, I better get up there. I'm sure she's cooking breakfast. I should see if she needs any help. See you later, Chris."

There was something soothing about the way she said his name; it sounded soft on her lips, and he caught the most distinctive hint of her Southern accent then.

As she turned to go, he said, "Robin."

Turning back to him, she asked, "Yeah?"

"Thanks for talking to me this morning. I'm sorry if I invaded your quiet time."

"No invasion. I enjoyed it."

Robin walked into the kitchen to find Emma sitting at the island, her view through the window ensuring she had seen her with Chris.

"Good morning," Robin said, knowing Emma was about to grill her.

Emma smiled. "Good morning. I see you were talking to Chris."

"Yes, I was talking to Chris."

It was obvious that Emma wanted to see her pair up with him, so Robin teased, "We're getting married this afternoon. I hope that's not too short of a notice for you."

Emma giggled at her silliness. "You know, he really seems like a nice man. It wouldn't hurt to get to know him."

"I am getting to know him. I'm just not planning on any kind of relationship, that's all."

"What do you know so far?"

"He's an art teacher, so of course he likes to paint. He spent his summers here at the lake when he was a kid. I've learned all kinds of things about him."

"Good. It sounds like you know enough to marry him."

With Robin out of the main house, Emma was up several times during the night. Each time she drifted off, she awoke with a start, fearing Robin would go out and swim. If she did, Emma would have no way of knowing if she was safe. Twice even, she went out to the porch and sat. It was a long night.

Emma asked, "How did you sleep?"

Nodding, Robin assured her, "It was good actually. No bad dreams."

"I'm glad to hear it. You know, Hummingbird, I've wanted to talk to you about Mike."

Looking at her watch, and as a way out of the conversation, Robin told her, "Hey, I need to get with Tommy about a few things. Can we talk about it later?"

"Sure, later."

She watched Robin escape through the swinging door. Emma knew she was trying to avoid even thinking about him, let alone discussing his release. What if he showed up at the inn? It wouldn't take long for him to figure out where she was. More than likely, he already knew. Walking back to the stove, she flipped the bacon and started cracking eggs. As she cracked them, she wished each shell were Mike's head. Nothing would give her more satisfaction.

Robin waited as Tommy made his way down the last few steps in the lobby. She could see he was still half asleep.

"Good morning."

"Morning," Tommy grumbled.

"Late night?"

"Yeah, pretty late. Have you seen Becky yet?" he asked.

He had tapped on her door, but she never answered.

"No. I imagine she's still asleep."

Becky had always been the most difficult for Robin to get up and around. It was the same the summer before.

"Maybe, but she's not asleep here."

"Really?" Robin thought she detected a look of disgust on his face.

"We were in town last night, and Becky hooked up with that Brad guy." Looking away, he added, "She left with him."

"Tommy..." She trailed off.

What could she say? Since early on, he knew Becky was interested in someone else. Still, he mooned over her, obviously hoping for more than what would ever be between them.

"Hi," Becky said.

Head bowed in embarrassment, she passed by them, sandals in hand, and made her way up the first flight of stairs.

As they both stood and watched her climb the stairs, Robin whispered, "Becky's home."

"Yeah, thanks."

"Look, Tommy," Robin kept her voice low. "She's an adult. I know you have a thing for her, but you may as well face it, she's going to do whatever she wants with this guy. No matter how foolish we may think it is."

Becky stood at the top of the first landing and listened to their conversation. With tears welling up in her eyes, she agreed – she was foolish. While with Brad the night before, she was still the same eager little girl she was the summer before. Obviously, he picked up on that. Much too late, after she had already left with him, she realized he was the same arrogant jerk he was the year before. He went on and on about himself, mostly the things he had, the things he would do, and his father's company. Not once did he ask her a question about school or what she planned or was studying to be. Why hadn't she noticed before leaving with him? While on the way to his house, though, it was as if her eyes were opened to the truth. Suddenly realizing he was expecting something she wasn't prepared for, she asked him to take her back. He refused. After a terrible argument, Brad dropped her in the middle of nowhere, and by the time she got back to town, Tommy was gone. So she stayed out all night, waiting for a fisherman to bring her back across the lake.

Walking slowly down the stairs, furious that they were discussing her behind her back, Becky protested, "I'm not as stupid as you both think."

Robin regretted talking about her with Tommy and offered, "I'm sorry. It's none of my business, and I shouldn't have been discussing it."

Tommy could hardly bring himself to look at Becky as he spat, "I'm not sorry. You deserve whatever you get from that guy."

His hands were trembling with anger, but when he finally did allow himself to look at her, he could see how his words had hurt her. In regret, he whispered, "I'm sorry, Beck, but don't you see what a jerk he is? He's a user and..."

"I know. That's why I didn't go home with him."

Suddenly uncomfortable talking in front of Robin, Becky asked him, "Can we go somewhere to talk?"

Lifting her hand, Robin turned to walk away. "I'm going. You two talk here."

Tommy just stood there, staring at her. Finally, he asked, "You really didn't go home with him?"

"No."

He walked over to her and put his hands on her shoulders, admitting, "I've been up all night thinking about you. It drove me crazy imagining you with him. You deserve so much more than just a one night stand. Don't you want more for yourself than that?"

"I want you." That didn't come out as she meant it. Smiling shyly, she touched his cheek. "I didn't mean it that way."

Hopeful, Tommy asked, "How did you mean it?"

"I admit it. I came here this summer hoping I would see him." The look on Tommy's face made her regret her honesty. So quickly she added, "When I went with him last night, though, I saw him for who he really is, what he always will be. Then I thought about you. How you make me laugh and how much you aggravate me."

She smiled. Tommy was everything she could want in a guy; he was smart and funny, and she was her happiest when she was with him. For the life of her, Becky could hardly understand how she missed it before. All night, she wondered what Tommy must be thinking of her and if it was too late for them. Several times during the night she was tempted to call him but was too ashamed for having left with Brad in the first place.

Smiling back at her, he asked, "I aggravate you, huh?"

"Yeah, a lot."

He gently tucked her hair behind her ear. She was looking up at him with those watery blue eyes, and he had no doubt he was falling for her. Leaning down, he softly kissed her cheek. Moving his lips near her ear, he whispered. "You aggravate me, too."

Relieved, she slid her arms around his waist. "I'm so glad."

Robin and Emma were peeking into the lobby as the two kissed. Giggling, they both hurried back through the dining room. Emma was still laughing as they walked into the kitchen.

Holding out her hand, Emma said, "Told you."

"I don't have it with me. I'll give it to you later."

Robin shook her head. Emma had predicted Tommy and Becky would get together and suggested a twenty-dollar bet.

"I'm glad you were right," Robin admitted.

"Me, too. Now if my streak continues, you'll end up with Chris."

"I'd be willing to raise the bet on that one."

Robin had no intention of getting involved with Chris. Though she liked him even more than she anticipated, she was safe in taking the bet.

"Okay, shall we say fifty?" Emma smiled at the smug expression on Robin's face.

Without hesitation, Robin agreed, "Fifty it is."

She was sure to win this one. They often made crazy bets like this, and for the most part, the winner would use the money for a night out together to eat or see a movie. Fifty dollars would make for a fine meal.

As Robin backed through the kitchen door into the dining room, she literally ran into Chris.

"Oh, sorry." Chris reached for her.

Robin was caught off guard, especially when he put his hands on her shoulders to steady her and keep from knocking her to the ground. They felt strong as he gripped her, causing her to feel all squirrely inside.

"No, I'm sorry. I wasn't paying attention to where I was going," she stammered.

He sniffed the air as he released her, asking, "Is that bacon I smell?"

She hid a grin and assured him, "Yes, Emma will be out with it in a minute."

"Good," he said as he went to the tall serving buffet. As he loaded his plate, he said over his shoulder, "I saw Tommy and Becky walking to the dock. Looks like things have changed with those two."

"Nobody ever listens to me," Emma said as she walked through the swinging door carrying a full plate of bacon. "I said they would get together."

Robin shrugged.

Pointing at Robin, Emma bragged, "She owes me twenty so far."

"So far?"

"Oh, ignore her." Robin handed Emma a biscuit, insisting, "Here, put this in your mouth."

Glancing at Chris, Emma winked. "She'll owe me fifty more before she knows it." Winking again, at Robin this time, she went back into the kitchen.

"What was that about?" He had a sense it might involve him.

"Nothing important. You know old people." Robin intentionally made the comment louder than necessary, certain Emma was listening in.

They sat at a table together, which for the first time didn't seem awkward. While he tried not to stare at her, he did notice how the sunlight streamed through the window and glistened through her hair. And those eyes – it was happening again, that melting down of brain cells like he experienced the first day he met her. Chris had to force himself to focus on his food to keep from morphing into some drooling, blabbering mess.

In an attempt to divert his mind, he asked, "So, is there anything to do around here at night? I know I haven't been here long, but I'm already getting a little stir crazy sitting around the cabin at night."

"I don't go out enough to know, but I'm sure there are a few places you might enjoy. I know Tommy and Becky go to a place over in Wolfeboro."

"I wasn't really thinking about a bar, if that's what you mean. I meant more of a restaurant or something."

"Well," she paused as she thought, "there are a lot of great restaurants. What do you want? Seafood? Steak?"

"I was kind of hoping you would go with me. I mean, nothing serious or anything, just grab a bite to eat."

Chris could see her mind was whirling and found it pretty amusing that he was holding his breath as he waited for her response.

At a loss for words, Robin realized she hadn't been asked out in many years, and she wasn't exactly sure what to say. "Well, I uh…well, I guess that would be all right. I mean, you said nothing serious."

Smiling at the cuteness of her response, Chris stuck a piece of bacon in his mouth, asking, "Great. How about tonight?"

"Tonight?"

All of the sudden, Robin realized what she had just agreed to. What had she done? Without question, she had made a serious mistake.

He found her expression amusing, as it reminded him of a deer caught in the headlights. Looking at him with those big doe eyes, she had no idea how adorable she was at that moment.

"Yes, tonight. You know, that time period between today and bedtime."

"I guess I could go tonight."

Hearing her own words, stammering though they were, she realized they had just agreed to something she wasn't at all prepared for. Hurriedly, Robin added, "I better let you know. I have several things…"

"Great, tonight it is. I'll pick you up at seven."

Without finishing his meal, Chris stood and left the dining room before she could change her mind.

Sitting alone at the table, Robin could hardly believe what had just happened. She had agreed to a date, and that was the last thing she wanted. Acknowledging she could have simply said no, she racked her brain trying to figure out why she hadn't. Closing her eyes, she put her hands over her face.

"Huh, wonder what I'll do with the extra fifty?" Emma said as she plopped down in the chair across from Robin.

"I guess you were spying on us?"

"Of course. Did you expect any less?"

Thrilled beyond anything she had known in eons, Emma was elated by Robin's decision to go. Had *Robin* not pressured *her* often about dating? "Oh, go," Robin would say. "It'll be good for you." Now that the shoe was on the other foot, her sweet girl was in over her head, and Emma was tickled pink about it.

"What am I going to do?" Robin asked, suddenly terrified when considering having dinner out with Chris or with any man for that matter.

"What do you mean?"

Already sensing her regret, Emma would do whatever it took to keep the date on track.

"I can't do this."

Emma asked, "Why not? He seems like a great guy."

She hadn't had the opportunity to talk to him as much as Robin, but the times she had, Chris seemed like a charming man. Forget about his looks even, though who could forget about that? He was an all-around nice guy, perfect for Robin.

"I know, but I'm in no position to date anyone."

Robin thought about Chris' smile; he had such a beautiful smile.

Trying to alleviate her own fears, Robin said, "He said it was nothing serious. Maybe he just wants some company."

"You mean, maybe it's not a date?" Chuckling at her, Emma waited to hear Robin's response.

"Yeah, maybe it's not."

"Okay, and I'll be seeing Santa Claus in a little while. I'll ask his opinion."

She reached out and patted Robin's hand. "Sweetie, just go and have fun. You deserve a wonderful night out with a nice guy. Just do it."

Groaning, Robin asked, "What will I wear?"

"I have plenty of dresses. Let's go upstairs."

Robin hesitantly followed Emma into her room and to her closet. Peeking in, she found Emma had dozens of beautiful dresses. Though Emma seldom went out, when she did, she always looked gorgeous. Surely they could come up with something.

She sat on the bed, feet dangling and swinging as Emma pulled one dress after another out of the closet. Robin turned up her nose at the first few, but finally there was one she liked.

"Aw, I love that one," she cooed softly.

After removing it from the plastic cover, Robin held the dress up to her. It was long, almost reaching to her ankles. The color could only be described as a buttery yellow, and the fabric was soft, smooth cotton. It had a vintage air about it the others lacked. Slipping it over her head, she was unsure of the color on her.

"I don't know if yellow is a good color for me."

Examining her, Emma shook her head in disbelief, saying, "Honey, with your looks, any color is your color."

Emotional, having never suspected she would see this dress put to use, Emma sighed heavily, exclaiming, "You look gorgeous."

"I don't think I've ever seen you wear this before. Where did you get it?"

Looking at her reflection in the full-length mirror, Robin decided it did look pretty good.

As if she had traveled back in time, Emma drawled slowly and quietly, "Oh, I've had that dress a hundred years, at least. And no, you've never seen me wear it."

Guardedly, Emma fought back tears as she thought of the last time she wore the dress. She had planned to be married in it, to Robin's father. How poetic it seemed that Robin was standing there before her with that particular dress on.

"Do you really like it?" Robin asked, feeling nervous and a bit self-conscious.

Having spent the past five years in jeans and shorts, Robin felt awkward wearing a dress. Even to church she wore pants.

"I couldn't imagine anything more perfect." Tears spilled over Emma's lashes.

"Why are you crying?"

As Emma dabbed a delicate handkerchief to the corner of each eye, Robin was reminded what a beautiful woman she was. Everything she did was glamorous. Even her little hankies were feminine and dressy. If only she could be more like Emma, elegant like a true Southern Belle. Instead, she was anything but that. Robin had always been more of a jeans and hoodie kind of girl. Can you be a tomboy in a girly sort of way? If so, that was the best description of herself that she could come up with.

"I don't know, sweetie. I guess I'm just glad to see you live a little. Hummingbird, you have to let it go."

Robin looked down at her bare feet sticking out from beneath the yellow fabric, admitting, "I don't know if I can ever let it go. I'm afraid it's part of who I am now."

Taking Robin's face in her hands, Emma disagreed. "No. It's *not* part of who you are. You're still who you always were before it happened. The real you is just hiding somewhere in there. Let her come out tonight."

"Should *she* go with no shoes?" Robin wiggled her toes as Emma looked down.

"No. You're cute and all, but I don't think you can carry off that look the way Chris can."

Emma knew better than to push her any further. Really, the few sentences she had just uttered were the most Robin had ever spoken of her time with Mike. It was a subject that was totally off limits.

Emma reached for a pair of matching yellow shoes.

Robin grimaced. "They may be a little much. Do you have anything a little simpler?"

"What about these? They will go nicely with a barefoot man."

Laughing at her, Robin did stop to wonder if Chris would wear shoes. Not once had she seen him wear them since he arrived. She slipped on the white sandals, asking, "Okay, so now I have an outfit, what about my hair?"

As Robin left to take the dress to her cabin, Emma felt herself glowing as if a lamp had been switched on deep in her soul. In many years she hadn't seen Robin so excited. Well, maybe excited was a bit of an overstatement, but Robin was smiling a genuine smile at least, not one of those superficial "I'm pretending to be part of life" smiles, rather a surprising "there is hope after all" smile. The light in the lamp grew brighter at the possibility of a new chapter in life for Robin. Chris may not be the answer, but he was at least the beginning of Robin daring to question again.

For five years Emma had tried to reach out to her, to somehow help Robin heal after the end of her marriage. Approaching her as a friend, her only option given the circumstances, the pretense of it all caused Emma to feel such shame she could hardly bring herself to look Robin in the eye oftentimes. Her truest desire was to comfort her as a mother, but she gave up that right when she placed her newborn baby in her best friend's arms. Emma would never have the luxury of such a connection with Robin.

While the circumstances of her arrival were horrid, Robin's decision to come to the inn and ultimately to stay on full-time was the most significant event to happen in Emma's life in the past thirty years. It was her secret "do-over," a means of really getting to know the daughter she gave away. Even though it remained a secret, in her heart she was Robin's mama. She found the greatest love she had ever known in her life—even beyond that of Robin's father—the one love she thought she could never live without.

4

Robin stood at the counter in the lobby, working on the list of reservations for the following week. All of the rooms and cabins were full, and there were no more guests expected, so when a woman walked in, Robin wondered if maybe she was lost.

"Hi, may I help you?"

The woman was in her late twenties, petite with short brown hair and dark, almond shaped eyes. Way overdressed for vacation, she wore heels and carried a purse the size of a small automobile. Her attire alone caused Robin to further conclude she was lost and looking for directions.

"Yes, I'm looking for Chris Wheeler. He's staying in a cabin here."

For the briefest moment, Robin was unable to speak. Finally, she stammered, "Yes, he's a guest here."

Raising her eyebrows, Vanessa said, "I know he's a guest here, sweetie. Can you tell me where I might find him?" Then smiling insincerely, she added, "I was supposed to be staying here with him but was unable to come at the last minute. I wanted to surprise him."

Robin smiled a much more sincere smile, saying, "Oh, I'm sure he'll be surprised all right."

Robin walked from behind the counter as she offered, "Come on, I'll take you to his cabin. I can't wait to see the look on his face."

"What do you mean?" Vanessa asked, curious about the clerk's tone.

Robin never turned back to the woman but shook her head as she said, "Oh, I just love being part of a surprise. That's all."

Sure, Robin could have directed the woman to drive to Chris' cabin, but where was the fun in that?

Moving along slowly, several paces in front of her, Robin's stride allowed for the woman's high heels in the grass. Admittedly, she felt a bit slighted, but Robin was more amused than anything. Since Chris asked her out, not knowing his girlfriend would show up, it would be humorous to watch him squirm, worth whatever offense she might have suffered. As they approached his cabin, she found him sitting on the front porch. Already his expression was hilarious. Robin smiled at him, and with her best *Price Is Right* arm gesture, said in an exaggerated tone, "And here he is."

When he saw Vanessa walking behind Robin, Chris jumped from his rocking chair and headed toward the stairs. Beating them to the bottom step, he asked, "Vanessa, what are you doing here?"

Happily, she threw her arms around him. "I wanted to surprise you. Are you surprised?"

Over Vanessa's shoulder Chris looked at Robin helplessly, his eyes apologizing.

With the girlfriend's back to her, Robin mouthed to Chris, "Surprise!"

Turning, Robin walked away, once again shaking her head.

Inside the cabin Chris and Vanessa sat at the small table.

"I'm so sorry about what happened. I guess I just freaked."

Chris sat, looking at her blankly. Of all the times for her to have a change of heart, it had to be the same day he had asked Robin out. Although Vanessa was talking, trying to explain, he had a difficult time concentrating on what she was saying. He kept picturing Robin saying, "Surprise!"

"What I said, about not being with you through..."

Holding up his hand to stop her, he protested, "You were right."

"No, I wasn't."

She was looking down at her hands. It had been the worst two weeks of her life. Never had she felt more rotten.

Chris reached for her hand. "I have to be honest with you. I don't think we should be together either. I know you feel lousy about the timing, but I think we both knew it wasn't working out between us, even before..." Chris trailed off. She knew his meaning. "Neither one of us would admit it though."

Moving from his chair, he knelt before her. "Sweetheart, you can't allow guilt to keep you with me anymore than I can be with you just because I'm in a bad place in my life." He touched her cheek. "I really care for you, but I'm not in love with you."

Momentarily incensed, Vanessa then realized that this was perfect. The end could come, but it would be on his shoulders, not hers. There was a great sense of relief to be let off the hook that way, and what he said was true.

While there was no longer the attraction there had been in the beginning, she felt obligated to stay with him, especially once his symptoms began and the diagnosis came. When he left Boston, she wanted it to be over, but as much as she tried to forget him and move on, she was consumed by guilt. The thought of him at the lake, hopeless and alone, had been a terrible burden on her.

"You know I care for you, don't you?" Vanessa asked.

"Yes, I know. Look, Vanessa, we've had some great times together, and nothing will ever change that."

Chris stood and walked toward the window. Looking out at the lake, he admitted, "I would rather us end this way, on a happy note." Turning, he smiled at her. "We've had some fun, huh?"

His smile made her want to rush to him, to throw her arms around him and try to make things better. She had never known anyone like him. Maybe that had been part of the problem, that he was such a good guy, he bordered on boring. There was no thrill or challenge. She needed more excitement than he offered.

"We certainly have," Vanessa agreed.

Regretfully, she stood and crossed the small distance between them. Putting her arms around him, she kissed him softly on the cheek, saying, "Call me when you get home."

"I will. Drive safely."

Chris watched as she picked up her purse and walked out the door. Now he just had to talk to Robin. The entire time he was with Vanessa, he could hardly get her off his mind, wondering what she must be thinking of him. Having agreed to go out with him so reluctantly, he supposed he lost out on the opportunity. Grabbing a towel, he decided to shower and dress for dinner just in case she gave him another chance.

Somewhat annoyed, Robin sat on the edge of her bed, foot propped up on the corner, painting her toenails. She had taken a shower and was now letting her hair air dry. The yellow dress hanging on the closet door seemed to be mocking her, but really, she was okay. Smiling to herself, she was just glad to know she had the courage to accept a date. The fact that it fell through this time was beside the point. What was most incredible was that in the process, she discovered there was still a tiny flicker of life left inside her, something she would have sworn didn't exist any longer. That was promising. Next time she might really go. Such a possibility caused her stomach to churn a bit. In truth, she knew she was far from ready to date and relieved things turned out the way they had. Still, though, the flicker was exposed.

She thought about Chris and for just a split second felt a twinge of jealousy. The woman was so beautiful it was easy to see why he was with her, and in his defense he had said "nothing serious." So he had a girlfriend; it wasn't the end of the world. As funny as it was, she was determined when she saw him next, she wouldn't make a big deal about the whole thing.

Walking on her heels, she went into the living room, and just as she passed by the door, someone knocked. A quick peek at the clock in the kitchen showed exactly seven o'clock.

"Surely not!" Robin whispered aloud.

When Robin came to the door, Chris was standing there, hands thrust deep into his pockets, dressed in the only respectable clothes he had brought with him. Half expecting her to slam the door in his face, he smiled apologetically, saying, "Hi."

She opened the door a little wider and asked, "What are you doing here?"

"I'm sorry. I thought we agreed on seven?"

"Well, I just assumed your girlfriend would have a problem with you going out to a 'nothing serious or anything' dinner with another woman."

His face took on a soft expression. "She's not my girlfriend. She's gone." Taking a step closer, he urged, "Please go to dinner with me. I'll explain it all then."

Standing there looking at him, Robin thought he looked so handsome in his khaki pants and blue shirt. The color of his shirt was nearly the exact shade of his eyes. It was the first time she noticed what an unusual shade they were, deep blue with pale gold streaks running through them. Hesitantly, she blinked, holding her eyes shut longer than necessary. Part of her really wanted to go, but the last thing she wanted was to get in the middle of some on again off again relationship.

"Maybe we shouldn't."

"Please, Robin, just dinner." Leaning his head against the door jamb, he added, "I'm all dressed up with nowhere to go."

"Can we agree this isn't a date?"

A bit surprised by her question, he agreed, "Sure. Just two pals having dinner."

"Pals?" The way he said it made her grin.

"Buddies, friends, compadres, whatever you want to call us. How about two hungry people eating dinner together at the same place at the same time? Are you hungry?"

"Yes." She swung the door open wider. "As you see, I'm not exactly dressed."

He smiled, saying, "I have all the time in the world."

When she turned to go into the bedroom, his smile faded. That wasn't at all true.

Seated at a table on the deck of one of the marina restaurants, Chris and Robin had decided on seafood, and this place was one of her favorites. Having supposed she would feel uncomfortable, she found herself instead relaxed and at ease with him. From the moment she got into his car, Chris kept the conversation light and fun. Already, it was shaping up to be an enjoyable evening.

"So, Robin, what did you do before coming to Lake Winnipesaukee?"

Looking down into her water glass, she said, "Oh, not much really."

"Independently wealthy?"

Chris noticed she seemed suddenly tense and wished he hadn't asked about her past. It was something he sensed already, but he let curiosity get the better of him. It had taken some time for her to let her guard down enough to talk to him at all. Noting his mistake, he was determined not to make a similar one.

Looking at him, she smiled faintly. "No, nothing like that. Actually, I was married."

Surprised, and detecting an unfamiliar expression in her normally inexpressive eyes, he regretted his question even more.

"I hope I didn't bring up a painful subject." Clapping his hands, he added, "I tell you what, let's change the subject entirely."

"That sounds good. Now, you tell me about being a teacher. Do you like it?"

His smile broadened. "Oh, I love it. It means so much to me, to really be able to make a difference in these kids' lives. Being a Christian teacher in a public school has its challenges, but I do what I can to show God's love to them."

Gazing out at the still water for a moment, he thought of Gloria Nelson, something he did often actually. Turning back to look at Robin, he shared, "You know, I was really on a bad road when I was young, until one of my teachers in high school saw something in me that I never saw in myself. Her belief in me changed my life completely. She invited me to church – of course, you could do that back then."

"Tell me about her."

He liked the way her eyes sparkled in the candlelight, and he could tell that she was really interested in what he was saying. There was a slight connection between her eyes and smile, a rare moment from what he had seen so far.

Leaning in slightly, he told her, "Her name was Gloria Nelson, and she was my music teacher my freshman year of high school. I had just moved in with my aunt and changed schools. It was a really difficult time for me."

Reminded of when they talked on the stairs about the summer his dad died, Robin noticed his eyes became cloudy, as they did that day. Wondering for a moment if eyes could be overcast like weather, she determined they could. His were. She had always heard the eyes are the windows to the soul, and for the first time she could visualize it. His eyes were more than just beautiful blue eyes, they revealed secrets about him, and she wondered if he knew that about himself.

Out of consideration, she asked, "Should we change the subject again?"

"No, I'm fine. It's just that when I think of that time, it's still a little painful for me. I suppose it always will be. My mom began drinking after my father died." Shrugging, he admitted, "I don't know, maybe she drank before and I was just kept away from it. Whatever the case, it was a horrible thing that only got worse. I eventually moved out."

He looked out at the water again. The image of his mother lying on the kitchen floor, passed out cold in her own vomit, was still a clear picture in his mind. For the first few years, when such things would happen, he would clean her up and get her to bed. After a while, though, he would just step over her to get to the refrigerator. Never knowing what to expect from her, he didn't invite friends over. The last time he did, he was so embarrassed by her stumbling behavior and drunken babbling, he swore he would never do it again. Life with her was lonely and he was in a constant state of upheaval.

Because of what he experienced, he had never touched a drop of alcohol in his life. Even the smell of it turned his stomach.

"Alcohol is a destructive thing." Softly, she added, "My husband began to drink. That changed everything."

Like a flash of lightning from out of the blue, her mind was struck with memories of his rage and loss of control. Though normally able to push such memories away, they were so fresh and real in that moment, she felt overtaken by them.

For a brief time they were both silent. It was as if they found common ground that only people who had experienced it could understand. In an attempt to drag herself from such an onslaught from the past, Robin tried instead to focus on this moment rather than what once was. As was her usual way of dealing with the past, she shoved it away, pretending it was indeed over and done.

"Thanks for coming tonight." Chris said, "It's getting pretty lonely, sitting in that cabin every night."

"Well, you did have company today."

Her tone was playful but curious. Although she wondered about the woman, Robin had resisted the urge to bring it up so far. This was a perfect opportunity, one she decided not to let slip by.

Chris smiled; embarrassed by how awkward the moment was when she led Vanessa to his cabin. There was a mixture of glee and what he later determined to be hurt feelings in Robin's eyes. Surprisingly, he had been more concerned with what Robin felt than the fact that Vanessa had driven two hours to see him. The look on Robin's face when she said, "Surprise!" was one he wouldn't soon forget. Unable to blame her for feeling hurt, all he could think of at that point was sending Vanessa on her way.

"That was Vanessa. We dated for about six months and just recently broke up. It went on for about three months too long, but somehow, neither of us wanted to be the one to initiate the split. I guess she was feeling a little guilty and wanted to set things right."

"Guilty? You mean she broke it off?"

"Yes, in a way. She was supposed to come out for the first week or so, but at the last minute she decided not to come. It was just a symptom of a bigger problem, and I knew it."

"What happened today?" Although she knew it was none of her business, somehow she felt comfortable asking.

"I told her I wasn't in love with her."

"And are you?"

"No, not at all."

Sitting there in the candlelight with Robin, and though he knew it was rotten to make such a comparison, Chris considered them both. Vanessa was as shallow as a puddle when compared to Robin, who had the unsearchable depth of the lake she was so drawn to. Early on while dating Vanessa, he sensed it and should have called it off. A verse came to mind, something about beauty being fleeting. In Vanessa's case, once the beauty faded, there wouldn't be so much to brag about. In fact, she was never even that kind. Men can be entirely stupid where a pretty woman is concerned.

"Don't get me wrong, she's a fine person, and we've had a good time together, but when…"

Suddenly, Chris found he was unable to go on. He had been prepared to tell Robin that he was sick, but the words hung in his throat. It was as if saying them out loud would make it all the more real. So far, it was still like a bad dream, one he knew would be over soon.

Noticing how abruptly he stopped, Robin decided not to question him further. In an attempt to once again changed the direction of their conversation, she told him, "You know, for two pals having dinner, we have gone way too deep. Let's go back to the surface."

"You're right. What's your sign?"

She chuckled. "Okay, a little deeper than that."

"When's your birthday?"

"March third, I just turned thirty. Yours?"

"July twenty third. I'll be thirty-eight." When spoken aloud, that number seemed awfully young to be his last.

"Hey, you'll be here for your birthday. We'll celebrate with you. Emma loves any reason to throw a party."

Amused, Robin considered how Emma would react when she heard what an enjoyable time she was having. If the night continued on as it was, she might even owe Emma fifty dollars.

Chris noticed how Robin suddenly seemed present and in the moment. It was one of the rare occasions when he caught a glimpse of real emotion in her eyes. So often, she seemed detached from what was going on around her, but tonight, he really felt as if she were right there with him.

"Most nights, we usually meet out under the gazebo. I mean, Emma, Tommy, and Becky. You're welcome to join us there anytime."

It was a time to decompress from the demands of the day. There was something special about that time together, like the coming together of a family under the stars. It was in those times that she most felt relaxed and at home.

Leaning in closer, she whispered pitifully, "I hate to think of you sitting there in that lonesome ol' cabin all by yourself."

"I'll take you up on that."

Having begun on such rocky footing, the evening turned out to be the most enjoyable he had known in a very long time. Without a doubt Chris preferred her company to Vanessa's. Occasionally she would giggle, and when she did, he was certain the entire room grew livelier. Even the candle on the table seemed to flicker brighter because of it. In rare moments when he could pull his mind away from how pretty she looked or how her eyes caused his stomach to flutter, he acknowledged the injustice of it all. There was no time to get to know her fully or to become known.

Having monopolized the table for longer than was appropriate, Chris finally paid the check and stood, saying, "I really hate to see the evening end."

"Yeah, me too."

Robin walked just ahead of Chris as they left the restaurant, and as they walked, he placed his hand on her lower back, guiding her through the maze of people waiting to be seated. The gesture felt overly familiar and caused her to walk a little faster.

Once outside, hoping to extend his time with her, Chris suggested, "We could take a walk around the marina."

"That sounds nice."

Even alone, Robin didn't feel as uncomfortable with him as she anticipated she might. Moving through the marina, they looked at the boats and marveled over the size of some of them. He showed her a boat similar to what his father had captained. Again, the word *comfortable* popped into her mind. He was kind and funny, a man any woman would be grateful to have, any woman but her. If she were totally honest with herself, she knew there could never be anything romantic between them. It was more than not being ready to be involved with someone at *that* moment. Robin was really quite certain she wouldn't be ready for an exceptionally long period of time. By the time she was healthy enough emotionally, she would be way too late for a summer romance with Chris. At that realization she decided her bet with Emma had been a safe one.

Finally, having covered every corner of the marina, they stopped at the end of the last pier. Robin leaned against a wooden post, sensing it was the moment to try and explain to him that for them, it was simply poor timing.

To Chris, the night seemed almost magical. The setting couldn't have been any more perfect as he watched the wind lightly lift her hair from her shoulders. For a moment he was reminded of the night he watched her standing on the small dock at the inn. How the wind blew against her, her gown creating a soft silhouette against her body. Without thinking he reached out to move a stray hair from her face.

Instinctively, Robin threw an arm up over her face and tried to move away from his approaching hand. For an instant she anticipated a strike to her cheek but quickly recognized what a foolish move she had made, as her sudden movement nearly caused her to fall into the water.

Reacting quickly, Chris grabbed her arms to prevent her from going over the edge and said, "Robin, I was just…"

He trailed off and stood there frozen. Did she think he was going to hit her? It became suddenly clear that Robin had been abused, and at that realization, his heart felt twice as heavy as normal. It quite literally felt as if it were sagging and weighed down.

Unable to look at him, Robin instead fixed her eyes on the worn wood of the dock. After a few awkward seconds, she whispered, "I'm sorry." Embarrassed, she pushed past him, saying, "Maybe we should go."

He stood for just a moment watching her walk away. It was then the pieces fell more securely into place. She had run from an abusive husband. That was what brought her to the lake, and the distant pain he was sure he saw was both emotional and physical in nature. Robin was even more wounded and fragile than he realized.

Jogging to catch up, he matched his pace with hers and quietly walked along beside her to the car. Once inside, he started the car and backed from the parking place. After putting the car into drive, he casually moved his hand to touch hers. Gently covering it, he held it as they drove home.

When Robin reached the bottom step of her cabin, Chris touched her shoulder, saying "Robin?"

Without turning to look at him, she whispered, "I'm sorry about what happened back there."

Tears burned her eyes. She hated to cry in front of him, so she blinked rapidly, trying to prevent it.

"Don't be sorry. You know I would never..."

"I know, Chris."

Even in the moment, she didn't actually believe he would hit her, so why did she flinch that way? She supposed it was because Mike had been so constantly on her mind. No matter how she tried to push his memory away, he dominated her thoughts and dreams. Her fear of him, even after all those years apart, was as fresh still as it was during their final year together. The constant uneasiness of doing or saying something that might set him off, even the thought of it at that very moment set her hands to trembling.

For several seconds he simply stood there with his hand resting on her shoulder. More than anything, he wanted to spin her around and pull her to him, but he knew better. Finally, she continued up the stairs, causing his hand to drop to his side.

Turning only slightly, she forced a smile and said, "Thank you for dinner. I had a lovely time."

He felt his heart beating up into his throat, and wanted to say something but was at a loss. Finally, he replied, "Thank you for going with me."

Sadly, he noted, her lifeless eyes had returned. Whatever brief time he caught a glimmer of some semblance of liveliness in them, it was now over.

Robin stepped through the doorway and closed the door quickly. Once inside, she leaned against it. Filled with a sense of embarrassment and guilt, she fought off the urge to cry. She hated to cry with a passion. Enough time had been spent on tears; and what had it produced? Nothing.

Going into the spare bedroom, she shifted boxes around until she came to the one she was looking for. As she peered into the box her favorite hiking boots came in, she sorted through her most important papers until she came to the ones she was looking for, her divorce papers. Sitting on the bed, she unfolded them and stared at the names at the top of the page. *Robin McGarrett vs. Michael McGarrett.* Stomach aching with regret, she flipped to the last page and looked at his signature. It was precise and legible, not his usual scratching signature. She always wondered why he signed them so easily. It was totally out of character for him. Still, he did. Why did that surprise her after all that happened that night?

At the moment she felt differently about seeing his signature than when she first received them from her attorney. All those years before, she felt something akin to hatred for him, though she knew she could never hate him in the truest sense of the word. She hated what he had become. She hated that he had destroyed their lives. She hated the memory of his blood all over her and the way he looked to her for comfort. How could he expect it of her? And where did her ability to give it come from?

Chris was sitting under the gazebo with Emma, Tommy, and Becky. He went there with the hope that Robin would show up, but she never did. Disappointed, he was anxious to see her again, to see if she was all right. By about ten, he was ready to give up and go back to his cabin.

Standing, he said, "Well, I guess I'll see you guys in the morning."

"Chris, why don't you stay a minute?" Emma nodded at the young people. "I'll see you two in the morning."

He sat back on the wicker swing. Once alone, Emma moved to sit next to Chris and patted his leg, asking, "Am I to assume the date didn't go so well?"

Chris smiled weakly and shrugged his shoulders, feeling tired and frustrated. "I had a wonderful time. But it wasn't a date," he corrected her.

"Humph! Seemed like a date to me."

"She said we couldn't call it that."

Grinning at how well she knew Robin and how she could easily see her saying such a thing, Emma wasn't surprised by that.

"You're obviously here looking for her."

Leaning his head against the metal chain, Chris sighed.

"Yeah, I'm not exactly sure what happened. I mean, I know, but maybe you can tell me how I might make it better."

He blinked and for a split second could see Robin flinching, obviously an instinctive reaction on her part.

"He hurt her didn't he, her husband?" Chris asked.

Unable to find her voice, and knowing if she spoke she would probably cry, Emma simply nodded.

"I reached out, just to move her hair from her face. She flinched as if I might hit her." Chris paused for a moment, and then asked, "How could he hurt someone so sweet?"

"I don't know. He wasn't always like that, but there at the end he became this monster. It was the drinking. He terrorized her and…"

She couldn't continue. What happened to her that night was like something out of a horror movie. Although Emma hadn't been given the specifics, as Robin was never willing to discuss it, the proof of Mike's brutality was pounded into every bruise and broken bone.

"Where is he now?"

Emma didn't know how much she should tell him. After all this was Robin's story, and Chris wasn't someone she knew all that well.

"He's still in North Carolina."

He could hardly understand how any man could raise his hand to a woman. Robin's face was so delicate, and she was so small, how could he hurt her that way?

Standing, pacing for a moment, Chris assured Emma, "I would never hurt her. I mean, if she were mine. I would protect her, and…"

And what, he wondered to himself as he trailed off, love her? Everything was getting muddled. He hardly knew her, yet he felt drawn into her story. At this point in his life, he was in no place to get involved with someone so fragile. How would she deal with what was ahead of him? He had nothing to offer her, no future.

Emma had moved to stand beside him. She suggested, "Just be easy with her. She has a very delicate spirit right now. It's not that she won't eventually heal; she will. She's a strong woman. Stronger than I could ever be."

Emma fought back tears at the recollection of all Robin had endured. It wasn't fair; none of it was fair.

Out of sheer frustration Chris shook his head. He couldn't allow himself to get involved in this; it was just too much. The thought no more crossed his mind when Vanessa's words came back to him. Those were the exact words she used – it was too much for her. He needed to think and pray through it all.

"I'm going on to my cabin, but thank you for talking to me."

"Chris?"

"Yeah?"

She smiled softly. "I'm glad you had a good time."

"Thanks."

He walked slowly to his cabin. Reaching the front porch, he never even went inside. Instead, he sat on the top step, kicked off his shoes, and just looked out at the water. To his left was Robin's cabin, less than two hundred yards away. To his right were the stone steps leading to the level clearing just before the lake. On one side she lay sleeping and on the other was the image of her sitting there at daylight, watching as the sun rose from behind the trees. Straight ahead was the small dock where she had stood, facing the wind just before diving into the chilly water. Feeling surrounded by her, Chris had to believe it was more than a coincidence he was there.

In truth, it wasn't too much for him, and he knew it. He wanted to help her heal. God had given him a particular insight into her, which in past experience usually meant he was being invited in. As he prayed and pondered, he began to sense he had been brought there for a reason other than his own. Clearly, he was encountering God's hand at work.

Quickly, Robin drifted off into a fitful sleep and immediately began to dream. As the dream usually started, she was running barefoot, dressed only in her nightgown, the chilly drizzle causing her to shiver as she raced down the driveway. She heard Mike screaming her name from the porch, and she knew without question he would find her; it was only a matter of time. He had always warned her not to run, and before she never considered it, but this night she was more frightened of him than ever. Somehow she knew that running was her only hope. Already, he had pushed her into the bathtub, and she feared her ribs were broken. With each step she took her chest cried out in excruciating pain. After yanking her out of the tub, he had hit her several times, the first backhand by far the worst. Her teeth ached still, and her cheek felt as if it were on fire. When Mike threw her on the bed and began loosening his belt, she believed him to be unsteady enough to topple. That was when she made the decision to run. With both feet she shoved him as hard as she could, scrambled off the bed, and began running. Now, she realized she had nowhere to go.

Robin bolted upright in bed, covered in sweat. Violently, she was kicking at the covers tangled about her feet. For a moment she wasn't sure where she was. The sights and sounds around her seemed foreign. Then suddenly it dawned on her, she was home, at Emma's, and she could run. There, she paid the price for running, but here, she could run.

Chris had been sitting in the silence for over an hour, so when that stillness was shattered, it took a few seconds for his brain to respond to what his eyes were witnessing. Robin passed by his cabin at full speed, barefoot and wearing only her nightgown. Immediately, he knew where she was going.

When he jumped from the porch he resisted calling out to her; instead, he followed her to the dock, where she stopped at the very end. Gasping for air, as she was breathless from her sprint to the lake, she lifted her arms, preparing to dive.

Quietly, Chris stepped onto the dock and pleaded softly, "Don't do it, Robin."

She froze but didn't turn to face him. "I have to."

Springing from the edge, she dove in and began to swim.

Chris walked to the end of the dock and sat, determined to wait for her This time he was close enough to hear her as she stroked through the water, until she swam so far out the sound faded.

He had no way of knowing how much time had passed, but it felt like an eternity as he waited. It was different from when he saw her do this that first week. Then, she was a stranger to him. This time, she was someone whose story had captivated him and drawn him in. Disoriented and out of breath already, Robin was far out in deep, dark waters. If she didn't return, he had no means of rescuing her and that terrified him.

When she did make it back, Chris held his hand out to Robin, offering to lift her out of the water. She took his hand.

Robin sat on the dock, draped her hair over one shoulder, and began to wring out the water. Chris hadn't spoken, and she was too out of breath to even try to explain. Conscious of the fact she was wearing a wet nightgown, she was thankful the moon was no brighter. Fortunately, it was bright enough only to allow them to make out the outline of one another, no more.

Genuinely concerned for her safety, Chris warned, "One night, something tragic could happen. You may not make it back."

She allowed his words to sink in and then replied honestly, "I don't know if that would be such a bad thing."

"Robin..." Unsure of what to say, only partially understanding what was driving her, he finally asked, "What makes you do this?"

Wrapping her arms around her knees, she gazed out at the water. "Some nights, I relive the end."

Her breathing had finally steadied but still her heart was pounding so hard in her chest, she could hear its echo all the way up into her ears.

He realized she was shivering from the cool night air and began to unbutton his shirt. Sliding it around her shoulders, he admitted, "You know, I saw you here on the dock when I first got here."

She looked at him, feeling something beyond embarrassment, something more akin to shame.

"You were standing there and then suddenly you dove in. I guess I thought you were... I don't know, trying to hurt yourself or maybe you were crazy." Hesitantly, he asked, "Are you trying to hurt yourself?"

"No. It seems to be the only thing that makes it better though. After I swim, when I come back I feel stronger. I may not be able to run away, but I can swim away."

"From what?"

"My husband." Standing abruptly, shutting down the conversation, Robin turned to leave, saying, "I'll see you tomorrow."

She had closed the door on further questions, so he dared not ask any more.

"It is tomorrow." He smiled and added, "Can I at least walk back with you?"

"Sure."

Walking with him, Robin remained quiet, and when they reached his cabin she wasn't altogether surprised when he continued walking on with her. Approaching hers, she slipped the shirt from around her shoulders and handed it to him.

"I'll be okay. Thanks, though."

"You should talk to somebody. You don't have to live this way."

"It's all I know anymore," Robin admitted.

She left him at the foot of the stairs, understanding how full of questions he must be. Ultimately, this was hers and there was no one who could help.

"See you for coffee?" he asked.

"Yes, I'll see you then."

As Chris watched Robin move through the doorway, he became utterly certain of why he was there. "You sent me here, Lord," he whispered aloud.

5

Early the following morning, just moments after the sun peered from behind the familiar tree line, Robin was sitting on the steps, looking out at the water. Out of the corner of her eye, she saw Chris approaching. In a way she felt embarrassed over what happened the night before, both flinching away from him and what he witnessed when he followed her to the dock. What could she say? There was no way to explain it to him. She barely understood what drove her actions. How could she expect him to understand?

Chris climbed the stairs slowly, and when he reached where she sat, he sat quietly beside her. Noticing the second coffee cup, he smiled. As he took the cup, he nudged his shoulder into hers. "Great service here." Then, after taking a sip, he offered, "I know someone who can help, someone you can talk to about this."

She never went back to sleep after their encounter last night. For hours she had been thinking about the things he said. When he suggested the possibility of something tragic happening and she found it wasn't something that sounded so bad, that was the point when she truly comprehended how far she had fallen into fear and despair. The truth was, she didn't want to live the remainder of her life the way it was, but she questioned if there was even hope for her. Assuming there *was* hope, how could she ever find her way back? Every excuse rose up and gave her reason to run from healing.

"You've seen my days around here. I don't have a whole lot of free time."

"He'll speak with you here."

"I could never afford that."

"He's really cheap. As a matter of fact, he does a lot of free counseling at my church."

Robin was skeptical. "He would drive two hours? Why would he do that for someone he doesn't even know?"

"As a favor to me. We're pretty tight."

Chris outmaneuvered her every attempt to avoid it and was prepared for every excuse.

"One session, that's all you have to do. If you think it helps, great. If not, then at least you gave it a try."

"Let me think about it," Robin said, trying to buy some time.

"Sure. Just let me know."

Surprised by Robin's semi-willingness, and fearing she might talk herself out of it, he felt it best to change the subject entirely, so he told her, "I think I'll take a boat out again today."

"What do you paint while you're out there?"

"Anything. Everything. My time is running out, and I want to capture everything I can while I can."

"You're here for another month and a half."

"I know. It seems to be flying by, though."

"Summer is like that."

"Yeah. Time flies by," he said thoughtfully.

Emma was in the kitchen watching Robin and Chris on the stairs. Smiling to herself, she hoped this could be a new beginning for her. More than anything, she wanted to see her happy. When Robin stood and came toward the house, Emma quickly moved away from the window, not wanting Robin to feel self-conscious. She poured herself a cup of coffee and leaned against the counter, trying to act casual.

"Morning." Robin said, dreading the probing questions that were sure to come.

Smiling sympathetically, Emma noticed how Robin's eyes seemed weak and heavy, so she said, "You look sleepy."

Robin pulled a twenty from her pocket and laid it on the counter. "For Tommy and Becky." Hesitating a second, she added, "I'm sorry to say, you won't be getting the other fifty. I'm just not ready."

"Then I'll never push you about dating again." Sad for her, Emma asked, "He is a nice guy, though, right?"

"He's a great guy, and I had a good time with him, but you know how complicated things are. I need more time."

"You take all the time you need."

Smiling half-heartedly, Robin asked, "So, where's my fifty bucks?"

Emma pushed the twenty back at her, saying, "I owe you the rest."

Robin moved into Emma's arms and they stood quietly, embracing. The turmoil she felt inside was worse than she had known in many years. Having hoped it would get better, instead, things seemed to be getting worse. Her greatest fear was that Mike would come for her and take her back, or worse. In the state she was in, she would hardly have the strength to fight him.

Robin moved through the remainder of the morning as if in a fog. For much too long she had spent days like this. The terrors would come, and she would spend the final hours of the night fighting sleep, terrified the dream would pick up right where it left off. Only once did she make it all the way to the end, and that was undoubtedly worse than the continual chase, much worse.

By early afternoon she was exhausted and went to her cabin to rest. After only half an hour of napping, she woke feeling refreshed and renewed. Sitting there on the side of her bed, she prayed her first heartfelt prayer in many years.

"I don't want to live this way anymore."

Deep inside, she felt something within her cry out for healing. She wanted it, but could she ever really find relief? Bound and gagged for so many years, could she ever find her way back when the person she once was seemed so far away? The life she previously lived, happy and secure, was surely shattered beyond repair.

"I know You're there," she whispered.

Chris had been out on the lake for the past three hours. Painting and praying, his constant thoughts were of Robin. Without any doubt, he knew she needed help, and something told him she was truly considering it. Her eyes that morning were tired and sad, full of pain, not distant pain as they usually were, but pain terribly present at that moment. Clearly, she was as low as she could possibly be, but wasn't that the best place for the Lord to begin a mighty work?

He had to admit, he was intensely attracted to her. If he wasn't, he would have never asked her out to dinner in the first place. So the attraction was something to be thankful for but greatly avoided. He felt certain God had brought him there specifically to reach out to her, and that was accomplished by the initial attraction. God was funny like that. Had Chris not been drawn to her, he would have remained within himself, concentrating on his own end.

As another example of the genius of God, in order to keep Chris totally dependent upon Him and his mind off his growing feelings for Robin, it would require clinging to Him and dying to self, the likes of which Chris had never known. God was still choosing to grow him spiritually even so close to death. Chris knew, in order to separate *his* feelings and thoughts from what was best for her, it would take dependence on the Holy Spirit each and every moment he was with her. How could he not marvel at the strategic wisdom of God?

When he arrived at his cabin, Robin was sitting on the porch, rocking. Dumping his paint supplies, along with two canvases of his not-so-best work, he joined her in the other chair.

Without looking at him, she asked, "Do you really think he can help?"

"I don't know about him, but I do know he'll lead you to the one place you can find some rest."

"Where?"

"To God. I know him well enough to know that's where he'll take you and your broken spirit. I also can tell you that healing can be found no other place. If you'll go to Jesus, it'll get better. Maybe slowly, but it will eventually."

"Have you talked to him?" Robin asked.

"Yes. He'll be here tomorrow. Is there any particular time that's best for you?"

"Lunchtime, I suppose. That way I won't feel the need to explain my absence."

"You mean to Emma?"

"No. I'll tell Emma, but I would rather not discuss it with anyone else."

"You shouldn't have to. This is between you and God and whatever you decide to tell the counselor."

"Chris…"

She sat for a moment trying to collect her thoughts. How could she say what she felt without it sounding as bad as it no doubt would sound?

"I don't know the way to God anymore. I used to, but I haven't in a very long time."

She had been a tremendous pretender.

"I know that."

He had anticipated this conversation and knew his observations about her would likely swell up a defensiveness in her that might prevent any further openness.

"At the risk of offending you, I'll tell you the way I see it. Since I've been here, you've left for church on two Sundays, and it seems less productive or beneficial than if you were going to the grocery store. At least from the store, you would bring back a sack of food, something of value, something to nourish you. Instead, you're practicing religious routines. You leave and come home empty handed."

She was silent, so he was unsure of how much more he should say. When he felt the boldness to continue, he asked, "Have you always gone to church?"

"Yes."

"Has it always been as it is now?"

"No."

"There is routine and there's relationship. The reason I know yours is routine is simple, really. Watching you jump in the water and swim, witnessing your apathy about your own safety, I understand the hidden meaning behind it: you want relief even if it's in the form of death. These things witness to your routine. You can't be in a close and intimate relationship with Jesus Christ and remain so tormented. I say this because I've experienced the same thing in varying degrees. I've thought long and hard about it."

Pausing for a second, he wondered if he could possibly express his thoughts in a way that might make sense to anyone but him.

"I've never articulated this, so cut me some slack in the presentation of it."

Her smile prompted him to continue. "There's no such thing as darkness. In actuality, darkness is the absence of light. Make sense so far?"

Nodding, she indicated it did.

"Similarly, chaos and torment are the absence of peace. The absence of peace means you've somehow stepped away from God. Make no mistake, He will never leave you nor forsake you, so absence means *you* have moved, if you are a believer, that is. For non-believers, chaos and torment is their natural state, parenthetically speaking, of course. They can never know the peace we're offered."

He looked at her, and the way she looked back caused him to momentarily stumble with the words. Trying to ignore what her eyes did to him, he went on.

"He's not the author of confusion. So anytime you feel that kind of commotion in your mind or in your heart, you have to determine what step you took away, or steps in cases where you feel far, far away. He is the Prince of Peace. He came to set the prisoners free. When you are in a close relationship with Him, you're free from that kind of turmoil. And you, Robin, are anything but free."

Amazed by his correct estimation, she said nothing in reply. Standing, she moved to the stairs. Hesitating on the bottom step, she asked, "Here, at noon?"

"Yep."

To her surprise Robin had a restful night of sleep. As she was soon to be in the process of churning up muddy waters, she anticipated a difficult night, but it was, thankfully, a night of rest. Sitting on the stairs, she wondered if Chris would come again. She brought coffee for him just in case. Within seconds, she saw him appear from behind the small row of trees leading from the cabins.

When he sat beside her, he thanked her for the coffee. After a minute of awkwardness, he admitted, "After the things I said yesterday, I wasn't so sure I'd be welcome this morning."

"You were right in everything you said."

"I thought about this all last night. You know what I've come up with?"

"What?"

"You've mended the veil."

Thinking for a moment, trying to figure out what his words meant, she finally gave up. "What does that mean?"

"When Christ died on the cross, the Temple veil was torn." Unsure of how much she had learned over the years, he decided going back to the basics might be helpful. "When you asked Him to come into your life and forgive you, from that point forward, you have had complete access to God. He died to offer you that. When you pray, you don't have to toss words up into the air and hope He catches them. You can sit right here with Him and simply talk." Patting the stone beside him, he suggested, "Here, every morning, He will sit with you. Standing out on that dock, He stands with you. Talk like you would to Emma or to me."

He considered how he used to pray versus his current way and hoped to give her a "for instance" that would make sense. "This morning for example, I said, 'Lord, Robin is in a mess, and I need the words to lead her to You.' I didn't use a whole bunch of churchy words. I talked to Him. Or, maybe I'll say, 'What do You think about this or that?' Then I wait and listen for Him to tell me. Mostly, He responds through His Word. Sometimes, He speaks into my heart, but always, always He answers, even when it's not what I want to hear. Honestly, a lot of times it's not what I want to hear. But still, He speaks."

This concept was foreign to her. Never, even before turning from Him had she prayed in such a way. If she had to explain what she experienced when praying, it was more like slipping words into a balloon, filling it with helium, and releasing it into the atmosphere in the hopes it would reach the right destination. When it mattered most, her balloon obviously missed heaven.

He continued. "All believers have this same access, and many of us use it. Some people, however, those who have been hurt or have experienced tremendous loss, spend their lives trying to mend the veil. What I mean by that is they build some sort of self-imposed wall between themselves and God. For many believers this process may happen inadvertently and over time, stemming from doubt that God is active in the lives of believers, doubt that He's close, or doubt that He cares. Stitch by stitch, they recreate the veil in their own hearts, giving them the sense that He's far away."

With his words she grasped a truth that she could have never identified on her own. What he said was an accurate description of what had happened to her over the past years. More than six years had passed since she was willing to look at God. That exact moment was burned so vividly into her mind and so engraved into her heart, she could feel the weight of it in her chest still. She had intentionally stepped away from Him. From the reasons he suggested, in her case it was all of the above: hurt and loss definitely, but mostly, she was convinced He didn't care. Had He not proven it by His inaction?

Chris could see how intently she listened and certain his words were ringing true, he went on. "With the wall in place, they mistakenly believe

God doesn't see them, or probably more accurately, they're hoping not to see Him. In this way they run from His presence rather than run into it. They live out the Christian experience missing the One they really need, Jesus. It becomes a lifetime filled with ritual and routine but never a relationship with Him."

"I've never heard anything like this."

"This is something I've pondered for years."

"Obviously!"

His thinking was so profound she could hardly imagine how she had missed his depth before. Then again, she had made it such a point of keeping him at arm's length, that a conversation at this level was all but impossible.

"In my case, I realized that I couldn't reconcile what I read of the God of the Bible with what I was seeing in the world and experiencing in my life. Doubting He was active in the lives of everyday people like me, I just installed a zipper, closed the veil, and went through the religious motions. That got me nowhere but miserable and defeated. Eventually, I realized I was seeing other people with what seemed to be a real relationship with Jesus, and I wanted that."

"What you said about stitch by stitch, that was probably more my case."

"That's what you need to talk about then, your stitches. Exposing them will begin the process of unraveling them. Until that veil is unmended, you can never be close and intimate with Jesus. Until you choose to move back into Him, you'll never know the peace and freedom He offers."

"I'm scared to talk about it. It terrifies me to relive it."

"There's a verse that comes to mind; it's about God being a candle shining a light into darkness. I'll have to look that up for you. Basically, what I get from it is that you have to allow those things into the light and He'll show you the way. He can heal them then, but if you keep them bottled up, you'll keep swimming in dark waters." He grinned at his pun.

"I don't want to swim there anymore."

"I know, and you're doing something about it. You've agreed to get help. You are *choosing* to move back where you belong, in His presence."

Though nothing had actually happened yet, she still felt some small sense of relief, as if help might really be on the way. Feeling some reservation about what she was about to say, she said it anyway. "While we're here and things are still quiet, I want to tell you something."

He turned to look at her, finding that he was caught off guard by how pretty her eyes looked. They had a tender sweetness about them she usually kept hidden.

"I was going to tell you the other night, but then I acted so weird." Flushing in her embarrassment, she looked back out at the water.

"What?" he asked.

"I'm not in a good place to date anyone right now. I think you're a great guy, but I'm just not ready."

"I get that." He gulped down the last of his coffee. "Honestly, I'm not either."

"Vanessa?"

"No, other things. How about I save the *other things* for some other time?"

"Agreed."

He stood to leave, bearing a deep sense of regret over their timing. If things were different, he would pursue her to the ends of the earth. Problem was, by the time she was saved from such a vulnerable place, he wouldn't be around to witness it.

With a few minutes to spare, Robin was nearing Chris' cabin. She felt nervous earlier, but after talking it over with Emma, she was more reassured. Emma had been thrilled to hear she would be talking to a counselor, amazed even that one was willing to drive in from Boston. Though Emma didn't grasp the Christian aspect of the healing Robin needed, still she encouraged her to talk openly. The things of God were not something Emma was ever open to. As long as Robin had been there, she had been going to church alone. Emma had no interest and had even asked her to stop inviting her. Looking back, how much good had it done her? No wonder Emma didn't see a benefit; Robin shown her none.

When she arrived at the cabin she was disappointed to see there was no other car there, only Chris'. Certain she hadn't seen anyone come in through the entrance of the inn, she feared the man wasn't coming. It had taken everything in her to agree to this, and now she was ready to get started.

Tapping on the door, she heard Chris invite her in.

"Hey," she said as she opened the door slowly and peeked in.

"I'm here. Come on in."

Chris was sitting in one of the club chairs by the fireplace. Of course there was no fire burning at such a time of year, but he thought it set quite a mood. Another chair was across from him.

"He's not coming?" As she asked, Robin tried to hide her disappointment.

"He's here, Robin. Have a seat."

"It's you."

It was a statement rather than a question. For some reason, the possibility that Chris was the counselor never even crossed her mind, but now as she thought about it, it made perfect sense.

"Does it bother you?"

"No." Pondering a moment, she added, "I don't think."

"Why would it bother you?"

She was wearing khaki shorts and a pink button-down shirt with a white t-shirt underneath. The previous summer, he had traveled with his church youth group to camp, and for some reason, with her in that outfit, he was reminded of that. Maybe it was that she seemed so young and vulnerable at that moment. While she still looked like herself, strong and determined, he had a new understanding of her. Inwardly, she was much more delicate than she appeared on the surface. Wasn't that the case with most people, though?

"I suppose it doesn't matter."

Momentarily uncomfortable, she tried to determine why. Just two nights before they were out on a non-date, maybe that was it. For the briefest moment she thought about the possibility of beginning something. She didn't know what to call it other than what Emma called it, a summer romance. Perhaps that was what bothered her at first. Whatever the case, he was willing and free, so she had nothing to lose by talking to him at least once.

"I have experience if that's what makes you hesitate."

"No hesitation. Just tell me how to begin."

Since their previous conversations, she suspected there was a vast depth to the man sitting with her, and she had barely scratched the surface. Apparently, there was godly wisdom and discernment beneath the surface of that handsome face of his. After so many years living the way she did, she had come to realize she wouldn't heal on her own. She needed help, and he was offering.

"Tell me your story. Help me know you more."

"You mean, like childhood, that far?"

"Sure. As far back as you want to go. Give me the highlights."

A slight smile tugged at her lips. "Well," this was an odd feeling for her. "I had a happy childhood, wonderful parents. They loved each other and loved me."

"Brothers or sisters?"

"No, just me."

"Milestones?"

Trying to come up with a milestone, she could think of nothing before her early teens. Childhood had been fairly uneventful.

"I kind of felt invisible for most of my early life, not at home of course, but at school. I had several good friends, but I wasn't wildly popular. Then one summer, I kind of blossomed. I grew a little taller and wore my hair a little differently. When I went back to school, things were different."

"You became more popular?"

"No, I didn't mean it that way. I guess I stopped feeling so invisible."

"Boyfriends?"

"One."

"What was his name?"

Moving her thumb to her mouth, she began to chew on her nail. *One.* That word echoed around in her heart. There had always been only one.

After another moment of hesitation, she whispered, "His name was Mike."

It suddenly struck her that she hadn't spoken his name aloud in many years. While it felt strange saying it to Chris, the sound of Mike's name was just as familiar as her own.

"How old were you?"

"Thirteen, we both were. It was middle school, seventh grade."

"Tell me what it was like to become visible."

❖ ❖ ❖

Balancing on an overturned log, Robin held a stick with a marshmallow dangling on its point. Trying to get it just right, she allowed it to catch fire then quickly pulled it to her and tried to blow it out. When she looked up, he was looking at her. His name was Mike. This was the same Mike she had been secretly watching since the beginning of the school year, when two separate elementary schools merged into the larger middle school building. This was a big deal to all the girls, as it afforded a brand new crop of boys to whisper about.

Robin noticed him the very first day of school, and as impossible as it seemed to her, he noticed her too. Often, she caught him looking at her during Social Studies. That was their only class together and suddenly her favorite of the day. His seat was over near the windows and behind hers, so that rarely allowed a chance for her to peek at him. She soon discovered that every time she dared a peek, he was looking her way. Then again, Shelly Masters sat in front of her. Who could help staring at her with her new figure? No girl but Shelly seemed to mature as much over the summer. Not only the new boys from West Elementary but the boys from her school noticed her *transformation* as well. As much as Robin tried to convince herself, something told her it wasn't Shelly Mike was interested in.

He was tall but not freakishly so. That came a few years later. Still, he was tall enough that she could see him over the other heads in the hallway between classes. His hair was brown, just a bit lighter than hers, and his eyes were dark blue or so they seemed from across three rows. Captain of the football team, every girl in school talked about him. As far as she knew, he had no girlfriend.

So there she sat, marshmallow ablaze, and Mike was smiling at her. It was then that he began to walk her way. Before making it to her side of the campfire, someone announced they were going to play Seven Minutes in Heaven. He halted his movements at that point. Disappointed, Robin had no idea what the game was, but since it kept her from talking to Mike, she already disliked it.

Watching as couples were paired up and sent behind a small group of trees for seven minutes, she suspected they might be kissing but had no way to be sure. This was, after all, her first boy/girl party. Her parents had only allowed her to go with the assurance everyone would be outdoors with adults present. After the third couple Shelly walked up to Mike and whispered something in his ear. Then she giggled, and Robin's heart sank. It shouldn't have surprised her since Mike was the most handsome boy in school, and with Shelly's summer "makeover," of course he would want to go with her.

Robin noticed him shake his head, though. Then he continued what she thought was his earlier trek over to where she sat.

When he reached where she was sitting, someone teased, "Mike and Robin," meaning they should be the next to pair up and go behind the tree line. Suddenly, many voices chimed in. Repeatedly, they chanted their names.

Where were the adults? Robin wondered. *Where was the way out?* She was unsure of what to do or how to react. If she ran toward the house, everyone would laugh at her. To go behind the trees with Mike, however, could be a fate worse than embarrassment.

Squatting down before her, Mike placed his hands on her knees and softly assured her, "We don't have to go if you don't want to."

On his face and in his eyes was a look of tenderness she would have never expected from a jock. Having daydreamed about the moment, in her version there was always an air of arrogance about him. This Mike, however, this huge football player, wasn't arrogant at all. Actually, he seemed very sweet.

Robin looked up at him, and without conscious thought of it, her head began to nod. What was wrong with her head? Did it not know her dad would kill her for an affirmative nod?

Extending his hand to her, Mike grinned playfully, saying, "Let's just do it to shut 'em up."

They walked hand in hand to the small clearing and for a moment just stood there. Someone had given him a flashlight, so it wasn't entirely dark; but it was still dark enough to be creepy.

Mike was the first to break the silence as he confessed, "I've been trying to get up the nerve to talk to you since the beginning of the year."

"Really?" she asked in awe of the moment.

Her heart was pounding and her hands trembled, and her entire body shook. It was cool out but not enough for the convulsions she was experiencing. *Did he notice?* Her mind was wandering, and all she could do was shake and grin like an idiot. He said something, but she missed it due to her crazy, wandering mind.

"Huh?"

Mike repeated, "I said I don't know exactly what we're supposed to do back here."

Chewing her thumbnail, she whispered, "Me neither."

What happened next was something that would cause them to roll with laughter for years to come.

He asked, "So, wanna be my girlfriend?"

"Sure." What else could she say?

"Can I give you a kiss?"

This time, "sure" wouldn't even come out of her mouth, so her rebellious head began to nod again.

Leaning down, he kissed her lightly on the cheek.

❖ ❖ ❖

Chris smiled. "That was a nice story. Did you date him for very long?"

After recounting the night they met, Robin realized how long it had been since she allowed herself to think back on such fond memories. Throughout the years, she had feared recalling the good times but found it less painful than she anticipated it would be.

"We weren't actually allowed to date until I was sixteen. Even then it was with serious restrictions." She grinned. "My dad was crazy overprotective."

"You were together for some time then?"

"We married when we were eighteen."

Chris sat there for a moment, for some reason surprised by that. Often, in cases of spousal abuse, signs of violent tendencies began prior to marriage. If Robin had dated Mike so many years before marrying him, surely there was some indication.

"What was he like back then?"

Gazing into the fireplace, Robin found herself wishing it was cold enough to have a fire going. That thought led her to remember she had agreed to take some firewood down to another cabin that afternoon. They were having a bonfire after dark.

"Robin?"

Robin glanced at Chris, unsure of what he had just asked. Without warning, she felt flush and unable breathe, so she jumped to her feet.

"I should go. I don't think I can do this anymore."

Standing, he moved between her and the door, saying, "If you're feeling uncomfortable, we can stop. I believe it was a good start, though."

He wanted to keep the door open for more sessions.

"Thanks for talking with me. I'm sure it'll help." Stepping around him, she reached the door.

"Tomorrow at noon?" he asked.

She muttered, "I don't think I can," and without another word, she left him standing there.

The remainder of the day, Robin tried to stay away from the others as much as possible. Though not upset exactly, she instead felt far away. Memory after memory flooded her mind, and for the most part, she simply wanted to wade in them alone. From the moment they met at the bonfire, all the way through school, she and Mike were inseparable. When she said she was no longer invisible, it was true. They were *that* couple in school, the one everyone wanted to be. Mike played football and she cheered. At every event, every homecoming and prom, they were at the center of them all, undeniably the perfect portrait of high school sweethearts. From sweethearts to marriage it remained ideal until their lives were shattered by loss and grief. Those were the memories that threatened to drown her.

She questioned whether she could go and speak with Chris again the next day. Sure, she could tell him sweet stories of middle school and high school. Even those first few years of marriage, though occasioned by separation, were beautiful and full of real and genuine love. It was the next chapter she feared.

Later that evening, Emma and Robin were sitting on the swing under the gazebo. Becky and Tommy had gone out for the night. Emma had encountered Robin several times throughout the day, but each time, someone was around, preventing her from asking questions. Finally alone, Emma asked, "So how did it go today?"

First, Robin told her that Chris was actually the counselor and Emma got a kick out of that. Then, Robin told her, "It was a start, I guess."

"That's all I get?" She patted Robin's leg, hoping for more.

"Today wasn't so hard. I know it'll get more difficult, though."

"But you'll stick with it, right?"

"I don't know if I can."

Emma sat for a minute before daring to bring up the subject. "We both know it's getting near time. Do you want to talk about it?"

"No. I just can't. Not now."

"Okay. I won't press you."

After a few quiet moments, Emma asked, "Are you sleeping well?"

"Last night, yes."

Chris was walking toward them and both became immediately quiet. "Mind if I join you?"

Emma stood, saying, "I was just heading in. You two enjoy the stars."

Her intention was no longer to set them up, rather to give them privacy to talk.

"You don't have to go on my account. I'm beginning to get a complex around you two." He smiled.

"Early mornings, you know." Pausing, she patted his cheek. "Have a good night, sweet thing."

Looking back at Robin, she smiled at her. "See you in the morning, Hummingbird."

"I'll come up early for coffee."

Both remained quiet for a moment after Emma left, until finally Chris asked, "Hummingbird?"

"She began calling me that when I was a little girl. I guess because of Robin."

"I see."

"Sorry to take off today. I guess I felt some things I wasn't ready for."

Taking the seat beside her, he turned to face her.

"There is no required amount of time. We will simply talk as you feel you can. No more, no less."

Staying away from any hint of the past, they chatted about senseless things. From weather to what outdoor activities they each liked, they kept the conversation in non-threatening places. As much as he wanted to help her, the truth was, he simply liked hanging out with her. Having no hidden agenda, simply being friends with her was easy to do. Appreciating her sense of humor, her sarcasm, and her kindness, he sensed she was good for him and helped to keep his mind off impending things. For as long as she was willing to be friends, he would seek her out.

Out until nearly midnight talking to her, time flew by. With her guard down, Chris found Robin to be one of the sweetest, funniest women he had ever met. It wasn't lost on him how compatible they were. From movies to sports, they had most things in common except football, and on that, they agreed to disagree. He hated the Panthers and she hated the Patriots. That was about as far as the dissimilarity went. Walking back with her to her cabin, once she went inside, he left feeling a bit let down. It was one of those perfect nights, one you hate to see end. If things were different…he stopped the thought mid-way through. It was safer that way. Things weren't different and never would be.

6

Robin sat in Chris' cabin feeling a little more comfortable than she had the day before. The night before was unusual, in that she dreamed of Mike, but not the end times. Instead, she dreamed of good times, times when she was her very happiest.

"We had a good marriage. No, we had a great marriage."

"No signs at all of violence early on? Or even when you were dating?"

"No, not at all." Hesitating, she added, "I can only think of one time he was even angry. In a way he became violent then, but he didn't hurt me."

"Tell me about it."

"It was our junior year. Something happened that really hurt me, so I broke things off. He didn't take it well at all."

Even the memory of it was unsettling. It was the first and only time he ever hurt her before he began drinking. Technically, it too was most likely related to drinking.

"What did he do?"

"He hit a locker a few times, nothing else."

"Were you standing near the locker?"

"Yes, but he wasn't angry at me. I think he was angrier with himself and maybe a bit jealous."

"Was he often jealous?"

Looking for common traits of an abuser, Chris thought maybe he had stumbled onto something. Jealousy was often something that drove spousal abuse.

"Then? No, not really. I suppose I had never given him reason to be."

"And this time?"

"I wasn't trying to make him jealous. It was just that this guy was talking to me, and Mike flipped out."

"Tell me what happened."

❖ ❖ ❖

Robin was standing at the foot of the staircase, trying to listen in on her dad's and Mike's conversation. Upon hearing his truck pull into the drive, and realizing it was nearly ten o'clock, she jumped from her desk and ran down the stairwell. Her father beat her to the door. With his hand he motioned for her to stay where she was.

"Just a few minutes." Mike pleaded. "I promise that's all. I just need to talk to her."

"You know how I feel about things like this."

Robin could hear the irritation in her dad's voice.

"Yes, sir. That's why I've never done it before. Just ten minutes – please?"

Stepping back through the doorway, her dad motioned for her, saying, "Just a few minutes. When I flick the light, you come in."

"I will, Daddy."

Robin kissed him on the cheek and rushed out to find Mike sitting on the top step. When he turned around and looked up at her, she grinned and whispered, "What are you doing here?"

"Come here and sit down."

Her heart began to pound and she suspected this wasn't good news, so Robin asked, "What? Is something wrong?"

Taking her hand, he pulled it over and rested it on his lap. For a moment he was silent. Finally, he began, "I didn't plan on going. When I went out with Tommy and Kevin, they wanted to go to Shelly's party."

It was Sunday night, and Robin had a paper due in her first class. Even when the invitation to Shelly's party began to circulate, she knew with it being a school night and church night, her dad would never allow her to go. So after church, she went home to finish her paper. She expected him to be at church as usual, but when Mike never arrived, she wondered if maybe he went to the party. If he decided to, it wasn't something that bothered her, until this moment anyway.

Suspicious, his tone giving her cause for concern, she said, "Uh huh?"

There was a smell about him, something different, so she asked, "Have you been drinking?"

He nodded but then shrugged his shoulders indicating it was no big deal. "A little, earlier."

She sat there, unsure of what to say. He had never drunk anything as far as she knew. His dad used to and Mike hated it.

"Did something happen at the party?" Immediately, as soon as the words were out of her mouth, she sensed she didn't want to know.

"Shelly kissed me." After a slight delay, he added, "I guess I kissed her back."

Saying nothing, Robin simply sat there and stared ahead. He was still holding her hand, and she lacked the presence of mind to withdraw it.

Mike turned to her and whispered, "I promise, nothing like that will ever happen again. I swear it."

"Why did you do it?"

Still, she didn't look at him. Instead, she tried to fix her gaze on the mailbox at the end of the sidewalk. Her breathing had become shallow and she feared she might cry.

"I don't know. She just moved in on me, and at first I was like, what the...? Then I don't know, she kept pressing in on me."

Robin could think of nothing else to say or to ask. Pulling her hand from his, she mumbled, "I should go in." At her words the porch light flicked off and on again.

Mike stood and caught her by the arms, assuring her, "I don't like her. Honestly, I don't even know how it happened. I just knew I had to tell you and ask you to forgive me."

She tried to turn from him, but he held her firmly.

"I can't lose you. Robin, I love you, and I swear I'll never do anything like this again. I'll never hurt you again."

Her dad opened the door so Mike had to let her go. Robin moved quickly through the doorway, never turning back to look at Mike. She didn't have to; the pained expression on his face was burned into her mind.

Moving up the stairwell in a daze, she mumbled, "Night, Daddy."

"Night, sugar."

The next morning, Robin was dressed and ready for school by the time her dad was leaving for work. Catching him at the door, she said, "I'll need a ride to school this morning."

"Sure thing. Is everything all right?"

She could tell he was puzzled. Since getting his license, Mike had taken her to and from school every day.

"Yes. Just need a ride, that's all."

During the ride, there were no more questions, though she knew he was curious.

Walking up the steps on the east side of the building, she saw Mike pull in and park where he usually did. Across the expanse of lawn she could see that he was watching her and was certain he had gone by her house to pick her up. Heartbroken, she turned away from him and hurried into the building and through the hallway to her locker. As she went along, she realized that people were watching her and whispering. Surely she wasn't imagining it. Settling the matter, her closest friends, Emily and Rachel, grabbed her and dragged her into the restroom.

"He's such a pig!" Emily spat.

Rachel agreed and added, "I'm so sorry. I wasn't even in the same room, but I heard about it."

They began to discuss the details between the two of them, who saw what, who should have said what.

"I've gotta go," Robin said to her friends, who were much too engrossed in the details of the night before to hardly notice she left.

She tried again to make it to her locker. At that point it became clear; it wasn't her imagination at all. All eyes remained on her throughout the morning. Plus, she heard several eyewitness accounts that painted a more disturbing picture than Mike's simple, "She kissed me, and I guess I kissed her back." Apparently, they were groping all over each other right in front of everyone.

By lunchtime she had heard all she wanted to hear. Whenever anyone approached, she threw up her hand and told them she knew. Mike had tried to talk to her on several occasions, but each time she hurried off, too hurt to even hear what he had to say.

Sitting at the lunch table with Emily and Rachel, Robin saw him approaching. By this point, with all she had heard, her mind was made up. Humiliated by the stories and hurt to her very core by his desire for someone else, she was determined to end things with him. Though she knew nothing else besides him, she felt she had no choice. It was his doing, not hers.

Mike straddled the bench next to her and moved in very close. For a minute he just sat, looking at her.

She noticed that others around, without any discretion at all, openly gawked in curiosity. Everyone knew about him and Shelly, and they seemed to be enjoying Robin's pain. It was the juiciest piece of gossip the school had known all year, and ironically, those who gladly put them up on a pedestal were just as happy to watch them topple over.

"Please talk to me," he pleaded.

Turning to face him, she said in as low a voice as she could, "It was more than a simple kiss. Do you know how many people were watching you?"

He nodded.

"It was stupid, and I can't do anything but tell you how sorry I am. Baby, I love you." He moved his hand to the back of her neck and pulled her to him. "Please forgive me, please." He rested his forehead on hers, reminding her, "I have nothing but you; you know that."

He was so close she could feel his breath on her face. His sad eyes revealed his desperation, but *his* eyes were not all she could think of. Literally, everyone was staring, watching this private encounter, eager to see what she would do. Even more embarrassed than before, she whispered, "I think we need some time apart."

Amazed at the courage of her own words, she knew deep in her heart it would never be as easy as she made it sound. Their lives were so intertwined that she didn't know where she ended and he began. Already having been together four years, he was all she knew, and still, even after all she heard about how he touched Shelly and how she touched him, Mike was all she wanted. Her weakness for him made her feel needy and pathetic.

"No, no. Don't say that." He held her firmly to him. "I'll do anything to make this up to you, anything."

"There's nothing you can do."

Pulling away from him, she took her tray, food untouched, and dumped it into the barrel trashcan. Holding her head high, with feigned strength, she left the lunchroom. Alone in the hallway, though, she ran all the way to the restroom, locked herself in a stall, and began to cry. Sitting there on the toilet, she went through half a roll of tissue before the end of lunch bell sounded.

After school during cheerleading practice, Robin was near to where Mike practiced football. On several occasions, she heard his coach yell at him, "Where's your head, McGarrett?"

Robin tried not to look, but when she did, she found Mike staring at her. Clearly, he was a mess, and it broke her heart for him. Once, when she had taken a fall during one of the stunts, she saw him begin to run toward her. Again, the coach yelled.

When her practice was over, she caught a ride home and waited for him to call. She knew he would. While they spoke on the phone, he begged and pleaded, but she refused to relent. After their third conversation, her dad demanded Mike not call again. It was the worst night of her life up until that point.

At school the next morning, Robin was at her locker before first period when a boy named Jeff approached her. Already, she was being propositioned, but didn't take it seriously, since she knew Mike and Jeff had a few clashes over the years. He was only talking to her to spite Mike.

When Mike caught sight of him there with her, he slammed his locker door and stormed toward them. The look of fury on his face sent Jeff moving away quickly.

As Mike reached where she stood, he spun her around to face him, saying, "I know you better than this. You would never go out with him just to hurt me."

She looked up at him, aware that he was hurting just as badly as she was and felt no sense of defiance by that point. He was right; she would never do such a thing to him. Even though the hallway had gone virtually silent, as onlookers watched their exchange, she no longer felt embarrassed as she did the day before. Instead, she wanted the whole thing to be over, the argument, not the relationship. She loved him and had come to conclude during the sleepless hours of the night, she would forgive him anything.

Grasping her by the shoulders, he pressed her against the lockers and moved his face nearer to hers.

"I swear to you, if he touches you, I'll kill him!" With that, he slammed his fist into the locker next to hers multiple times.

She jumped at the sound of the pounding next to her ear but never once considered he might hit her. He stood there, towering over her, breathing hard and swearing under his breath. While she had never seen him so angry before, still, she felt no fear of him. Looking at his hand and noticing his knuckles were bloody, she reached for it, saying, "Look what you've done."

He never looked at his hand. Instead, his eyes were trained on hers as he said, "I don't care. I don't care about anything else, only you. What happened with her will never, ever happen again. Please don't leave me."

Mike's voice was anything but quiet. His eyes were moist with tears, and she considered the fact that all of their friends were looking on still. Yet, he was unafraid to fight for her or plead with her, right there in front of them all. He loved her enough to make a fool of himself, and she loved him even more for that. Slipping her arms around his waist, she rested her head on his chest, saying, "I could never leave you."

❖ ❖ ❖

Robin sat with Chris, reliving the moment even then. She could hear Mike as he whispered in her ear, "Never again. Do you hear me? No one but you."

From then on that was the way it remained.

After hearing of her relationship with Mike, Chris felt a peculiar sense of jealousy. He had never known a love like the one she described and grieved the absence of it. Though he had been in what he would call "love," it was never that deep and lasting kind of love he hoped for. There was a reason he was still unmarried at thirty-seven.

Obviously in her case, it was no more lasting than his had been. So having heard stories of their early relationship and how good things were, he was more than a bit curious to learn how things took such a drastic turn, leaving them divorced and her so damaged.

He suggested, "Tell me about your marriage."

She sat there, biting at her lip, trying to muddle through the onslaught of memories. Going back to the good times was like a journey home after being away for so many years.

"Mike enlisted in the Marines right out of high school, so we married before he left for basic training. I stayed with my parents and started classes at a community college nearby. Immediately after, he was deployed to Afghanistan for a year. It certainly wasn't easy, but we got through it."

"And then?"

"When he came back, he was sent to Camp Pendleton, California. Things were great between us. It was really our beginning as a married couple. We had never been away from home, but somehow, being so far away from family caused us to grow even closer."

Recalling that season of life was gut-wrenching. Mike was all she had ever wanted, and at the time she truly believed she was living out her happily-ever-after. Nothing could have ever prepared her for what was to come.

"Then he was deployed again for another year. That year was much more difficult. I was all alone there in California. It was too expensive to fly home often and too far to drive. I got a job and continued taking classes, which helped me somewhat."

Chris' suspicion was leaning toward post-traumatic stress disorder. Some soldiers came back from war with it. For a man to transform from what she had described so far to a violent abuser, some event or series of them had to trigger it.

"Once he returned home, he only had another six months left and decided not to re-enlist. We moved back to North Carolina after that."

The look on her face when she spoke of Mike told the story of her love for him. Chris was surprised at how much more open she was; she seemed almost animated. Her eyes sparkled, danced even, as she recounted stories of their early years together. Only in rare moments, as if she suddenly remembered the love story she recounted no longer existed, her eyes would cloud over with that reality.

"What was he like when he came home the second time?"

"Different from the first time. He wasn't sleeping well and often seemed agitated." Feeling the need to defend him for some reason she couldn't understand, she added, "He was never ill with me. He just wasn't like that. You would have to know him then to understand."

She sighed, filled with regret over what was lost.

"He treated me as if I were his whole world. That's how it always was."

She stopped for a moment, lost in the memory of how much he loved her. He did love her.

Noticing how far away Robin seemed, Chris suggested, "Are you okay? Do you need a break?"

"A break would be nice. Actually, can we pick back up tomorrow?"

Something was stirring in her chest, something she needed time alone to process. A tidal wave of emotions washed over her, causing her to long for those days. No such longing had occurred in many years, and she was unsure how to filter out the good from the bad, the happy from the sad.

"Your rules, remember?"

"Again, sorry about yesterday. I shouldn't have taken off like that. Thanks for not giving up on me."

Grateful, Robin realized how fortunate she was to have this opportunity. Opening the door to her past was painful and frightening but necessary if she ever wanted to live again. Chris was giving her that chance, and she was more than appreciative of it.

He smiled at her sweetness. "Oh, I imagine it won't be the only time you try to run. I'm patient, though."

"Thank you so much. I wonder how I could ever repay you for this."

"You don't have to repay." Then thinking better of it, he changed his reply. "Who knows, maybe I'll think of some way. I'll let you know."

"You do that…anything you say."

As she cleaned one of the second story guest rooms, Robin was left alone to think. Her mind traveled from place to place back in time. Giggling, she thought about the donuts. After all those years, it still made her smile.

❖ ❖ ❖

Robin sat nervously on the side of the bed and looked up at Mike. He was standing there before her, grinning awkwardly.

"You know what this reminds me of?" He sat beside her as he spoke.

"What?"

"Seven Minutes in Heaven. Remember how we didn't know what to do?"

"Are you saying you don't know what to do?" she teased.

They had waited to be married before being together, and though it wasn't easy on either of them, they made it through. After what happened their junior year, Robin was easily able to trust Mike again. Something changed between them then. Out of his regret and her heartbreak, there developed a deeper level of intimacy. Their love had become stronger and both felt a greater sense of commitment than ever before. Now, on their wedding night, it was finally okay to make love, and there they sat, both nervous, afraid of not knowing what to do or how to please the other.

"I think I'll figure it out," he said as his grin broadened. Moving in to kiss her, he whispered, "I've waited years for this. You better believe I'll figure it out."

It was sweet and beautiful, and at times even funny. They giggled in the darkness as they explored each other and all that was finally open to them. It was worth the wait and something tremendously more than either anticipated. They shared something few people ever find, and both were aware of that fact. His love for her ran deep and wide, and she was certain nothing would ever change it.

The next morning she woke up alone. The hotel room was small, so when she found he wasn't in the bathroom, she suspected he had gone out to get them something to eat. Wrapping herself in the sheet, she plopped down in the middle of the bed and turned on the TV. Within a few minutes, she heard the key slip into the lock, and Mike walked in carrying donuts and two jugs of milk. It was their first breakfast together as man and wife.

❖ ❖ ❖

When Mike returned home from overseas the first time, Robin picked him up at the bus station. Since she was living at her parents' and wanted privacy for his first night back, she booked them a room at the same hotel. On the way there he pulled into the parking lot of the donut shop. Smiling mischievously as he put the car into park, he assured her, "So we don't have to get out in the morning."

Alone in their room, he knelt before her and said, "I want to tell you something. Married guys were hooking up with some of the women there. It happened all the time, but I never did. I would never do that to you. There isn't another woman in the entire world for me."

Sliding her arms around his neck, she demanded, "Promise me."

"I promise – no one but you."

That night was different from their wedding night and the few weeks before his departure for basic training. There was an intensity in the way he made love to her that shook her all the way to her soul. Nothing could ever take that kind of love away; she was sure of it.

The next morning, they sat in bed and polished off an entire dozen donuts. It became their thing, donuts, and because of it, she hadn't eaten one in years.

❖ ❖ ❖

Robin knocked on Chris' door, and when he didn't answer, after another minute she turned to leave. They had agreed to meet so she was surprised to find him gone. On the way back to the house, she saw him heading up from the dock.

Lifting his hand, he shouted, "Sorry, I lost track of time."

In that moment she became aware of something she should have recognized before. He was there on vacation, paying handsomely for the cabin rental, and here she was taking up his time with free counseling. He was rushed from his morning out on the water to get back to meet with her. She felt incredibly selfish.

Meeting him halfway between the cabins and the dock, she stopped and admitted, "I just realized how I've monopolized your time. I'm so sorry I haven't seen it before now."

"Monopolized my time? What are you talking about?"

"You felt rushed to be back here to meet with me when you should have no schedule to keep. I'm so sorry."

He chuckled. "You have to be kidding me." Passing by her, he added, "Come on."

She fell in behind him, still concerned. "Are you sure?"

When they reached the cabin, he dropped his backpack on the porch and moved to sit in one of the rockers. Pointing to the other, he smiled reassuringly, saying, "Sit."

She did so. For a moment she was quiet, still concerned that she was invading his vacation. How could someone, a virtual stranger to her, give so much of his time to a woman he barely knew? Chris was one of the kindest men she had ever met, and Robin couldn't help but compare him to the other men in her life. By comparison, she found the others to be lacking. Her dad was a good man but could be abrupt, even harsh. Mike was fun-loving for all the time she had known him, up until that final year, but she would never have described him as kind necessarily. Chris was kind through and through. There weren't many men like him, of that she was certain.

Finally, after a few moments of pondering his kindheartedness, she became curious, asking, "Have you always been this way, so giving?"

He smiled shyly. "I don't know that I would call myself giving."

"I would."

"So, where shall we begin today?" she asked.

Rocking slowly, he inquired, "Are you ready to tell me about the hard times?"

"Maybe." She squirmed a bit in her seat.

"When was the first time he hit you?"

Looking away, staring out at the water, Robin wasn't at all prepared to talk about it, but knowing there would be no relief over the end without taking him through the beginning, she began.

"I went to work for a car dealership as a receptionist. One night after closing up, my car wouldn't start. Of course I tried to call Mike, but he never answered. He had been going out after work drinking with the guys. At first it was just occasionally, but before long, he went out a few nights a week. I imagine he was ignoring my calls because he didn't want me asking when he might come home. I did that a lot.

"I wasn't sure what to do. One of the sales guys offered to drop me off, and I thought it was no big deal."

She was quiet for a minute. The memory of that night, the beginning of the end, brought with it an indescribable ache deep within. It reached a hidden place she was certain had become numb. In that moment, however, she felt the stabbing pain of disappointment and loss, assuring her she was anything but numb.

"Even after I got home I tried to call, but he still never answered. When he came in a little while later and heard I had accepted a ride home, he went off the deep end. It was like nothing I had ever seen in him before. He began accusing me of cheating and threatening the guy. I didn't understand what was happening. I kept trying to explain, and it seemed the more I did, the angrier he got."

A shiver ran along her spine at the recollection it.

"He reeked of stale beer and cigarette smoke from the bar, and at one point, he grabbed me and tried to kiss me. I was so disgusted by him in that moment, I shoved him away."

Hesitating, she recalled how he looked at her after she pushed him. It was the very first time she saw his anger directed toward her. Up until then, he was simply angry at everything. Burnt toast might cause him to throw the toaster. Lost keys would result in upside down furniture and slammed doors. In those moments, she would rush in and try to help diffuse his anger. That night, though, she was the target of his rage and no one was there to help her.

"After I pushed him he slung me across the kitchen and into the counter. I think maybe I cracked a rib. The bruising and pain lasted for weeks."

She stopped, unable to go on. That night, from there on, things only got worse. He never hit her or pushed her around again, but it was the first of many times he forced himself on her. Not in a violent way, but as some means of trying to make up with her, he began kissing her, telling her how sorry he was and how much he loved her. Even while she tried to stop him, he held her firmly in his grasp and continued kissing her until finally she gave in to him.

Afterward, and all throughout the next day, she lived in stunned silence, as if the entire thing had been a terrible dream. No matter how much she tried to push the memory away, the bruises on her wrists where he held her down were evidence of its reality. Even worse was the memory of how she responded to him, desiring him as much as he did her.

"That night, was there anymore violence?"

"No," she lied as she looked back out at the water. Some things were too humiliating to discuss.

"What happened afterward?"

"He was so drunk, but eventually he realized what he had done. He cried and told me how much he loved me. I became the typical, stand-by-your-man woman."

Robin snorted at her own stupidity. In truth, she believed him when he said he would never hurt her again. Of course she believed him. He had never lifted a finger to harm her before. How could she ever anticipate what was to come? For nearly a year it happened, not every day or even weekly but enough to make life so completely miserable that even when he was stable and not drinking, she lived in fear that he would snap or that something she said might set him off.

"Did he hit you only when he was drinking?"

"Yes."

"How long did it go on?"

"Nearly a year."

Chris stopped rocking and leaned up. Clasping his hands together, he told her, "I'm glad you got out when you did. Many women stay for years. Some never make it out."

She admitted, "That last night, I had no choice, or I would have never left him on my own."

"What happened?"

Shaking her head, trying to ward off the bloody memories of it, she whispered, "I can't, not yet."

"Okay, I understand."

He noted how the color drained from her face and knew better than to push her about that final night.

"After that first night, how long before it happened again?"

"A few months later. Honestly, I'm surprised it didn't happen sooner than it did. He was becoming more and more volatile. Everything upset him. Even sober, he had this incredibly short fuse. I never knew what might set him off and felt as if I was walking on egg shells constantly. I became nervous and jumpy, knowing something was terribly wrong. Then one night, it happened again. Actually, the second time he backhanded me...several times. The next morning, I was pretty beat up."

Out at a movie one night, a guy from one of the classes she had attended while Mike was on his first deployment, someone she barely knew really, came up and began talking to her. As he was about to walk away, he reached over and hugged her. When he did, Robin stood frozen, noticing the look on Mike's face. He was beyond furious. Stepping forward, he grabbed the guy's arm and shoved him. Though the guy apologized, Robin knew it wasn't over. Mike ignored her as she pleaded with him to stop, but he took a swing anyway and sent her former classmate flying into a wall.

The entire way home he grilled her, asking if she had gone out with him, if she had slept with him. Crying, Robin begged him to believe that nothing happened between them. Once inside, Mike ranted and raved then finally he left. When he came home much later, he dragged her out of bed and the whole thing began again. It was different than the first round. In his drunken state, many times he shoved her, and eventually he began to hit her. Until that final night, it was the worst of all the times.

"Did you call the police?"

"He was the police," Robin mumbled.

Just after returning home from the Marines, Mike got on at the Sheriff's Department. The friends he drank with were all deputies. Even if not, she would have never called and risked getting him into trouble. His job was everything to him, since being a cop was all he had ever wanted to be. She would have never taken that from him.

Looking at her, Chris shook his head and sighed. "Did you tell anyone?"

Pulling her legs up, propping her feet on the chair, she wrapped her arms around her legs. Resting her head on her knees, she admitted, "No."

"Were you scared to?"

"I don't know, I guess." Thinking, she added, "Not scared. It wasn't as if he threatened me if I did. I just didn't want anyone to know."

"Why do you think that is?"

Shaking her head, she shrugged her shoulders. By the time the abuse began, they had been married over five years. In all those years, she and everyone else believed them to be the happiest of couples. Was that what kept her silent, her embarrassment?

"Did anyone at work notice?"

"I never went back to work after that first night. From then on he was extremely jealous, so I simply stayed home. It was easier than the accusations and fights that arose when I did go out."

Her mind drifted between the two Mikes. When he was sober, though he was different from the man she married, he was at least remorseful over the things he did while drinking. In a drunken state, however, he was a total stranger to her, and treated her as if she were a stranger too. In either state, he lived with some sort of new fear, bordering on obsession, that she would leave him. He often said so, and it was something she could never understand. Never, not once had she threatened or even considered doing such a thing. Robin was willing to suffer the abuse as long as she was with Mike.

"Did you go to church then?"

"Yes." She stood and moved to the railing. "But not when I had bruises."

Millions of women lived that very life every day, but Chris' deepening feelings for Robin brought the reality of it painfully close to his heart. Standing, he walked to where she stood. She was gripping the railing, so he placed his hand over hers.

"I'm sorry you had to live that way."

Sighing, she agreed, "Me too. I was so sorry things became what they did." Closing her eyes, she admitted, "I loved him so much."

Looking back at Chris, as if trying to convince him of something she was certain of, she added, "He loved me too. I never doubted that, but after he came home, he was never the same. I've always wondered – what if I would have gotten him some help?"

"You can't blame yourself. I'm certain you did the best you could with what you had at the time. We all look back at our past and make sound judgments of what we could have done differently. Then we spend way too much time beating ourselves up over what we didn't do."

On the heels of a stirring deep within his stomach, Chris removed his hand. When he placed it on hers, it was an innocent gesture of concern, but after a minute he realized he was allowing it to remain there simply to be touching her. Clearly, the lines were getting blurred, and he would never do anything to jeopardize her trust in him.

"I know," Robin sighed. "Honestly, there are many things I would do differently if given the chance."

Thinking for a moment she asked, "Ya know what?"

"What?"

"Looking back, I can see it happening. Every strike was like another stitch, until finally, I could see nothing of God at all anymore."

After Mike would hit her, and then the things that would often follow, she would lie in bed and cry herself to sleep. The power he had over her mentally, emotionally, and especially physically was so traumatic, she was losing the desire to even get out of bed most mornings. Early on, she would wonder if God was looking on, watching what was happening in their home. Eventually she thought of no such things. At some point, though she wasn't sure when it finally happened, she stopped caring if God was watching or if He even cared at all. It was then that she started to truly die inside and eventually became numb to life altogether.

"Hindsight gives you great insight. It'll also help you heal. You can see what caused you to turn from God, and in knowing that, you know what barriers have to be removed."

His head was hurting, so he went back to sit down. Rubbing his temples, he admitted, "I may have to call it a day."

"Are you okay?" She went to him and squatted down. "Can I get you something?"

He was feeling a bit nauseous and needed to lie down. The headaches were becoming more frequent, but the nausea was new.

"I think maybe I'm coming down with something. I'll go in and sleep it off."

Concerned, she offered, "Please let me know if you need anything. Can I leave you my number?"

"Sure."

Chris went in, trying not to make too big a deal of things and pointed to a pad of paper on the table. "Just write it there."

Without another word he went into the bedroom and closed the door.

Standing there in the middle of the room staring at the closed door, Robin wondered what had just happened. Was he suddenly that ill? Leaving quietly, she felt uneasy. He was fine one moment and practically staggered to the bedroom the next.

That afternoon, Robin went about her work, but by dinnertime she was concerned enough to go by and check on Chris. When he answered, she was relieved to see he looked much better.

"You had me worried," she admitted.

He laughed. "Sorry about that. It came out of nowhere, but I'm better now."

Headaches were common, especially upon waking and were what led to his diagnosis, but the intensity of the one he suffered during the afternoon was like nothing he had ever experienced.

"Would you like to come up for dinner? Emma's cooking, and she wanted me to invite you."

"I feel privileged. If it's anything like her breakfast, consider me in."

"Great. Come up in about half an hour."

"I'll be there."

When Robin left, Chris went and sat on the sofa. He should have told her then that he was dying or at least that he was sick. Many times he considered how he might tell her, but every time, he acknowledged it would likely derail her progress. Out of concern for his condition, she would feel the need to give him his space, or something to that effect. Deliberating on it regularly, he wasn't so sure he would tell her at all. With only two weeks remaining there at the lake, there was no reason she would ever have to know.

7

In her room alone, Emma sat on her bed with her phone in hand. Having just hung up from the sheriff, she felt a terrible sense of dread over impending things. He agreed to call and find out when Mike would be up for parole, promising to get back with her when he knew. Certain that Mike would show up at the inn, Emma briefed the sheriff on his and Robin's history, in part anyway. Even with the sheriff's assurance that everything would be okay, Emma knew better. Mike could be at the inn long enough to do serious damage before a patrol car would arrive. He was this massive man, strong and determined, and because he was so completely consumed by Robin, his intention would be to take her away. How could any of them stop that?

Emma walked down to the lobby, hoping to catch Robin alone and at least let her know she had placed the call. Instead, Tommy and Becky were behind the counter, Tommy working on Robin's computer.

"Where's Robin?"

"I'm not sure. I think she's with Chris."

Walking into the kitchen, Emma sat on a stool and looked out through the large picture window. She could see them out on the dock talking. They had been meeting for a few weeks, and there were some signs of restoration in Robin. Emma was incredibly thankful for the progress she was seeing and for Robin's willingness to seek help. There seemed to be something brighter in her outlook and attitude.

Chris had begun going to church with Robin, and once, Emma even dared to go with them. When the roof didn't cave in, she decided she might give it a try again sometime. She had always believed in God and gone to church as a girl, but it had been many years since she thought of such things. Recently, witnessing the miracle that was happening in Robin's life, Emma felt as if she were catching a glimpse of Him in action. Something about that gave her hope for her own heart and almost a willingness to seek God for some restoration of her own.

"Emma, there's a call for you." Becky was peeking around the kitchen door.

"Thanks, sweetie."

As she stood and followed Becky to the lobby, Emma thought of Robin again. She had tried on several occasions to talk to her about Mike, but every time Robin changed the subject. Whether she was prepared to face what his release might mean or not, Emma was surely not going to sit idly by and let him surprise them. Her plan was to take a proactive approach. If she had to hire full-time security, she would do it. Robin meant that much to her, and she would pay any price to keep her safe.

When Emma answered the phone, her greatest fear was confirmed. Mike's parole hearing would be in two days, even earlier than anticipated, a fact which caused Emma to cry

Becky and Tommy were exchanging looks. Neither had ever seen Emma upset like this. As they quietly began to walk from behind the counter, she shook her head *no*.

Emma held up one finger and mouthed, "Stay here." Hanging up the phone, she wiped her eyes with her handkerchief.

Becky felt this sense of dread wash over her. "What is it?"

"Robin's ex-husband will likely be out this week."

"Oh, no!"

While she didn't know the whole story, Becky knew he was responsible for the nightmares Robin experienced. Emma at least told her that much the summer before.

Although it was Robin's personal business, Emma realized it would affect them all, so she felt compelled to share with them. "He'll show up here. I have no doubt."

"What can we do?" Tommy wondered aloud. While he wasn't exactly the confrontational type, he would do whatever he could to help protect Robin.

"I'll kill him." Emma said without hesitation.

Emma would indeed kill to protect Robin. Having known this day would come, she was prepared to do whatever it took to keep Mike from ever harming her again.

"Emma, you can't…" Even while she protested, Becky could see Emma's resolve by the expression on her face.

"Oh, yes I can!"

"Look, we'll just watch out for him."

Tommy wasn't sure what they would do if the guy showed up, but killing the man wasn't the answer.

"I have to talk to Robin." Without another word, Emma rushed away to find her.

By the time Emma reached the bottom of the stairway, only Chris was left standing on the dock.

"Where's Robin?" she called out.

"She was heading in to shower before dinner..." Chris trailed off, as he watched Emma immediately spin around and make her way toward the cabins. Her sense of urgency wasn't lost on him.

As she left the bathroom, Robin found Emma sitting on her bed. Clearly, by the look on her face and her lack of color, she was upset.

"What's wrong?" Robin asked.

"I want you to move back up to the main house. Now!" As she spoke she glanced down at her hands and noticed how badly they were trembling. There had never been a moment in her life where she felt such overwhelming fear and dread.

"Why?"

Even before asking, Robin knew it was about Mike.

"He's up for parole this week."

Understanding the implications of his release, Robin sat heavily on the bed beside Emma. Determined to never put Emma in harm's way, she suggested, "Maybe I should leave."

Unable to contain herself any longer, Emma burst into tears, pleading, "Please don't leave. I hate to imagine life here without you. You're all I have."

Wrapping her arms tightly around her friend, Robin consoled her. "I'll stay. I just don't want to cause any problems for you here, since I honestly don't know what he may do." Deep down, Robin knew what Mike was capable of.

Taking Robin's face in her hands, Emma sternly said, "This is *your* home. I won't allow him to drive you away."

After dinner Chris spotted Robin standing alone on the dock. With her back to him, he could see she had her arms wrapped around herself, as if to ward off the chilly evening breeze. Her hair whipped and flew in the wind, and her shoulders appeared rather downcast.

For just a moment he hesitated. Should he invade her solitude? He seemed to do that a lot. Considering all the old memories she was dredging up, having to process so much, he knew that time alone with God was where her real healing would begin. Not with him. Hanging his head, he wondered what he was thinking in the first place. How had he allowed himself to feel this way for the troubled woman standing out there on that pier? As if life away from this place had no sting of reality, he had allowed himself to become consumed by her and her story. When had it actually begun? He thought back to the night he saw her run toward the dock and dive in. No doubt, it began then and grew artfully, disguised in his simple determination to be her friend. Undeniably, he had come to the place where he wanted much more than her friendship. But what did he have to offer her? Certainly not a future.

Feeling the dock sway slightly, Robin knew someone had joined her, and even without turning, she knew it would be Chris. He had a way of being near when she needed him most.

He stood quietly beside her, hands dug deep into his pockets. She smiled up at him acknowledging his presence but remained silent. That was unlike her.

"Tell me what's going on in your head. I want to help."

When she leaned her head against his shoulder and sighed, it felt unusually intimate, so he slipped his arm around her and rested his hand on her shoulder.

"It looks like my past is about to catch up with me."

"What do you mean?"

"Mike."

For the moment she could say nothing more than his name. The fear of him was so overwhelming she could barely breathe, let alone speak.

"You think he's coming here?"

She nodded. She knew he would come for her. Not once had she ever doubted it.

"Emma was looking for you earlier. I could tell she was upset."

"He's in prison, but she found out he's up for parole this week."

Startled by her revelation, Chris asked, "Prison?"

In all the weeks they had spoken, she never mentioned he was incarcerated. Chris had assumed she left him. So far, she had talked about many things but never the last night. She was petrified of it, and this latest bit of information shed even more light as to why.

"The last time..." Nervously, she raised her hand to tuck her hair behind her ear. With her eyes cast down at her feet, she continued, "The last time, he went to prison for what he did to me."

Turning her to face him, Chris moved his hand up, lightly touching her cheek with his fingertips.

"I can't imagine how anyone could hurt you that way."

When she glanced up at him, those big brown eyes filled with fear, his stomach sank. She was alarmed, and after what he had heard so far, she had reason to be.

"Do you really think he'll come here?"

Robin turned to face the water, saying, "I'm sure of it."

Mike sat stiffly in the small wooden chair. Facing the parole board for the first time, he was unsure of what to expect. When they met a day early due to weekend travel plans of one of the members, he was anxious about the outcome. Though he had completed only five years of his seven-year sentence, his attorney was confident the parole hearing would go well. With his prior history with the Sheriff's department and good behavior during his five-year incarceration, it looked as if he would walk away a free man that day.

"Mr. McGarrett, we have reviewed your file and with no prior history of criminal behavior..." Robert Henry removed his glasses, smiling. "Actually, your record with the Sheriff's Department was exemplary, and you've served as a trustee for the past two years without incident. Mr. McGarrett, we are granting your request for parole."

From that point forward Mike never heard another word. After five solid years of staring at gray walls, he would finally be free. Night after night, he had lain awake, wondering where his wife was and what she was doing. Already, his only thought was of finding her. Soon after he arrived at the prison, his mother had written, telling him Robin had left town. His suspicion was that she went to New Hampshire to be with Emma. After so many years, would she still be there? That's where he would start.

Back in his cell, gathering his few personal belongings, Mike pulled the worn photo of Robin from the wall. Peeling off the wad of tape from the back of the picture, he looked at her sweet face. How had things gotten so out of control? From the time he was thirteen until that very moment, he loved her more than life itself. Caught in a spiral of anger and confusion, then alcohol and abuse, he demolished their lives entirely. Nothing could have convinced him early on that their marriage would end in such a way, or end at all for that matter. Robin was right; he became his father after all. All those years he was so confident that he was a better man than his dad, but Mike learned a humbling lesson: he was no better at all.

His brother Trevor picked him up and took him home. Loyal to a fault, he had been to see him every month since the very beginning, the only one to visit him besides clergy. Even when he told Trevor he didn't have to make the drive so often, he did anyway. Their history had created a bond few other brothers might maintain throughout adulthood. No doubt, they would always remain close. Grateful for the five years of rent-free living, Trevor was more than willing to help him get a new start. Though by no means well off, he offered what he had to his older brother, knowing it wouldn't be easy to find a job and rebuild his life.

Mike appreciated the way Trevor maintained his home while he was away and how he took care of their mother in his absence. Fortunately, he stepped in and took care of many things that needed to be done. Mike would always be grateful for that and offered Trevor the option of staying on as long as he needed.

Once home, reality settled heavily upon Mike. Years passed and life went on for everyone else, but for him, time stood still. There was always some unrealistic expectation of what he would feel and experience. The hope of going home, though, proved to be a cruel deception. While it promised to be a better place than he had known in five years, it was instead, extraordinarily lonesome. Unprepared for the onslaught of emotions he would feel in Robin's absence, soon after arriving home, Mike quickly had to get out of the house.

Standing at the bottom of the steps leading to his mother's house, Mike recalled how growing up, all he had ever wanted was out. Now, he was back, tail between his legs. When he married and left home, he remembered thinking with a sense of confidence, or more correctly arrogance, that he would never live as she did. Her poor decisions and inconsistency had driven him crazy all his life. Yet there he stood, newly released from prison, with the hope she would at least be glad to see him.

Kathy McGarrett was standing inside, arms crossed, looking at her son through the screen door. Without much in the way of enthusiasm, she said, "I thought you got out tomorrow."

Mike hesitated a moment before continuing up the steps. No matter the difficulty of their relationship, he had missed her and was glad to see her. Finding that she looked exactly as she had the last time he saw her, he acknowledged what a pretty woman she was still. Young to have a son thirty years old, she had barely turned seventeen when she gave birth to him. Her hair was the same dyed-blond shade she had worn for years. Now though, her roots were revealing her natural color of dark brown, his color. Her blue eyes were lighter than his, and for the first time he noticed how much her age was showing around them.

"They moved the hearing up to today. Trevor came to pick me up." He paused at the door, unsure if he was even welcome. "I just wanted to stop by and say hi and thanks for all the cards and letters."

Though she hadn't visited him once, she was faithful about staying in touch.

"I figured you would make it by."

As much as she wanted to throw her arms around him and welcome him home, all she could see was Walt standing there. Mike looked exactly like his father, where Trevor looked like no one really. Pushing the screen door open for him, she patted his arm as he passed by. Something about him looked different. He seemed unusually humble. *He should be*, she thought.

"I have some dinner on the stove. Are you hungry?"

He sat quietly at the table waiting for his mother to join him. Appreciating the food she prepared, he realized just how much he missed sitting at a real table with real food and family. Though he hadn't lived at home in many years, and no matter how glad he had been to be away from her, she was still his mother, his family. After he married, Robin was all the family he thought he needed. How time changed things.

"You going by the feed store? I talked to your uncle, and he said he would put you to work."

Noticing how her boy's hands trembled as he ate, Kathy recounted the countless nights she had spent, lying in bed, wondering if he was getting enough to eat. He had always been a big eater. At six feet, five inches and nearly as broad as he was tall, the boy could put away some food.

"I'll call him first of next week."

"What about tomorrow?"

Mike looked down at his plate, saying, "I have something to do first."

She dropped her fork, the sound of it startling them both.

"I know you don't think you're gonna go find Robin."

"Yes, ma'am, I am."

Standing abruptly, Kathy left the room.

Alone on the porch, Kathy thought back to that terrible night five years before. Once Mike and Robin had been carted off by ambulance, she was left to clean up the mess, she and Trevor. The house was covered in blood, and it was hard telling whose blood was whose. From the side porch through the kitchen and into their bedroom, there were splatters and puddles. Even after all that time, the mere thought of it nauseated her. She had never seen anything like it and hoped she never would again.

"It's not what you think, Mama."

He stood inside, looking at her through the screen door.

"Don't ya think you've done enough?" She turned and glared at him. "She should have killed you. Then at least she wouldn't have to worry about you comin' after her."

"I would never do anything to hurt her. Not again."

Storming toward him, she shook her finger, saying, "That's what you said the day you married her, remember?" Hanging her head, she began to cry. "You promised me you'd never do what your daddy did."

He looked away, unable to watch her cry.

"I don't know how it all started."

"It's the drinkin'!" she shouted. "I told you never to start that."

"I know, Mama."

"She never came back, and I don't blame her."

Though she only heard from her once after she left, Kathy would always love Robin. She was a sweet girl, one of the few people to ever treat her with any kindness.

"I didn't figure she would come back, especially after her parents moved away. If I had to guess, I would say she's up at the lake with Emma."

Kathy guessed the same. That was where Robin's only letter was posted from, but that had been years before.

"I think ya ought to leave well enough alone."

"I need to see her."

His palms grew sweaty just thinking about such a thing. It was what he thought of most over the past five years. With no hope of ever having her back in his life, he at least wanted to tell her how desperately sorry he was for the way he treated her. All he wanted was to see her one more time and to beg her for forgiveness.

"Why?"

Shaking his head, he muttered, "I need to ask her to forgive me."

Kathy nearly laughed at such a ridiculous statement. After the mess he made of both of their lives, she would be surprised if Robin, even as kindhearted as she was, would be able to forgive him. Though she appreciated his need for forgiveness to get on with his own life, she was concerned that seeking her out would only serve to upset Robin's. As for any real possibility of getting on with his life, she wondered what the future could possibly hold for him. Everyone in town knew he had served time in prison. Other than working for his uncle, what was there for him?

"I think you better think twice about going to see her. Are you even allowed to leave town?"

"No, ma'am, but it doesn't matter. I plan to go and come right back. If I get caught, it'll be worth seeing her."

As Mike pulled onto the highway, just beginning the sixteen-hour journey north, he smiled as he opened the cooler sitting next to him. Though she didn't agree with his decision to go, the instincts of a mother trumped her disapproval. Having filled the cooler with leftovers, she brought it by the house later that evening and wished him well. Mike never questioned his mother's love for him, but he knew how hard it was for her to show it, so the gesture meant a lot to him.

Since he had no money of his own, he had to borrow gas money from Trevor, but at least having plenty of food, he wouldn't have to stop often or spend much. With no real plan he drove toward New Hampshire, at times hopeful, at times hopeless, wondering if Robin would even talk to him. If she refused to, he could hardly blame her.

When he reached the mid-point of his journey, Mike stopped again for gas before going on to a rest station to eat. At the moment he was sitting on his tailgate, eating cold chicken, going over and over what he might say to Robin. Even as he rehearsed the possibilities, nothing he came up with could possibly undo the damage he had done. During that last year, he was so out of control, he remembered very little of the things he said and did to her. It became a common occurrence to wake up, after tying one on, to find bruises on her face and arms and things broken around the house. No matter how many times he swore it would never happen again, it did. Losing his wife was exactly what he deserved.

Having had the past five years to think it over, he agreed with his mother; Robin should have just killed him. At least then, he wouldn't be making this foolish drive, knowing he could never get her back. The only thing that mattered at this point was that he see her and tell her how sorry he was and that he found Jesus on the way to the hospital that night, or more correctly, Jesus finally took hold of him.

On many occasions Mike had tried to piece together the fuzzy details of that last night. He had been dwelling on it for years. He drew a total blank before the moment he laid there on the kitchen floor, with her holding his head in her lap, and he remembered the ambulance ride. No other pieces ever came together.

Several days later he was conscious again after a string of surgeries. The police, even the North Carolina Bureau of Investigations were there questioning him. It all became muddied in his memories. What he did remember most vividly were the photos of Robin that the district attorney showed him. Her image was burned into his memory for life, her face nearly twice its normal size, her nose broken, and both eyes swelled shut. It was enough to make him sick to his stomach. He learned that several ribs were fractured and her shoulder was dislocated. That was the point at which he agreed to plead guilty. Requesting she not be subjected to all a trial would involve, he made an agreement with the DA at his bedside and never even appeared in a courtroom. He was moved directly from the hospital to a prison infirmary.

8

As Robin worked behind the counter in the lobby, she froze when she heard a frighteningly familiar sound, a distinct grinding, squeaking, and a hard slam. Instantly, she was taken back to her former life. Her stomach sank and bile rose up into her throat, and for a moment she stood there paralyzed, looking toward the front door, waiting to see Mike's face. When his large frame filled the doorway, she felt her knees buckle out from beneath her, so she grabbed for the counter trying to steady herself, and she staggered sideways toward the back door. She watched in horror as he pulled the screen door open and stepped inside.

As desperately as she longed to escape, she realized she had no control over her legs. In her head were echoes of her brain shouting, "Run!" but there were also his words of warning that it would be worse if she did. As this scene unfolded in slow motion, Robin's mind was spinning rapidly, and then it all came back to her, her plan. Different from being at his mercy that final night, she could run. With that in mind her legs carried her clumsily toward the door where she might find help. Just as she pushed through the door, she heard Mike call after her, but her own screams drowned out his words. Haunted for years by this possibility, Robin had repeatedly planned her escape. Hour after hour, she pushed herself to swim farther and faster. Now the time had come, so if only she could reach the water, she could get away from him.

Slamming through the door leading from the back porch, she sprang into mid-air as she jumped over the back steps. Secretly, when no one was around, she had practiced this jump, always recognizing it might mean living or dying. Landing perfectly, she never missed a step as she continued across the lawn and toward the stone stairway. Having considered and experimented with the quickest route, she discovered she could slide down the hill much more quickly than she could take the steps.

Chris was passing the edge of the tree line when he heard faint screams off in the distance. Picking up the pace, he had a sinking feeling and moved as quickly as he could toward the main house. As if watching a movie play out in slow motion, he witnessed Robin sliding down the steep hillside, nearing the bottom. His first thought was that she must have fallen, until something else caught his eye. Mid-way down the steps was a massive man jogging down at a rapid pace. Suddenly, it dawned on him; it was Mike chasing her.

Chris moved swiftly, knowing for certain he could do nothing to stop the huge man without a weapon, so his only hope was to slow him down long enough for Robin to escape. With adrenaline pumping and his heart pounding, he was prepared to do whatever it took to save her; he had nothing to lose.

Though running as fast as his legs would carry him, he watched helplessly as Mike closed the distance between them. There was no way Chris could get to her first. Robin was so close, the dock merely inches from her when Mike reached for her. As Chris considered her path of escape, her late night swims came much more clearly into focus. The water was her getaway plan, probably had been for as long as she swam alone.

Chris witnessed the most unsettling sight of his life unfold. From afar, he watched Robin crumple to the ground, vulnerable and exposed to Mike. As he drew nearer, though still not near enough to be of help, he saw Mike simply stop and stand over her. Without saying a word he sank heavily to his knees before her and began to weep.

Approaching the two slumped figures, Chris knelt close beside her, saying, "Robin, it's Chris."

Softly, Chris placed his hand on her back. She was kneeling with her head buried into her knees and her arms covering her head for protection.

Hoping to reassure her, Mike reached out to take her hand, saying, "I'm not here to hurt you, and I surely didn't mean to scare you."

All he wanted was a chance to talk to her, but as she ran, the sad realization of how terrified she was of him caused him greater pain than any he had known in the past five years. Instinctively, he had followed her, but now, seeing the way she cowered before him, he understood what a mistake it had been. Never, even to satisfy his own need for forgiveness, would he have pursued her if he had known how traumatized she actually was.

Holding out his hand, Chris stopped Mike from touching Robin, saying, "You shouldn't have come."

Ignoring the man, Mike whispered, "I had to tell you how sorry I am. Please forgive me."

Again, he broke out into loud disturbing sobs.

Slowly, Robin raised her head, and in doing so she could see what Mike couldn't. Standing directly behind him was Emma holding a rifle. The look on her face was determined; she was prepared to fire.

Weakly, Robin whispered, "No, Emma."

"I'll kill you for what you've done."

Although her hands trembled, Emma's heart was set. If Mike wasn't so close to Robin, she would have fired already. Without doubt, it was the opportunity she had longed for over the past five years. Images of Robin's battered face surfaced in her mind, riling her up to an even greater level of fury.

Mike stared at Robin vacantly. "It doesn't matter. Let her do it."

Early on Mike had seen Emma out of the corner of his eye as she descended the stairway, but he genuinely had no concern for his own life. After all that had happened between him and Robin, having lost everything that ever mattered to him, to live or die wasn't a matter that troubled him. If he died, maybe Robin would be at peace.

"I'm asking you to please put the gun down," Robin pleaded, knowing what it felt like to carry Mike's blood on her own hands. It was something she wished on no one else, especially Emma.

"I want you to stand up and slowly move away from her," Emma demanded with a steady voice.

Hoping for only a minute more, just enough time to express the things he had rehearsed during the drive, Mike assured Robin, "I've been sober five years now." His face wrinkled as he fought back more tears. "I can't explain how or why I did all that, but I'm begging you to forgive me. Not a day has gone by that I've not thought about you or about what I put you through. I needed you to know, I found Jesus, just like you said."

He stopped and sighed heavily. Her face was expressionless, as if he weren't speaking at all.

"I don't know how we got here, Rob. I just know it was all my fault."

When Mike spoke the name of Jesus, it took Robin back to that night and the look of fear in his eyes as he lay on the floor, blood gushing from his abdomen with every beat of his heart. It was all she knew to speak to him, her only hope for him, his only hope. Now, looking into his eyes, she felt a wave of compassion for him, seeing how desperate he was for her to hear him.

Lowering her eyes, and with a shudder she caught sight of his hands resting on his knees. At the sight of them something happened in her mind, like a deafening roar of thunder. In that moment there was no one there but the two of them. Emma and Chris had faded away. Reaching out, she almost touched his hands, the same ones that gently lifted her lifeless baby from her arms all those years ago and handed him to the paramedic. Lightning joined the storm in her mind, and with a vivid flash she could see the scene and hear the sounds of the moment. With her arms empty, knowing they would never feel the warmth of Michael in them again, a cry escaped her, and along with it the very breath of life from within her. From that very moment she too ceased living. While looking at his hands, Robin realized that on that very day, Mike began the process of dying just as she had. She withdrew into herself and away from him, and because she did, he died without her by drowning himself in a bottle.

This was it, the moment she dreaded for the past five years. It wasn't retaliation or revenge on his part that frightened her. Deep inside, she feared facing the tremendous emptiness of her arms since the loss of her child. She feared having to see Mike again and relive it over and over. She feared that someday she would have to go back to that house and face the one moment of her life she had tucked away safely in some deep recess of her heart.

When she moved to touch him, Mike held his breath, anticipating the touch of her skin on his. There was a glimmer of Robin veiled behind the blank expression on her face. For a split second he caught a glimpse of her, not the Robin he had always known but the grieving mother who eventually became a stranger to him. When she withdrew her hand, Mike exhaled softly, hope pouring from his heart like the draining of a bathtub. He felt it swirl round and round 'til finally all hope was gone and all that remained was the gurgling sound of the last drops escaping him. During the long journey to see her, his mind was certain all was lost, but still, deep inside, in a place where he had no control, hope floated around wondering, "What if?"

Mike wiped his nose with the back of his hand and turned to look at the man standing nearby. Clearly, he was in love with Robin, and no matter how much that hurt him, Mike knew he was the only one to blame. She had moved on without him and well she should.

"Just take better care of her than I did."

Without another word Mike stood and moved toward the stairway.

Robin looked at Emma, assuring her, "I'm okay," and then watched Mike as he started up the stairs. His shoulders hung low, so low in fact, he hardly looked like a tall man at all. Holding to the railing as he ascended the stairs, it was clear, he had little strength to make it to the top.

"Mike," she called after him.

Turning, he waited as Robin moved slowly toward him. Her expression was altered. No longer was there a look of alarm as in the beginning or the emptiness of a grieving mother but rather something closer to tenderness, similar to the look she wore when she once gave him a second chance he didn't deserve.

"I'll walk with you."

Quietly, Robin walked in step with him. As they moved slowly up the stairs together, she thought back to a time when she loved Mike more than life itself, a time when she couldn't imagine living without him. Before the drinking and violence and misery, she loved this man with all her heart. Maybe he could be that man again. Without question, it was too late for them, but maybe he could start fresh, with someone new. She wanted that for him, to begin again.

As they walked, they both remained quiet. Oddly, it wasn't at all awkward. He was the one person who inhabited the planet that she knew better than anyone else, and he knew her that way. Two people who shared a common history that no one else could enter. That recognition caused her heart to burn with regret, and she was certain there could never be another living soul who would know her that way.

At his truck he stopped and turned to face her. She finally spoke. "I hope you stay away from the booze, Mike."

This wasn't a moment she ever prepared for. When she played out the scene in her head, it was always the worst possible scenario. After all that happened she thought it could never come to this, a simple good-bye. Well, not quite so simple. The tearing she felt in her heart was anything but simple. As if literally being torn in two, her heart longed for the days when they were so happy and more deeply in love than anyone she had ever known. But the reality was, that life was gone forever and nothing could ever resurrect it.

"I will."

As hollow as it may have sounded, he truly meant it. His life was so drastically altered by the events of that night that he would never be the same man he was then. The chaos in his head was gone, and he no longer felt the compulsion for alcohol. Being apart for so many years, there was no way he could expect her to understand, in one mere encounter alone, the change that had occurred in him. He was a different man entirely, but to her he was the one who nearly killed her.

Leaning against the truck, Mike covered his face. Sliding his hands across his rough chin, he whispered, "I know there's no way to undo it or make up for any of it, but Robin, I just need you to know…" He hung his head, unable to even look at her. "I've always loved you more than anything in this world. Still do."

She looked away. "Don't, Mike."

At his words the pain searing through her chest became even more unbearable. For so many years she loved him just as he described, more than anything in the world. There was nothing she placed above him, but in the end their love was never enough. Standing near him after so many years apart, even after all that happened between them, her instinct was to move into him. Knowing what it felt like to be wrapped in his strong arms, to be molded against his body, she could feel the very sensation of it on her skin if she allowed herself. How could such love still linger amid their circumstances?

"I'm not asking for anything. I know it's too late for us."

He looked down at her, and when he did he could still see that young girl he fell in love with all those years ago. Reaching for her hand, he found it trembling in his.

"I just had to see you, to tell you how sorry I am. That's all."

Before this day Mike's memory brought with it fear and torment, but finally, standing there with him, all that remained was sadness so real and palpable it caused her mouth to go dry. Choking out the words, she whispered, "I'm glad you came. I think we both needed this in order to move on."

The expression in her eyes nearly caused his knees to buckle. Large dark eyes conveying such deep emotion, they expressed her boundless grief.

For twelve years when she looked at him, he found nothing but love and devotion, but this day, only sorrow remained. Her words, "to move on" suggested something he would never attempt. Without her, there was no such thing as moving on. He would gladly live in the past with her in his heart rather than face the prospect of a future without her.

"About the house. Trevor is moving out next week. I can't afford to buy you out now, but I'll come up with the money as soon as I can."

He would work two jobs if that was what it took to stay in the home they made together. Everywhere he turned, she was there. It was the only place he would ever feel at home. Their son was born there and died there, and every memory that mattered was in that house. Never could he imagine living anywhere else.

Holding up her hand, she shook her head, saying "No. I don't want any part of it."

"It's half yours."

Actually it was more than half hers. They saved for a down payment, but when they came back from California, her parents paid the rest. It wasn't much of a house back then, just a rundown little farmhouse, but they worked tirelessly on renovating it. It was theirs.

Mike stepped closer to her and, without thought of the propriety of it, circled his arms around her. To hold her again, even if it was just for a moment, was worth the drive.

"I'll always love you, Rob."

Tears streamed down his face and tumbled onto her shirt, as he said, "Words can never tell you how sorry I am."

As she always had, she felt so tiny in his arms. How could he have hurt her the way he did, nearly killing her? This was the same girl he danced with at every prom, holding her in his arms in this very same way, the girl who knelt over him on the football field, crying when he blew out his shoulder, ruining all hope of a scholarship. This was the same girl he saw that first day of school, convinced she would someday be his. This was the woman he married and planned to spend the rest of his life with, the mother of his only son. How could he have destroyed what they once shared?

He held to her so tightly Robin could barely breathe, yet strangely, she had no desire to pull away from him. For the first time in many years she didn't feel quite so misplaced. It was a feeling that lasted for only a split second, but in that second she felt less empty. From out of the blue, though, roaring to the forefront of her memory, violent scenes flashed across her mind, causing her to pull away.

Out of words and void of hope, he whispered, "I won't bother you again."

Releasing her from his grasp, he moved quietly to his truck and slid behind the wheel.

Robin went back and stood on the porch. Watching his taillights bounce down the gravel drive, she whispered, "Goodbye, Mike."

Chris watched Robin and Mike from inside the inn. He didn't want to invade her privacy; instead he wanted to make sure she was safe. When she turned and began to walk toward the inn and Mike started his truck, he moved away from the window. Feeling slightly uneasy, he made his way back to his cabin.

Robin and Emma talked for over an hour before she finally went to see Chris. Mostly, she felt embarrassed about how she had acted earlier, but even more she considered Chris' reaction, how quickly he ran to help her. His concern touched her, reminding her how selfless he was. Without regard for himself, he reacted and was prepared to take on Mike, something that said so much about the man he was.

After tapping lightly on his door, she turned to face the lake. The sun was just setting, and the sky shimmered with a brilliant orange glow. It was as if the outer edges of the earth were ablaze, and in that moment, she wished she could capture the memory and keep it forever. Suddenly, all things were new. No longer would she anticipate or dread an inevitable encounter with Mike. What she had feared most was behind her, and up ahead of her was a new life to be lived. Somehow, somewhere along the way, hope had crept up inside her and the implications of it seemed limitless.

As Chris opened the door, he noticed she was standing with her back to him. Something about that gesture increased the uneasiness he already felt since watching her walk away with Mike. There was something about her long history with him, though turbulent to be sure, that troubled Chris. Hidden in the way they looked at one another was a deep level of intimacy. The way they walked in unison, it was an old familiarity that he didn't have with her and never would.

"I'm glad to see you're all right."

Turning to face him, she nodded and smiled halfheartedly.

"Yes, I'm all right." Embarrassed, she looked down. "I guess I overreacted a bit."

Without returning the smile, he disagreed. "I don't think it was an overreaction. Based on your history, I think it was perfectly normal."

"Now, there's nothing to worry about, not anymore."

He looked over her shoulder, not wanting to look her in the eye, and asked, "So what does that mean?"

She noticed the coolness in his tone, something she had never heard from him before.

"What are you asking?"

"So, are you going back to him?"

When Mike wrapped his arms around Robin, the way she melted into him, Chris didn't doubt she still loved him.

"Are you serious?" Taking another step toward him, she asked, "How could you think that?"

He looked down at her and his stomach fluttered. Her soft brown eyes caused the same reaction in him every time he looked at them, and their effect on him was becoming more difficult to ignore.

"I don't know." Shaking his head, he mumbled, "I don't know anything anymore."

Sensing Chris was upset, Robin was at a loss for what to say. Finally, she asked, "Are you saying I should?"

Even with the pain and regret she felt when Mike was driving away, never once had she considered going back to him.

"No, not at all."

His feelings for her were blurring his judgment and quite possibly his advice. Should she go back? It wasn't a question he had even contemplated so to advise her either way would be a mistake.

"That's something you have to decide."

"I'm not even considering it."

Something was going on, though she wasn't at all sure what. He seemed unusually pale and maybe even distant in a way she had never known him to be.

"Do you think we need to stop counseling now?"

"No, absolutely not."

Sitting in a rocker, he began to move slowly. He acknowledged he was crossing a line he should never cross. Well, his heart was anyway. No matter how he felt for her, he would never undermine her openness with him by exposing his feelings.

"You still haven't told me how you got to where you are today, either of you."

No doubt, she had been avoiding the most difficult revelations. Yes, she shared how Mike had changed when he began drinking and how the violence began, but she had yet to find herself strong enough to tell him about Michael.

"There *is* something I haven't told you yet. I've been thinking about it a lot, and I believe it was the very first stitch."

By the look on her face, he was certain they would need privacy. Often they sat on the porch and rocked, but he sensed this wouldn't be one of those days. Standing, he indicated she should follow him.

"Tell me now."

Following him inside, Robin took her usual seat. When Chris was seated across from her, she began, "When we moved back from California, I was pregnant, three months. We were so excited and could hardly wait to be settled in and begin our family. My parents were overjoyed at the thought of their first grandchild. They helped us pay for our house so I wouldn't have to work."

Chris sat waiting, knowing the worst was to come. Either she lost the baby or the baby died. Whichever it was, he was beginning to understand her first stitch a little more. She had been through so much heartache and pain, there was little wonder why she was in the shape she was in.

Robin sat for several minutes, unable to go on. When this happened, he was always patient with her and waited for her to begin again. Chris never pressed her. Finally, she whispered, "His name was Michael, and he was the sweetest little baby you've ever seen. Big," she said soflty, "he was really big even when he was born."

Chris watched Robin as she spoke; already tears were rolling down her cheeks and falling onto her shirt. Earlier, when Mike was there, his did the same – ironic how their tears were being mingled again over the one thing that caused the greatest heartbreak of their lives.

"Tell me how he died."

"They call it SIDS."

She gripped the arms of the chair and closed her eyes. With them closed she could see Michael so clearly.

"When I approached his crib, he was just lying there, cold and not breathing. I picked him up and held him to me. There was this sound, this loud and shrill sound, and I kept wondering what could make such a horrific noise." Opening her eyes, she told Chris, "It was me. I screamed until nothing came out anymore."

Pulling her knees up to her chin, Robin wrapped her arms around her legs and buried her face in them. In her mind she could see every aspect of Michael's room vividly. She could feel the soft material of his terrycloth pajamas on her hands and smell the distinct scent of baby powder.

Chris sat quietly. Her shoulders were shaking, and he wanted to go to her and comfort her. If he thought he had what it would take to bring her some relief, he wouldn't hesitate, but there in that moment, he discerned how much deeper her trauma was than what he had the wisdom or power to overcome.

"Lord," he prayed, "do something. I'm in way over my head."

The sights and smells and sounds of that day threatened to send Robin over the edge of some emotional cliff. This penetrating and excruciating pain was what she had been avoiding for years. Jumping to her feet, holding out her hand toward Chris, she whispered, "I can't do this. I can't do this."

She began to sob, her breath catching in her throat. In her mind she could see Michael's lifeless face. There was no smile of recognition, as when she normally lifted him from his crib. His eyes were closed, as if sleeping peacefully, but he wasn't sleeping; he was dead and she was screaming.

Dropping to her knees, Robin continued to weep. She doubled over and rested her face in her hands on the floor, saying, "I was sleeping. Why was I sleeping?"

Chris was unable to understand her. Her words came between racking sobs, and at times were indistinguishable from her cries. Kneeling beside her, he placed his hand on her back and suggested, "Take a minute, just breathe."

For several minutes she rocked and cried. Finally, unable to look back at that day any longer, she rose up and looked at Chris. Out of breath and nearly in as much pain as she was the very day it happened, Robin admitted,

"My baby died while I was sleeping." Tears fell from her face and onto the floor. Shaking her head violently, she cried, "I never, ever took naps, no matter what. Why was I sleeping that day? If I would have been awake, I could have saved him."

Still kneeling there with her, Chris wrapped his arms around her and held her close. The look of anguish on her face was beyond anything he had ever encountered. Her words expressed more than grief; they actually spoke of the guilt she carried.

"No, there was nothing you could have done."

"I prayed and begged God to give him back to me."

The anger she felt toward God was as fresh in the moment as it was the day she watched the first scoop of dirt land on that tiny silver casket.

"God wasn't there."

"Yes, He was. He has promised to never leave us or forsake us. No matter what your eyes saw or your heart felt, He was there. Look back and tell me what you see in that room."

"It was just Michael and me."

Moving his lips close to her ear, Chris whispered, "The Psalmist said, 'The LORD is close to the brokenhearted and saves those who are crushed in spirit.' He was there, Robin. No matter what it felt like, He was there."

He prayed aloud, "Father, give her eyes to see You when You seemed to be hidden. Mend her heart and bring her near to You."

The peace of that prayer washed over her. In all those years, not once had anyone prayed over her that way. Robin wiped her tear-streaked face with the back of her hands. Her voice became very soft. "I've looked back for years now, and all I see is me sitting in that rocking chair, holding my dead baby. There was no one else."

"God never left. He simply didn't answer the way you wanted."

What question was asked any more than why God would allow a baby to die while his mother begged Him for life? Chris would add that to his list of questions for when he got to heaven, though he suspected, he would understand fully when he stood in God's presence.

"If He was there, I would have my little boy."

Contrary to what Chris believed, she knew God turned a deaf ear to her. Year after year, she relived the anguish of that day, and undeniably, she was alone. From then on she was angry, and the truth was, from that very moment she never asked God for another thing, ever. She stopped talking to Him altogether. Later on, when Mike would come home drunk and violent, she never prayed for God to help her, determining it was pointless.

The day she held her ten-month-old baby in her arms, with no life left in him, she knew she was done with God. Why she continued to go to church, she could never fully understand, maybe because it was expected or because that was just all she knew. How she felt was always her secret. During and after Michael's funeral, when someone would try to console her with Bible verses and well-intentioned words of encouragement, she would nod while tuning them out. She despised them for trivializing her son's death that way. Michael's death was a zipper, not a stitch. From then on she refused to look at a God who had the power to save and yet refused.

Appreciating he was standing on holy ground, Chris spoke the only words he knew on the matter. "His ways aren't our ways, and His thoughts aren't our thoughts. There's no way I can explain this to you. I can't answer for God. But I do know this, He sent me here for you. He loves you and wants you back with Him."

"*He* left *me*," she spat.

"No, He's right here, and He wants you to see Him."

Unable to receive his words or believe what he said to be true, Robin whispered, "I don't want to see Him."

With that she stood and left the cabin.

The remainder of the day Robin avoided Chris. Unable to even pretend to keep busy, she told Emma she needed time alone in her cabin. Later, once it was dark, she went out to the water's edge and stood looking at the moon reflecting off the water. Lifting her eyes to the heavens, faced with the twinkling of a million stars, she demanded, "Where were You?"

The next morning, Chris went out early, even before the sun came up, to sit on the dock. He wasn't sure if Robin would be out early or even at all. After the day before he felt inadequate to counsel her. As much as he wanted to help her, he realized he didn't have enough experience. Talking with people, getting them to open up was his gift, and he often used it to help God's people, but in Robin's case, more than informal counseling was needed. Surely, someone with training could reach her. As soon as he returned home, he would find additional help for her. He would pay any price. All he knew how to do was to point her back to Jesus. Spiritually, that was what she needed, and no matter what she believed or felt, God was there with her and for her. But how could she break through the pain long enough to see Him? It was beyond him.

The night before had been torturous for him, and the few hours he did sleep were fitful. He thought of nothing but Robin and came to realize, somewhere along the way he had fallen desperately in love with her. No matter what he felt, though, his motives remained pure. They had no future together, so for her to ever know his true feelings would be pointless.

Thinking back to their first session together, he recalled how jealous he felt by her and Mike's love story, acknowledging he never had one of his own. Now he did, and it was too late or poor timing, whatever it might be deemed. He felt something for her he had never felt for another woman. It went beyond the desire to save her or help her overcome her past. Assessing the sum of her qualities, he loved everything about her. Her strength, even in the midst of such mind-numbing heartbreak, was something that caused him to marvel. *How was she even standing?* he wondered. She had determination that was unlike that of most people, and he knew it was the Spirit within her fighting to be heard. Never once had he doubted God's power of restoration. She would be well, and he would be but a small part of it.

Ultimately, he determined, loving her wasn't pointless. It was a gift, something God gave him there in the final months of his life. He deeply regretted not having the opportunity to share a lifetime with her, but realized for him, it *would* be the remainder of his lifetime. In his heart he knew if given a miracle and more time, he would pursue her and do everything imaginable to make her fall in love with him. As it was, he would take the gift of love over the certainty of death. Love would be his focus and the fact that his Savior cared so much about him that He would allow him to experience it in this way. Love would be the last and greatest emotion he would know, the greatest of all things to cling to.

Finding Chris sitting on the dock rather than the steps, Robin decided to join him. The night before, something happened that she could barely understand herself, let alone try to explain to him. While alone in bed, something came over her and made her know, not just suspect, that God indeed sent

Chris to help her, and as comforting as that was, something else happened, something like the tinkling of a familiar song playing off in the distance, where you can almost remember the words but not quite. God's presence felt almost familiar, as if she had never turned away from Him. It didn't last long, but it was present long enough to stir up a yearning she didn't realize existed inside her anymore.

As she sat, she greeted him. "Hi."

Robin handed Chris his cup of coffee, admitting, "Yesterday was tough, more than I expected."

"I agree. It was tough"

He took a sip of the steaming liquid. Feeling inadequate, he said, "I wish I knew how to help you more. Honestly, I'm afraid I'm in over my head."

"I disagree. The mere fact that I've talked about this means something. I wouldn't have opened up to anyone else. You've asked me some tough questions, ones I needed to ask myself."

Patting his hand, she assured him, "I wish I could explain it better, but for now, all I can say is that I feel something in me coming back to life."

Chris could hardly speak for a moment. Humbled beyond his ability to even grasp at the time, he prayed and thanked God for any progress she was experiencing. "Lord, please heal her," he whispered in his heart. Considering again his earlier thoughts about finding another counselor, he determined it would have to be something he prayed about. Once he left the lake at the end of summer, God would lead the way. Chris trusted that.

"Have you ever played 'Would You Rather'?"

"I don't think so."

"It's a game where you get two options, and you have to choose one."

"I didn't know it was an official game, but I suppose I have."

"I was thinking about what I should cling to, and it brought me to a question for you. This is something serious. Are you in the mood for that?"

"Maybe."

She wasn't at all sure, as her feelings were still so raw, but for once she understood how much bringing the past out into the light helped. In the weeks she had been talking to Chris, she felt so much less burdened than before.

He looked at her sympathetically, asking, "Would you rather have ten months with the pain of losing him or to have not known Michael at all?"

Shocked by his question, she drew in a sharp breath and without hesitating, whispered, "Ten months with the pain of losing him."

"I have a new way to frame this for you. I'm not sure it'll help, but I'll try it."

He turned to where he was facing her.

"Stop holding on to Michael's death, Robin. That's your entire focus – *that* day, *that* moment. Instead, hold on to the love you have for him. Hold on to his life." Chris felt a bit uncertain but continued anyway, "I didn't even know about him until weeks after I met you. I should have known. Somewhere between moving home and the joy of your new house you could have told me, but you intentionally left it out. You are so busy trying to somehow comprehend the incomprehensible, wondering why God didn't save him, that you've stopped remembering him or his life.

"This may be an odd comparison, but the Lord brought it to my mind last night. So I feel it's worth sharing. If you consider Job, he lost all his children, plus everything else, but I imagine the loss of his children was his truest grief. If you were to ask him now if the sorrows of this world pale in comparison to eternity, you know his answer would be yes. If you asked him if the millions of people over the years who have benefited by the story of his loss of so much and his refusal to curse God and die were worth all he suffered, he would say yes.

"Don't get me wrong. I'm not trying to compare you with Job, but rather Job with Michael. If you were to ask Michael now if his limited time here on earth was worth the mighty works God would do in his mother and father, he would tell you yes. Robin – with his current, eternal perspective, he would tell you yes."

Holding his hand up before she could speak, Chris added, "I'm not saying God caused Michael's death. The simple fact is that we live in a fallen world. There was some genetic abnormality in his little body that caused him to stop breathing while he slept. God wasn't the cause, but the effect was that He would use the tragedy and pain of it to show Himself to you. Even then, you didn't know Him, Robin. If you had, you would have turned *to* Him for comfort. When you know Him, you know beyond a shadow of a doubt and beyond what your circumstances tell you that He's your only place to run. Only He has the arms that can heal such a broken spirit, but you turned away, testifying that you never knew Him at all."

Robin sat silently, the things Chris said turning over and over in her head. He was right; she never truly knew God before. She knew some facts. She believed Jesus was God. She believed He saved, but she never *knew* Him, and she still didn't. Finally she was willing. If that was truly the place of healing, she wanted to go there, to get to know Him.

"Say something. Have I hurt you?"

Her face held no expression. He couldn't imagine what she might be thinking but winced with regret that he may have hurt her feelings, or even worse, broken her heart.

Stammering, she admitted, "Again, you're right. I don't want to keep holding on to Michael's death. Tell me then, how can I cling to that love?"

She held one hand out to him and tapped it with her finger. "Put something in my hand that helps me do that. I need something, an action to help me get started."

Finding such pain and uncertainty in her eyes, there was no moment before when he wanted to hold her any more than then. If there was any way humanly possible for him to lessen her pain, he would do it. He was helpless and knew nothing he could ever do would make a great deal of difference. In all his life, his adult life anyway, he had never experienced a moment where he felt as powerless to help someone who so desperately needed it.

"Go talk to Emma," he suggested. "Tell her all the funny, sweet, and silly things you can think of about Michael. Describe his laugh and his personality. Remember his life. Thank God for every day of those ten months. Then thank Him for the things He will do in and through you because of knowing Michael. After that, each and every day, find a way to hold on to his life, if only on the inside."

"I can do that."

"Sure you can."

Looking into her eyes, Chris saw the glimmer of what she must have been talking about earlier. There was a spark of life in them he had yet to see before. God was awakening her spirit, and it was the most amazing sight he had ever seen, let alone been a part of. Something about that moment assured him that she would indeed live again.

Later in the afternoon, after lunch, Robin found Emma in the kitchen cleaning. It was where she spent most of her time. Having remodeled the room two years before, it had become her resting place. That seemed odd with the flurry of work that went on there, but for Emma, it was her place. She said the warmth of the pale yellow cabinets made her feel as if she were standing in the sunshine.

"Do you have a minute?" Robin asked.

"For you, all the time in the world."

Robin poured them each a cup of coffee and said, "I'd like to tell you about Michael."

Dropping a cookie sheet into the large white sink, Emma moved to a stool and sat. Stunned, she stammered, "I would love to hear anything you want to share."

Emma had only seen the baby twice. Holding her grandchild was like a sweet, undeserved gift. Because he looked so much like Robin as a baby, he served as a painful reminder of what she had given up.

Robin began and went on for more than an hour. She tried to recount every memory she had of him, and it was the sweetest therapy for her wounded soul. From his smile and giggles to his temper when he was hungry, she shared all she could remember. It was, in a sense, like pouring cool water on a burned hand, painful, yet soothing at the same time.

Afterward, Robin experienced something akin to laying down a heavy load. It was more than emotional relief, it was physical as well. Suddenly, she felt less alone. For years, she had kept Michael hidden in her heart, but this day, it was as if he filled the air around her. Having pondered how this particular therapy could be so effective, she determined that love is sweetest when expressed, and that was what she had done that day. She expressed her love for Michael, something she would continue to do from that point forward.

After dinner Robin sat alone in her cabin and opened up her Bible for the first time in many years. On Sundays she would turn to whatever passage the pastor directed her to, but she never read along. She went through the motions, just as she was taught to do as a little girl, bowing when they said bow, opening her Bible just as everyone else did, but it was like being a little child again, as she stayed in her own world, thinking of other things. Keeping her mind closed off to God had kept the veil securely mended.

Prior to Michael's death, she had thought herself so faithful. If the doors of her church were open, Robin was there. Still, what Chris said about her not knowing God before Michael's death was accurate, and she knew it back then. She served and worked but recognized something was missing. It was most obvious around particular women, those who had a passion for Jesus that she didn't. It was clear to her when they spoke of their love for the Lord, that somehow, she was lacking something they had attained.

Within the past two days, Robin had seen Mike and had openly spoken of the loss of her son, Michael. The extremes of her emotions and the turmoil she felt inside could have easily overtaken her. Instead of running this time, she would take them to God.

Turning to Job, she looked up a verse Chris had given her. Even before he began to counsel with her, he mentioned it. Her version was different from what he had written out for her. His was from the King James Version.

> "Oh that I were as in months past, as in the days when God preserved me; When his candle shined upon my head, and when by his light I walked through darkness; as I was in the days of my youth, when the secret of God was upon my tabernacle."

Hers read:
> "How I long for the months gone by, for the days when God watched over me, when his lamp shone on my head and by his light I walked through darkness! Oh, for the days when I was in my prime, when God's intimate friendship blessed my house."
> Job 29:2-3

Chris' version called it a candle, hers a lamp. Both were beautiful images and made her hear that sound again, that familiar tinkling in her head. There was a momentary lightness in her heart, and for an instant, she felt less burdened. Any given moment before, heavy of heart would have best described her state. At long last, she yearned for the days when she didn't feel so far away from God and finally believed there may be a way back.

9

Another week passed and all that remained of Chris' vacation time was one week. He had rented the cabin through the end of July, which was fast approaching. His progress with Robin was nothing short of miraculous. Over the past week she had been so open with him, and for the first time, willing to take steps toward God. She asked questions and spent several days telling him about her son. Slowly, the veil was being unmended, as she was open to the Lord removing the stitches she had sewn. Still, she had far to go, but to see any progress at all was proof of God's handiwork in her life.

When he wasn't with Robin, Chris was praying. He had spent more time in prayer during that summer than he ever had. Strangely, he caught glimpses of God like never before. Not only was God actively working in Robin's life, He was working in his own. At a time when any man would question and fear, Chris felt a closeness and intimacy with Jesus like he had never known before. Though he would have considered himself, at the beginning of the summer, a man who walked with God; by the end of it he was prepared to declare he was a man who lived in God's presence. He had shown up in nature, in His work with Robin, in settling his apprehension about the end, so much so, that Chris considered the possibility that God lived full-time at Lake Winnipesaukee.

Finally, he didn't fear death or even dwell on it for that matter, for he knew what was to come and was at peace with it. Only once had he even considered another opinion or chemo or radiation, and that thought, or more correctly momentary sense of optimism, was in hopes of adding more time to his life so that he might spend it with Robin. He finally settled the matter in his heart not to seek any of those alternatives. He had been diagnosed by one of the best oncologists in Boston, and a second opinion was given by another who was highly recommended. So to pursue treatments would only postpone the inevitable. Without question the brain tumor was inoperable, his death certain. Somehow, assuredly divinely bestowed, he was at peace in his spirit.

Recently, his symptoms were becoming more problematic, and his head hurt so horribly at times, he would begin to vomit. He had yet to have seizures as he was warned he might, but he knew his illness was progressing quickly. Having not yet decided if he would tell Robin, he wavered back and forth from day to day. The place he stood for the moment was not to tell her.

Her progress was such that if she heard something so disturbing, she could be right back where she began —wondering why God wouldn't save him? It was a possibility, and he wasn't prepared to be the reason she questioned Him again. Chris knew that God had a plan, even when it wasn't evident. Actually, in his case, the plan was becoming amazingly clear. Without the illness, Chris would have never come to the lake. Without his attraction to Robin, he would have never gotten to know her. Without getting to know her, he would have never recognized her wounded spirit. Every step was in order beginning with his impending death. God was not One to figure out, merely One to stand in awe of when encountering His providence.

Having taken pain medication earlier, Chris was at least capable of meeting with Robin. The day before, he had to cancel. In doing so he again aroused her concerns about taking up his vacation with her problems. He smiled to himself, appreciating what a thoughtful woman she was, so concerned with others that she had left herself out for many years. Finally, in God's all-knowing manner, having recognized Robin would never put herself first, He intervened in her life and was bringing her freedom.

Tapping on the door, Robin turned the knob and asked, "Are you ready?"

"I am. Come on in."

He was sitting in his chair waiting for her when she knocked. The curtains were drawn and the lights were turned off to ward off another headache, so he hoped she wouldn't mind the dim setting.

She moved to the chair across from him. Sitting on the edge of her seat, as if she might bolt away at any moment, she acknowledged, "I'm running out of time, I know. It's time to get it over with."

Understanding what she meant, Chris nodded for her to try again. She had tried on several occasions to tell him of her last night with Mike. Not once was she able to get more than a sentence or two out. All he knew so far was that she was washing her face before bed when it began.

"Usually, I would hear his truck. I guess with the water running, I missed it that night. Normally, when I would hear him pull in, I would try to prepare myself for who might walk through the door. I never knew what to expect. That night, I didn't see it coming until it was too late.

"He grabbed me around the waist and threw me into the bathtub. I was tangled up in the shower curtain, and the rod fell and hit me in the face. Blood began to pour from my nose and all over my nightgown. At that point he wasn't even looking at me. Instead, he was hitting walls and even crashed his hand into the mirror over the sink. Glass was everywhere and his hands were bleeding.

"When he finally turned his attention back to me, he reached down and grabbed my wrist. He yanked me out of the tub and dragged me into the kitchen. There, he pushed me down into a chair, and that's when I saw them, a pack of birth control pills on the table in front of me."

Chris noted as she spoke, Robin looked as if she were in a trance. There were no tears, and she seemed unusually disconnected from the story. The only time he had ever seen her cry was when she spoke of Michael. He always found it a little curious under the circumstances. A few times, he was sure he saw tears well up in her eyes, but she was always able to blink them away.

"I'm not certain how he got them. All I can think is that he must have been at the drug store and the pharmacist thought he was doing me a favor."

"You were on the Pill and Mike didn't know?"

"Yes."

Her heart sank when she thought of the many months he was so hopeful that she might be pregnant. Each time, she knew better and still allowed him to hope. Even before the violence began, she had secretly gone to the doctor to get the prescription.

"He smashed them with his fist and began screaming at me. The things he said were terrible and true."

Holding her finger up, indicating she needed a minute, Robin leaned back in her chair and recounted Mike's words, ones that had resounded in her heart for years. She could hear them ringing in her head even at that very moment.

"All I've ever asked for is another baby, and you refuse me that." He slammed the pills again. "You were sleeping while our son died. He died on your watch! Not mine. These past months, you've let me hope…" Stopping abruptly, Mike began to weep openly, and with his tears came an explosive sort of anger like she had never witnessed before.

She began again, saying, "He flipped the table over and pulled me out of the chair. Dragging me into the bedroom, he threw me on the bed, and he…" She closed her eyes and drew in a deep breath. "He hit me in the face a few times.

"I had never run from him before since he threatened that if I did, he would make me regret it. This time, though, he was different. I had a feeling if I didn't get away, he would kill me. He began taking off his belt, and I knew what he was about to do."

Looking away, a knot formed in her stomach, and for a moment she felt queasy.

"So I took both feet and pushed him into the wall. He was drunk enough that it seemed to stun him for a minute. It was my chance to run.

"At the front door, I grabbed my purse and kept running. I dug around, but my keys weren't in there. Most likely, he took them; he had done that before. As I ran down the driveway, I heard him come outside, but he wasn't chasing me yet. He just stood on the front porch screaming my name. He was so angry."

Stopping for a moment, Robin sat, gripping the arms of the chair until her knuckles turned white. Even at the memory of it, her heart was pounding, and she could feel the chill of the night air and the jagged rocks beneath her bare feet. She shivered.

"I was barely dressed, and it was drizzling out. It was cold, and I was shaking so badly I could barely keep running. When I ran out onto the road, I knew I was out of his sight for a moment. I made it to a large group of trees and into some thick brush. It was muddy out, and I could see I was leaving a trail, but there was simply nowhere else to go. The moon was bright, and I was too visible. He found me easily enough."

Chris sat there, suddenly nauseous. He supposed it was this traumatic, but hearing her tell the story, it affected him more deeply than he anticipated it would. The dread of hearing more made him want to stop her, but he knew healing could come no other way than for her to allow it out into the light.

"Back inside the house he took me to the bedroom and forced himself on me."

Gazing into the fireplace, she avoided making eye contact with Chris, not wanting to see the expression on his face at her admission.

"He raped you."

Her way of expressing what Mike did was, in a sense, lessening the significance of it. It was rape.

"It wasn't the first time, but that night was nothing like before." Ashamed of what she could only consider some sick perversity on her part, she admitted, "The times before, I gave in to him, responded to him even." Hesitating a moment, she whispered, "I know how that must sound."

"What do you think it sounds like?"

Embarrassed, she regretted telling Chris about it at all. At the memory of it, her breathing became labored, and she could nearly smell stale alcohol in the air. Mike would whisper in her ear, telling her how much he loved her. Always, he would say, "I need you to love me." Even the recollection of it caused the hairs on the back of her neck to stand on end and her heart to thud erratically.

"He would change, become like the real Mike again. He would tell me he loved me and how he couldn't stand the thought of losing me. Then it would turn from something ugly to what it used to be."

"Do you feel ashamed that you responded to him?"

She nodded.

"He was your husband, Robin, the man you loved. If your heart or even your body responded to him once he became tender and loving toward you, it wouldn't seem so out of place to me. Maybe you wanted what *used to be* so desperately that you were willing to reach for it in that moment." Shifting in his seat, he moved in closer to her. "Shame is something that keeps people in darkness, especially women. Your body responded how it had always responded to your husband. Determine this very moment that you have nothing to be ashamed of."

She nodded again, grasping his words as some new revelation that might ease her shame. "All I ever wanted was our old life back. When I could catch a glimpse of it or of the old him, I clung to it."

"This night was different, though?"

"Yes. The tenderness never came. The way he looked at me, it was as if he didn't see me at all, exactly as if he were looking at a stranger. At one point he told me since I would no longer be on the Pill, he would do that to me every night until I got pregnant."

Closing her eyes, Robin placed her hand over her mouth, recalling how that terrified her. For a moment she was unable go on. What happened next was like a nightmare she couldn't shake. Finally, she whispered, "When he was finished, I said something really foolish. I knew better." Her heart began to beat rapidly at the memory of it and her breathing quickened.

"What?"

"I told him he had become his father. There was no crueler thing I could have said. When he was a little boy, his father used to beat his mother, Mike, and his little brother. So when I compared Mike to him, he totally snapped. He wrapped his hands around my throat and began choking me, screaming at me to take it back. Then he lifted me from the bed and held me against the wall with my feet dangling above the floor."

Robin stopped and looked at Chris. The memories felt so real in the moment; every detail was vivid, causing her airway to actually feel constricted. "You wanna know what I was thinking?"

He nodded.

"I kept thinking, 'I hope I die, so I won't have to live this way anymore.'"

Up until that point, Chris had been holding back a rising tide of emotions. At her admission, though, he stopped fighting them and found himself crying quietly. He thought of the times she swam alone in the dark. Having lived so many years full of torment and anguish, no wonder relief seemed possible only in death. This was the woman he loved telling this story, not some stranger. This was the woman he would marry if God would only give him a miracle. For a moment, while she was quiet, he tried to regain his composure. Rubbing his face, he wiped his eyes with his fingers.

"Something happened." Robin sighed, still trying to figure out how things took such and abrupt turn. "I don't know. All of a sudden, he let go of me and jumped back as if he'd been scalded. For some reason he rushed from the bedroom. When I fell to the floor, I lay there gasping, trying to catch my breath. I could hear him in the kitchen throwing things, and I figured he would come back. But everything got really quiet, and it was then that I looked on the dresser and saw his holster.

"I could barely stand, but somehow I got up and went over to the gun. I took it out and turned off the safety. I hardly remember walking into the kitchen, but next thing I knew, I was standing there watching him bent over the sink vomiting. I waited until he stood up, and when he turned around to face me, he didn't seem at all surprised. I was holding the gun out, and it was shaking so badly I could barely aim. I guess I never realized how heavy it was. He just stood there, looking at me. He never even made a move to stop me. There was something different in his eyes by that point, maybe resignation or regret; I'm not sure what.

"Finally, I pulled the trigger, and the sound of the blast was deafening. After the first shot, he looked down at his stomach and then back at me. So I shot him again and again. By that point it was as if we both were moving in slow motion. He put his hand over his stomach and slumped to the floor. I dropped the gun and went for the phone. While we waited for the ambulance, I sat with him, and he kept telling me how much he loved me. He just kept saying, 'I love you, baby. I'm so sorry.'" Even after all that had happened, she knew he meant it.

Robin's expression was entirely blank, as if she were retelling a movie she had seen rather than a scene in which she had participated. There were no tears or emotion. She simply retold the story in such vivid detail that Chris was certain she must relive it frame by frame day after day.

Looking directly at him, she admitted, "I did it on purpose. He wasn't coming after me again. I *meant* to kill him."

She allowed the wicked truth to linger in the air between them. Self-defense was the term the police used, as did her parents and Emma, but the real truth was that she sought him out to kill him. Just before pulling the trigger, she could hear his words ringing in her head, *he would get her pregnant.* He was consumed by the thought of having another baby, but it was the one thing she would never allow.

"Once we were taken to the hospital, I never saw him again – until he showed up here."

Now, discovering Robin had shot Mike, no wonder she thought Mike was coming to kill her. After hearing the story he could view their encounter by the lake with new perspective. Understandably, she was hysterical, having waited years for his retaliation. Mike was broken, remorseful for the terrible things he had done to her. Even Emma's actions took on a new dimension.

She was prepared to kill Mike. Had Chris known the gruesome details, he might have felt the same way.

"Can we stop now?" she asked, feeling too drained emotionally to say anymore. She stood, feeling unusually calm, and with a heavy sigh said, "It's in the light now."

He stood, too, and placed his hands on her shoulders. "Yes, Robin. It's in the light. Now, you've given God something to work with."

"I'm glad it's out. I've told that to no one other than the investigator who came to my hospital room."

"How does it feel?"

"I'm not exactly sure yet. Can we talk about that next time?"

"Yes."

He was feeling ill and knew he needed time alone, so he suggested, "Maybe tomorrow or the next day."

"I'll see you in the morning for coffee?" she asked.

"Sounds good."

Just as she closed the door, Chris rushed to the bathroom. He spent the remainder of the night in his cabin. Tommy stopped by to invite him up to eat, but he declined. With the way he was feeling, Chris was beginning to wonder if he would even last the final week.

Over the past few days, Robin and Emma had been making plans for a birthday celebration. Emma, feeling as if she owed her very life to Chris, was probably the most excited. In the weeks since he had been counseling Robin, something miraculous was beginning to happen. The change in Robin was evident. As the nightmares had ended, Emma hoped she would move back to the main house, but Robin chose to stay in her cabin where she said she was seeking God.

Emma was beginning to see something of God in her. A concept she deemed "her parents' kind of thing" was beginning to find some basis of reality in her daughter. Never one to believe God was active in ordinary and everyday lives, Emma was witnessing proof that something powerful existed. Chris was the one to draw Robin back to Him. If it could work for Robin, it might possibly work for her too. She had gone to church a couple of times with them and was considering, as foolish as it seemed, going with Robin more often.

The day of the party, while busy in the kitchen cutting veggies for a veggie tray, Robin admitted, "I had the hardest time keeping the secret this morning. I thought I was better at keeping secrets, but every time I opened my mouth, I almost blurted out, 'We're throwing you a party.'"

They had met for coffee and the sunrise as they usually did, and he seemed quieter that morning than ever before. At first she was concerned about him, but by the time they parted, he was much more like his normal self.

"I never knew you were so bad at keeping secrets either. I'll remember that."

Emma finished icing the cake and put the cover over it. As she hid it in the storage pantry, she said, "I'll run to the market later for a few things, but for the most part, we're set."

"Great. Let me know if there's anything I can do to help."

Robin was excited about their surprise but still a little worried. When Chris turned down the invitation to dinner the night before, she began to worry about their plan. What if he did the same this night? Trying to come up with an alternate plan was what kept her mind whirling over the past few hours.

"I hope he comes," Robin said.

"Me too, but if not we'll celebrate without him. I made him my favorite cake."

"I noticed that." Robin giggled at her. At times, Emma was just like a kid.

"Not knowing what his favorite is, I had to pick something."

White cake with white icing, though some may call it plain, was her favorite. Not just any white cake would do but her aunt's recipe. She had never tasted another like it.

"I may be a little worried about him," Robin told her.

Emma stopped what she was doing and asked, "Yeah, why's that?"

"He's acting differently, like something's wrong."

"Have you asked him?"

"No. I don't know. There's nothing I can put my finger on, just a sense I get."

"I'll watch him tonight and see if I feel the same thing."

As Robin walked toward Chris' cabin, she found him sitting on the front porch. He smiled and raised his hand. At first glance he appeared better than he had that morning, but when she reached the porch, she thought he still seemed pale. Sitting next to him, she asked, "Do you mind if I ask you a question?"

"No, not at all."

"Are you okay?"

He paused for a moment. "Sure, why do you ask?"

"I don't know. You seem a little different."

"I'm okay. Question is, how are you? Yesterday was a tough one."

"It was. I don't know why I waited so long. Afterward, I felt lighter somehow."

"I can understand that."

"What's next?" she asked eagerly, ready to take any step necessary toward healing.

"I've thought of a few things, like, how you felt afterward for one. I suppose I'm curious."

He never let her rest. His questions were like picking at a scab. She would think, *whew, it's over*, but then he would pick at the wound, and it would open again and begin to hemorrhage.

"If I had to describe it in one word, it would be disappointment. I was disappointed about life, every aspect of it. Mike had let me down. God had let me down." She stopped and smiled at Chris. "Maybe my mind is changing about that. Time will tell." Continuing on, she said, "My town let me down. I felt as if there was nothing left, absolutely nothing."

She stopped rocking and pondered a moment. "Truth is, I thought I had life figured out. I never saw any different future than being with him. Suddenly, there I was in the hospital, well, both of us in the hospital. We had nearly killed each other, our marriage was over, and I felt stunned. After that night I didn't know who I was anymore. I guess I've felt like that all these years afterwards too." She began to rock again. "That was who I was. Here, in this life, I feel like I'm pretending. This isn't who I am. I lost me along the way."

"Maybe this is the new you. Not necessarily the *you* you had planned on but you under new circumstances. You seem to have a great life here. Emma loves you. Someday, I imagine you'll find romantic love again." His stomach turned at such a thought.

Turning over what Chris said in her mind, Robin thought about him and how, for about a minute, early on, she wondered if they could fall in love, but very quickly she knew that wouldn't be the case. Not only was she not ready, ultimately, she wasn't prepared to give her heart to another man. She may never be ready for that. It was similar to her feelings about having another baby. To bring another child into her life would be like saying Michael never mattered or existed. It was the same with Mike. Their family was real at one time. She could never pretend otherwise.

"Maybe this is the new me." She looked at him thoughtfully. "Have you ever been somewhere and just have a sense you don't belong?"

"I think we all feel that at one time or another."

"At times, I feel like I belong here, especially since I've been here for several years now, but more often than not, I feel like I'm out of place, like a misplaced object."

"Have you considered moving back to North Carolina?"

"No, never."

"Maybe it's not a physical out-of-place you're experiencing. Maybe it's spiritual."

"How do you fix that?"

"Keep doing what you're doing. Keep seeking God. Keep reading your Bible. Keep going to church. Find your faith again."

He had a sudden thought and was certain it was from the Lord. Having been so ill the night before, he had little time to process the things Robin told him, let alone pray about what to say.

"Tell me, when you look back to that final night with Mike, can you see God?"

The question startled her, and she became immediately irritated and spat, "Of course not."

"You said something happened and he let go of you like he had been scalded. Could that have been the hand of God?"

She gasped and her hand flew over her mouth. A hollow or swollen feeling, she couldn't distinguish which, rose in her chest, as if her heart might collapse or burst at any moment.

"Could it have been?" she wondered aloud.

Closing her eyes, she tried to look back on the scene. Mike's eyes while he choked her were filled with anger, but then there was this softening, a spark of recognition as if he was suddenly seeing her, and following that a look of panic registered in them. He released her.

"I believe it was. I believe He has a plan for you. He saved you that night. God was there."

Robin jumped to her feet. "Why didn't He stop it all?"

Shaking his head in frustration, he acknowledged, "Here we go again. I can't answer for God, but I say again, we live in a fallen world. Mike chose to do what he did, but God spared your life." It then occurred to him. "Like Job, I suppose. Remember, the Lord allowed the circumstances, but He determined that Job's life would be spared."

"I just read that."

"And?"

"I don't know." She sat back down for a second, trying to comprehend it all. Finally, she admitted, "I'm confused."

"That's understandable. This isn't easy, and you have so much to sort through. There's a season of healing ahead of you, one that'll be between you and God. Just don't hesitate to ask the difficult questions. He doesn't cringe at our tough questions, neither does He apologize for who He is or His plan for mankind. Even when we can't comprehend it, we're each a smaller part of a bigger whole. In the days, weeks, even months to come, take every single feeling and emotion before Him. Hold nothing back. If you're angry, tell Him. If you have doubt, say so. Ask Him questions and then watch and wait for an answer. Will you promise me that?"

Nodding to indicate she understood what he was saying, she knew she was in for a long and difficult journey. Finally, after years of running, it was a journey she wanted to take.

Chris assured her, "I know one thing; the place you must begin is forgiveness."

She allowed his words to sink in for a moment. Then, as if a movie played in her mind of when he came to the lake, she could see Mike crying, begging her for forgiveness. Unable to extend it that day, neither could she do so at the moment. Not only did he destroy their marriage, he nearly killed her. How do you forgive such things?

"How could I possibly forgive him? How can I just forget and act like it never happened?"

"Forgiving is not forgetting. The memories will come. They always do. The difference is what you do with the memories when they do come. Forgiveness doesn't mean you are saying what he did isn't wrong. What he did was *wrong*. Forgiveness isn't a feeling. You may not feel like forgiving. Still, for your sake you have to."

"For my sake?"

"It'll release you. What happened is now between him and God, but as for you, you'll find freedom in forgiveness." He paused a moment, then continued, "I know this one by experience since I had to deal with it concerning my mom. For years I was incredibly angry at her for how she messed up our lives. She stopped being my mom because my dad died. I lost both parents at almost the same time. Forgiveness didn't come easy."

"How did you do it?"

Before his admission forgiveness seemed impossible, but considering what Chris had gone through gave her reason to believe if he could forgive, then maybe she could too.

"It took longer than necessary, simply because I didn't know how. For me, when I finally got to a point where I could empathize with my mom, that was a first step. I tried to put myself in her position, what she was feeling, and that broke my heart for her. Then I started praying for her, regularly. Something about that gave me tremendous freedom. From there, I don't know, it became a choice to forgive her. I chose it. So when an ugly memory would surface, instead of allowing anger to control me, I chose to recall how damaged she was, I prayed for her, and I reminded myself that I forgave her. After some time it became part of how I dealt with bad memories. I did this over and over until eventually it became so automatic, that I didn't have to even think through it. I went from ugly memory to automatically recalling I had forgiven her."

"How long did it take?"

"For me, over a year. Like I said, though, I didn't understand the process I just explained to you. I was going through it without the benefit of this hindsight I'm sharing. For you, I hope it takes less time than it took me. Will the same approach work for everyone? I'm not sure, but it worked for me. Now, I can see my mom, and trust me, she's in really bad shape, and I'm able to love her."

"I don't want to ever love him again."

"I'm not saying you have to, not in the way you did, but you still have to forgive him. Oddly enough, you *will* love him again, but it'll be God's love not something you're capable of on your own. Remember, this is for *your* freedom not for Mike in any way." Chris sighed, knowing her greatest hurdle wasn't forgiving Mike. "Before you get to that point, I think you have an even bigger issue."

"What's that?"

"You have to forgive God for disappointing you."

She had no reply, mainly because she wasn't sure how she felt about that. Thinking back to that last night with Mike, suspecting God may have saved her after all, made her realize she would need to go back and look for Him with Michael. It would be a process, one she wasn't sure she knew how to navigate.

"You'll be gone soon."

He nodded. "I know."

"How will I do this without you?"

"I'm recommending another counselor for you."

"I'm glad to hear that. I don't think I can do this alone."

"You won't have to." Standing, he said, "Hold on, I'll write it down for you."

He went in and when he returned handed her a piece of paper, saying, "This is who I recommend."

Glancing at the paper, she looked back up at him. "Are you sure?"

"Positive," he said.

"I trust you."

"It's not me you should trust."

Robin was sitting on her bed with her Bible in her lap. It was not long before dinner and Chris' party. Opening it, she turned to the book of Isaiah. It read,

> "For to us a child is born, to us a son is given, and the government will be on his shoulders. And he will be called Wonderful Counselor, Mighty God, Everlasting Father, Prince of Peace." Isaiah 9:6

Chris' version was different, and she decided she liked his better.

> "For unto us a child is born, unto us a son is given: and the government shall be upon his shoulder: and his name shall be called Wonderful, Counsellor, The mighty God, The everlasting Father, The Prince of Peace."

His reminded her of being a small girl. Every Christmas, these were the words she heard, yet somehow she missed the significance of them. In all her life Robin had never known God in any of those ways, not one. Chris had made a note below the verse which read,

> *You will know him as Counselor first. Then, the other ways will come. Eventually, you'll know Him. Once you do, you'll never be shaken again. I promise.*

Robin believed him.

The table was set and Chris was on the way. Tommy had gone to get him. At least Robin and Emma hoped he was on the way. After Chris' refusal the night before, they were uncertain. With the dining room decorated and the place full, they were having a party regardless. They had discreetly spread the word to the other guests, and who were they to refuse a party? So providing the guest of honor arrived, it promised to be a great surprise.

Chris followed Tommy up the stairs, looking forward to a good meal. He was feeling better than he had in a couple of days, so dinner sounded appealing for the first time. Noting the lights were out in the dining hall, he continued up the stone stairs and toward the back porch.

"Looks like they don't know we're coming."

Tommy smiled in the dim light, certain Chris wasn't suspicious.

"We ate in the kitchen last night. S'pose we will tonight too." Coughing, Tommy tried to stifle a nervous laugh.

As they walked into the main lobby area, Chris thought he heard whispers. Just as he rounded the corner toward the dining room, the lights flashed on, stopping him in his tracks, and a crowd of mostly strangers began to sing "Happy Birthday."

Embarrassed, he looked around for Robin. Remembering he had mentioned his birthday when they went out to dinner that one evening, he knew it must have been her doing. Going to her, Chris hugged her tightly.

"I can't believe you did this," he whispered.

"I can't believe you didn't think I would."

Chris went to Emma and Becky and hugged them. When he got to Tommy, they settled for a knuckle-bump.

There was a long banquet table in the middle of the room with BBQ and every side imaginable. On the buffet was his birthday cake, his favorite, white. Shaking his head, he prayed, "Lord, You thought of everything."

Since late afternoon, he had been feeling better. The night before, there was no way he could have attended; the headache was too severe. For the moment, however, he felt perfectly normal. There was no way of knowing how long he would feel this way, but he would take it while he could get it. With only a few days remaining at the lake, he wanted to enjoy every last moment of it.

After dinner he asked Robin if she would take a walk with him. Having decided he should tell her about his illness, he wanted to get her alone so they could talk. Since he wouldn't be able to stay in contact with her once he returned home, she needed to know why. His intention in not telling her had been to protect her, but he had to trust the Lord to care for her. She was His and in capable hands.

They walked out onto the dock and Chris sat. When she did the same, he asked, "You remember when I said I would tell you something later, why the timing wasn't right for me either?"

The morning she told him she wasn't able to date him, that was when he said it. "Yes," she said.

"I guess it's about time."

It was difficult. Since receiving the diagnosis, he had only spoken the words aloud three times. He told his aunt, Vanessa, and the principal at his school.

"I'm sick. That's why I came out here for the summer."

"Oh," was all she could say.

She had no idea what to ask, but the way he framed the statement left no room for doubt, it was serious.

"I'm dying."

Her breath escaped her as if she had been kicked in the stomach. She reached for his hand, asking, "How long do you have?"

"A few months, maybe more."

"And there's nothing they can do?"

She knew it was a silly question, but she wanted to know more and wasn't sure how to ask.

"Radiation or chemo would only prolong it but not stop it." Squeezing her hand, he admitted, "I don't want to live my last days here on earth fried from radiation or throwing up from chemo. I just want to die peacefully. That's the way it'll likely happen."

"Is it a brain tumor?"

"Yes."

"You have headaches. I've seen you rub your temples and pinch at the bridge of your nose. I just thought it was regular headaches."

"They've been pretty bad lately."

It explained a lot. Especially over the past week, he wasn't the same.

"Thank you for trusting me with this."

"Once I left, I knew you would never hear from me again, and I couldn't stand the thought of you thinking I don't care about you. I do."

"I know you do. I would have never thought that."

They sat for a moment, still holding hands. After some time, he asked, "You are going to be okay, aren't you?"

"Yes." Smiling, she added, "I won't let you down."

"Let me down?"

"We've begun a good work."

"That's scripture, you know. He who began a good work…"

"I know. That's why I said it. We have…God, you, and me. I'll keep seeking Him."

"That's what I wanted to hear."

Looking out at the water, he felt relieved knowing he didn't have to worry about her swimming out there alone or the thought that maybe she would swim out and never return. Each day, he was certain he witnessed more strength in her than the day before. Not so slowly, she was indeed beginning to live again, beginning to walk with God.

"Where will you go now?" she asked.

"To my aunt's house. I sold my condo." He laughed a sort of sarcastic laugh, admitting, "Funny, at the end of things, you realize *things* really do mean little. All the junk I had accumulated over the years, I just gave it away. Why sell it? What would I use the money for?" He turned to face her. "The end is simpler than I thought it would be."

"How so?"

"Well," he grinned at her. "I took the summer and had the best time of my life, doing things I would never normally do. I rested, painted, watched the sun come up, had coffee with you, and went barefoot when I could."

She laughed. "I wondered why you showed up barefoot."

Grinning, he asked, "You noticed that, huh?"

"I did."

"I was driving down the road and my shoes felt uncomfortable, restrictive in a way I had never noticed before, so I leaned down while I was driving, pulled them off, and threw them in the back seat. I've hardly worn any since."

"I've noticed. You did to dinner that night, and you're wearing them now."

"Special occasions," he assured her.

"Both *very* special occasions," she agreed.

She thought of how handsome Chris looked that night, which brought Vanessa to mind. "Vanessa...she broke it off with you and you're dying?" It wasn't necessarily an accusation, but the timing caused her to speculate.

"We had only been seeing each other for three months when I was diagnosed, and even those three months were not the greatest. At that point in her position, can you imagine breaking it off right away? As for me, I was confused and a bit scared then. It was simply easier to keep things as they were. I don't blame her at all. If she would've loved me, she would have wanted to be with me no matter what was ahead. Same with me." Considering the implications of that, he admitted, "If we had stayed together, I would have never met you. Well, we would have met but never have gotten this close."

"That's true. I'm glad she dumped you."

"She didn't exactly dump me," Chris argued.

"Oh, you got dumped." Laughing, she added, "And I really am glad you did."

Wondering if he had any idea what his entry into her life meant, she asked, "Do you realize what you've meant in my life?"

"Honestly, yes. I see something happening in you, and I know God brought me here to help that begin. He will finish it, but He allowed me the privilege of the beginning. You know, I was thinking about this the other day, I've felt more purpose in my life this summer with you than I have in my entire life combined."

Taken back by such an admission, she could think of no reply. Finally, after a moment of silence, she admitted, "I don't know that I have ever felt that, well, maybe when I had Michael, but since then I haven't. For your sake, what a gift."

"That's exactly what I was thinking. It's been a gift. I'm not saying my only purpose on earth was you, but my final one was."

He looked up and asked, "Wanna play "Would You Rather"?"

"Sure."

"Would you rather have a short life with great purpose, or a long life with little purpose?"

"Short life, no doubt."

"Me too. Maybe that's why I'm okay with the end."

Tears filled Robin's eyes as she asked, "Will you be there waiting for me?"

"You bet."

"Are you scared?"

"Maybe of the pain but not of dying."

Thinking for a minute, she asked, "Chris?"

"Hmm?"

"Can you stay longer? Have you ever seen the fall colors here at the lake?"

"Yes and never."

10

There were good days and bad days, but for the most part the good days were more prevalent. As anticipated, the fall colors were spectacular, a masterpiece by the Master, so Chris spent as much time outdoors as possible. Though he tried to capture the radiance of the oranges, reds, and gold, he realized no manmade paint could ever accomplish such a task. The intensity of color, the variation of hues, only God could create such vividness. He sat day after day trying to grasp a small piece of His brilliance but failed.

"That's your best one yet."

Robin had been watching Chris from the kitchen window. The wind was whipping in off the lake, causing him to grab for his canvas many times. Still he painted.

"I think it's spectacular," she added.

"I wouldn't say spectacular."

"Marvelous?"

"I can live with marvelous."

When she handed him his coffee, he thanked her and took a sip, admitting, "I should probably go in now."

"You've been out for a long time. Are you hurting?"

She and Emma watched over him like mother hens. Emma was even worse than Robin.

"Yes and feeling a bit sick."

"Let me help you gather your things." She did so.

"Just lay them down on the dock for now."

He placed the canvas on the dock, wet paint side up, hoping the wind wouldn't catch it again as it had several times already that morning.

"Can we just sit for a minute and drink our Joe?" he asked, dreading the conversation ahead.

"Sure we can."

Robin took his cup and waited until he was seated and handed it back to him. His coordination was failing, and she tried to help when she could, always mindful though to allow him his dignity and independence. He wasn't a child, and she forced herself not to treat him as such. Early on, after learning of his illness, she was much too worried, hen-pecky even. Once, he called her on it, and when he did she swore off mothering him. So far she had kept that promise. She helped him as needed, allowed him space when needed, and remained available for whatever he might require.

Sitting beside him, she asked, "How many times will you paint this view?"

"Until I get it right."

"You must see something I don't. It looks right to me."

"I see something with my heart that I can't see with my eyes. That's what I'm trying to capture."

"What do you mean?"

"I don't know; there's a feeling I get here that I want to be able to take away with me."

"Take away?"

He looked at her, and when he did he sighed deeply. Early in the summer, he was attracted. Mid-way through, he was smitten, at the end, captivated and completely hers. So by the time fall arrived, he was so helplessly in love with Robin that he felt as if she were a part of him, as if she always had been. Maybe that was the feeling he wanted to capture, his love for her. It was the purest love he had ever known. There was nothing physical between them, nor would there ever be. That was the simplicity of loving her. Nothing more was necessary. It was the love of a lifetime, and that was all that was needed. There in his final months, he found his very own love story. She was an astonishing last gift.

Finding it nearly impossible to say the words, he finally forced them, blurting out, "It's time for me to go back to Boston."

"Oh."

She looked away, out across the lake. Her eyes were stinging, so she blinked rapidly to chase away the tears.

He watched her intently, sensing she was about to cry.

"Don't be hurt."

Prepared to say she wasn't hurt, she decided not to. It would be a lie. He had become such a vital part of her life, it did hurt, or maybe it scared her to consider letting him go. From June through October he was part of her every day. Suddenly, he would leave and that would be that.

"I need you to understand. I have some good-byes there, too. It has nothing to do with wanting to leave you. Honestly, I've put if off for far too long."

"Are you going to your aunt's?"

"Yes." He paused a moment. "I called my mom. She'll be coming to stay for a while."

"That's a good thing."

"Being here with you – and Emma – has been one of God's greatest gifts to me. These past months, reading together, studying together, and just watching you grow with the Lord, Robin, I'm humbled and grateful to have been a part of that. But they need me, too."

"I'm sorry."

"For what?"

"For being so selfish."

Chuckling, he said, "You're anything but selfish. The way you've taken care of me when…"

He didn't have to finish. She had helped him more than he wanted. When he had been his sickest, she was right there with him.

"You're like an angel."

She giggled. "An angel, really?"

By her tone, he knew she was mocking him.

"Pretty corny?"

"Pretty corny. But I like corny sometimes."

"How 'bout now?" he asked.

"Yeah."

Robin reached for Chris' hand. The moment was so strikingly similar to the evening he told her of his illness, it was slightly disturbing. In the brief time she had known him, she had come to love him deeply. Emma had once asked her if she was in love with him, and the honest answer was no, but she loved him with the same intensity she loved her family and Emma. It was simple love. He was the least complicated thing in her life, and she liked that.

"I'll drive you back."

He had one seizure not so long ago, and from that point on was no longer allowed to drive. At the emergency room he was warned it could happen at any time.

Without room for discussion, Robin added, "I'll call Tommy. I can drive your car and he can bring me back."

While he began to protest, not wanting to put her out, Chris decided against it. Instead, he would be grateful for any time he had left with her. Deciding to go back to Boston was one of the most difficult decisions of his life. With every fiber of his being, he wanted to stay with Robin, but for her sake, he was leaving. Lately, there was a sense the downhill slide was approaching. He felt it deep in his spirit, as if the Lord was giving him fair warning. The end would be the very worst of him, something from which he wanted to spare her.

After that day Chris remained only two days more while packing up and preparing his heart to leave her. Having noticed how quiet she was about his departure, he realized she was hurting because of it. He was certain she loved him, though he was just as certain her love differed from his, and that was okay. In truth, if her love reflected his own, then his death would be much more painful for her. God spared her that, something for which he was truly grateful.

The morning they loaded his car it was raining. How befitting it seemed. By the time they reached the highway, the rain cleared out, and the sun rose high and bright overhead. The mood in the car changed with the weather. All the way, they laughed and reminisced about the summer. It seemed as if they had known each other for years and years like family. As a family on the way home from a vacation might do, they listed the highlights and mentioned even the worst moments of their time together. The two-hour trip sped by in what seemed like minutes, much too quickly for either of them.

Once in Boston, Chris invited her in, and though she planned to spend more time with him, Tommy arrived much earlier than expected. Not wanting to keep him waiting, as she knew he was busy with school and work, Robin left after less than another hour with Chris.

Leaving him was more painful than she prepared herself for. When Chris walked with her to the car, just before she climbed in, he pulled her to him and held her tightly for several minutes. He was crying, which made her cry. Neither said a word in all that time but just sobbed and held on, knowing this was possibly the last time they would see each other on this side of heaven. Finally, when he pulled himself away, he kissed her on the cheek, turned unexpectedly, and went back into the house. Intentionally, he didn't turn back to look at her. Robin waited, but he never did. As if ripping away a bandage rather than pulling it slowly, he left her standing there, dazed and longing for more of him. When he closed the door, she sat down heavily in the passenger seat. Bewildered that he would leave her so abruptly, she knew his intention was to protect both of their hearts. He didn't want to let her go any more than she did him. While it would be excruciatingly painful either way, he obviously believed the rip and run approach to be his only option. Without question, he loved her.

For the first half of the trip back, she quietly reflected on her time with his Aunt Tina. Surprised by how young she was, only ten years older, she was a mere twenty-five when she took Chris in to live with her. What an unusually selfless act for someone of that age. She wasn't married at the time, but she loved Chris and his mother enough to give up her freedom to become the parent of a teenager. On the drive back to Boston, Chris had told her stories of how difficult he was to deal with during those days, leading Robin to believe that Tina must have regretted her decision early on. Eventually, they both began going to church, and something happened to Chris that truly changed him at an early age.

Having described him as young as eighteen, Tina said he was the godliest man she had ever known, even that early. Robin wasn't at all surprised as he was the godliest man she had ever known, too. With ease he found a place in her heart that would always be held for him. He was the first time she truly saw God. Thinking back to how he walked away, the bandage analogy, she smiled to herself. He was God's bandage in her life. Though unaware herself, she was hemorrhaging on the inside. God knew, and He sent Chris to help her begin to heal.

When Chris said God sent him to help her, at the time, she was distraught and could in no way process the implications of his revelation, but later, his words permeated her heart and her mind. The realization that God actually hand-picked a man such as Chris to bring comfort to her, proved His love for her, His active "I'm in the middle of your business" kind of love. The stitches in the veil began to unravel the very moment of that revelation.

Still, there was a journey ahead, but one she looked forward to with much less fear. The few times while reading her Bible, when she actually felt God was speaking to her intimately and personally, caused an intense longing for more. From those times on, she opened His Word with great anticipation and excitement. She not only read; she studied and poured over the Scriptures, watching for Him at every turn.

They had left Boston an hour before, and already, they were stopping for gas. Tommy was pumping while she sat lost in thought, wondering how things were going with Chris and Tina. She speculated when his mother would come. Her prayer was that she *would* come. "Please, Lord, give her enough presence of mind to see her son." From what Tina suggested, it wasn't at all likely.

"We're set. Sorry, I should have filled up before picking you up," Tommy said.

"Don't worry about it."

Tommy had been unusually quiet, out of character for him since getting to know him better. He mentioned Becky a few times, but when he did it was cryptic. As far as Robin knew, things were still going well with them, since Becky called occasionally with an update on life. Strangely, they were immediately like family, so the assumption for them all was that they would both work the summer again.

"Anything you want to talk about?" The question popped out before she thought better of it.

Immediately defensive, Tommy asked, "What? Has Becky said something?" He knew they talked, and he had often wondered if Becky told Robin things were not going so well between them.

"No, nothing. You just seem quiet. I'm not picking you for information or anything."

He drove in silence for a minute more before admitting, "I think we're having problems."

"You think?"

"She's pulling away. I can feel it."

"I'm sorry, Tommy."

She was, and she was surprised too. When Becky called, she acted as if Tommy was the love of her life. Robin anticipated marriage someday.

"Why do you think she's pulling away?"

Shaking his head, he sighed. "I don't know if pulling away is the right way to describe it, but there's something going on. When we're together, she acts stand-offish. There's some hesitation I don't understand." Scratching his head, he went on. "I wonder if she thinks about that guy."

Uh oh, Robin thought. *Why did I ask if he wanted to talk?*

"Not this summer of course, but last year, they...um, they were together. You know?"

Fearing he might be fishing to see if she knew anything, Robin sat paralyzed. She was Switzerland, neutral as neutral could be. She didn't nod; she didn't move her head just in case it appeared to be a nod. Her suspicions about Becky and Brad were confirmed, but she had no intention of discussing it with Tommy.

When Robin gave no reply, Tommy continued, "Anyway, what if she wants to be with him? She says she regrets it. At least she was honest about it. Actually, she was more than honest; she's real broken up about it. I think she's pretty ashamed."

He didn't take a breath, instead, he kept on and on with his observations for nearly the last hour of the trip. Robin simply let him talk. By the time they reached the inn, he had talked himself out of breaking things off with Becky before she could do it first. His rambling was sweet and crazy and as full of love as Robin had seen a young man in many years.

At the thought of silly love, Mike's image danced through her mind. It was a moment she hadn't thought of in many years, a memory she thought had long since faded; one she cupped in her hands and peered into. It was sweet and brought her back to the day Mike asked her to marry him. He rambled on and on about how he would take care of her somehow and how cops didn't make much money, but he could hunt if he had to. At the memory of him suggesting he would hunt their food, she smiled. It was young, sweet love, just like Tommy and Becky were experiencing. The remainder of the drive, even while Tommy listed every pro and con of his relationship with Becky, Robin found herself wading in puddles and reflections of the early days, times when life held a promise more so than pain. Her heart was filled with "if onlys," and she wished more than anything she could go back and live that life differently.

Back at home, life would never be the same, and Robin knew it. She and Emma both grieved the loss of Chris' presence. They tried to fill the hours with games, chatting, reading, and any other activity they could think of, but his absence screamed loudly in the quiet house. Emma had taken no more reservations, even for the weekends. So it was just the two of them, as it was throughout each winter.

Robin talked to Chris often, but in the past week, he hadn't called. She tried calling on two occasions, but he didn't answer his cell phone. Tina called once in between the two calls saying he was sleeping more than before, but she would have him call soon. Still, nothing. After Thanksgiving, Tina called again, but it wasn't what Robin hoped for. The call was instead to inform her that Chris was moved to hospice care. Robin packed immediately and drove to Boston.

At Chris' bedside Robin wasn't sure if she would be able to talk to him at all before he passed. He was sleeping mostly around the clock. The next step, she was told, would be a coma. Being in his room with him was surreal. The sleeping form wasn't the man she knew, the one she laughed with and cried with. He was already gone and she missed him terribly. Time, she discovered, there was never enough of it.

Mostly alone, as Tina worked during the daytime, Robin read aloud to him, especially from his Bible. Flipping through it, she found verses he had circled and read them to him. Many of them, he had read to her while he was still with her at the lake. Tucked inside were folded sheets of paper, but she was careful not to open them. Assuming they were his personal study notes, she moved them to the back of the Book.

Once, he woke up long enough to smile at her, but quickly he drifted off again. Hour after hour she waited for another waking moment, but one never came. To pass the time, she talked to him. She poured out her heart to him, from the serious to the silly. One morning, she was thinking about Becky and wished she could ask his advice. He would know how to handle things.

"There's something going on with Becky, and I'm worried about her. When Tommy took me home he said things weren't going so well, but when I talk to her, she seems so in love with him. One thing he said keeps coming to mind; he thinks she's ashamed." Waving her hand, Robin stated, "That's a whole other story, but if that is the case, how do I help her?"

Leaning in, she confessed, "I want to help her the way you've helped me. I want to help people like you did." Pondering for a moment before going on, she finally confessed, "You know, I think I've been helping Emma, at least some. There's something different in her here lately. She's finally open to hearing about Jesus and how much He loves her. Trust me; that's such a big deal for her.

"I keep thinking about what you said one day…that you felt more purpose over the summer than you had before. That's what I want, to know my purpose. So far, I really don't think I have one. How sad is that?"

"As for Becky, though, I know she'll come back in the summer, and I want to reach out to her. I wish you would wake up and help a sister out." Smiling, she reached for his hand. "I miss you."

During her third day there, Robin sat quietly reading a book that Tina brought her the night before. When she heard a distinct "psst," she looked up. Chris was grinning as much as his condition would allow.

"Hi," he whispered softly.

He felt terribly weak, but the sight of Robin there gave him strength he hadn't known in the past weeks. Knowing the end was so near, his main prayer had been that he might see her once more before he died. Thankfully, she came. Deep inside, he knew she would.

Robin leaned in and grinned, saying, "Well hi there, sleepy head."

"I want you to take that." He was pointing to his Bible on the bedside table.

At first considering refusing it, certain Tina would want it, Robin thought better of it. "It'll be my prized possession."

"I know. That's why I want you to have it." He drifted off momentarily. Waiting, she stayed close by, hopeful he would open his eyes again.

When he did, he smiled again. "I think I fell asleep."

"Just for a second. It's okay. I'm not going anywhere. Sleep all you need to."

He shook his head and motioned for her to come nearer. When she did, he reached his hand up and placed it behind her head, drawing her even closer. "It's time to pay up."

"I don't understand."

"You said you could never repay me. I said I would think of something."

She smiled, "You're right, and I said anything."

"Anything?"

"Anything."

"Forgive all things, Robin."

"I'm trying." A lump formed in her throat even as she said it. The counselor was back, and he brought with him tough matters.

"Forgive Mike. Remember empathy. Forgive God for taking Michael too soon. For in Him we live, and move, and have our being…look that up. It was something I wanted to share but kept falling back asleep. I think I wrote it down. I don't remember. "

Robin began to cry and tried to move back. He wouldn't allow her, though, and his strength in holding her was surprising.

Chris' voice was fading. "Finally, forgive yourself for taking that nap and for pulling that trigger."

Her tears began to drop onto his face, and when they did, he pulled her the rest of the way and kissed her cheek. He softly whispered, "I love you, Robin."

Looking up into her eyes, he was reminded of sitting with her on the dock the day he told her he would be going back to Boston. He called her his angel, and though he would never tell her at the moment, certain she would mock him if he did, he was sure again she was his angel. What better gift could the Lord supply to usher him into His arms?

"I love you, too, Chris. God sent you for me."

"Please don't leave me," he whispered in her ear. "I want you to be here with me when I go."

"I won't leave you. I'm right here."

Robin moved onto the bed and lay there with him. The hand holding her head loosened its grip and fell limp. He was asleep again. Lying with him that way for over an hour, she prayed for mercy. She prayed for the Lord to take him home so he would finally be healed. How different this prayer was than the day she held Michael. Finally, trusting God's plan, she prayed His will be done above all else.

Later that evening, Chris slipped into a coma and never regained consciousness. The next day, he was gone. She was lying next to him when he went to be with Jesus.

At Tina's house Robin was thumbing through Chris' Bible. Curious about the pages she had moved to the back, she took them out. They were all for her. He had been making notes since leaving the lake. In that moment with her emotions so raw, she was unable to read them, though she was certain they pertained to her healing. Even in his own death his concern was for her. "Lord," she whispered, "how could a man be so selfless?"

She hugged the Book tightly to her chest. Once she returned home, she would read every word he left for her. For the time being, though, she would do her very best to be a comfort for Tina, and possibly his mother, *if* she showed up for the funeral. Just as Tina predicted, she never made it to see Chris. He died without having seen her at all.

11

After the funeral Robin arrived home with a tremendously heavy heart. The journey ahead of her had felt less intimidating while Chris was alive. He had become such a close friend in such a short span of time that it truly felt as if she had lost a close member of her own family. Emma had driven up for the funeral, and Tommy and Becky came, too. As much as they tried to recount fun stories of him together, they could never stir up the joy they hoped for. He was too young to have been taken. None of them could quite grasp the reality of it. It seemed surreal until they lowered his casket into the ground. At that moment it became all too real.

What was evident that day was that Chris had purpose that spanned well beyond his understanding. The church was filled with hundreds of people, so many in fact, it became standing room only. Many were students whose lives he had touched. Members from his church were a large part as well. He was loved, as he had loved well.

On a personal level Robin considered her own impact on people and the world around her. Had that been her coffin and her funeral, other than her parents, Emma, and maybe Tommy and Becky, who would attend? At church she snuck in and out, mindful not to make connections. Her existence was inconsequential for the most part. How can one person make such a great impact and another mean so little? It was a choice he made; she was fully aware of that. Consciously, he chose to look outside of himself, even to the very end, where she lived life looking inward and backward. No wonder she had no idea where she was going since she never looked at the road ahead or the possibilities God placed before her.

For several days Robin tried to get back into the groove of daily life. It was impossible. Nothing would ever be the same. Both she and Emma sensed it. It was early December, and the usual excitement of the holidays seemed unbefitting. Her parents weren't coming, so it would only be the two of them. At a time they would usually begin to decorate, neither had the heart for it. This would be a sad Christmas. They both felt it.

Sitting in the kitchen one rainy afternoon, they shared a piece of pie. Both were unusually quiet.

"What now?" Emma sighed and rested her fork on the plate.

"I think I'll go back to school."

Robin had been thinking of taking classes and finishing her degree. She had finished one year while Mike was on his first tour. Then while in California, she was able to complete a second year.

"School for what?"

"I'm not exactly sure. I have two years behind me, and I might as well do something about finishing."

Chris' contribution into the lives of others had made a lasting impression on her. As much as she desired to help others the way he helped her, she was certain there was a long road ahead for her own healing. Still, there had to be a beginning point, a point at which she set a course to do what she felt such a strong desire to do.

"I think that's a great idea. Will you begin in January?"

"If possible. I've been checking into some schools that offer classes online. I may be too late to begin by this semester, but if not, I think I'll try it that way and see how I do. I may be a bit rusty by now."

Emma reached over the counter and took Robin's face into her hands. "Hummingbird, if anyone can do it, you can. I believe in you."

Smiling, her cheeks squeezed between Emma's fingers, she asked, "Really?"

"Really. You can do this, and I'll pay for it."

The argument over who would pay continued until Robin registered. All through Christmas, even up to the point of writing a check, the battle raged. Emma won out and paid for her classes and books. Robin was only taking two to begin with, but she quickly learned two was enough for someone so out of study practice. It was the best decision she could have made, turning the normally dreary winter months into something challenging and exciting.

New England weather in the earliest part of the year was dreadful. Robin stayed in so much, she was certain that when the spring thaw occurred, she would have forgotten how to interact with people. Other than trips out for groceries and going to church, they both hibernated. The one and only thing that could draw Robin out of the warm house was her treks to Chris' cabin. Once or twice a week, she went there for counseling sessions, and just as she had done with Chris, she sat in her chair. At the onset his empty chair caused such grief she could hardly pray or make progress, but eventually, she found the Wonderful Counselor had taken Chris' place. In meeting with her new Counselor, Robin envisioned Jesus seated in the chair across from her. Just as Chris suggested, she talked as she would to him or Emma. She asked the tough questions and often unfurled the ugliness that was trapped in her heart, such as bitterness, anger, and disappointment. One thing she observed in how the Lord dealt with years' worth of pain: all matters were not to be dealt with at once. He would take her through seasons, a season for bitterness, a season for anger, and so on. It progressed that way from the very beginning.

One day, she read a verse about not conferring with flesh and blood. The Lord used that verse to hammer a truth deep into her heart – He was her source of healing and finding another human counselor wasn't her answer. Jesus Himself, inside of her, was to counsel and guide. Once that concept was revealed to her, she never looked back again. She would use Chris' study notes and ponder all the things he suggested, but her main source of counsel would be the Spirit and the Word. Whether or not she made it to the cabin, each and every day she sought God through her Bible, and His Word soon began to come alive to her.

The upside to the cabin in the wintertime was that she could have a fire. Always, she began with that. Once it was blazing warm, she would begin by reading at whatever place she left off the day before. Trying to keep a normal flow of reading was the key. If she had questions, she learned that looking for the answer could lead her to frustration. It was too precarious to find a verse that seemed to be the answer to a question or concern she faced and try to apply it to her circumstance. Instead, she found that if she simply placed her question or care before the Lord in prayer, then read in her usual manner, the answer would come. While it may not be that day or even within several days, an answer always came. It was the anticipation, the excitement that kept her reading and studying His Word daily. He always showed up, and to her, that was one of the first real and significant truths she learned about the character of her God. He is faithful.

She began reading Chris' notes just before Christmastime. They were so personal and intimate in knowledge of her heart, that she found them at first to be intensely sorrowful. They brought her more grief than gain in the beginning, but eventually, through the strength of the Spirit, she was able to study them. Over time the Lord used what Chris wrote to lead her through treacherous waters. While navigating along, she would sometimes imagine Chris sitting quietly with the Lord, asking Him how to best advise her. It was a very sweet and comforting image to contemplate. He cared so much for her, and because he chose to put so much effort into her, she was becoming well.

His first lesson recorded a verse he spoke to her in the hospital. He had said, "For in Him, we live, and move, and have our being." On the study page he took the many verses that preceded it and dissected it for her. It was from Acts 17. Toward the goal of her healing over Michael's death, his point was that God determined the begin date and end date of his life on earth – He determined the bounds of his habitation. He gives all things breath, and it's His right to determine such things.

> "That they should seek the Lord, if haply they might feel after him, and find him, though he be not far from every one of us…" (27)

Regarding this verse, his notes expounded the most. As he had done while he counseled her, his assurance again was that God was present in the moment of her greatest pain. No matter what her eyes saw or her heart felt, Jesus was there. Her heart was trying to believe, but her mind couldn't see it so far. She held on to hope that it would come. Of all that lay ahead of her, she knew this was the one area that would require God Himself to open up her understanding and plant that belief in her heart. Her emotions over Michael were still as raw and tender as the day she began talking about him. It was the longest road ahead.

Another of Chris' notes dealt with Mike and forgiveness. He suggested that, in order to have a reference point for empathizing with him, and in doing so traveling the road of forgiveness, she research post-traumatic stress disorder. It wasn't something to be used as an excuse for his behavior, but it might help her to better appreciate what he experienced when he came home. His compulsion to drink could be better comprehended once she more fully understood the catalyst for it. His reminder, too, was that Mike also lost his son right there in the midst of tremendous mental trauma that was already dragging him under.

There were many notes, ones he had obviously poured so much of himself into. As the winter passed she worked through each of them, some many times. It was in late February that she spent the most time on forgiveness. His words to her, "forgive all things," were the theme for that season of her life. Having done as he suggested and read as much as she could find on PTSD, she found empathy came easily. The effects on the brain were enough to convince her of Mike's inability to control what was happening to him. Then, with the trauma of losing Michael, he was sent over the edge entirely. Alcoholism was a common occurrence in those with PTSD, as a way of self-medicating. Tragically, in his case, the alcohol led to unexpected aggressive and violent tendencies. For whatever reason, as it was with his father, alcohol made him a different man entirely.

Forgiveness, something she was positive she would never grasp, arrived and remained. More than able to forgive him; she began to pray for him, that his mind would remain restored and that he would never again turn to alcohol. More than any other thing, she prayed his heart would heal over losing their son. As much as she still grieved Michael's loss, she knew Mike did as well. It was in praying for him that she found her truest freedom. No longer did she feel haunted by the end of their marriage, rather, she could look back on those times with a new level of compassion for him.

Hour after hour she reflected upon how much he lost too, his sanity, his son, his wife, his freedom. Even though he was released from prison, she had no doubt that their final year kept him just as bound as it had her. She prayed for Mike's healing and that he might somehow forgive himself. Memories of the pain and sorrow she saw in his eyes when he came to see her often stole sleep from her. Never had she seen a man more broken

In a continuation of the season of forgiveness, she felt the Lord leading her toward empathy for the woman who pulled that trigger. It was at Chris' suggestion that she go back and evaluate her life, especially from the point of Mike's drinking forward. In doing so she was better able to capture the truth, the hidden motive behind her deed. Gaining insight from retrospection, she acknowledged that her ability to take such violent action stemmed from Mike's promise that he would get her pregnant again, no matter her feelings about it. Though a drunken threat, it was likely one she could regard as true. That prospect flipped a switch in her mind, and in the moment, it drove her to proceed out of her fear. It was more than the unbearable thought of bringing another child into such an abusive and chaotic home, it was the idea of another child altogether. After Michael's death she never wanted another child. The thought of such a thing was terrifying. That fear arose long before Mike began drinking. It was immediate and one she acted on in such a deceptive way that its revelation nearly killed them both.

Robin had to forgive herself for her deception, as well as for picking up a loaded gun and intentionally trying to kill the man she loved. Revisiting her actions through hindsight, she discovered empathy came relatively easy for her too. Just as Mike was out of his mind, being chased by his own demons, she too was bound by oppressive fear and grief. When looking back, she felt such sympathy for both of them that her heart remained heavy and her prayers were ones filled with tears and pity. They were a young, lost couple, trying to wade through a sea of grief and misery. Sadly, both were drowning and neither had the means of helping the other. The only Life Preserver was out of reach for them both. She had turned her face from God, having mended the veil in her distrust and disapproval of His ways. Mike had no such option, for he knew Him not at all.

Healing was beautiful and painful and undoubtedly worthwhile. The moments she spent with her Lord were similar to surgery at times, when there was a cutting away of what deserved no place in her heart, such as fear and unbelief. At other times it was comparable to sitting in soothing waters, warm and comforting, when He simply tended to her wounds. Then there were moments when grief and loss covered her in darkness, and it was during those times she saw Him as most mighty. When all seemed dark and she couldn't see Him clearly, she was assured it was then that she was resting in the shadow of His wings. To see Him would have meant moving from His embrace. Certain times required the dimness and sanctuary of His encirclement. He was wrapped around her so securely that she felt no need to see Him. He was in her and with her, no matter what her eyes saw or how her mind tried to advise her. Her spirit knew. Like hugging a parent in your distress, you bury your head in their chest so that you have no field of vision. So in order to see, you must lift your head, which would remove the source of comfort. "Remain in the shadow of My wings," was what she often heard, and that was what she did.

One day in particular, she considered Chris' words before they even began counseling. He said, "And you, Robin, are anything but free." Back then, she knew she was wounded. She knew she was damaged. She even knew she had a broken spirit. What she didn't know was how utterly bound she was. Indeed, she was anything but free. Just the day before this reflection of her lack of freedom, she read a verse.

"But whenever anyone turns to the Lord, the veil is taken away. Now the Lord is the Spirit, and where the Spirit of the Lord is, there is freedom." 2 Corinthians 3:16-17

After so many years turning away from Him, finally, by the simple act of turning back, she was free. While she would have never considered herself such, the truth was, she had been the Prodigal all along. Typically, the thought of the Prodigal suggested an image of one falling into a life of outward sinfulness. In her case, turning away from God and closing Him out of her life, she was every bit the same, just as far away as if she had traveled to a foreign land to spend her inheritance.

There was something about this revelation that caused her to love Jesus more than ever before. Never once had she had the mental image of God waiting for her with outstretched arms. Ever after though, it would be what she saw of Him when she looked back to the days of her brokenness. He was her Father, and He waited patiently, until one day not intending to wait any longer for her return, He sent Chris to find her and guide her home. That illustration of His love for her caused her to fall into Him in such a way she knew she would never be the same.

As the pages of the calendar were turned and the cold ground began to thaw, life became new at the inn. Robin was new, as was Emma. In April, after going with Robin to church regularly for some time, Emma asked the Lord into her life. It was Robin's greatest joy to lead her to the One place where healing was found. Emma needed as much restoration as she had. It was the beginning of her journey, and Robin was honored to be used, even in small ways along the way.

By late spring reservations began pouring in, and soon Tommy and Becky returned. Cabins filled and the guest rooms were booked for most of the summer. Chris' cabin, however, was never rented. Instead, when the weather was warm enough, Robin moved her things there to stay. No more was it about disturbing guests with her screams. Rather, it had become her shelter and sanctuary. Out of a sense of propriety, she slept in the other room, not Chris'. It felt wrong somehow to sleep where he had slept, intimate in a way she never thought of him. In that place he was everywhere; his memory was there in his chair, his wisdom on the porch. God continued to use the things he said and the questions he asked to draw her near to Him.

The summer was the best she had known in many years, certainly more years than she had been at the lake. Always before, she had felt as if she were a part of the periphery of life, no longer involved in it. This year, though, there was an openness, a willingness to engage and invest in the lives of others in a way she had never experienced before. Besides Becky and Emma, whose spiritual and emotional welfare were her causes over the summer, there was something new in the way she related to the guests. Intentionally, she reached out to every one of them in some way. Even if it was encouraging them or granting a request, she did all things with a new approach. Without question her desire stemmed from Chris' funeral. The image of the mass of people ever followed her, and out of the overflow of his impact on others, she wanted to touch lives the way he did, so she made every effort to do so. In this new way of dealing with others, she was catching an inkling of her purpose. Though not clear enough to pursue, there was something distant on the horizon, God's plan for her.

By the end of July, nearing Chris' birthday, they decided to have a huge celebration in his honor. The event was held outside and rivaled any Fourth of July party. It was not only an appropriate commemoration of his life, it was a way to bring all the guests together and share with them who Chris was. At the end of the party, Emma, Robin, Tommy, and Becky walked to his cabin, Tommy carrying a ladder. Each cabin had a wooden plaque over the porch with its name engraved into it. Tommy got up on the ladder and took the name *Willow* down and replaced it with *Chris' Cabin*. It was officially his, a gift from Emma. Robin was merely a guest there for the summer.

When time came for Becky and Tommy to leave at the end of the season, Robin felt assured of God's hand in their lives. She had done what she called mini-counseling with Becky. Throughout the winter the Lord had given her insight into Becky's shame and regret over giving herself to someone she would never marry. One afternoon, while sitting by the empty fireplace in the cabin, she was praying for Becky. The Lord took Robin back in time to her own wedding night and the sweetness of the gift of purity she and Mike were able to offer one another. Becky was grieving the loss, or more correctly, regretting that she had given that gift to someone who had no heart for her. A gift she wanted to give to Tommy was something she no longer possessed.

Over the course of weeks talking with Becky, Robin helped her to prepare her heart to receive the Lord's forgiveness and to find her way through forgiving herself. Having been raised the daughter of a pastor, a life filled with what she considered unachievable expectations; Becky carried an enormous measure of condemnation and guilt due to her sin. The load was so burdensome it prevented her from experiencing God's grace early on. Finally, admitting she would forgive and extend mercy to another if in her position, Becky began to extend herself the same.

It was in the last weeks of the summer that the Spirit began a work in both Robin and Becky that would ultimately lead to the greatest freedom either would ever know. In contemplating the whys of Becky's decision to be with Brad, they both came to the conclusion that it was her need to be loved. Stemming from that thought, they discussed how her true desire was not human love or one that any man could offer; her truest desire was to know the love of God with such certainty that human love would forever pale in comparison.

Flood gates opened in Robin's own heart, bringing her face to face with a truth that took her back to seventh grade. Most precisely, that was the moment she sewed the very first stitch in the veil, separating herself from God. Mike was the first stitch; he became her god. She called him her rock when Jesus should have been her Rock, deemed him her first love when Christ was to be first in her heart and in her choices. He was her hero, when only One could ever truly save. Mike was her idol and her god. How had she missed it all those years?

One morning, in her normal course of reading and in the exact providential way of God's dealings with her, she read,

> "For although they knew God, they neither glorified him as God nor gave thanks to him, but their thinking became futile and their foolish hearts were darkened." Romans 1:21

Her thinking futile and her heart foolish, there could have been no better description of her for all those years. She had known God, or at least at such a tender young age was growing to know Him, when Mike came into her life and stole all desire of knowing Him more. In thinking back she recalled the difference in herself even at church. When Mike began going with her, her entire focus was on him, never what was being taught. If it wasn't on Mike, it was on what others thought of him. The envy of every girl she knew, Robin recalled how she reveled in being his and the way they wished they were. Mike was her god; that realization rang over and over in her head until it became a pounding conviction she could hardly bear.

There came a day when the simplicity of the solution became apparent. Sliding out of her healing chair, Robin knelt and made a commitment before the Lord. Aloud, she prayed, "I will have no god before You." It was something so intense and personal, that she spoke it over and over. Even when she finished saying it out loud, it chimed in her head and in her heart for hours to come. Something new happened that day. It was nothing she could identify externally, but internally there was a shift – her heart belonged to Jesus in totality. *My Beloved is mine and I am His*, became the song of her heart.

Once the summer season was officially over, life became slower for a time. When fall colors ramped up, so would the reservations again but for the time being, it was a time to breathe and rest. Both Robin and Emma needed the break. The heat that year had been oppressive, so the slightly cooler temperatures drew them outdoors more often. Sitting on the covered porch, sipping coffee together one September morning, Robin shared, "There's something I've been sensing. I believe I should say it aloud just to hear how it sounds."

Curious, and always eager to hear Robin's perspective on things, Emma encouraged her, "By all means, say it aloud."

Robin's depth in spiritual matters was mystifying to Emma. Over the past year something beyond extraordinary had happened to her. Emma watched with great joy, and sometimes with envy, how Robin became free and unbound by her past. While Emma desired the same, the shame she felt went beyond what Robin ever had a reason to.

"I've forgiven Mike, of that there's no doubt. I've realized, though, that never telling him has been a mistake. The Lord has laid it on my heart that he needs to hear it."

"Will you write to him or call?"

"Neither. I've tried. Several times, I've pulled out paper and a pen and then just sat there, staring at the blank page. I've actually held the phone in my hand to call him but can never dial."

Feeling a bit uneasy about what she knew Robin was suggesting, Emma asked, "What will you do then?"

"I'm supposed to go and see him face to face. I know it."

Beyond all shadow of a doubt, the Lord was moving her in that direction, and the mere thought of it scared her nearly to death.

12

After shifting into park, for a moment Robin sat looking at her former home. Though it appeared much the same, one major difference was that it now had a silver metal roof. It was what they wanted to put on when they first moved in but couldn't afford it at the time. Pale yellow with white trim, she recalled how Mike and Trevor painted it over the course of two weekends that first year. It looked like a little doll house, and the sight of it stirred up a sense of accomplishment mixed with a deeper sense of regret.

When her parents first brought them out to see the place, she knew it was the home for her. Mike was happy as long as she was happy. Even before they moved in, they were there every afternoon working and cleaning up. Having been vacant for some ten years, just to clear out the weeds and debris from around the house took two days. It had been worthwhile, though. Nestled in a little valley between two hills with tall trees, the rear of the property was edged by farmland. There was a long gravel driveway that led from the two-lane highway up to the house, and she noticed on the drive up how well maintained the yard was.

Sighing, she gripped the steering wheel and prayed, "Lord, I don't know if I can go through with this," but she knew she could, no matter how difficult. Along with the sight before her came a flood of memories, good memories, ones that made her want to go back in time when they were so in love. Tears pooled in her eyes as she recalled walking up that set of steps with Mike, him holding Michael and shielding his eyes from the sun when they brought him home from the hospital. All the best things in her life had happened in this place.

Robin stepped from the car and walked tentatively up the stairs to knock on the door before she lost her nerve altogether. Though there was no answer, his old blue truck was in the drive and she smelled burgers on the grill, so naturally, she moved down the stairs and toward the left side of the house. Not having an official back door, theirs was instead a side door.

At the side of the house, she hesitated. There he was, standing over the grill flipping burgers. It was like old times. He wore a white t-shirt and jeans, and something about the familiarity of the sight made her want to turn and run. Instead, she moved closer, saying, "Knock, knock."

When Mike looked up and found Robin standing on the other side of the fence, his hand went limp and he dropped his spatula on the ground.

"Robin?"

"Hi."

She walked nearer, stopping at the gate. Fumbling with and finally unhooking the latch, she continued on to the patio where he stood staring at her. Reading such surprise on his face, she simply smiled, unsure of what to say next.

He could only stand there, too. Too shocked to speak, all he could do was stare at her. Purely convinced just one minute before that he would never see her again, his heart was pounding so hard in his chest he found he could barely breathe. This was *the* last thing he ever expected.

"I was hoping to talk to you for a few minutes." Noticing several burgers on the grill, she added, "But if you're expecting company, I can come back."

Finding his voice, he stammered, "No, no. I was just making enough for the next few days. Are you hungry?"

The burgers were nearly done, but he had no way of getting them off the grill.

"Hold on a sec," he said and ran into the house.

Once inside, he reached for another spatula. Before turning to go back outside, Mike bent at the waist, grabbed his knees, and drew in a deep, steady breath and then let it out slowly. Quietly, he whispered, "God, how I still love her."

As he placed the hamburgers on a plate, he stood there looking at her. Dazed by how pretty she looked in her Panthers t-shirt and jeans, he was again struck silent. Of course he remembered that shirt, along with how she kept things for so long, too long. She had ratty t-shirts from all the way back in high school. He grinned at such a ridiculous memory.

"I don't want to keep you from eating."

"Will you join me?"

He shifted from foot to foot. Tempted to grab her and hug her, he instead gripped the plate of burgers tighter in order to save him from such an unfitting thought.

"I don't think so," she said, but then her stomach grumbled. The smell of charcoal in the air reminded her that she hadn't eaten since breakfast, and it was well after one o'clock.

"Well, maybe one."

For the life of him Mike couldn't stop grinning. He knew how dorky he must look, but the stupid smile was plastered to his face. Oh, he had no misconceptions about her visit. His first guess was that she was ready to sell the house. Having lived there for more than a year, he had wondered when this time would come. Although he considered going for a loan and sending the money to her, he could never bring himself to do it. Something about that seemed so final, since all that was left between them was the house. Apparently, he would be forced to soon.

Robin discovered that following Mike inside proved to be a mistake on her part, and she wished she would have waited on the patio. The familiarity of it was overwhelming. It was her little home that she made ready for her husband and her son. As she looked around the kitchen, she noted it wasn't filled with bad memories of their final year as she would have expected. Instead, she was reminded of the joy they shared there. Bittersweet was the term most appropriate to express the stirring in her heart.

The cabinets were painted white and the floor was hardwood, original to the home. She noticed that Mike had installed a dishwasher, something she never had when she was there in that kitchen washing dishes by hand. Not as if she minded. In her mind she could still envision what it looked like to have pots and pans and baby bottles drying on the counter, a memory that nearly sent her over the edge.

Trying to shift her train of thought, Robin took two plates from the cabinet but then stood there staring at them, again spiraling down some deep hole of regret and missing what she once had. Tracing her fingers along the edge of one, she sighed. They were a wedding gift from Emma, as were most of her dishes. While they were simple white plates, they were hers, and she had forgotten how much she loved them.

"You can have them if you want," Mike offered.

He had watched her intently. The look on her face caused his heart to break, for he appreciated what it felt like to be seeing all these things again after many years away. While living there, Trevor kept everything as it was. He was meticulous in the care he took with their home. For the most part, the house looked the same when Mike returned home. His first night there alone, he cried in nearly every room. Everywhere he looked he saw Robin and recalled how excited she was when they first moved in. Every coat of paint or the smallest change he made sent her over the top. He could hardly remember her ever being so happy. With the baby on the way, being back near her parents, and having her own home, she was happy and content. But he destroyed all that.

"No." Sliding the plates back into the cabinet, she asked, "Do you have paper plates? Then you won't have to clean up a mess."

"Right here."

He pulled two plates from the same cabinet she originally chose for paper plates. Did she notice, he wondered? As much as he could, he had kept everything just as Robin had left it.

Once they filled their plates, they moved outside to eat on the patio. There, she found she was able to recover from the onslaught of memories and turmoil she experienced inside.

Small talk was easy for them. They knew so many people in common, and that seemed to be a safe enough topic. He caught her up on his family and she on hers.

"I got my old job back, though I never dreamed such a thing could be possible. I had to go before the town counsel for a vote. It was the most unnerving thing I've ever done, and I didn't dare to even hope, but they said yes."

"I bet it was unanimous."

Nodding, he asked, "How did you know?"

"Everyone loves you here."

Finished with half a burger remaining, Robin leaned back in her chair and said, "That was wonderful. Thank you."

When he pointed to the second half and arched his eyebrows, she knew he wanted to eat it. "Go ahead. I'm full."

He had already eaten two burgers plus her half. She was astounded when he ate another with no bun. "You'll be sick."

He chuckled. "You obviously have a bad memory."

Immediately, he regretted saying it, as he had tried to be careful not to bring up anything about the past or things that might be painful for her. Quickly, he added, "I still eat like a horse."

Unable to avoid it, Robin noticed how much bigger Mike was than when she saw him the year before. His chest was so broad that his t-shirt fit snugly, more so than she had ever seen in past years. Once, when he reached across the table for the mustard, his sleeve slid up over his massive bicep, exposing the bottom of the letters of his tattoo. It was her name, and she wondered what it must feel like to look at it every day. It made her sad, causing a knot to form in her stomach, and from that point on she could hardly help but wonder what his new life was like, the one where she had no place.

Within seconds of her arrival, he saw she wasn't wearing a wedding ring. He had spent many an hour wondering about the man who ran to her side that day at the lake and if Robin had married him. Mike was pretty sure, too, that she noticed he still wore his ring. It was in with his personal belongings when he was released from prison. Since slipping it back on that day, he hadn't taken it off and had no intention of it. Although propositioned often, actually almost daily, he had no interest in any other woman than his wife. There wasn't a great deal of single men around town, so he seemed to be the target of more than a few lonely women. He avoided them like the plague when he could. Though they knew of his history, it didn't seem to deter any of them, which was perplexing to him.

When she became so suddenly quiet, Mike couldn't help but wonder if she was trying to find a way to bring up the house. Hoping to help her, he offered, "If you're here about the house, I told you before, it's yours to sell or whatever you want to do with it. If you'll give me a little time, I'll check into a loan. Or if you want it back…"

Holding her hand up, she stopped him. "No. I'll never move back here. You keep the house. I'm glad you've been able to start a new life here and thankful that Trevor stepped in and took things over the way he did."

Trevor was two years younger than Mike. With the history of chaos and upheaval they shared, they remained close, the only constants either of them ever knew growing up. So when she realized she would be staying with Emma indefinitely, Robin called Trevor to see if he would move in. Releasing her of the responsibility of it, he took care of the maintenance, utilities, and taxes, everything she would have had difficulty doing from such a long distance.

Though her admission stung, it didn't surprise Mike in the least, having never anticipated she would return. What was left for her here?

"Trevor was able to save up a down payment for his own house while he was here. I know he's really thankful for that." Realizing he hadn't told her earlier, he added, "He's getting married in a few months. Great lady. She has a little girl from a previous marriage. He's crazy about them."

"Tell him I wish him the best."

"I will."

The moment had finally come, and no matter how difficult it seemed, she headed straight into it. "Look, Mike, the reason I came is that I wanted to tell you something. When you came to see me that day, you asked me to forgive you, and I never responded to that."

Leaning up in his chair, he propped his elbows on his knees and looked at her intently. His heart began to pound even harder than when he first looked up and saw her standing by the fence. "You don't owe me anything, and you sure didn't have to come all this way…"

"This is for me," she interrupted. "I need to say this. I need you to know that I forgive you. It has taken a lot of soul searching and a whole lot of time with the Lord, but I do forgive you."

He was on the verge of tears, afraid if he started to cry, she might too, and she hated crying. Actually, she always said he was much more girly than she was since he would choke up at a movie long before she would.

"I also need to ask you to forgive me for shooting you."

Her words brought with them vivid memories of the sight of him lying there, blood soaking through his shirt and pouring out onto the floor. At the recollection of it, she began to weep openly, admitting, "I can hardly believe I did it. Your gun was just there, and the next thing I know I was pulling the trigger."

Moving quickly from his chair, he knelt before her. Though he had no right to touch her in such a familiar way, he took her face in his hands, saying with great conviction, "Don't you ever blame yourself. I nearly killed you that night." He began to cry with her. "Baby, I saw the photos of what I did to you. Saying I'm sorry could never be enough. But as for you, don't ever regret it. That's the night Jesus finally got to me. I've never been the same since. I'll never be the same."

After years in and out of church with Robin, it took that night to finally open his eyes and his heart. Once he began to serve time, having been a cop, he was kept in isolation most of his incarceration. He did very little but read his Bible and whatever other books about God he could get his hands on. Since then, all things within and without were new.

He wanted her to know. "That night, I was so scared of dying. Not as much of dying as I was of going to hell, which I knew I would, and I knew that wasn't where you would be. I think that's what scared me most."

With his hands still holding her face, he moved his thumbs to wipe the tears from beneath her eyes. "I have to tell you, and somehow I just know this deep down inside, if I hadn't called on Jesus that night, He would've let me die. I certainly deserved it."

His words completed the unraveling of a stitch. Memories of picking up that gun and walking into the kitchen haunted her as much as the beating that came before it. It was forgiveness that she needed. She had already been forgiven by God, and she had even learned to forgive herself, but ultimately, she longed for Mike's forgiveness. Able to look back with great pity on the girl who was so tormented and battered that she could be driven to such an act, this day would be her final release.

Though she hadn't planned to tell him, and it was something she never even admitted to Chris, she felt led to say, "After I shot you, I planned to turn the gun on myself. I remember thinking there was nothing left. After Michael, then what happened between us, I was certain there was nothing else to live for."

He wept as remorsefully as the day he knelt with her at the lake. Sitting back on his heels, hands still resting on her knees he allowed her to finish.

"But there you were, blood pouring out onto the kitchen floor, and I knew I couldn't let you die. So I called an ambulance with every intention of shooting myself afterward. But when I came back to you..."

Covering her face with her hands, for a moment she was unable to go on.

"You don't have to do this," he whispered.

Reminiscent of the day they buried Mikey, he wrapped his arms around her while they both sobbed. It was a rare occasion to see her so devastated. Holding her close, he allowed her to cry as long as she needed. With her head resting on his shoulder and his cheek pressed against her hair, lightly, he stroked the back of her head.

Eventually, she raised her head, knowing she had to continue on. It had to be brought out into the light. "I don't know how much you remember, but you were conscious, just barely. I kneeled down beside you and lifted your head into my lap. You told me you loved me and asked me not to leave you. I realized then I had to stay with you until help arrived. I could never leave you alone and so scared.

"Next thing I knew, there were police and paramedics. People were shouting and it all became a blur. Once they put us into separate ambulances, no one would tell me anything about you. For the longest time I thought you must be dead."

Resting his head on her lap, Mike continued to cry. Over and over he told her how sorry he was, begging again and again for forgiveness.

Robin stroked the back of Mike's head just as he had done hers, trying to comfort him. His hair was thick and coarse and reminded her she knew every inch of this man. This was her husband.

Several minutes passed, until finally he stood and moved back to his chair. Wiping his face with a napkin, he sat looking at her, amazed by her words and by her heart.

"You're the kindest woman I've ever known."

He meant it. After the way he battered her, a black eye one day, bruises on her wrists another, he knocked her around and demoralized her, still she actually asked *him* for forgiveness. Not a day went by that he didn't think of her, and pray for her, regret the things he did to her, and especially grieve her absence from his life. Always, he remembered the good things about her, and those memories were the source of great joy and great sorrow simultaneously.

She whispered, "I'm so sorry that things turned out this way."

"I'm sorry too, Rob."

Recovered enough to drive, and anxious to get to her next destination, she stood, saying, "I should go now."

He stood and walked with her to the car. Opening the door for her, he asked, "Have you gone to see Mikey yet?"

"No. That's where I'm headed now."

"Do you want me to drive you? I know it'll be difficult."

"I think I should go alone."

"I understand."

He couldn't help but wonder where she would go afterward, so he asked, "So, where are you staying?"

"The Ramada."

"In Raleigh?" he asked. There were hotels nearby, so he found it strange she chose to stay so far away. It was best that he not ask.

"Yes, in Raleigh."

"Be careful on the drive back then."

When she sat down in the car, he squatted beside her, regretting that he didn't hug her good-bye. This would be the last time he saw her, and that realization caused tears to spring to his eyes again.

"You okay?" she asked.

Reaching out, she stroked her hand along his cheek. It was rough and unshaven. Smiling at him, she was struck afresh by how handsome he was. He was beautiful, with a smile that caused her to melt even still. Always he was the most attractive boy in school, in the town even, and he used to be hers.

Mike only nodded, not trusting himself to speak. Finally, after swallowing hard to choke back his tears, he told her, "I'm so grateful you came. This means everything."

"Thanks for letting me come and clear the air."

"You're welcome here anytime."

When she made no further comment, he said, "Drive safely."

He stood, shut the car door, and watched as she started the engine, made a loop around the tall oak near the driveway, and roll slowly away. The moment compared to the day they lowered Mikey's casket into the ground, that feeling of a forever good-bye. His heart went with her and his chest felt painfully hollow.

Inside the house he went and stood before Michael's closed door. Though he entered occasionally, it was usually only to dust. Each time he did, while in there, he felt the air to be too heavy to breathe. Turning the knob, he pushed the door open and simply stood in the doorway without going fully into the room. For the most part, all his son's things were packed away upstairs. All that remained in the blue room was the crib, dresser, and a rocking chair sitting beside the window.

The day Michael died, Robin called him hysterical, saying he wasn't breathing. Mike beat the paramedics to the house, and this is where he found her, holding their dead baby in her arms, rocking him. From that moment on nothing was ever the same. A part of her died too that day, and for him, each day became a struggle to hold on to the one thing he had left, his wife.

When the feeling of detachment from Robin set in, along with it came the most alarming sense of resentment he had ever known.

"God, forgive me for how much I hated You."

Mike had said it a million times, and deep down he knew he was forgiven, but anytime a memory such as this stirred him, he reminded the Lord of his regret. If only he had known Jesus then, Mike would have healed and been able to help his wife heal. Instead, he battled God and lost.

Mike sat in his truck at the cemetery, debating whether or not he should leave. He was parked beside Robin's rental car. Having waited more than an hour before leaving home, he assumed she would be gone by the time he arrived. The fact that she was still out in the cemetery and it was getting so close to dark concerned him. As much as he didn't want to interrupt her, he made his way to Mikey's graveside anyway to check on her.

For several moments he stood quietly behind her, until he finally said, "I'm sorry. I thought you would be gone, or I would've never come."

She was sitting on the grass with her knees bent up to her chest, hugging her legs. Without turning to look at him, she assured, "It's okay. I didn't realize I would be here so long either."

He sat near but not too near her. "I feel guilty when I leave," he admitted.

Turning to him, she nodded. "That's exactly what I feel, like I'm leaving him here all alone. I can't make myself stand up." Tears sprang to her eyes, so she rubbed them away with the sleeve of her shirt.

She knew her son wasn't there in that grave. Rather, she knew he was in heaven and this was just a place where his little body rested. Still, to stand up and walk away made her feel as if she were abandoning him.

After he died she came to sit beside his grave nearly every day. Mike never knew. Always, she would wait until he was gone to work, and with nothing at home to give her purpose anymore, she would drive out and spend hours on end. When she finally accepted the job at the car dealer, she reduced her trips to the weekends. It was a small step toward moving forward, or at least she thought so at the time.

Though he would have been certain just moments before he couldn't possibly cry anymore, again, Mike was on the verge of tears, so he just sat quietly and watched his wife look at her son's grave. How many times had he watched her do this very thing? After Mikey died she came faithfully. It took some time for him to realize just how often, but after a week or two, he discovered she was going every day. Regularly, on his lunch break, he would drive out, knowing he would find her there. He never approached her, but he watched her, concerned she may never recover. It was after the first two months that he began falling to pieces along with her, never sure which was worse, losing his son or watching his wife come undone. From there forward he simply felt as if he were falling down some giant hole and there was no bottom to it.

After several quiet moments Mike told her, "You and I are the only ones who can understand this grief. I know other parents grieve lost children, but I mean him, Michael. No one else can understand what it feels like to sit here by his grave, knowing we will never see him again." Reaching out, he rubbed his hand across her back. "I've been here so many times this past year and each time I wonder, will it ever stop hurting this bad? Today is the first day it doesn't hurt quite as much. I think maybe because you're here, and I know that you share this with me." Looking at her, he asked, "Does that make sense at all?"

"Yes, I think it does."

She vividly recalled what it was like to stand over the fresh grave of her son. Then, Mike was by her side, and somehow that made the day bearable. Otherwise, she was certain she could have never made it through. Mike had always been her rock. That recollection led her to pray silently, "Now, You are my Rock, Lord."

Taking her hand, he lifted it to his lips and kissed her knuckle. "I'm so sorry I couldn't help you through it. I was never sure of what to say or do or how to make it better for you."

She considered telling him of the things she had researched about PTSD, but the grief of the moment prevented it. It was suffocating her, so all she could say was, "We both did the best we could with what we had at the time."

He continued holding her hand, and for a moment, he really did feel whole again. The years without her had been incredibly empty. Though he knew the Lord was ever with him, he felt her absence always. Appropriately, the verse about it not being good for man to be alone came to mind. No, it wasn't good at all. Sometimes, though, man orchestrates his own solitude.

"I never napped. I can't for the life of me remember why I took a nap that day."

The expression on her face tore at his heart. "Don't do that."

"If I had been awake, I would've known something was wrong."

"If you had been awake, you would have been doing laundry or cleaning. You would have thought he was sleeping. He always slept well. You can't possibly blame yourself."

Thinking for a minute, he tried to remember, finally he did. "You were up, off and on during the night. That's why you took a nap."

"Why?" She couldn't remember.

"I don't know. You just couldn't sleep."

It would always make her wonder. How could she have been asleep while her baby needed her?

"I know I said a lot of horrible things when I was drinking, but I need you to know that I never blamed you. It was never you. I was angry at God." Reaching for her, he pulled her closer to him, saying, "I'll never figure it out, why He took our son. Sometimes I feel like maybe it was because of me. If I had believed earlier, maybe He wouldn't have had to get my attention that way."

For years he had played the "what if" game. What if he were a godly man? Would it have made a difference?

"This one place is where I stay stuck." She had tried and tried to get past it. "Things with us, I've found my way out of the darkness, but this, this still envelopes me. It's the one stitch I can't seem to unravel."

He was unsure exactly what she meant, but he understood enough. His son's death had been the beginning of his undoing, and his only way to reconcile it was to believe God is good, even when He doesn't show up and save a baby.

"I met with a counselor, and he gave me this one thing, this way of remembering that has helped. He showed me that I was clinging to Michael's death rather than the love I have for him. So now, I try to remember the good things, the sweet little baby he was. Like, I loved how he would rub my chest while he was nursing. It must have been soothing for him."

She was warmed by the memory of it. Grinning, she asked, "Do you remember how his eyes would roll back in his head and he could barely stay awake long enough to finish?"

Of course he remembered, but for a moment he could hardly find his voice to say so. Sitting close, with no space between them, Mike draped his arm around her and rested his hand on her leg. There in that moment, he clearly felt the presence of the Lord, knowing He was healing deep and agonizing wounds within them both. This was a moment to be cherished, and in hindsight, would likely be considered holy. Squeezing her slightly, he finally replied, "I remember well. He sure was a good baby."

"He sure was," Robin whispered, knowing she was talking about her son with the one other person who knew him and loved him as she did.

Mike kept thinking of her words, of how she had been clinging to Mikey's death rather than her love for him. Was that what he had done? It was something he would spend time in prayer about. Admittedly, he could rarely think of his son because of the depth of sorrow his memory brought.

They sat for a while longer in this way, together, reminiscing about their son. At one point Robin considered how the Lord prompted her to make the trip in the first place. He knew it was exactly what she needed to begin to truly live again. Most likely, it was the same with Mike. As mysterious as her future was to her, she had no doubt that God had good planned for her, and Mike too. This would be a crucial step for both of them to finally heal.

As they repeated their earlier good-byes, Mike stood by Robin's car wanting desperately to hold her. His arms ached to wrap around her and feel her against him one final time. Pressing his hand against the car door, preventing her from opening it, he whispered, "Can I have a hug?" He felt silly for asking.

Robin turned to face him, saying, "That's easy enough," and wrapped her arms around his waist and rested her head on his chest. His heart was pounding erratically in her ear, most likely because he was holding her so close. She found that to be very sweet. For as long as she could remember, she affected him that way. Just as relieved to be held, she found the smell of him familiar and comforting, which triggered memories of who they used to be and how they once held to one another with no intention of ever letting go. Remembering *them* caused a stirring deep within her belly, something she could scarcely identify. If she allowed herself to give it a name, she would call it a distant longing for that lost love.

With Robin nestled in his arms, she felt so small. Mike squeezed her as tightly as he dared, wishing desperately he could pull her inside of himself and never let her go. Then, for a split-second, guilt surfaced. How could he have raised his hand to someone he loved so much, someone who trusted him the way she did? Shoving the guilt away, he refused to spend the very last moment of the very last hug thinking such thoughts. He simply wanted to feel her near him. Pressing his lips to the top of her head, he gave her a long secret kiss. How many hundreds of times had he openly done that? Being more than a foot taller than Robin, it was where he could most easily reach, so from the time they were thirteen on, he often kissed her there. She used to find it endearing, but with her heart in such a distant place from him, it wouldn't likely be as well received.

The following morning, dressed early, Mike made the trip to Raleigh. He had spent most of the night awake, thinking of Robin and all that transpired the day before. Finally, by sunrise, he found himself sitting at the kitchen table drafting a letter, actually, many versions of a letter to her. She had said she was staying at the Ramada, and he had to assume it would be the one nearest to the airport. His hope was to drop the letter off at the front desk.

As anticipated he found her rental car in the parking lot and went inside the hotel. He was taking the chance that since he was in his deputy uniform, they would be sure to give her the letter. Speaking with the only clerk behind the desk, Mike said, "I need to drop this off for Robin McGarrett. She should be checking out this morning."

The clerk began typing. "I don't have a McGarrett registered." Offering no further help, he went back to what he was doing.

Mike's heart plummeted. He was sure the car was hers. When she pulled out of the driveway the day before, he had stared at the car long enough.

"What about Jacobs? She may be registered under Jacobs."

Typing again, the less than courteous man advised, "Yes, we have a Robin Jacobs."

Sensing the man wasn't entirely interested in making sure Robin got his letter, Mike towered over him and warned in his most intimidating voice, "Look, I'm leaving this here for her, and I'm holding *you* personally responsible for making sure she gets it. Do you understand me?"

Eyes growing larger by the second, the clerk replied, "Yes, sir. I'll hand it to her personally."

Sitting in his truck, Mike saw her exit the hotel with his letter in hand. After she loaded her bags into the trunk, he watched her get into her car and open the letter. She smiled; he was pretty sure. When she pulled out of the parking lot, he sat there a minute longer, realizing, if she found him watching her it might seem kind of creepy. Laughing at himself, he had to admit, it probably *was* pretty creepy.

Robin's flight was delayed, and the drive back to the inn was long. By the time she reached home, she was in no mood to field Emma's questions. After a brief summary of her trip, she headed down to Chris' cabin to think – and to read Mike's letter again.

Though it was mid-September, the weather was still unseasonably warm. Robin loved it though. In some parts of the state, there was a touch of fall color arriving, but at the lake it was still a while away. Each year, she held on to every last trace of summer, dreading the changing of the seasons. Though fall was magnificent, another New England winter wasn't something she looked forward to with enthusiasm. Once the real cold set in, she would move back up to the main house with Emma, but for as long as she could, she would stay where she felt closest to God.

Robin sat on the porch and inspected the envelope again. It was addressed to Robin McGarrett. Since her arrival in New Hampshire, she had taken her maiden name back. Even prior to having divorce papers drawn up, she signed her name as Robin Jacobs because the sight of Mike's name in print was so devastatingly painful for her. Today, seeing Mike's name there was another reminder of how much had changed over the years. She was a lifetime away from that campfire and burnt marshmallow.

Sliding the single sheet of paper from the envelope, she scanned his writing. How many letters had she read and re-read when he was overseas? During the two and a half years they were apart, they lived and loved through their letters. From telling the most trivial details of their day to sharing the deepest loneliness each was experiencing, both hung onto every word the other would write. His letters were all that got her through each deployment. She had them still, tucked away in a box at the bottom of the chest in the spare room, untouched for years. Pulling herself from the past, she read his letter again.

> *Dear Robin,*
>
> *Words can never express my gratitude. The fact that you forgive me is a reminder to me of God's grace. The fact that you felt you needed to be forgiven reminds me of your tenderness. After you left I realized, in all the arguing I did that you didn't owe me an apology, I never said these words to you – I forgive you. I always did. Just as I needed to hear you say those words, if what you need is to hear them, then I'll say them again. I forgive you.*
>
> *I know our early life together is now a lifetime away, but to sit and talk with you was proof that it actually did exist once. Sometimes, I wonder if things really were as I remember them to be. I ask myself, were the good years really that good? Now I know.*
>
> *What I've found most difficult is that the one person who was my best friend all those years was just gone one day. Even though we may no longer be friends in the normal sense of the word, while you were here I felt like I had my best friend back. I've missed simply talking to you.*
>
> *When I got home last night, I realized I left the food out, so there went my leftovers. Nothing about yesterday turned out as I expected, and I can honestly say, for someone who never much liked surprises, yesterday was a good day.*
>
> *It brings me joy to know you are happy where you are. You deserve all the happiness in the world. It's what I pray for you each and every day without fail. I hope you don't mind that I'm bringing this letter to you. So as much as I feel like a stalker, I'll try the airport Ramada and look for your car.*
>
> *Well, I have an hour drive ahead to find you, so I'll close.*
>
> *Thanks again and again.*
Mike

Robin had re-read the letter once on the plane and again this time. Knowing him as well as she did, she knew he agonized over every word. His letters from Afghanistan were frequent, but brief. He wrote something to her nearly every day and would let them build into a few pages before sending them. So for him to sit and write out so much in one sitting, took tenacity on his part.

She smiled and wondered if she should write in return.

13

A week passed after Robin's visit, and for the life of him, Mike couldn't get back into the normal groove of things. It was as if he walked around in a daze. Work was a good distraction, but being at home caused him to recount their conversation over and over. For hours on end he would sit on the patio and imagine her sitting there, hearing in his heart the words she spoke. Many nights, long into the night, he would sit and look at the empty chair where she had cried, and he prayed for her.

The contents of his letter concerned him, too. Did he say anything that upset her? He had wadded up and thrown away several versions before settling on the one he delivered, all the while hoping he wasn't out of line for doing so. Still, he wondered and worried.

After spending the morning at his mother's place, mowing and working on whatever odd jobs she found for him, he was heading home to mow his own yard. He still hadn't told his mother about Robin's visit and wasn't sure if he ever would. Somehow that time together was so personal, it seemed nearly sacred to him. He didn't even want to open up the conversation with her. No telling what she would say, nothing encouraging to be sure.

Pulling into the drive, just far enough that his tail-end was out of the road, Mike stopped and put his truck into park. At the mailbox he opened the door and stood frozen. There on top of the stack was a letter from Robin. Even though there was no return address, he recognized her handwriting immediately. Reaching for the letter, he held it and looked at it for a minute or two, unable to open it. Turning, he went back to the truck and drove on up to the house. He took the letter and sat on the porch, and when he flipped it over to open it, he saw that she had written her return address there. Opening it carefully, so as not to tear the address, he slipped the letter out and unfolded it.

Dear Mike,
Thank you for your thank you, but no thanks are necessary.

He smiled at her words. When he was overseas, he could always expect some sort of silly opening. Though not quite so prepared for it this time, it made him tremendously happy that she remembered.

Thank you for so graciously offering your forgiveness. I'm sure it's not often that people in our unusual circumstance force apologies on one another. Nothing has ever been usual for us.
Sorry about your burgers. It was the best I've had in some time. If I had known you cared so little about them, I would have smuggled them out in my pocket. And I agree – it was nice to talk again as friends.
I wanted to tell you, I really am happy that you were able to get back on at the Sheriff's Department. For as long as I can recall, you've wanted to be a cop. I remember all the way back to ninth grade and the career fair. We all had to make a display of what we wanted to be. Yours was all about police work. I should know; I did most of your poster board, and you're very welcome.
As for receiving your letter, I admit I was surprised, but not in that you-were-a-stalker kinda way. It was a pleasant surprise.
Speaking of surprises, when I came home, Emma told me she'll be baptized next Sunday. I don't think I told you that she's been going to church with me for quite some time. For as many years as I've been here, she has been closed off to the things of God. It wasn't until last summer that she agreed to go. She was saved in April but hasn't felt ready to walk the aisle and join the church yet. She worked up the nerve while I was gone. I wish she would have done it with me there to see, but at least she did it. So rejoice with me. I am so happy, as I love her more deeply than you can imagine.
Well, I should close now. We have weekend guests due soon, and I have some last-minute things to do. Things are slow now during the week, but weekends will still be busy.
Have a good week and stay safe.

Robin

For a moment he was taken back in time. That was exactly how she wrote when he was overseas, answering paragraph by paragraph. Though he noticed she skipped one. The one paragraph he agonized over the most, the one where he mentioned their early life together, was the one she didn't

Unmending the Veil

respond to. What did he expect, though? The fact that she replied at all was more than he could have asked.

Scanning through her letter again, he found what he was looking for. One thing he was unable to get off his mind was about that career fair project. He tried to remember what she did her display on but couldn't recall. After reading the letter through again, he was determined to remember.

Several days later, his mind was still occupied with the things she said. Her words tumbled over and over in his head. She even agreed it was nice to talk as friends. Certainly, he was overanalyzing it. Mostly though, he kept wondering if the fact that she included her address meant she might welcome another letter. Hopeful, he sat down more than once to write one, but then thought better of it, as she was likely just being kind in her response. It was just the way she was.

Finally, at the one week point, the question about the career fair began to bother him more. No matter how hard he tried, he couldn't remember what she wanted to be. He had racked his brain to try and recollect, and eventually realized he simply may have never known. That disturbed him even more. How could he be with her so many years and not know or care what she dreamed of becoming? Was he really so caught up in his own dreams that he overlooked hers?

Throughout school, he anticipated he would go to college on a football scholarship. Everyone did. His plan was to study criminal justice and go into law enforcement. Once that hope was shot, there was no money for school. His grades weren't good enough for an academic scholarship, so going to school right away was out of the question. After 9/11 all he could think of was joining the Marines. Besides serving his country, he knew it would give him money for his education. Going to school was still his plan when they moved back home from Pendleton, but once there, he was able to get on as a deputy. Things seemed to fall into place for him, and she was right there beside him every step of the way.

Thinking back, she was behind him at each stage of a hope or dream. Whether it was training for football, shipping out to war, or spending nights alone that first year he was on the job, she was always there, rooting for him. But what did she want to do and be, and why did he never even try to find out?

Early Monday morning, just after the sun had risen, Mike sat ready to give a letter another try. Convinced she wouldn't have given him her address if she wasn't open to another letter, he began.

Hey, Rob –
First, and most importantly, I think I would've noticed you smuggling the burgers out in your pocket. I'm a trained professional. I have an eye for that sort of thing. Actually, I have you to thank for my career. Without that poster board at the career fair, I most certainly would never have become the fine officer I am today. So I thank you indeed.
You know, I've been racking my brain this week, trying to figure something out. During the career fair, what did you do your display on? What did you want to be? Taking a slight turn toward the serious, I have to say, I can't for the life of me remember. I'm ashamed to admit this, but I think maybe I was so caught up in what I wanted to be that I never asked you. I know it's a little late, but I would really like to know.
Speaking of surprises again, I'm so glad to hear about Emma. I may be able to top that one, though. My mom went to church with me Sunday. I have no idea why. She just showed up. You should have seen the looks on the faces in the church that day. You know my mom…she didn't care. She finished her cigarette on the porch and walked right in like she owned the place. It was weird and funny, but really nice, too. So pray for her.
Glad to hear things are busy. That's a good thing, right?
Will stay safe, and you do the same.

Mike

Relatively happy with the outcome of the letter, Mike read it again to make sure it made sense. Considering the tone of her letter, he went for the same general, upbeat feel. He hoped he made the mark.

Robin had spent the entire day with Emma but was glad to have a few minutes alone. Regretfully, it was Emma who checked the mail that day, and when handing the letter from Mike to her, she wore a deep scowl on her face. Who could blame her really? What Emma witnessed when Robin arrived all those years ago was bound to set her at odds with Mike for good. The pieces of her heart were scattered about, and it was Emma who began to pick them up and help her to put her life back together. Emma knew firsthand what Mike was capable of.

Upon receiving another envelope with his handwriting, she found herself excited. It was as he implied in his first letter; you can't be best friends with someone so long without a tremendous gap emerging in their absence. He got her jokes and she got his. Without question there was a history with him she could never have with another living soul. She hated that she had to hide her true feelings about receiving the letter. When Emma handed it to her, she tried to act as if it were no big deal. But it was.

Alone in her cabin, she started a fire and sat in Chris' chair to read the letter. Seeing the words, "Hey, Rob," caused her to stop reading altogether. Closing her eyes, she fought back the urge to cry. There was a lump in her throat, and she swallowed hard to try to clear it. When he called her at home before they married, that was his usual greeting. It felt like a lifetime ago, and then again it felt like yesterday. She could hear the tone of his voice ringing in her head. "Hey, Rob." Finally shaking off the memory, she continued on with his letter.

His trained eye, that was funny, causing her to giggle aloud. Unexpectedly, and after having been so thrilled by his letter, she came to his question about what she wanted to be back in ninth grade. Though he could have never known its impact, it caused her to weep openly. At no time was he caught up in himself, as he included her in every aspect of his life. The truth was, and she could understand how he could have missed it, she wanted to be exactly what she was – his.

From the moment they began dating, she wanted to be his wife and the mother of his children. No one ever believed they would stay together throughout school. She knew, though, and so did he. Within weeks of the campfire, they began talking about a future. At first her parents thought it a crush, one that would pass. It took at least two years before they became overly worried, then worry became acceptance. When the two decided to marry at such a young age, no one, especially her parents, was surprised by it. They loved Mike, everyone did.

Her mom was a stay-at-home mom. She was there for her every minute and never seemed too put out by the constant demands: baking something last minute, no problem, hemming a dress, no problem. While her mom didn't necessarily make it look easy, she made it look rewarding. To Robin, it was as noble a profession as being a doctor or nurse, so her poster board back in ninth grade was on being a homemaker.

Reading his question again, she knew she would never be able to respond to it. It was something too painful for both of them; some things were better left unsaid.

Robin spent all week thinking about Mike's letter, and though wanting to reply, she put it off for another week. It was similar to eating ice cream. At first you are enjoying it tremendously, until you get that pounding in your head – brain freeze. She had heart freeze. Certainly, she enjoyed his letters, how could she not? Before he was ripped away from her, he was the absolute foundation of her life and existence. Long before the night they last saw each other, he was gone. Nearly at the first drink she lost him, and she had missed him every moment since he became that stranger.

With her new understanding of PTSD, she often thought back to when he returned from his second tour. Admittedly, he was different at first, but then they found out about the baby and quickly the move was upon them. After a few months he seemed okay, or at least better. Still, he wasn't exactly right, and she knew it deep down inside. Figuring there would have to be some effects from war, she assumed it would be something he would get over. What if she had been more inquisitive? Would things have turned out differently?

Mike sat alone in a booth at the diner staring at the full plate of food in front of him. For the first time in as long as he could remember, he found he had no appetite. Having not received a response from Robin in nearly three weeks, he had to assume their correspondence was over. In constant prayer, he thanked God for the one thoughtful letter she had sent. When viewing things in proper context, he could expect no more.

"You seem miles away."

He hadn't noticed her approach, so when Shelly slid into the booth across from him, Mike was a bit startled. Always uneasy in her presence, he opted not to respond. Newly divorced, she had made it a point to let him know on several occasions. Though still a pretty woman, he found nothing about her attractive. The circumstances of her divorce were common knowledge around town. Her husband caught her cheating and apparently the boyfriend didn't stick around long after. It was no one Mike knew. What he did know was that she had set her sights on him, since every time he turned around she was there. Even at the gym, she began going at the same time he did, and while he tried to avoid her, she was everywhere.

"I was just leaving." He reached for the check, but when he did, she placed her hand on his.

"Don't you ever get lonesome out there all alone?"

The way she looked at him conveyed her real intentions. The realization occurred to him, she would show up at his house sooner or later if he failed to put a stop to this now. The last thing he needed was her out there with him alone. Although he trusted himself fine, he didn't trust her at all.

Ashamed by his actions, he recalled her birthday party all those years before. Though he never told Robin, it was his first time to drink, and that day he drank way more than he should have. By the time they got to the party, having been drinking since midday, he was totally out of it. While not passing out drunk, he felt unlike himself. So when Shelly came on to him and he responded to her as he did, it wasn't what it seemed to her. Clearly she thought he was interested, but truthfully, the entire time he was with her, he was envisioning Robin. They had gone no further than kissing in all the years they dated, so when tempted in such a way, combined with the effects of the alcohol, he lost himself in the moment. By nine o'clock he was throwing up, mainly due to regret over his actions and the fact that he might possibly lose Robin because of it.

Quickly, Mike pulled his hand from beneath Shelly's and assured her, "As a matter of fact, I don't. I'm content just as I am, so I want to be up front with you; I'm *not* interested in a relationship."

Biting seductively at her lower lip, she whispered, "Who said anything about a relationship?"

He understood her meaning. She was offering herself with no strings attached, as if that were possible. While he felt sorry for her, since her desperation was as sad as it was pathetic, he had no intention of allowing a door of possibility to remain open.

Mike leaned in to ensure no one would overhear and sternly reminded her, "I said no seventeen years ago, and the answer is still no."

He was referring to her proposition at the bonfire the night he met Robin. What Shelly suggested they do for seven minutes was downright filthy for kids that age.

Infuriated by his rejection, Shelly spat, "Yeah, I guess there's no accounting for taste. How'd that work out for ya, Mike? Where's your precious Robin now?" Standing, she added, "If you're still pining away for her after all she did to you, then God help you."

Watching her leave, Mike realized how much he must have hurt her. Though not his intention, he knew he had to be firm and clear. An apology crossed his mind, but he suspected that if he acknowledged her at all, he would only be opening the door for more trouble. Considering her angry words, "pining away," he admitted the truth of them. For years he had and for life he would. And what did she mean when she said after all Robin did to *him*?

Once home, Mike went through the same routine as he had over the past weeks. This time, though, instead of disappointment awaiting him, inside the mailbox was a letter from Robin. "Thank you, Lord," he whispered aloud. He felt like a kid again, like when they first began going together – that was what they called it. Her parents wouldn't allow her to date, or even call it dating until they were seventeen. Smiling at the recollection of those times, he thought of how they passed notes back and forth during school. In the hallway, at lunch, constantly, they wrote to each other throughout the day, just short notes, ones describing how boring a class was or how much they missed each other. Did he appreciate those notes then the way he did now? Maybe not quite as much, having such tragedy in their wake to cause him to see her willingness to communicate with him as nothing short of miraculous, but even back then, he would feel a thrill of excitement when she slipped a folded sheet of paper into his hand.

Speeding up the driveway, he came to an abrupt stop, excited, relieved that she had finally answered his letter. Without bothering to put his truck into park, Mike tore into the envelope. Unfolding the small sheet of paper, his heart plummeted when he read the brief note.

Hey, Mike –
Still praying for your mom.
*   Robin*

He sat for several minutes, staring at the one sentence. What did he expect from her? Without a doubt, she had been more than gracious as it was. What more could he want from her? Did he really believe that something could begin again after all that happened? Sure, he secretly hoped, but deep down, he had known better. Robin's willingness to reply to his first letter was more kindness than he deserved, but no matter how he tried to frame it or put it into perspective or talk himself out of being disappointed, the simple truth was, he was devastated.

Moving slowly into the house, as depressed as he could ever recall being, he slumped into a chair and sat. Evening came and still he sat. Without energy even to get up and turn on a light, he just sat with the Lord, seeking comfort. His prayers were more for her than for himself. "God give her a better life than I offered her."

Stir crazy, Robin volunteered to go to the market. Having anticipated a letter in return, she found herself disappointed when none came. It had been more than a month since she received Mike's second letter, and she was beginning to believe she wouldn't hear from him again. Maybe he discovered a way to move on. She hoped so for his sake. Maybe someone new had come into the picture, and yes, the thought of that stung her heart, but ultimately, she had to know it would happen.

As handsome as he was when he was young, Mike was even more so as he matured. What was once smooth and soft young man's skin had become more weathered and creased. When he smiled, tiny lines formed in the corners of his eyes. There was wisdom in them and new found tenderness. Something about his presence altogether seemed more assured and confident. It struck her – it was godliness – that was what made him so much more attractive. He had become a good and godly man, and it flowed from him in words and actions. He was so broad and beautiful, how could any woman not be attracted to him? Robin would be a fool to believe any less. Knowing how life worked in their small town, Robin was certain he was the object of much affection. This realization would prompt her to take more conclusive steps in allowing it to be over. No matter what comfort or connection with her former life his letters brought her, she had to let him go.

As much as she said it was over, so far for her it hadn't been. Maybe that was why the Lord was so heavy handed with her about going to see him personally, to allow some healing. They both needed closure to move forward. He needed to be set free as much as she did. She could see it in his eyes when they were together on the patio. Of course she would give him that.

As she turned into the market, her phone slid from the console and onto the passenger seat. Once parked, she stretched over the gear shift to reach for it when something caught her eye. There, between the console and passenger seat was an envelope. Squeezing her hand between the two, she caught the paper with the tip of her fingers and dragged it upward. It was her last letter to Mike.

When she took his letter to the post office, she had a bundle of mail from the inn and had haphazardly tossed it all over onto the passenger seat. So of course she failed to notice one missing envelope when she carried the stack in. Sighing heavily, she tried to put this in perspective with her earlier thoughts. She had waited two weeks before writing, and a week later, she sent a simple note telling him she was praying for his mom. For all he knew she had only sent the one note. Was that why he never wrote back to her? From his viewpoint, she never replied to his last letter.

Skipping the market for the time being, she rushed over to the post office. From her console, Robin pulled a small piece of paper and scribbled,

Thankfully, I'm a wild driver. My phone went flying when I made a turn just now, and when I reached for it, I found this letter. Sorry this is so late.
Robin Andretti

Inside the post office Robin purchased a blank envelope and addressed it. Folding the misplaced letter, along with the note, she tucked them inside. As she handed the envelope to the clerk, she silently prayed, "Please don't let him think I simply ignored his letter."

Back in the car, she felt a stinging sense of conviction. The way she took her letter with the mail from the inn was, in a way, a form of deception. In truth, she hadn't wanted Emma to know she was communicating with Mike regularly. Though she had not fully come to understand her motives in keeping it secret, she had some inkling of an idea. In one way it was Emma's disapproval of Mike that prevented Robin from being open about it. Prior to her visiting him, Emma had done nothing but discourage it. Understandably, she was still so bitter against him that no matter what Robin said about the need to see him face to face, Emma tried to dissuade her.

Another truth she had to admit to herself was that she didn't want to be one of *those* women, the type who gets knocked around, and then when her man comes around full of apologies, she goes back for more of the same. While she knew the circumstances were different entirely, still, she felt the reluctance of appearing that way. It was something she was trying to work through. Its name, as difficult as it was to admit, was pride.

The fact of the matter was that she enjoyed having Mike back in her life. She loved seeing his handwriting and being able to envision him sitting there, choosing every word so carefully. She wanted to know what was happening in his life, even if it meant he would soon share something as painful as falling in love again. After all the years apart and all the grief and pain, they could be no more than friends, but she wanted that, and she desperately hoped he did, too.

While putting groceries away in the pantry, she realized she would have to be honest with Emma. No matter how she reacted, Robin was determined to keep the lines of communication open with Mike, and Emma would have to try and understand. It would likely run its course and eventually dwindle away. So what was the harm?

Mike had spent more time at the church lately. During the spring and summer, he spent his Saturdays there, maintaining the lawn and whatever else needed to be done. Since fall was fully upon them, not as much was required of him. Still he went and did odd jobs that other people avoided – anything to keep him out of the house.

After his release from prison, he went to church that first Sunday, Robin's church. Then, he considered it hers because, when they were younger, his only motive in going was to be with her. Her dad wouldn't allow them out together unattended, so church was three extra times per week he was able to see her. Wednesday night, Sunday mornings and nights, he showed up with only one thing on his mind – Robin. Then when they returned home from Pendleton, he went while she was pregnant and while Mikey was still alive. After that, though, he found any and every excuse to stay away. Other than a major holiday, he stayed home and watched ball or worked around the house.

That first day, walking back in after five years in prison, he wasn't sure what to expect. What he did know was that God was leading him there, and while he fought it at first, the prompting was too strong to ignore. To his amazement, he was welcomed by most everyone. It was certainly a God thing. A man with his history of abuse, especially against a woman who had attended their church all her life, could hardly expect much of a welcome. There, though, he found a new family and had grown to love them more and more over time.

Easily enough, he became close friends with the pastor. Since Tim was single, he spent more time at the church than a man with a family might. That allowed them to get to know each other better. Since Tim arrived during Mike's incarceration, he wasn't as familiar with the history, other than the gossip, so Mike was glad to have someone who was willing to get to know the new man rather than the one who did the things everyone else remembered.

This day, having finished early, Mike went home. Making the drive out of town, he didn't relish the idea of a lonesome afternoon at home. He had stopped waiting and hoping for anything more from Robin, and finally, he was at peace with it. God gave him that peace. So this time, opening his mailbox, there was no expectation. Maybe that was what made the sight of her letter so much sweeter. Reaching for it, he noted how his hands trembled and laughed at himself. Moving to his truck, he lowered the tailgate and sat there to read it. It was chilly out, but he barely noticed with such warmth stirring inside. Noticing the bulk of the envelope, he could tell it was no simple page inside. He tore into it anxiously and first opened the small piece of paper.

Mike smiled broadly as he read the note explaining the missing letter and was relieved to know she hadn't simply ignored his last letter, and her signature, Robin Andretti, was hysterical. For years he called her that. When they were out together he drove, having always feared her getting pulled over for speeding with him in the car. A deputy with a reckless driving wife, how embarrassing would that have been?

Opening the sealed envelope, he pulled out the page and began.

Hey, Mike -
An eye for that sort of thing? Really? So while you were busy stuffing your face with half a cow, you think you would notice? I hate to say I doubt your abil-

ity, but my memory is not all that bad. I've seen you eat. You go to a faraway place, you and your food.

Resting the letter on his lap, he threw his head back and chuckled. She had always given him a hard time about how much he ate – everyone did. No matter how much grief she gave him, though, she confessed on more than one occasion that she loved to cook for him and watch him eat. Cooking came naturally for her, and he missed it. Closing his eyes, he swallowed hard. He missed everything about her. In his mind, when he read her words, he could hear her voice and that served only to make him miss her more.

Continuing, it went on to say,

Finally! My work is acknowledged. Though I've had no reason to make a poster board lately, I'm confident I still have the gift. As for mine then, it was nothing to write home about. Actually, Bobby Taylor went before me and went on and on. So I never did mine, and Mr. Howell never noticed, probably bored to tears. Obviously, I wasn't about to mention it. If you remember, I was terrified of talking in front of the class. Somehow, I dodged the bullet. So now, I guess innkeeper would be the answer.

Speaking of surprises again and again – that is a huge surprise. Your mom, really? I have to say, "And me of little faith," though I shouldn't have been. When God begins to touch a life, amazing things happen. I'm so happy, and I hope she continues to go with you. We both know she's lived a hard life, so if anyone needs Jesus, your mom does. I'll be praying for her.

Thinking back, all I can say is that she was kind to me. Though you and everyone else found her so difficult, for some reason we got along well. I was always glad about that. Somewhere beneath that hard exterior, I saw something others didn't see. Maybe she saw something in me, too.

Okay, the cigarette thing kills me. Well, at least she put it out first. That proves there's a God. I can still see her now, eating dinner with a cigarette burning in the ashtray. She would stop and take a puff, then continue eating. How can you not find that funny?

Things here are slower. I know now we are on the downhill slide into winter. It has rained a lot, too much. I've been cooped up too much. These next few months will drag on and on. At least I have Thanksgiving and Christmas to look forward to. My parents will fly in for Christmas, but I suppose Emma and I will spend Thanksgiving alone. Or possibly, we will be joined by a handsome veterinarian who has wooed and pursued Emma until she's finally on the verge of breaking. Will keep you posted.

Have a safe Halloween. I know that's when the crazies come out. Will you work that night?

Well, going to throw a log on the fire. Will be moving back up to the main house tomorrow. Too cold for a Southern girl.

Blessings to you!

Robin

He read it again and again. Sitting there on his tailgate, he believed he might possibly be the happiest man alive. Clearly, the way she asked questions, her letter opened the door for him to respond. In hers, she was open and sweet and funny, everything she always was. It reminded him that she was his best friend, and he was willing to settle for having her back in his life this way. He had his chance at more and blew it. But this, this new whatever-it-was, was enough. Without hesitation, he would take even the tiniest little scrap she would give him.

14

When Emma handed Robin Mike's letter, there was a new, softer expression on her face. Gone was the critical, *I hope you know what you are doing* kind of look. After feeling so guilty about keeping something so significant from her, Robin admitted they were writing. Emma didn't seem at all surprised. Once Robin explained how she was feeling, conflicted, yet comforted by having a part of what she had lost restored, Emma's attitude changed from then on. The day Robin opened up to her, Emma simply nodded, saying, "Of all people, I understand."

Her words saddened Robin. They reminded her that Emma still longed for what she lost all those years ago. It was the truest kind of love that could span three decades.

"In your next letter to him, tell him I said 'hi.'"

Smiling at Emma, Robin took the envelope. "I will."

Robin went into the dining room and sat at a table by the wall of windows. What had been a relatively gloomy day was taking a brighter turn. Before she could get the letter open, Emma walked to the table and sat a cup of steaming coffee before her.

"I thought you might enjoy this."

"Thanks."

Anxious to read his letter, Robin could hardly wait to see what he had to say about her missing letter. Chewing on her thumbnail, while grinning at the same time, she read,

Dear Ms. Andretti,
Half a cow? Whatever. It was two and a half burgers. The last one didn't count since there was no bun, and you, you still eat like a bird. Get it, Robin - bird? Okay, I'll work on my humor.
As for my faraway place, I'm unable to visit often. I still don't cook much, and I'm so overdone with diner food. You know us cops, we do eat a lot of donuts,

but what does the Good Book say? "Cop does not live by donut alone." I may be paraphrasing a bit.

That's right, I remember Bobby's presentation. It was the longest, most boring thing I've ever heard in my life. I think Gina's career choice of underwater basket weaving or whatever it was, was even more interesting than his. What was his, microbiology?

Okay, so you didn't do yours, but you still never reminded me what it was about. Being an innkeeper now doesn't count. That's new news. Still, tell me more about that. What do your days look like, summer and winter? And what did you mean you're moving back to the main house?

About my mom, so far not so good news. She hooked up with some guy and hasn't been back again. That's typical, but still I will hope. I just don't press her about it. It wouldn't make a difference if I did. You said, "And me of little faith." I understand that. I guess I still feel that way. I shouldn't, I know, but she has been like this all my life, and I guess to expect some drastic change is hard to wrap my mind around.

Though I shouldn't have been, I was always surprised at the way she was with you. She was different, and of course she saw something special in you, everyone did. You were always so sweet and compassionate with others. When everyone else, including me, judged her, you accepted her. That had to have meant something to her. In hindsight, I should have learned from you, and maybe things would've been better between her and me.

I can hardly imagine what the winters are like there. I remember the summer I was there was beautiful, but the winters must be brutal. As cold natured as you are, how do you survive it?

I can hardly believe that Thanksgiving is a week and a half away. The year will be over before we know it. It's turned out to be an exceptional year, though.

Stopping, taking a sip of her coffee, Robin wondered what he meant by an exceptional year. Did it have anything to do with her? She noticed he didn't mention what he would do for Thanksgiving, and she speculated. In years past his mom never had dinner at her house. While they were together, he always came to her house. Beginning at fifteen, they were together every year for Thanksgiving dinner. That was a really hard year for him, the year his father went to prison.

Can't wait to hear more about the vet. Is he an old guy? What's he like? I suppose I just want to know more details of your life if you're willing to share them with me.

Halloween was crazy for sure. I requested off work so I could serve at the church. We had almost every kid in town there, or so it seemed. I worked the caramel apple table, which in review wasn't the best assignment for someone with my appetite. Miss Allen said next year I can't work a food table. Most likely, I'll be stuck face painting or something. Know how you would always say, "You're gonna be sick, eating all that"? Well, it finally happened. I was so sick at my stomach that night and even through lunch the next day. Looking back, I've determined eating seven caramel apples wasn't such a good idea. I wrote myself a reminder for next year. (Now is where you say, "I told you so.") Remember to tell me about the move to the main house. Where were you before? A cabin, I guess?

Okay Southern girl, stay warm and dry, and write back when you get a chance.

And Rob, I'm glad you wrote. Honestly, I thought maybe you were sending me a message by not sending me a message. If it ever gets to that point for you, please just say so. Finding an empty mailbox is worse than knowing up front. Blessings right back at ya,

Mike

Robin decided this was his best letter yet. He was open and funny, while in his prior letters, she sensed his restraint, as if he feared saying the wrong thing. This time, he wrote as an old friend and didn't tiptoe around old subjects. He simply spoke from his heart. Every bit of it made her smile, or maybe glow was a better way of explaining it. She felt as if she were glowing, radiating sunshine right there in the dining room. Snickering to herself, she acknowledged how sappy she became after reading his letters; maybe sentimental was a better term. Whatever she called it, it was the same feelings as when they wrote back and forth during his deployments. As if she rode the waves of the ocean, his letters could make her soar high, and sometimes, they took her heart to the very depths of despair.

Having finished her coffee, she went into the kitchen for more and found Emma there.

"How was your letter?"

"It was sweet and kinda funny."

"Are you sure you know what you're doing?" Her tone was not disapproving, rather, more protective than anything.

"Not at all."

Robin took her letter and tucked it into her coat pocket. After bundling up she slipped her hat on and went down to the dock. No matter how cold it was, if it wasn't raining, she went there to pray. Besides the cabin, it was the place she felt closest to God. Each morning, while watching the sun come up, even if only from the warmth of the kitchen window, she was reminded of His faithfulness. Something she discovered, a revelation from Him that amazed her still, was that all that time she felt so compelled to sit before the water and watch the sunrise, it was actually the Spirit drawing her back to Him. At night when she ran, it was the water she ran to. He is the Living Water. He was calling her to the depths with Him, as if to say, "Come to Me and live."

In the mornings only the sun could cause the shadows of the night to flee. He was the Son she looked for. Somehow, her physical world and what she ran toward was ever symbolic of her deepest spiritual longings. It was always Him. With eyes open to how relentlessly He pursued her, she fell helplessly and entirely in love with Him. *He* was her love story, only she missed it for the first thirty years of her life. Astonished He could love her so much and even more so that she was able to love Him with such a feeble heart, she looked out at the water and whispered, "I love because You first loved me."

Robin had been out on the dock for nearly an hour and while she was there, she read Mike's letter again. Something in it disturbed her, and the more she read it the more troubled she became. Grappling with it, she finally acknowledged that she was jealous. There he was, living his life, at her church, in her home, and she was far away in the coldest place on earth, practically. He was eating caramel apples until he was sick, and she missed another fall festival. In no way was she angry at him, it was his home and his town, but it was no longer hers. That hurt terribly.

Realistically, she knew she could never go back, not with the way things ended there. After the shooting she became the most hated person in town. He was their hero, the football star who led them to the state championships, the war hero, the sheriff's deputy everyone adored, and she was the one who shot him. The things they said about her and to her caused her cheeks to flush in humiliation still.

After she was released from the hospital, she went directly to her parents' home. Once there, she didn't dare go out of the house. No one saw what she looked like in the aftermath of that night. Maybe if they had, attitudes would have been different. No one knew of his history of abuse, not even her parents. So the town was in shock, and with no coverage in the paper and no trial, they blamed her, not their hero. It began with phone calls at all hours. People were cursing her and her parents. They would wake up to find trash on the lawn and worse. Soon after, her parents packed her up and took her to Emma's. At the time she had no intention of staying permanently, but while there, her parents made the decision to move to Phoenix where her aunt and uncle lived. Within a few months she realized she had absolutely nothing there to go back to, so she simply stayed in New Hampshire. It wasn't what she chose, rather where she landed. As if a tornado picked her up and flung her hundreds of miles away, she was the victim of a storm that destroyed her home and left her no place to return, a misplaced object.

Later that evening, Robin sat in the gathering room before the fireplace. Emma had gone up to bed, and the house was quiet. It was then she decided to answer his letter.

> *Dear Apple Glutton,*
> *That was by far the longest letter I've ever seen you write. I laughed, I cried, I mocked... Seriously, it was a great way to catch up. Thank you for so many details...really rare for you.*
> *Your humor, "eat like a bird..." Stop, you're killin' me. Not! Okay, I'll have to admit your "Cop does not live by donut alone" was good, actually, really funny.*

Stopping abruptly, Robin wondered why she hadn't noticed before. Did he think of the implications when he mentioned donuts? Something unusual and unsettling happened within her. There was a stirring inside she hadn't felt in many years, a longing for him unlike anything she had experienced since he was overseas. She sat the paper aside, afraid of what she was feeling, unable to continue on.

It would be days before she could finish. When she finally did, Robin took the letter to the post office and watched carefully as it slid into the blue box. No more mishaps with her letters, she decided.

It was Thanksgiving Day and Mike was home alone. Although he had been invited to the homes of several families from church, he couldn't bring himself to go. So instead, he would do what he did the prior year, which was sit around and watch football. He at least had a turkey sandwich, but that was the extent of his holiday festivities. Without family the day didn't mean so much. His brother went with his girlfriend to visit her family. As for his mom, who knew where she was?

Unable to keep his mind on any game, he went and got Robin's letter out of his bedroom. Sitting in the recliner, he read it again. The wait had been excruciating, but when it finally came he was amazed by its length and content. She was her but a totally different her, and he found he was so proud of the woman she had become. The things she said were so deep and meaningful, it made him conclude that she had become a better version of herself without him. Obviously, he held her back all those years. In his estimation looking back at the entirety of their lives together, it really was all about him. She was unable to remember what she wanted to be, likely because the focus was ever on him, what he wanted, what he dreamed of becoming. How could he have been so selfish?

Again, he read her words.

Dear Apple Glutton,
That was by far the longest letter I've ever seen you write. I laughed, I cried, I mocked... Seriously, it was a great way to catch up. Thank you for so many details...really rare for you.
Your humor, "eat like a bird..." Stop, you're killin' me. Not! Okay, I'll have to admit your "cop does not live by donut alone" was good, actually, really funny, but don't quit your day job.
Having seen you, I have to believe you are being fed and relatively well. I would feel sorry for you, but I really believe you can follow a recipe. Start at the top and work your way down. It's really kind of satisfying to eat a meal you've prepared for yourself, one that doesn't come from a box. I can hardly

imagine, though, that you could be tired of the diner's food. From what I remember, their food was quite good.

Gina's career wasn't underwater basket weaving. She wanted to be a designer. Where did you get that? Too funny.

As for mine, I simply can't recall, but if it helps, I really don't want to be an innkeeper, well, maybe half and half. What I really would like is to become a counselor of some sort. I've been taking classes to try to finish my degree. I will someday, though I may be ninety-seven by then. But hey, old people can counsel, too.

I had a friend, Chris. He was here at the inn last year and helped me work through some difficult things. Although he passed away last year at this time, he left a lasting imprint on my life. It was he who led me back to God and toward forgiveness. Something he taught me will be part of how I help others. During one of our first conversations, he talked about mending the veil. Though the veil was torn when Christ died, allowing us access to God, some people spend their lives trying to mend the veil, so they don't have to see Him. In my case, I did so stitch by stitch. Michael was among the first I suppose, then the things that happened between us. Though I once was open to God, as a result of all the pain, I shut Him out of my life. I want to work with people like that and help them to unmend the veil the way Chris helped me, stitch by stitch.

Some people, when they're saved later on in life, come right in and install a zipper. Some of this, the Lord has revealed to me through talking with Emma. When she was saved, she had complete access to God, but instead of seeking Him, immediately, she began to hide from Him. There are things in her past that keep her from opening up to and trusting Him. I know the reality of being stuck there, which makes me think maybe God has me here for this very reason, for her. Just so you know, she's making tremendous progress, and not because of anything I'm doing but what He's doing through me. So…that's what I want to be when I grow up, a counselor…I think.

What do my days look like? Now, they're dull and uneventful. We piddle around and do this and that and laugh a lot. I drink a lot of coffee and wonder why I'm jittery. We sometimes get online and look at warm beaches and swear we're going, though we probably never will. I have a women's group that meets here on Tuesday evenings. That, I love. There is a great group of women here, even if they do talk funny.

Summer here is fun and busy. Typically, we stay at full capacity throughout June, July, and early August. There are usually kids everywhere. I like that. We have great guests and crabby guests. Each and every day is different. I would think it's like your job in a way, as you encounter different people and situations every day. There's nothing repetitive during the summer, which makes up for the drudgery of the winter.

My move to the main house – no big news. I was staying in a cabin, but once colder weather arrived, I knew I couldn't survive by hauling in tons of wood. I'm not exactly the lumberjack type. I still lean toward the girly side.

Hmm, some new guy? We will pray for her anyway. No, don't press her. You know that would push her away even more. Give it time, as I would have to believe that seeing the change in you has to make her think twice about God and such things. I saw the difference. I'm sure she does, too. How could she not? Keep being who you are, and someday, through God's grace and mercy, she'll come around. Just love her. Lost people act lost. While I know how frustrated you get about the choices she makes, the simple truth is, she's just looking for Jesus. She doesn't know it, but that's the "thing" she keeps searching for. Men will never fill that void, but Jesus will. Let's just pray and pray. That's not the only thing we can do; it's the most powerful thing we can do. "The prayer of a righteous man is powerful and effective." You're a righteous man. Pray!

I'm still cold natured but have become a bit more hardy. I don't know if I will ever get used to January and February weather here. It's beyond cold; it's, frigid.

The vet is on schedule for T'giving. I can hardly wait to see Emma that day. Already, she's flittering around like a school girl. He's a widower with four grown children and ten grandchildren. I know I'm putting the cart before the horse when I say this, but I would sure like to see her fall for him. She has never had a family of her own, and she is so amazing with children. It doesn't have to be too late for that. She would have a ready-made family, grandchildren and all.

The fall festival sounded really fun. I miss those. I was at every one from the time I was a little girl until we moved to California. Face painting next year, really?

What you said about if the time comes that we should stop writing – I would let you know. I would never just leave you hanging. I ask that you do the same. I realize there will come a time when someone special will enter your life, and when that happens, I would think she would feel uncomfortable with this. So we will keep that in mind.

So now, my hand is fully cramping. I'll close. I hope you have a wonderful Thanksgiving. Don't eat so much; you'll be sick. Haha.

With His love,
Robin

Mike sighed heavily. Reading the letter for the first time, his heart soared with every line, with every word even, until he got to the end. *There will come a time...* Though she didn't say as much on her side, when she assumed he would find someone special, she was likely preparing him for when she did. He could read between the lines and see she was setting the stage for when they had to stop writing. As much as it killed him to even consider it, had that not been his prayer for her, to find someone? Mike never entered the church without going to the altar and pleading for her happiness. She was a tremendous wife to him, and someday she should have the opportunity to be a wife again and hopefully a mother. There would *come a time* for her but never for him.

Taking her letter, he went into the kitchen and pulled some paper from the drawer. Paragraph by paragraph, he responded to all she said.

Dear Counselor,
I did come up with a long letter before — how rare for me. So did you. I asked you to share details of your life, and you did that. Thank you, and thank you for being my friend still.
Yes, I am being fed, just not as well. I eat out too much, and I know that's not good for me. I'm working out a lot and stay hungry 24/7. The new pastor at church, his name is Tim, has been working out with me. We meet after work every night and even hit the gym some Saturdays. I'm pushing him, and in doing that, end up pushing myself, too. It relieves stress and clears my head after a long day. All that to say: that's the reason I'm the size I am. I've grown out of most of my clothes and had to...gulp, go shopping. It was dreadful, so traumatic, in fact, I can hardly talk about it.
I've tried to cook a few times, and it turned out okay. Honestly, though, I just don't like it much, plus I end up with too much food for just me, which means

I eat too much. I try to use it for leftovers, but when I know it's in the fridge, I'll eat on it all night. It calls my name. So, I gave up.

A designer? Where did I get the basket weaving part? I don't know. It was the second least interesting is what I remember most.

This counselor thing, wow, I'm amazed at you. So why haven't you told me about school before now? Are you actually going, or are you doing it online? And what does it matter how old you are when you finish, as long as you finish? Rob – I'm really so proud of you. After reading your letter, I realize how much I held you back. I'm incredibly sorry about that. Now, you seem to be able to fly.

In truth, I've always wondered about the guy I saw there. He must have been Chris. I'm sorry you lost such a good friend, and I'm thankful for how much he helped you. His words are wise.

I installed the zipper. I've been thinking about this unmending the veil thing since reading your letter. In prison (and I'm sorry if this is too uncomfortable a subject for you) I really sought hard after God. Maybe it was my military background, but I had no trouble calling Him Lord. I got that, and a heart of obedience came easily. But there was this one area where I simply could never connect, or maybe a better word is relate to Him. I could hardly see Him as my Father. I brought too much baggage, I guess.

Did it ever cross your mind that I was in the same prison as my dad? I never saw him, but I thought about him often. I slowly began to pray for him, and eventually, I learned to forgive him for how he treated my mom and us. Now I can say with hindsight and the use of your terminology, the veil was unmended. You can't imagine the freedom I feel. It began to reshape me. Now, I joyfully call God my Father. I needed one my whole life, and after all these years, He is mine. Pursue this dream of counseling. Don't let it go. I'll pray for you.

I can hardly imagine you as a major coffee drinker. You never used to drink it at all. Hot chocolate – that I can see. Do you still have a sweet tooth? I do. What are the warm places you dream about?

Tell me more about your women's study. What are you studying? Do you lead it? I ask for a reason. Tim has asked me to lead a men's group on Wednesday nights. So far, I haven't said yes. I feel way too inadequate. I can't imagine he would even ask me. I can't imagine anyone would come. They all know…

I just got this mental image of you in a red flannel shirt chopping wood. Ha! Funny. You are very girly indeed, but that isn't a bad thing.

Your insight about my mom is right on track. I can see how broken she is now. When I remember how my dad knocked her around and then just up and left her, I feel a deeper level of compassion for her than I ever did. Occasionally, I remember a little more about her from when I was younger, like really young. There was a time she was tender. It has been a really long time, though. You know, like she was with Mikey. There was a time she was like that with Trevor and me. It's in there somewhere.

How are things going with the vet? Any love connection as of yet? This is T'giving Day, so by the time you receive this, you can tell me how dinner went. Tell me the menu, too. I'll live vicariously through your stomach. I decided not to do the big dinner thing this year.

No way, I won't try face painting. You've seen me draw and can agree, I have no art skills. Miss Allen is old. She'll forget all about it by next year, even if not, I'll still try for something food related, just not apples. I just gagged a bit at the thought of it.

You said something about there coming a time… If that happens with you, please let me know. It's my greatest prayer that you find happiness. And I understand that, at that point, there will be no place for me in your life. I'm more than grateful for this friendship you're offering me. I certainly don't deserve it, and will never take it for granted. So for as long as you are willing, I would like to continue writing.

Love,
Mike

Robin stood on the dock shivering. It was barely above forty, and she was foolish to be standing out in the gusty wind. Rain was on the way, which would certainly add to the gloominess of the day. The day was not only overcast and dark, it was plain sad. Mike's letter was tucked safely in her coat pocket, and having read it so many times, she had no need to read it again to recall the sadness of it. Did he realize how poignant it was? His openness and sincerity gave her greater insight into the new man he had become, and along with that insight, came a longing to know him more.

Taken off guard by his story of his father, she grieved again for him, just as she had all those years ago. They had been together just over two years when his father killed a man during a bar fight and was sentenced to life in prison. Though she never met him, after hearing stories about him, she decided she never wanted to. He was an alcoholic, abuser, and a womanizer. He had been brutal to Mike's mom and to both boys. Finally, he left when Trevor was ten and Mike was twelve. From that time on Mike was mostly in charge of Trevor as their mom began an endless pursuit of men and often wouldn't come home for two or three days at a time. They ended up on government assistance, something he was mortified by, but they did what they could to get by. At fifteen Mike went to work at his uncle's feed store and continued to work there until he left for the Marines.

His story was sad, the early one and then what happened to them after Michael, but in between the two stories, he thought he had made it out of the turmoil and chaos. So did she. Mike insisted he would never be like his dad, and once he got on at the Sheriff's Department, he was confident he would make a difference and be a better man. Somehow, no matter how much he tried to overcome it, he became a version of his dad after all. Life took that tragic turn once they buried Michael, for both of them, but by God's grace, he didn't have to remain that way.

Her thoughts drifted to how he said he feels inadequate. Then he said, "They all know." She wondered what that must feel like for him. What was it like to live in such a small town where everyone *knows* something so ugly about you? Sure, she had experienced a small taste of it, but she fled. Mike, though, was able to go back and carve out a new life for himself in spite of it all. Knowing the human heart and how the enemy tries to make you second guess your every move, especially in matters of service, she was certain his struggle was a great one. So her prayer for him was that God would give him wisdom and courage to do what He called him to do, if that was indeed His call.

Lastly, and this was the point at which tears stung her eyes, she imagined him alone on Thanksgiving Day. While she, Emma, and Stan laughed and ate until their bellies hurt, Mike was there alone, in their home. She was sure he watched football; it was what he always did. Even in their teens, she helped her mom in the kitchen while Mike, Trevor, and her dad watched football.

This wasn't the first stirring, but it was the most intense and painful of her heart's longing to go home. No matter what she felt, she never could. After all, they did all know.

Later that evening, Robin began a note that would take her but a moment.

Dear Inadequate,
You are inadequate for the task. When we are weak, He is strong. What does He say? Has He told you to lead this class? If so, what is the verse He used to speak to you?
Your friend still and always,
Robin

Mike read Robin's brief note and was amazed at the simplicity of it. He had heard and he did know.

Dear Robin,
You sound just like a counselor. Yes, I am inadequate, but He isn't. Thank you for the reminder. He says so. Without doubt, He has told me to feed His sheep. What a humbling thought.
Pray for me.
Mike

The day after he received her note, Mike received another envelope. He sat in his patrol car, having just eaten lunch, and read it again, planning his responses. Ironically, he found that the more they wrote the more he missed her. Seems it should be the other way around. Somehow, though, as she shared her daily life through her letters, he felt jealous that he wasn't able to see those things in person, that he was unable to live them with her. He knew the details of her life would always be secondhand. Even so, it was enough.

As long as he had known her, she was always spiritual. Now though, she was such a godly woman, as if she took all the things she knew in her head before and moved them down into her heart. It was application – she applied her lifetime of church to life and hearts, and because of it she would make a great counselor or whatever she felt led to do.

Still, in her letters she was as funny, if not maybe more so than she ever was. When he read her words, he knew exactly where to apply sarcasm and teasing. Then when her tone turned to one of tenderness, he could hear her sweet voice saying the words. She turned him into a big pile of mush, and oddly enough, he didn't mind one bit.

Dear Mike,
I didn't realize you had a new preacher. What happened to Brother Billy? Tell me more about Tim. I think it's cool that you are working out together. Is he as into it as you are, or are you forcing him?
Me, I try my best to avoid that kind of exercise. I have a gym allergy. I like to walk and bike and other outdoorsy things. No gym for me thanks.
Shopping? What have you done with Mike?
I should have been a fly on the wall while you were cooking. Yes, you can grill – well established – but I would like to see you make a casserole. Now that I think about it, what do you take to covered-dish dinners? Are you one of those show-up-empty-handed guys, or a store-bought-cookie guy?
I'm taking online courses. I only take two per semester, which is plenty. I just started in January, so I have forever to go.
Mike – what you said, you never held me back, never. I was content as things were. Yes, now there's something new, but you never stood in the way of it. It simply wasn't my desire then. As for flying, I don't know about that. It still seems like a faraway dream, a place I'm not sure I'll ever reach.
Thank you for sharing your story with me. You have never talked much about your dad, but when you did, I knew how much it hurt you. I'm so grateful to God for your healing and forgiveness. You are free!
I'm happy you've found your Father. Because my dad was so great, that wasn't an area where I struggled as much. Who knows, maybe I did in some ways. Now that I think about it, because I did have such a good dad, I didn't feel as much of a need for God as Father. It was merely a title. Over the course of this year, though, I found Him to be the Father who took me into His lap and consoled me. Hey – we have the same Father!
It did cross my mind about your dad being there, and I did wonder if the two of you ever saw each other. Have you seen him since you've been out? I suppose that would be hard to do. Your forgiveness may begin to reshape him, too.

Thank you for your prayers, and I will continue to pursue this. Honestly, I'm not sure if I'm supposed to be a formal counselor, or maybe it'll be something I use as ministry at church. I'm open to His leading. I think of the verse in Isaiah that says, "Whether you turn to the right or the left, your ears will hear a voice behind you, saying, 'This is the way; walk in it.'" I'm beginning to hear God more and more, and I understand His leading in a way I never used to. So finally, I feel secure in simply following as I feel led. I try not to stress about what's up ahead.

Coffee? Yes, and too much of it. I don't know, I tried a cup one day and thought, "Hey, is this what I've been missing all these years?" So now, I'm trying to make up for lost time. I do switch to decaf later in the day; but still, I drink it and drink it until my eyes are floating.

Do I still have a sweet tooth? Absolutely! I try not to bake much because I eat until I'm sick. (I know - the hypocrisy of it.) When we have guests, we have sweets and pastries for breakfast, and I find it difficult to say no. I try to stick with proteins, as I know that sweets cause me to feel as if I'm running on empty by ten.

The places I dream about are anywhere warm and sandy. Maybe someday I'll come there to the beach. We used to go on vacation when I was a little girl. I have no idea why we stopped, but I can't recall going after I was about nine. I'll have to ask my mom why.

My women's study is still going strong. We meet here because we have so much room, but no, I don't lead it. We've recently done a study on Jonah and just began one about contentment. Since I replied already about your study, I simply can't wait to hear what you decide. Keep me posted. The ones who are supposed to be there will come. You can't allow those whispers to prevent you from obeying.

While I don't own a red flannel shirt, I can see how the image in your head would cause you to roar with laughter. Remember when we went four-wheeling and got stuck. If you recall, I refused to use the outdoor restroom, and by the time we got back into town, I was nearly in tears. If I didn't think you would've made fun of me, I'm certain I would have officially cried. I don't believe I'm quite so girly now, but no survivalist either.

Your mom and Michael, that was sweet. You're right; there was something different about her when she held him. Maybe she could look back and see you, before things got so bad between her and your dad. There is something special inside of her, but I doubt she believes that. I believe your dad may have stolen that from her.

The vet? What a difference a dinner makes. If you can imagine, they were like teenagers together. Emma let down her guard and simply enjoyed the day. Oh, he's more than smitten. I think he would marry her tomorrow if she would agree. Honestly, I have a feeling that things will go well. He is a really nice man, and he makes her laugh and compliments her in sweet ways while she blushes like a school girl. I want this for her so badly.

Dinner was just okay: Turkey was dry, dressing gooey, potatoes lumpy, and sweet potatoes not-so-sweet. I hope that helps your envy. It wasn't at all true, but maybe that will help. Why? Why didn't you go somewhere for a big dinner? I know how the ladies at church operate, so you could have. I'm sure of it. It made me terribly sad to think you were all alone for Thanksgiving. Each and every holiday, knowing you're alone, I've grieved for you. Have I said too much?

Miss Allen really is old. The last time I saw her she looked a hundred. Is she still in charge of events? See, even at ninety-seven, I'll have purpose. Really, you gag at the thought of apples, apples, apples? Sorry, but I find it rather funny.

Mike – before I loved you, I liked you. There will always be a place in my life for you. While I can't imagine what that will look like in the time to come, you'll always be my friend. Our history is too long to undo. These letters have reminded me of why I like you. So thank you for being my friend, too. And you shouldn't take me for granted because I did your poster board which we all know led to your lucrative career.

I should go now. Maybe I should start typing these letters. I may be getting carpal tunnel. Have a good week.

Love,
Rob

15

Another day later, the day Mike mailed a very difficult letter to Robin, he received a package from her and could hardly imagine what was in it. Tearing into the brown paper, he found a box filled with chocolate chip cookies, his absolute favorite. She used to send them to him when he was in Afghanistan, and by the time they arrived the chocolate had melted and reformed many times. Then, it was like having a little piece of home to hang onto. In a way, standing there looking at those cookies, he felt the same way, as if he had a small part of his old life there in his hand.

Why had she done such a thing for him? Was she missing him at all the way he was missing her? He knew better, but still his mind pondered the question. What he knew was, if he hadn't loved her before, he would love her now. With every letter he fell in love with her all over again. How could he not?

After recently sending Mike a care package of cookies, Robin had begun to question the decision. Was she somehow setting up expectations for more than was available to them? The gesture was similar to when she was waiting for him during his deployments, too similar. Her fear was that she was unknowingly giving him hope that was unrealistic. As often as she began to doubt her actions, she would then remember the joy she felt while baking them for him. It took her back to a time when she had nothing but hope for her future. There was something in the act of baking that made her feel hopeful or maybe whole, she was unsure which exactly.

The day his letter arrived, she knew it was too soon to contain anything about the cookies. She would have to wait to see what he thought of them. Hopefully, they would be better shipped to North Carolina than overseas. Emma was out with Stan for the evening, and Robin had held on to his letter so she could read it privately. The more they wrote, the more intimate the letters felt. Anyone else who might read them would never depict them as intimate, but they were becoming so much more personal, she wanted to cherish them without someone looking on.

It was already December, and they had been writing since mid-September. Receiving letters weekly, with the exception of the weeks when her letter was lost, she felt almost constantly in contact with him and in some ways better in touch with his life. She welcomed each letter and found that she had so much to say in return; it was as if no time had passed.

Going up early to her bedroom, she got into bed and opened the envelope.

Dear Robin,
This is not a reply to the letter I have just received. I'll reply to that next. This is something different, something I've felt led to say for a few weeks now. I refuse to run from it anymore, as I feel I owe you some explanation for my actions, as weak as it may seem.
A few months before coming home from my second tour, a friend of mine was killed. He was the one guy I trusted most. Just that morning we were laughing and cutting up, and by lunch, he was lying dead beside me. It could have been me. Often, I wondered why it wasn't. His name was Chuck, and he had a wife and four kids. It was the last half of his third tour. He was a dedicated husband and father; and somehow, I just couldn't move past what happened. Why him? I had friends killed prior to that, but with Chuck, it was different. We kept each other accountable. We both had wives we loved, and we both knew how lonely it could get over there. I told you once, people were hooking up and neither one of us wanted to be part of that, so we kinda helped each other stay strong.
For the remainder of my time there, I spent every waking moment in fear of not coming home to you. Every mission I went on, everywhere I went, it was in the forefront of my mind. I became convinced that something would happen at the last minute and I'd be killed. I would lie in bed at night and wonder who would take care of you if I never came home.
Obviously, I came home, but I couldn't get my mind straight once I was there. My brain never shut down, and I wasn't sleeping most nights. No matter how hard I tried, I could never seem to get back to who I was before. Once you became pregnant and we moved back home, it gave me something to focus on

besides the mess that was going on in my head. I did everything in my power to pretend I was okay, but I was far from okay.

Then Mikey died. You know, when he was a tiny little baby, probably just a week or two old, I sat with him one night rocking. Looking at him, I realized he would bind us together for life. I'm not exactly sure why I felt as if I needed that so badly, but I did. Thinking of it now, I suppose it was due to the turmoil in my parents' marriage.

Early on after he died, we really clung to each other, then that stopped and you seemed so far away. I became more and more angry. Anger began to consume me. As I told you when you were here, I was angry at God, never at you. It has taken me years to figure this out, but you were the only God I had ever seen. So I lashed out at Him through you. He knows this and is my witness; I'm so sorry, both to you and to Him.

Once you went to work, I think that's when I really lost it. I remember a moment when it occurred to me: Michael no longer bound us together. You were working, so it was only a matter of time before you left me, too. That was when I started pressuring you to have another baby. I have foggy recollections of how I forced myself on you. I raped you. Forgive me! Please forgive me for how I hurt you and how, instead of being your protector, I became the perpetrator. I wasn't thinking clearly at all. I was so much worse than when I came home from war. I was so lost.

When I first started drinking, it seemed to take the edge off. What I didn't anticipate, though, was how it would begin to overtake me. I became angrier when I drank but was unbearably agitated when I didn't. The more I tried to drown out what I was feeling, the more I felt as if I were drowning. I lost myself somewhere along the way. Then I lost you. Even before that final night, I knew I had lost you. I could see it in your eyes every time you looked at me. You were disgusted with me and disappointed in me. Even then, I could hardly blame you. That afternoon when I went to the pharmacy to get something for my shoulder, the pharmacist saw me there and gave me your prescription. I went crazy. I left my shift without even calling out and went straight to the bar, and well, you know the rest better than I do.

Dear God, I am so sorry.

Robin, that night was surreal. After all I had done to you, do you remember the things you said to me there on the kitchen floor? You told me Jesus would forgive me if I would ask Him. You held me when I was certain I was dying. I nearly killed you – and what you did was purely in self-defense whether you accept that or not – still, you led me to Jesus. I asked Him to come into my life while I was in the ambulance, and I've never been the same since.

Now, I realize a lot of guys have come home messed up, and I wouldn't dare try to use that as an excuse; but I need you to know my mind wasn't right even before I got home. Brother Billy came to see me soon after I got to prison. After we talked, he arranged for someone nearer the prison to come out and talk to me once a week. It was a good start for me to begin to understand what was happening in my head. The greatest healing, though, came through God's Word. There's a verse in the Psalms that I now own and always will, it says, "He sent forth His word and healed them." That's what happened. He healed me.

I apologize for laying such a heavy load on you. It has never been my intention to justify my actions in any way. Instead, I know I've been prompted by the Lord these months we've been writing. I tried to be as thoughtful as possible with how I've written this. The last thing I want is to drag your mind back to such dark days. I was the cause of them, and I know it. Forgive me, Rob.

With all my love,
Michael Sr.

By his signature he was reminding himself and her that he would always be Michael's father. Sometimes she had to remind herself she was still a mom. Even though she had no child to mother, that painful fact could in no way take her title away. Apparently, it was the same with him. He probably needed to see proof of Michael's existence occasionally, and by his own name he could remember. Tears dripped onto the sheets of paper. Not one page remained dry.

"Lord, how could I not have known how sick he was? How did I miss it?"

Did she miss it really? Thinking back to his homecoming, she did sense something amiss. Not that very first day or two, as a matter of fact, that first day was the sweetest day she had known with him up until that point, but after that, she knew something was the matter. Over the years she had considered what she could have done differently, how she might have helped him before things spiraled so far out of control. In the moment, though, the pregnancy and the move overtook her, and quite simply, she never wanted to admit that her happily-ever-after life might be in jeopardy.

After reading Mike's letter, that night she didn't sleep well, and when she did she dreamed of him. The next morning, Robin remained in a fog for hours. Memories of his homecoming floated along with her throughout the hours of the day. It was her most vivid dream from the night before. They were in the large auditorium. Mike, along with all the others returning home, stood at strict attention. The ceremony was unnecessary as far as the Marines and their families were concerned. She remembered thinking, *Stop the music and just give me my husband already.* All the while, he was looking directly at her, and peeking from behind that serious expression of a dedicated marine, she could see a trace of a smile. He was just as anxious as she was.

When they were finally released, he ran to her and circled his arms around her, lifting her off the ground. As he did, she wrapped her legs around his waist and clung to him, as he would later say, like a monkey. From that moment on he never put her back down. He even stooped over to grab his bags with her still clinging to him. They walked to the car in that manner, and along the way, someone said to him, "Now I get it."

He grinned and held her and juggled his bags all at the same time. Once behind the car, he dropped the bags and walked with her to the passenger side. When he opened the car door, he chuckled at the box of donuts waiting for him.

She giggled and hugged his neck even tighter. "I don't plan on getting out in the morning."

As planned, they spent the next few days snuggled up in each other's arms and what she thought was glorious happiness.

That afternoon, Robin went to Chris' cabin and started a fire. Once settled in, she began to pen what she knew would be her most difficult letter to date.

Dearest Michael Sr.,
I'm rocked to my soul by your letter. I knew something wasn't right, and yet I did nothing to help you. I wanted you to be okay, so I think maybe I buried my head in the sand. I had no idea you were going through such difficulty

and turmoil. I thought it was what was to be expected from war. Mike, why didn't you talk to me?

I have an admission of my own. After Michael died, even before my milk dried up, I went on birth control pills. I believed I would never love another baby the way I still love him. I was terrified of the thought of getting pregnant again. I didn't want to forget him and move on. I only wanted him. When you began to talk about having another child, I was scared to tell you. You had become so explosive that I feared your reaction, so I hid it from you. I'm tremendously sorry that I deceived you in that way. Thinking back to how you would get your hopes up each month, I so regret allowing you that false hope. It was wrong and cruel, no matter my motives.

And in case you haven't finally realized, Michael will bind us together for life. You will always be the father of my son.

I understand your anger at God. I felt the same, only my anger was expressed by rejecting Him, by not allowing Him access to my heart anymore. Just as you were, I've been healed of that, and I love, love, love the verse you shared. I'll own it as well. He did send forth His word and heal me, too.

I was never disgusted or disappointed with you. While I was disappointed at how our lives turned out, deep inside, I held on to my memories of the real you. When you weren't drinking, I could still see you and I longed for things to be the way they were in the early days.

The things that happened that terrible night will always haunt us. I don't doubt that. I think, though, what matters is what we do with the memories when they come. The whispers still come. Now, when they do, I call out to Jesus. He never leaves me defenseless.

This is indeed a heavy load, but shared, it's something we can both withstand. Now I ask you to never apologize again. When you do, after having received my forgiveness, you're saying you don't trust my ability to forgive. I can forgive because I'm forgiven.

With a heart full of love,
Michael's Mom

P.S. Okay, I know how morbid this will sound even before I write it. Will you please take a photo of Michael's grave and send it to me? Not being able to go there is the worst part of living so far away.

Unmending the Veil

When Robin took her letter to the front desk, she found another from Mike waiting for her. She smiled and held it up to her nose. Why, she wasn't exactly sure. Did she expect perfume? She giggled at herself and caught Emma staring at her from the dining room door.

"Are you falling back in love with him?" Emma asked gently.

The something new in Robin's demeanor was obvious. Emma had never seen her glow as much as she had over the past few weeks. Even on her wedding day, she wasn't so sure Robin was as full of love.

"I'm realizing that I may have never fallen out."

"What will you do about this?"

"I don't know. Right now, I just want to love him this way."

Robin knew one thing for certain, she could never go back there, and for Mike to come to New Hampshire would mean he would have to give up what he loved most. No other law enforcement agency would dare hire him with such a conviction. She would never ask him to give up what he had wanted since he was a little boy. There was no easy answer.

Alone, sitting out on the back porch, Robin tore into Mike's latest letter.

Hey Rob –

Brother Billy retired two years ago, before I got back. Tim is a great guy and has really turned this place around. There's a new excitement that I can hardly believe. It's nothing like you remember. Obviously, he knew part of the story. Gossip line is still working well here and we still know each other's business. But Tim welcomed me as if I were anyone else.

Now, he does like working out. Not so much at first, maybe because I pushed him so hard. He was such a little girl then, but it was worth it, and he admits it now. He feels better and has dropped some unneeded weight.

I know you never liked working out. I remember. Since when do you like outdoorsy stuff?

I've never tried to cook a casserole, and I don't plan on it. I think I would lose my man card if I did that. I'll stick with grilling meat and baking potatoes in the microwave. That's what real men do. With head hung low, I admit I'm a store-bought-cookie guy. Then, once I'm there I eat the homemade stuff. Kids eat my cookies, so it all works out.

> *Speaking of cookies — you are the greatest! I just got them this morning and have eaten half of them already. Not feeling sick at all, so no lectures. I don't know what possessed you to do such a thing, but whatever it was, keep it up. I never tire of chocolate chip, though I do remember you make a rockin' oatmeal raisin, too. Really, I'm merely doing my part. I know how you like to bake, and since you said you eat too many when you do, I'm willing to take one for the team. I'll eat them. (Sigh) Yes, I do know how selfless I am.*
> *Tell me more about the classes you're taking. Well, unless it's boring stuff like underwater basket weaving. If it is, just give me the highlights.*
> *You mentioned your dad, and I have to tell you, you couldn't possibly know how much he meant to me, him and your mom. All those years, I always felt so welcome there. It was the closest to a normal family I ever knew. Exactly, you do have great parents. After all that happened I won't even allow myself to consider what they think of me. I hope someday you'll share with them how much they meant to me and maybe even how much I've changed. Do they even know you're writing to me? They're coming for Christmas, right?*
> *I've thought about going to see my dad. I just haven't worked up the nerve yet. Trevor has seen him and says he really is a different guy. Good thing for the McGarrett men they don't serve booze in the pokey.*

Robin chuckled at his words. Some things about him never changed, and she was glad that his sense of humor was one of them. Always, from the very beginning, he made her laugh.

She continued on.

> *Proteins? You're talking like a gym rat. There's hope for you yet.*
> *Someday — to the beach here? That would be something. If you ever do, would you mind if I met you there? Maybe we could have dinner or something. I'm not talking about a date or anything, so don't go getting your hopes up there, desperate girl. Just two friends eating dinner at the same place and time.*

His words reminded her of Chris'. She wondered what he was really thinking when he asked that question. Was he feeling as desperately in love as she was? Was he trying to hide his true feelings, or could he possibly be content with having their friendship restored? Why had she made that statement at all? Would she really go?

My men's study began last week. There were ten there that first night, and I was scared to death. We are reading through a book and discussing it. It went really well. Guess who was there? Jeff. Yes, the same Jeff I threatened to kill if you went out with him. Funny stuff, huh?
Rob, thanks for your words. Deep down, I knew I was supposed to do it, but I was scared. The whispers...I know exactly what you mean by that, hard to tune them out sometimes. You always know what to say, always have. How did you get so wise?
Yes, I remember the four-wheeling disaster. I thought you were a very good sport about it. If you had cried, I would've never made fun of you. You always amazed me that way. You almost never cried. That was one thing I always wondered about. My mom cried a lot, just never when anyone was around. Were you like that? I know I made you cry with the whole Shelly thing. Seeing you cry that night nearly killed me. What I'm wondering is, when no one else was around, did you cry more?
Any more news on Emma and the vet? Does Emma still hate my guts? That was an odd lead in, wasn't it? I can't help but wonder.
Thanks for the dishonest Thanksgiving recap. Why did I stay home? I couldn't imagine sitting at a table with someone else's family. I would feel out of place. So I stayed home. Yes, you said too much. You have to stop telling me things like you were grieving for me, because when I answer you, I feel something – I don't know, stupid or I would say vulnerable if I were a girl, but I'm not, so I'll go with weak. Please, never grieve for me. I do have joy and contentment that is surprising and surely from the Lord. Yes, holidays are hard, but I'd rather be at our home alone than somewhere I don't belong. Still not past the apple thing. Even the thought of apple pie makes me nauseous. See, this has become serious!
Before I loved you, I liked you, too...I think. I don't know for sure; I loved you so quickly that I can't swear to it. I think I loved you when I saw your marshmallow burn up. You were looking at me, and there it went, up in flames. That would have been funny to me had I not been so nervous about talking to you. That night, I was determined you would be mine, no matter what it took. Did I ever tell you that?

There will always be a place in my life for you, no matter what life looks like in the time to come, always.

These letters have reminded me why I like and love you. You are a funny, funny girl, and sometimes, when you aren't picking on me, you can be very sweet. Please, no typing. It's much more personal this way.

Always,
Mike

Her response was immediate.

Dear Always Mike,
Tim sounds great. Glad to know you have a friend like him.
Okay, I didn't mean I like outdoorsy as in the go mountain climbing kind of stuff. I imagine that sounds like fun to you. We play volleyball in the summer and go out on the boat. I've decided I like to fish. I don't want to bait my own hook or take the fish off, but I like the thought of catching them.
I suppose real men, like you, should only grill and use the microwave. Since I remember you like chili, which is a relatively manly thing to cook, I'm including a recipe in with this letter. Just put it all in the slow cooker before work and when you come home, you'll have dinner waiting.
I'm certain your cookies are gone by now. Maybe I'll send you some more soon. And my, how selfless of you to offer to eat my cookies and keep me from overindulging. You are a real team player.
This semester, pretend it's underwater basket weaving. Nothing interesting.
You'll have to let me know if you decide to go and see your dad. I'm sure he would love to see you.
Hope for me to become a gym rat? Hardly.
The beach – with the weather here now, it sounds like a wonderful dream. If I ever do make it there to the beach, a buddy-old-pal dinner would be very nice. Thank you for offering.
Jeff? Seriously? How is that working out? You two never got along, and I never fully understood why. He seemed like a pretty nice guy. And surely you knew I would have never gone out with him.
I'm glad your group went well. I don't know that I would call me wise, just learning.

I didn't cry much and am not sure why, just wasn't me. This past year, I've cried a lot. I think I needed it. I spent too many years with things bottled up inside me. Now, I feel lighter on my feet. Who knew tears weighed so much? Emma and Stan are like two kids in love. It's just been a few weeks, but you would think they have known each other for years. Recently, I asked if maybe they're moving a bit too fast, and she informed me that they're on an accelerated calendar. She said, "Honey, at this age, you can't afford a long courtship." I take that to mean they're already talking about a future together.

Does she hate you? No. She was worried at first but not now. She understands how much this means to me.

Glad to hear you have joy and contentment. I told you, that's the subject of my current Bible study, so I'm working on contentment myself.

I fully understand what you mean about feeling out of place if you went to someone else's house. I'm just sorry you were alone. That's all.

I'm mailing you an apple pie. Kidding. This does sound serious, though.

No, you never told me you made up your mind that first night. I wish you would have. That would have been a sweet memory to carry all these years. I'll treasure it now, though.

Notice – I'm writing by hand and not typing.

Always too,
Robin

P.S. Decided to make cookies tonight, so I'll send with the letter tomorrow. Hope you enjoy. I ate three when they first came out of the oven. I am a very good cook.

After reading her letter, Mike noticed Robin left out any mention of her parents. He could hardly blame them for hating him. If he had to guess, he would suspect they didn't even know about the letters, and he understood why she would keep it from them. In a way it clarified something for him. The fact that she hadn't even told them assured him that this was friendship and nothing more. If she were feeling something deeper than that, she would have at least told her mom. More than once, he reminded himself it was enough. Before September he had no hope of friendship even.

The day before, Tim cornered him at the gym, trying to get him to open up. He had only briefly mentioned they were writing, and for the most part, Tim never asked questions. Yesterday, though, he pursued the subject more than Mike was comfortable with. Tim's concern was that maybe this would prevent them both from moving on. Mike wondered if he was indeed preventing Robin from moving on. It was no prevention on his part, as he had no desire for any other woman but her, but the idea that he might somehow keep her from meeting someone who would love and cherish her in a way he would never be able to, made him feel terribly selfish. Wasn't it his selfishness that was exposed when they first began writing? Had he not overlooked what she wanted and what was best for her when they were together, focusing solely on himself? No longer that same man, Mike wanted more for Robin than he wanted for himself, a fact that would require something of him, a level of selflessness he wasn't so sure he possessed, but after doing all things the wrong way for his entire life, for once, he wanted to put her first.

The thought that maybe he was preventing her future happiness plagued him. He had prayed all morning about it. Should he leave her alone in the hopes that the right man would come along? While he tried to begin a letter to her, he found his heart was too heavy to even write. Throwing away what he had so far, he called Tim instead. Meeting down at the church, they prayed together at the altar.

Once he arrived home, he felt better able to do what needed to be done, still sad, but able.

Dear Robin,
I've been thinking about this and praying so hard about it. I'm at a loss here – and worried. Are we doing the right thing? This friendship means the world to me. My fear is that it'll somehow prevent you from moving on. That's been what I've asked God most for you, to find someone who will love you. I don't want to interfere with that, and if I stay in the picture it may never happen. For once, I want to do what's best for you.
I received your letter, and as much as I want to reply, I think maybe I shouldn't. I'll wait until I hear back from you. Think this over. Pray about it. If you think we should stop this now, I'll go along with whatever you want.
A thousand times thank you for the cookies. They're almost as good as choco-chip. You are a gifted cookie-maker indeed.

Mike

P.S. I'll send you the photo you asked for. I can understand why you need it. The years I was away, that was one of the most difficult aspects, not being able to go there and sit with Mikey.

Robin sat with a blank piece of paper before her, perplexed. Should she? Scribbling out a few words, she quickly sealed it in an envelope and drove it directly to the post office, afraid she would change her mind if she had to wait all morning for the postman. Afterwards, she had some last minute Christmas shopping to do. Emma was leaving to go to upstate New York with Stan to visit his daughter and her family. Robin's parents canceled after Emma had already made plans. Though Emma insisted on staying home with her, Robin wouldn't hear of her canceling the trip. This turn of events would leave Robin all alone for Christmas.

Had she just made the biggest mistake of her life? She wondered. Shaking her fears away, thankfully, she knew it was too late to change her mind. What was done was done.

Mike found Robin's letter in the mailbox and knew it was too soon to be a reply to his question. Sliding his finger underneath the seal, he pulled out the small note. He read the words again and again, certain they couldn't possibly mean what they said.

Dear Mr. Solo,
What are your plans for Christmas? Is it too last minute? Call me.
Solo Too

He whispered, "Is this real, Lord?"

Reading her note again, Mike laughed out loud. It was real, and she even included her number.

Sitting at the kitchen table, it took him two tries to get the number right. His hands were trembling from sheer excitement, knowing he was about to hear her voice.

Robin was sitting in front of the fireplace, curled up under a blanket. When she saw the 919 area code, she inhaled and held her breath for a second, acknowledging how excited she was. She answered, "Hello."

"Hey, Rob." His heart was racing with anticipation.

"Hi. I guess you got my note?"

Suddenly, she was thirteen again, sitting there grinning and chewing on her thumbnail.

"Yeah, and I'm not doing anything for Christmas."

"My parents canceled and Emma is going out of town. I was wondering if maybe you would like to come here and spend Christmas with me?"

He closed his eyes and drew in a deep breath. "I can't think of anything I would like more."

"I was thinking maybe the day before Christmas Eve. Would that work?"

"Yes. I'll have to talk to them at work, but I don't think it'll be a problem."

He would personally pay someone to take his shift if he had to.

"So, okay then. You're coming."

Her stomach was flipping and flopping, and she wondered if he could sense the goofy smile on her face.

"This will be my first holiday with..." He was about to say family but stopped himself. "This will be the best Christmas I've had in a very long time."

"I'm looking forward to it."

Having agreed he would check flights and get back to her, they ended the call. After hanging up he grabbed his coat and headed out to shop. The week before, he had bought her a gift but had no intention of sending it until he heard back from her regarding his last letter. Then it struck him, she would receive the letter and likely be a little confused. Should he call her back and try to explain?

During their next phone call, Mike gave Robin his flight information and added, "I, um, sent a letter the same day I received yours. I'm not sure if I should tell you to forget it, or to think about it still."

"Why, what did it say?" The tone of his voice made her uneasy.

"Just read it. I'm sorry if it seems silly."

Emma was calling her from the top floor. "Hey, I have to run for now, should I call you back to discuss this?"

"No. It was no big deal. We'll talk soon."

"Okay."

She felt a bit uncertain, but then Emma called again in a tailspin about another packing crisis. Nervous and excited about meeting Stan's family, every detail, no matter how small it was in actuality, became a big deal to Emma.

Two days later, only four days before Mike was to arrive, Robin received the note he must have been talking about. He asked if they were doing the right thing and said he was worried that their friendship might prevent her from moving on. Those two statements were enough to disturb her, but what he said about wanting her to find someone who would love her — that was what caused her chest to feel terribly heavy.

Obviously he was thinking of moving on. Maybe there was someone there he was interested in already. Finally it registered with her, saying he wanted her to find someone to love her was his way of saying he didn't. He was trying to gently set her straight.

Feeling foolish for having invited him, Robin regretted it completely. So why had he agreed to come? She had known it was a mistake. The entire relationship was a mistake. Where could it lead after all? Never could she go back to North Carolina, and he didn't belong in New Hampshire. With no reason to ponder the subject any longer, she picked up the phone and dialed.

Sitting at the diner with Tim, Mike reached for his vibrating phone. When he saw that it was Robin's number, he grinned broadly, saying, "Hello."

He hadn't slept the night before and was running on sheer adrenaline. In front of Tim he tried to act casual, but he was beside himself with excitement.

"Hey. Are you at lunch where you can talk for a minute?" Robin asked, feeling really stupid.

Standing, he moved for the front door and out onto the sidewalk. "I sure am."

"You don't have to come," she said rather abruptly.

Though she expected she would be nervous, she wasn't. If anything, Robin felt relief that it would soon be finished. She had been irrational to think they could continue on the way they were.

Leaning against his patrol car, Mike exhaled and closed his eyes, extremely disappointed. All along he feared it was too good to be true.

"I already have my ticket," he whispered softly.

"Maybe this isn't a good idea after all."

He wasn't about to argue with her. If she changed her mind and didn't want him to come, he would cancel his flight. Then it occurred to him. "Did you receive my note?"

"I did."

He noticed the coolness of her tone, so he asked, "And?"

"And maybe this *is* a mistake. You don't have to worry about me holding on, or missing out, or whatever you fear I'm doing."

In her voice he thought he detected a hint of hurt feelings. Having known her as long as he did, he had messed up plenty. Of course he knew the you-have-hurt-my-feelings,-but-I-will-pretend-I-don't-care voice.

Smiling sheepishly, he asked, "What do you *think* I meant by what I said?"

"I'm not exactly sure, maybe that I need to move on because you are. Don't worry, I can do that. If I would've known you were feeling this way, I never would have invited you, and if you were feeling this way, you never should have said you'd come."

He grinned at how she read way more into his words than he intended, but that was exactly what he often did when she wrote.

"I meant precisely what I said; I just don't want to prevent *your* happiness, nothing about me moving on."

He was glaring through the window at Tim.

"I'm a guy. There's nothing deeper or hidden in my message. I said something simple, and I meant it exactly like I wrote it."

She tried to speak, but he interrupted, saying, "It was a dumb thought that someone planted in my head. Forget it. I don't want to stop writing to you. I don't want to cancel my flight. As a matter of fact, I have my ticket, and I'll be getting on that plane. If you aren't there to meet me, I'll rent a car and drive to the inn. If you aren't at the inn when I arrive, I'll sit out in the freezing cold until you get there.

"So now, I'm going to hang up the phone before you have a chance to tell me no. I'm coming, and I'm so excited I can hardly see straight. See you in four days at noon. Bake me some cookies. Bye." Quickly, he hung up the phone.

Back inside the diner Mike sat across from Tim and asked, "Really, you get paid to help people?"

"What?" Tim shrugged innocently.

Robin sat listening to silence. Finally, she whispered, "Whew."

He would be there in four days, and her heart began to pound with the anticipation of seeing him. Of course she would be at the airport to meet him. His being there would be the greatest gift she had ever received for Christmas.

16

Since they hadn't spoken after the day he assured Robin he was coming, Mike walked through the terminal of the Concord airport, uncertain of what to expect. While he had no way of knowing if she would be there, truthfully, it didn't matter. If not, he would go to her and straighten things out. That stupid note, why had he sent it? Certainly, he learned a great lesson about doubt. Although things were going along so well, doubt crept up in him, which in turn gave her reason to doubt. From his point of view the note expressed his concern for her. Obviously, his message was unclear, and she had taken it as some means of escape on his part, which was the craziest thing in the world. If she only knew what he was really feeling deep inside, how desperately he loved her still.

With all of these thoughts rolling around in his head, in an instant, all deliberations faded. In his field of vision, about fifty yards ahead, was the answer to all his wonderings over the past few hours. As if encountering a mirage in the desert, he blinked his eyes, trying to make perfectly sure he was seeing what he thought he was seeing. Robin was there, smiling at him, no mirage at all. Wearing a long black sweater with jeans tucked into tall black riding boots, she waved at him shyly. Her hair was down, with the ends curled and draped over her right shoulder. Quite literally, the sight of her took his breath away. He felt suddenly winded.

Moving toward her quickly, nearly knocking people over in his path, he chuckled softly when he saw her move her thumb up to chew on her nail. It was something she did unconsciously when she was nervous or excited. Likely, it was a little of both, as he was feeling the same way. As beautiful as she looked, what most captured his attention was the way she smiled at him, assuring him she was happy he came. He stopped just in front of her, wondering if it would be okay to hug her. As if answering his thought, she reached up on her tip toes to slide her arms around his neck. Having longed to feel her in his arms, he stooped down and slid his arms around her waist. Standing, he lifted her off the ground and squeezed her hard.

"Aww. You *are* here," he whispered.

"And you're here."

With her face tucked into his neck, she breathed in the scent of his aftershave. He smelled clean and fresh and familiar. For the first time in many years, she felt whole again, in a way she had forgotten was possible. In her heart, she prayed, *"Lord, I've surely missed him. Thank You for bringing him here."*

"I told you I would be."

"What was the deal with that note?" she asked.

He sat her back down on the ground.

"Doubt, and I'm so sorry I even sent it. I never meant to hurt your feelings or make you doubt me." Reaching for her hand, he added, "That's the last thing I ever want to do."

She sighed, leaned back in, and rested her head on his chest. How could she doubt him?

"Let's forget it then," she suggested.

When he circled his arms around her, she closed her eyes and slipped her arms around his waist, nestling into him as she had done a million times before.

"Please, let's do."

Holding her to him, his fears of the past few days slipped away. Nothing about holding her was a mistake. How could he have ever thought such a thing? For as long as she would allow him to be part of her life, he would be. It would have to be her who pushed him away.

Anxious to get home, she took a step back and asked, "Are you ready?"

He stood there looking at her as if he hadn't heard her question, and she wondered what he was thinking.

Finally, he whispered, "You look so beautiful." He touched her hair, mesmerized by the sight of her standing there. "Have you always been *this* beautiful?"

She grinned and blushed, noting that the look in his eyes was like nothing she had ever seen before, as if he were seeing her for the very first time. Somewhat similar to when he approached her at the bonfire, then though, he was much more bashful. Feeling as nervous as she had that night, she realized now, just as then, they were about go off together, and she hadn't a clue of what they were supposed to do alone. For several not-so-awkward moments, they just stood there, looking at each other. This was likely the beginning of something more than friendship, and they both knew it.

Eventually, she asked, "Do you have bags to collect?"

"Yes."

"You travel heavy."

Slipping his hand around her waist, he began to lead her down the corridor, saying "I come bearing gifts."

"Good. I've been a very good girl this year."

"So I've heard."

"Who told you?"

When she wrapped her arm around his waist, she tucked her thumb into his belt loop, something else she had done a million times in years past. Such a trivial detail brought with it unexpected comfort and familiarity. Snuggled against him as they maneuvered through the mass of Christmas travelers, they were as good as alone together.

Their conversation continued on as playful and flirty all the way to claim his bag, throughout the walk to the car, and along the drive to the inn. Each moment, he was intentionally and prayerfully grateful to be with her. Continually, he gave thanks in his heart, sometimes even shouting at the top of his spirit in gratitude. Since waking up in the hospital, he knew nothing would ever stop his heart from loving her, but he could never have anticipated how much more he would someday. Astounded by this intense, patient devotion he felt toward her, he realized, it was a love only God could give him. It was the love God constantly extended toward him.

Once Mike was settled into his room, he came back downstairs with a stack of gifts and found Robin waiting in the main lobby area.

"Where's your tree?"

"I haven't gotten one yet."

Surprised, he asked, "*You?* You're crazy about Christmas."

"I was thinking we could go get one together."

"Aww, I like that idea." The thought of it brought back a flood of memories of past Christmases together. She was like a kid when it came to decorating the tree. "I'm glad you saved it for us to do together."

It would be the first family Christmas he had known in six years. While he visited his mother the afternoon of the previous Christmas, and

Trevor came too, it didn't feel right to him. Robin was his family, and only she could make the day feel complete.

"Me, too." Pointing to the parlor, she said, "We'll set it up in there if you want to take the gifts on in."

It thrilled her to see the gifts. Not that she wanted presents but that he took the time to shop for her. It wasn't at all surprising, though; he always was overly generous at Christmastime. Even when he worked at the feed store for nearly nothing, he made a big deal over Christmas, saving for a whole month to buy her something. It was the year they were seventeen that he gave her a promise ring on Christmas Eve. Smiling, she thought of her dad's reaction and how he nearly flipped, but then eventually settled into the idea.

Once in the parlor he spotted a stack of gifts sitting near the fireplace and decided to place his alongside them. When he got nearer, he realized they were all for him. Though he couldn't care less what was in them, to know she went out and picked things out for him caused tears to form in his eyes. Chuckling aloud, knowing if she caught him misty eyed he would never hear the end of it, he quickly blinked them away.

Scattered around the room were boxes of ornaments and lights. Sadly, none of them were theirs. Their attic at home was full of decorations and ornaments, ones they had collected over the years, even as teenagers. She always loved Christmas, so each year he took her to pick out new ornaments. Decorating a tree in her bedroom at her parents' home, she placed their ornaments on her tree, certain that one day they would have a home of their own and a tree they picked out together. Bearing in mind what he lost, a knot formed in his throat and the tears returned. This time, however, he was unable to blink them away. Rubbing his face, he heard her come in and stand quietly behind him.

"Feels like old times." Understanding his unchecked emotions, she smiled at him. "This feels right, doesn't it?"

Nodding, he could hardly trust his voice to answer. When she moved near to where he stood, he wrapped his arms around her and held her to him. After a minute or more, he finally whispered, "Nothing has ever felt more right."

They walked the lot looking for just the right tree. Robin had definite standards and Mike was eager to please. Where one was the perfect height, it was too scraggly on one side. If one was the right width, it was too short. He patiently walked with her, realizing the little things in life are truly the most important. There wasn't a thing in the world he would rather be doing than searching for the perfect tree with her. Finally, happening upon the elusive flawless tree, they tied it down on Emma's Subaru and headed back to the inn. With the tree indoors and secured in its holder, they worked first on the lights.

Stopping in the middle of the fifth strand, Mike exclaimed, "I'm starving! I skipped lunch."

"Why didn't you tell me? I'll go in and make us something."

With the next day being Christmas Eve, he didn't anticipate going out. "Why don't we go out to dinner instead? We can eat here tomorrow."

"I thought you were sick of eating out." She planned to cook for him after such a poor, poor me routine.

"I'm sick of diner and fast food. We can go out for a real dinner, like a steak."

"That would be nice." Looking down, she asked, "Do you mean like a go-get-nice-clothes-on kind of dinner?"

"You look great as you are. I'll grab a different shirt."

After freshening up, Robin met Mike at the stairwell going downstairs. She had given him a room on the second floor, so when she reached the bottom of the second set of stairs he was standing there waiting for her. They walked down the last flight together, both grinning, excited by the prospect of the evening.

Wearing a black shirt with royal blue pinstripes, his sleeves were rolled up to just below his elbows. She noticed he had changed into nicer jeans and dark loafers as well and looked as handsome as she had ever seen him. To her astonishment, his eyes still, after so many years, made her heart flutter just as they did that first night over the campfire. They were dark blue, and something about the color of his shirt made them pop. They sparkled almost when he smiled at her.

On the way to the steak house, the conversation was light, and never once did she feel uncomfortable. Several times she realized that, though it was never said, this was a date. Whatever you might call it, she felt at ease with him, and he seemed just as relaxed.

Mike drove as he always had, and while riding and talking with no distraction of the radio, he simply listened as she chattered away about various things. Thinking back, he wondered if he had ever listened to her so intently. With this new whatever they were sharing, he listened closer, trying to catch any glimpse into her heart that he could. Although he had known her over seventeen years, now, his greatest desire was to know her more.

Once, while she was describing some of the more colorful characters around town, he casually reached over and took her hand. Glancing her way, he asked, "Do you mind?"

Her heart was beating much too quickly. Evidently, his touch still did that to her. "No," she answered. Looking at his hand and how it dwarfed hers, she stammered a bit, saying, "I've missed you holding my hand."

He couldn't help but wonder if anyone had held it besides him. Many times still, he thought of Chris. Had she felt as comfortable with him? Did she allow him to hold her hand this way? Reading people as well as he did, he knew that Chris was in love with Robin. When she had written in her letter that he had died, it eased his jealousy somewhat but never fully took it away.

Rubbing the palm of her hand with his thumb, he admitted, "I'm sorry I haven't been around to do this."

"Me, too."

The drive became suddenly quiet, each lost in regret and a strong desire to go back and undo the damage of that last year together.

Conversation over dinner was again relaxed and comfortable. As if they had requested the best table, Mike and Robin were seated in a private place out of the way of the main commotion of the restaurant. People were out in droves as they did last minute shopping, so the parking lots of most restaurants they passed were full. This place, though, was quiet, and their table was secluded, giving them freedom to talk openly.

Peeking over his menu, he suggested, "Order the larger steak." He knew she would pick the smaller.

"Are you that hungry?"

"Starved."

"Why didn't you just tell me? I would've made you some lunch before going out for a tree."

Mike grinned shyly. "I couldn't have eaten a bite then. Now, I'm feeling a bit less nervous."

"You were nervous?"

How could she find that anything but sweet? He never showed it on the surface.

Resting the menu on his lap, he admitted, "Yes. Weren't you?"

"Yes," she admitted and glanced back down at the menu. "What vegetable do we want?" She giggled.

"Anything, I'm not picky"

Placing his menu on the table, he reached for her hand and said, "I can hardly believe I'm here."

"Me, too." Noticing the server approach, she quickly added, "This wasn't a mistake, was it?"

"No. This was no mistake at all."

Trimming the tree was as much fun as Robin had had in years. They spent as much time on the tree as if it would stand there forever. Obediently, Mike moved the ornaments around in the higher places just as she directed. She found no need for a ladder for the first time since leaving North Carolina, as he was easily able to place the star atop the tree without even standing on tip toes.

"You're quite a nice helper."

"I just do what I'm told. So what's next?"

"I was thinking a movie."

Gleeful was the word he would use to describe her at the moment. With her still standing beside the tree, he was reminded of when they were much younger. Of all the things he could recall, her excitement at Christmas was one of his favorite memories of their holidays together. He moved closer to her.

"I've missed you, missed this." He slid his hand behind her neck and pulled her into him.

Resting her head against his chest, Robin could hear his heart beating hard and strong. "I've missed you, too. I don't think I realized just how much until today."

She gripped him tighter and buried her face into the fabric of his shirt, sighing softly. Tears were burning her eyes and her face felt flush. Inside, she felt a mixture of excitement at being held by him, along with alarm at how right it felt. Her own heart was beating clear up into her throat, and the rhythm blended with what she was hearing in his chest. Just as he had done at the cemetery, she felt him press his lips to the top of her head and kiss her softly. Until he did it that day, she had forgotten how much she loved it. As he did then, he did so discreetly today, as if not wanting her to know. She smiled.

"Does this scare you?"

Robin nodded, and without looking up, whispered, "A little." Then, after thinking it through, she admitted, "A lot."

He stood there holding her to him, amazed that he was fully wide awake, not dreaming. How many dreams had he dreamt where he held her this way? Over the years, probably hundreds. Upon waking, he never once believed it would happen again. It was real this time, so in his heart he prayed, *God, You are so good to me when we both know I don't deserve it.*

"No need to be scared. We'll take things slowly." Lifting her chin to look at him, he promised her, "I'll never give you a reason to be scared again. Never. You say back off, I'm back. You say draw near, I'll be here."

A sudden uneasiness began to form in her stomach. As much as she feared getting close to him again, fear in the context that she knew there was no future for them; her truest desire was to move in closer and kiss him. Apprehension, though, became so much stronger than desire, she found herself taking a step back.

Sensing her hesitation, Mike clapped his hands together and asked, "So, what movie?"

When she quietly moved to where the movies sat on a shelf, he closed his eyes, wondering, *What am I doing here? I know this must be a set-up for a fall.*

They watched two Christmas movies. Both, of course, were stories of miracles and love, which gave him impossible and irrational hope. By the time the last film ended, it was eleven o'clock. Agreeing to go to bed so they could get up early and make the most of the day, they walked together up the stairs. Upon reaching the second floor, he took her hand, preventing her from continuing up the next flight of stairs.

"Rob…" He rested his forehead on hers. "This has been the best Christmas Eve eve I've ever had."

"Me, too."

"I know you felt uncomfortable earlier. I'm sorry I made you feel that way. We're friends, and that can be enough for me if that's all you want. You've always been my best friend, and you always will be."

"You'll always be my best friend, too. Right now, beyond that, I don't know what to think."

"Don't think. That's when people get into trouble."

Parting was difficult for him. In a strange place, in a strange bed, he found it nearly impossible to sleep. Or maybe it was the knowledge that she was in a room sleeping just one level above him. Even early into the morning hours, he found his mind full of memories. He could close his eyes and see exactly what she looked like sleeping, grinning, he recalled drool and all.

"Lord, other than salvation and forgiveness, I think this may be the best gift You have ever given me. Well, and Mikey. Thank you for this. I still can't figure You out. I suppose I never will, but I do know this – You are beyond good to me."

It was after nine when Robin finally knocked on Mike's door. Tapping lightly, she called out, "Hey, sleepy head, you're missing the day."

Mike lifted his head and blinked rapidly, trying to clear the fog from his mind. The clock read nine twenty.

Groggily, he mumbled, "I'm up. Sorry."

Robin cracked the door open and told him, "Breakfast is ready, so hurry on down.

"Give me five minutes."

He found her in the dining room setting plates onto a table near the window. It was the first he noticed it had snowed the night before. "Amazing!"

"We'll have a white Christmas. Have you ever had one before?"

"A dusting maybe but nothing like this."

Sitting at the table, just as he had done the night before at dinner, he took her hand and gave thanks for the food. When he had done so the night before, she found it sweet, but this morning, his prayer caused a lump to form in her throat, and for a moment, she was unable to eat. Recalling the man he was before, she knew he would have never done such a thing. Only she blessed the food before a meal. Once apart, though, he had become the exact man she had always longed for him to be. This was truly the man of her dreams. As desperately as she wanted to love him and trust him again, too much had happened, and their history was so ugly, it seemed a great gulf stood between them.

Mike sat quietly for a moment. By her silence he could tell she was lost in thought, and he wondered if she was regretting having invited him. She sat looking at her food but not yet eating. When he had reached for her hand to bless the food, once he was done, she gave it a slight squeeze and smiled at him. Something about that tiny gesture reassured him at least a little.

Before him was a plate full of eggs and bacon. On another small plate was toast with butter. She had set out little containers of jellies.

"You're a great hostess."

"I should be. I do it enough."

"Why not in the winter? I would imagine people would come in droves to see a sight like this."

The lake did look spectacular surrounded by snow. From where they sat he could see clear across the water to the other side. Pine trees were draped heavy with snow, a perfect picture, as if he had opened the largest Christmas card ever and propped it up beside the table.

"Since I've been here, Emma hasn't had winter guests. She says she needs to recharge, and I don't blame her. The spring through fall months are crazy. I didn't know this until I came here to live, but she doesn't have to rent out at all."

"Really?"

"Oh, she's loaded. You know, not like Rockefeller kind of rich but enough to simply live here in a place like this and not need an income."

"Hmm…I had no idea."

It was the grandest home he had ever been in. Growing up, Robin's was about the nicest home he had ever been inside. Although he had a few friends with nice homes, the Jacobs' home was nicer by far. His own home had always been run down and reeked of stale cigarette smoke. Since his mom worked two jobs most of the time and he and Trevor were left without supervision, the place stayed a mess. As he got older, he began to help out. Still, it was never what he would call nice.

"You must like living here. This place is grander than anything I've ever seen."

What he was really thinking was that it was grander than anything he could ever offer her.

"Yes, I suppose. It's been good for me these past years."

Sensing he was about to head down the road leading to the past, he made no comment. Instead, he asked, "So, what did you get me in there?"

"I'm not telling."

"Will we keep tradition and open one tonight?"

"Absolutely." She was scrapping the rest of her eggs onto his plate as she asked, "So, what did you get me?"

"A puppy."

Giggling at him, she suggested, "We may have a problem then."

When she laughed, he felt the warmth of it settle into his chest. Since arriving, he continually was waiting to wake up, waiting to find it was all some spectacular dream. While he knew he didn't deserve a second chance with her, there he sat. As hope of a future mixed with the warmth of her laughter, he found it to be an emotionally charged combination. Fearing he may cry and upset her, he tried instead to refocus his thoughts by asking, "Was there anything you wanted? I almost called and asked, but I didn't think you would tell me."

"I can't think of anything."

Inside, she knew her gift was being with him for Christmas. In truth, she was happy when her parents canceled. Even if Emma had remained home, Robin would have invited Mike. While it would have been much more uncomfortable with Emma watching on, she could hardly stand the thought of Mike spending another holiday alone.

Grinning at her, he wrapped two pieces of bacon in his toast and ate nearly half in one bite.

Robin laughed at him again.

He shrugged and mumbled, "What? I'm a growing boy."

"I know, Mike." She smiled softly and looked down at her plate.

Noticing the tender expression on her face, he could tell his statement took her back in time. It was the first time he realized that she must think back fondly on the early years just as he did. "Rob?"

Peeking back up at him, she feared he could read her thoughts. She was as hopelessly in love with him at that moment as she was sitting on the bed during their honeymoon, eating donuts. Back then, he shoved an entire donut in his mouth and said the same thing.

"I hope you made me cookies."

Thankful for the way he redirected the conversation, she ordered, "Finish your breakfast."

Their day together proved to be even more fun than decorating the tree. They played out in the snow, built a snowman, bundled up in the afternoon and went out for a walk, and they even ventured out to see the lights around town. The worst part of the day was how quickly it passed. Sitting in the parlor after dinner, she handed him a gift, and picked up the one he wanted her to open. Tearing into the package, she found a set of three coffee mugs. One said Hope. One said Faith. One said Believe.

"I love them. I'm a big coffee drinker, don't ya know?"

"I've heard that rumor. I thought we could use them in the morning."

There was a forth mug in the set that said, Love, but he decided to keep it for himself as a means of staying connected with her. While he wasn't a coffee drinker, he was thinking of becoming one. He would try it the next morning. Surely with enough sugar, he could drink anything.

Mike went next. When he opened the box, he found his cookies." Jumping up, he grabbed the "Hope" and "Faith" mugs and started out of the room.

"Where are you going?"

Without stopping, he said, "To get milk. Where else?"

Settled back in with a mug of milk for each of them, Mike said, "You'll never top this gift."

He dunked a cookie into the milk and put the whole thing in his mouth then held the box out to her. "I suppose I can spare one," he mumbled.

Robin took the cookie and dunked hers just as he did. Inside, her heart was so full of joy and contentment. For the past few years at Christmastime, she never felt as if she belonged. While she loved Emma and Emma loved her, she wasn't home. Even the two years her parents came to visit, she felt very alone. Now she realized, what she was missing was Mike. He was her husband, and she would likely always feel his absence.

Noticing how deep she was in thought, Mike sat and stared at Robin. She was sitting just to the left of the tree, and the lights were twinkling behind her. After opening their gifts, they were seated on the floor still, just a few feet from the fireplace. The fire had died to a low crackle, and the sounds of it made him realize just how romantic the setting was. The lights were dim, and they were alone, and she was the prettiest thing he had ever seen sitting there by the tree. So far, the night was a perfect blend of excitement and tradition.

Curious, he reached out and grabbed both of her ankles and slid her nearer to him asking, "Why did you invite me here?"

The atmosphere around them had taken a sudden turn. Biting at her lower lip, Robin stared into his penetrating eyes. *Longing* was the word that echoed in her head. In his eyes she could see it, and longing was the only way she could describe what was churning within her. She longed to be his again.

"I didn't want you to be alone for Christmas."

Mike reached out and touched her cheek. "Is that the only reason?" Sliding his other hand behind her back, he drew her a little closer.

She swallowed hard. Gazing into his eyes was a mistake, for she became lost in them. She shook her head no and admitted, "I wanted to be with you for Christmas. I *needed* to be with *you*."

He slid his hand behind her neck and pulled her nearer still. "I'm about two inches away from crossing the line of this friendship."

Mesmerized by the melody of his words, she could only stare at his lips. His breath smelled sweet like cookies, prompting her to say, "Draw nearer."

He kissed her softly and intentionally. This was a moment he had dreamed of since he lost her, and he had no desire to rush things. Even more so than their very first kiss, this kiss was the most exquisite moment of his life, and he wanted it to last. Moving his other hand to her face, Mike held her there steadily. When he touched her cheek she sighed softly. That was what he felt too, a sigh of relief, a sigh that he was holding her as he used to, a sigh that, for the first time in a very long time his lips touched hers. Cupping her face with both hands, he pulled back for a second, rested his forehead on hers, and whispered, "It's always only been you." This time, he pressed his lips onto hers again, but her response was unexpected.

Sliding her hands up to the back of his neck, Robin held him to her firmly. Breaking contact for only a second, she breathlessly whispered, "And there's only you," as she moved to sit on his lap.

What began as something tender and deliberate turned quickly into an intense, enflamed moment. He held her so tightly, Robin could barely breathe. Kissing her face and her neck, he whispered again and again how much he loved her. His whiskers were rough and scraped the smooth skin of her neck. How she missed the feel of his face pressed against hers and his lips on her neck. As she had always been, she was lost in him and was, without any hesitation, prepared to give herself to him, right there, right then. All the doubts she felt before faded the moment he kissed her.

The ringing of the phone was something they at first ignored. Finally, he gripped her by the shoulders and pushed her away from him. "You better get that."

Grinning at him, she stood and moved quickly from the room.

Breathless, he found he was barely able to regain his composure. Since arriving, he had wanted to kiss her more than anything else. When given the opportunity, at the onset, it was his only intention. Once she responded as she did, though, his only thought was of making love to her. No doubt, that was exactly where they were heading. Their circumstances were such, that he knew it would be a mistake.

Needing fresh air, Mike went outside to wait for her on the back porch. Although the temperature was in the low twenties and he wore no coat, he still found himself overheated. His heart was pounding at the mere thought of her lips on his and the way she dug her fingers into the skin of his neck. In his mind he could still hear her soft words, "I need you. I need you." Inhaling deeply, he grabbed onto the railing of the porch and prayed, "Lord, I want her more than I've ever wanted anything in my life. But I know things are too uncertain between us. While in my heart she'll always be my wife, and I believe in Your eyes she is, we're no longer even married. I can't allow myself to be with her like this. Not when she's not mine. I need You to give me strength, or I may make the biggest mistake and end up losing her again. Please don't let me lose her."

While on the phone with her parents, Robin watched Mike go outside, glad he did since she had allowed her parents to believe she was alone. As much as she hoped to find the courage, she simply couldn't tell them about him. They had suffered too much heartbreak and upheaval in their lives after what happened, and because of that, it wasn't at all likely they would understand her spending time with him.

During the call, she felt as if she caught a chill, and from that point on, she didn't feel herself. It was warm in the house, but for some reason, she still shivered. Supposing it to be nerves after her encounter with Mike, she found her heart racing at the mere memory of it. Being in his arms caused her to forget all her uncertainty and apprehension. The intensity of desire she felt for him was quite unexpected, as if an explosion had happened in her heart, and she was momentarily prepared to open herself up to him fully. Even at that moment, the recollection of his warm hands on her face caused another shiver.

Robin cracked the door open and asked, "What are you doing out there?"

Moving back in through the open door, he admitted, "Cooling down." He smiled down at her as he reached out and rubbed his hands up and down on her arms. "I want you to know, that was never my intention in coming here. Up until a few minutes ago, I never even thought about trying to get you into bed. I promise you."

"I don't think that."

Mike chuckled, admitting, "I'm thinking about it now for sure."

He paused and reached for her hand. His heart was pounding still, and she looked so beautiful standing there looking up at him all wide-eyed. Putting the brakes on would take more than he had in his own strength. Mike asked, "Tell me, can you honestly say you know where we stand?"

"No, not at all."

"As long as you have any uncertainty, I don't think we should go in that direction."

Robin rested her head on Mike's chest. "I agree."

She felt worse every second and knew she needed to go and lie down. Whatever brought on the chills wasn't nerves after all.

Disappointed, yet understanding how she must feel, Mike wrapped his arms around her and admitted, "I couldn't be with you that way and then simply get on a plane and go home as if it never happened. When it does happen," he corrected himself, "*if* it does happen, it has to be forever. Agreed?"

She nodded.

For a minute more she simply stood there, head buried in his chest. When Robin shivered again, he asked, "Are you okay?" He lifted her chin to look up at him. "You're pale."

"I don't know. I'm not feeling well."

"Let's get you upstairs to bed." Mike chuckled softly, "You know what I mean, to sleep. I'll come back down and take care of the fire and turn out the lights."

Walking with her up the first flight of stairs, he made the turn with her, continuing up the second flight. He would stand for nothing less than getting her settled into her room. What concerned him most was that she went from looking fine to frightfully pale in the matter of a few minutes. He wondered if the phone call had anything to do with it.

"Is everything okay? That phone call?"

When they reached her bedroom, she went and sat on the side of the bed.

"Oh, that was just my parents."

Lying back, she pulled the quilt over her and said, "While we were talking, I got a chill. I hope I'm not coming down with something."

"Hey, the guy at the tree farm," he reminded her.

"Oh, no!" she groaned quietly.

While they were tying the tree onto the car, the man who helped them was obviously sick, because he complained and hacked and coughed in their direction the entire time.

"I'm not coughing, though."

He pressed his hand to her forehead. "You feel warm. Do you have anything you can take?"

Without sitting up, she pointed to the bathroom. "Medicine cabinet, and there are paper cups under the sink."

When Mike returned, he said, "Here, sit up long enough to take this."

She did and then rolled over onto her side and pulled the quilt up to her chin.

Sitting on the side of her bed, Mike wished things were different. As he sat there in her bedroom looking around at all the unfamiliar things, he realized he was an outsider. Even though he had known and loved her for more than half the years he had been alive, here, he wasn't a part of her world at all. He was a visitor, and in that moment he felt like a stranger, unable to even find an aspirin. In the entire room all he recognized was the photo of Mikey's grave he recently sent and a photo of him and Mikey. It was sitting on her bedside table. Stunned that she had a photo of him, he reached for it and studied it. Of all the pictures of Mikey alone, why had she brought this one? He sat it back down as an unusual wave of emotion washed over him, and he was reminded of the worst truth of his life; his family was gone. He still felt like a dad and husband, yet he had no family. Nothing was more tragic to him than the loss of his wife and son.

Reaching for her, longing for what used to be, he stroked her hair softly, asking, "Can I get you anything else?"

"No, I think I just need some rest. I'm sorry to cut the evening so short."

He stood to go, admitting, "Probably safest. I'm sorry you feel bad. Will you come get me if you need anything?"

"Yes," she barely mumbled.

Mike leaned back down and kissed her lightly on the forehead. "Good night, sweetheart." When she didn't answer, he realized she was already drifting off to sleep. "I love you," he whispered.

"Love you, too," she whispered back.

Certainly, he hadn't expected her to reply, but when she did, he knew she meant it. If only it could be the kind of love they used to share, though that was something altogether unlikely.

Just after seven the next morning, Mike made his way up to Robin's room. He had been up for two hours, and every minute of it he wondered if she was okay. Tapping lightly on her bedroom door, he asked, "Robin, are you awake?" Cracking the door open slowly, he found her wrapped up in her quilt and shivering.

"I'm so sick. I've been throwing up most of the night."

Rushing to her bedside, he pressed his hand to her forehead. "You're burning up. Why didn't you come get me?"

"I couldn't," she said through chattering teeth.

She was so cold and weak there was no way she could have made it down the stairs.

"Aww, baby." Leaning down, he kissed the top of her head. "I'll get you some more aspirin."

She slept off and on for hours, and he stayed there by her side the entire time. It was Christmas morning and she could hardly even sit up, let alone go downstairs. There was a small TV sitting on her dresser, so Mike watched it with the sound muted throughout the morning and past lunch. There was nowhere else he would rather be than with her. Feeling so ill still, she was unable to eat and would barely drink anything. At one point when her temperature reached 103°, he suggested they go to the emergency room, but she refused, assuring him she would sleep it off.

Each time she awoke, Robin found Mike there, sitting next to her in the bed. Most times, he was holding her hand or rubbing her head. As often as she apologized for ruining their Christmas morning, he shushed her. Next thing she knew, she was drifting off again. At least the vomiting had ended. Her last episode was just after he came in that morning. All the while she hovered over the toilet, he hovered over her, holding her hair back, whispering how sorry he was that she was sick. His tenderness toward her was a reminder of years past, when she was so sick early in her pregnancy with Mikey. Those times, too, he stood with her and held her hair, a memory that made her cry.

Not understanding exactly why Robin was crying, Mike simply held her and whispered softly that he was there for her. Because she was rarely so emotional, he found that he rather enjoyed the moment. Not that he would wish her to be sick, but it did give him reason to hold her, a privilege he had forfeited so many years ago.

At three that afternoon Robin awoke again to find Mike gone. When she heard the sound of him throwing up in the restroom, she moved quickly from the bed. Finding he was kneeling in front of the toilet heaving, she reached for a washcloth, wet it, and pressed it against his forehead.

Waving his arm, he demanded, "Go get back in bed."

Ignoring him, she ran her hand along his back. "I'm sorry."

For several minutes he was sick, and for a brief moment, she was reminded of the many times he vomited that way after drinking, especially when he first started going out after work. Intentionally, Robin pushed past the painful memory and prayed silently for him instead. It was what she always did when the whispers came. She reminded herself, this wasn't that Mike; he was dead and gone.

Finally, coming to a point where he knew there could possibly be no more to come up, Mike fell back against the wall, took the cloth from her, and wiped his mouth. Smiling weakly, he offered, "Merry Christmas. Can you wrap up a toothbrush?"

She laughed softly. Reaching into the drawer, she pulled a new one out and said, "Merry Christmas."

They shared the sink as they brushed their teeth and then made their way back to the bed. After taking aspirin with a shared cup, they climbed under two quilts and shivered together. He dragged her to him, wrapped himself around her, and within seconds, they were both drifting off to sleep.

The evening wore on like this with Robin feeling better first. She was far from well, but at least her fever had broken. Knowing he must be starving, she slipped from the bed and slowly made her way down the two dreaded flights of steps. Making him dry toast and opening a can of soda, she dragged herself back up the stairs. Back in her bedroom, she sat on his side of the bed. Rubbing his forehead, she asked, "Do you think you can eat something?"

Peeking an eye open, he asked, "Are you better?"

"Yes, some."

He reached for her hand and pulled it to his cheek. "I don't like being a visitor."

At first she wasn't sure what he meant but then concluded he must wish he were home in his own bedroom and could hardly blame him. It was miserable to be sick while traveling.

"Can you eat?"

Shaking his head, he rolled over and went back to sleep.

It was the next morning before either was able to be up and around for long, having lost an entire day in bed. While Robin stayed in her room to shower, Mike went downstairs to his own to clean up. Afterwards, he waited in the parlor for her. By the time she came down, he had plugged in the tree lights and started a fire.

When Robin entered the room, she found Mike sitting on the floor, leaning against the same club chair he had on Christmas Eve.

"Merry Christmas," she said softly.

"Merry Christmas. Is this our do-over?"

"I suppose it is."

Though he was due to fly out that afternoon, he was considering calling work for an extension of his time off. He wanted to stay longer and make sure she was healthy enough. Since Emma wouldn't be home for several more days, he hated the thought of leaving her there sick and all alone.

Sitting near him, Robin asked, "How will you travel today?"

"I'll be okay, but should I stay until you're better?"

"I'll be okay, too. You need to get back to work. I know this was last minute to begin with."

He took her hand in his. "You're still pale."

She grinned and informed him, "You are, too."

"I need to eat something and get some energy back. I'm not sure I can stomach anything, though."

"I have some biscuits in the freezer. Let's start with that."

They had a small breakfast together and went back to the parlor to open gifts. Time was against them and both felt rushed. It wasn't at all what either had expected their Christmas together to be.

He gave her the first gift, the one he was most excited about. "I hope this is okay."

Inside, she found an iPod and at least a dozen CDs. "This is too much."

"No, it's not. You don't have one?"

"No."

"I know how you used to listen to Christian music back home. It's all I listen to anymore. I got you the CDs for some of my favorite songs, but from now on, you can just download music online. I was thinking it would be something we could share." Laughing, he clarified, "Not share the iPod but share the music we like. When you find something new you really like, you can let me know, and I'll download it."

She was sitting on the floor beside the tree. Moving onto her knees, she crawled over to him and hugged him. "Thank you for this. I like the idea of sharing music." While she didn't say it, she was surprised. Mike was always a rock fan and could hardly tolerate what he called her Jesus music. This was an interesting new side of him.

Unmending the Veil

When all the gifts were opened, both sat for a moment without speaking. With shirts, including her new red flannel one, socks, and books scattered about, there was also a new air of sadness that filled the room. Their time together had come to an abrupt end, and neither was ready for it.

Mike gazed out the window at the layer of snow settled upon the window ledge. The idea of facing that chilly weather caused the most terrible sense of dread to fill his heart. This time with Robin was the closest to home and family he had known in many years, and he could hardly believe it was over already.

"I'll call a taxi. I don't want you to get out in this weather."

"No, I'll take you."

"Please, it's cold out, and the roads are slick. I would rather say goodbye here. It'll be more difficult at the airport, and on top of that, I'll worry about you driving home, so please."

Sitting there without arguing, Robin was perplexed. It was hard letting him go, and she wondered what their relationship might look like going forward? After the closeness they shared during their illness the day before and, she recalled with cheeks flushing, their kiss on Christmas Eve, was a simple friendship even possible anymore? What else was there for them, though? They lived nearly eight hundred miles apart, and neither could afford to visit often enough to maintain a relationship. Could she expect any kind of reasonable future for them? When deliberated with even the slightest bit of reality, she knew the answer was no.

Robin's silence disturbed him, as her mind was clearly spinning. On her face was a mixture of disappointment and sadness, mirroring his feelings at that very moment. Reaching for her, tucking her hair behind her ear, he pleaded, "Talk to me."

"I don't know where we go from here."

"Where do you want to go?"

Her eyes were weak and she was so pale, even her lips had no pinkish tint to them. Mike hated the thought of leaving her in such a condition.

"I'm not sure," Robin admitted.

He looked away, knowing exactly what he wanted, for her to come home. He wanted to marry her again and to be a family like they used to be. Ultimately, she would have to want those things, too, and until she did, this was where they were, separated by time and distance. What they cautiously called friendship, was instead, a man loving his wife with all he had in him. Though he was confident she loved him, he feared that, after all that happened between them...after all he had done to her, her love for him wasn't enough. How could it be?

Unable to look at him as she said it, Robin looked away. "I think for now we should leave things as they are."

There were no other options as far as she could see.

"That's what we'll do then."

With his fears confirmed, Mike pulled her into his arms and kissed her forehead. His heart was breaking, and all he could do was hold her to him, knowing it would likely be the last time he would see her for months, maybe even longer. He loved her letters, and now, he presumed they would talk on the phone, but neither would satisfy his need to have her in his arms. Looking up at the grandfather clock in the corner, he held her a little tighter. Then, after a minute more, said, "It's time to get things packed up. Will you get me the number for a cab?"

She simply nodded.

His bags were by the front door and the cab was pulling into the lot of the inn. Wrapping his arms around her tiny little frame, he admitted, "If I have to be sick, doing it with you is my first choice."

She grinned. "Me, too."

"Thank you for inviting me."

"Thank you for coming."

Her face was buried in his coat, and the thought of seeing him walk out that door was tearing at her heart. A small part of her wanted to beg him to stay, but then the whispers came and she had no strength to fight them. *It's too late*, were the words that echoed in her mind. How could they ever piece back together any sort of a life?

Mike found it difficult to let her go when he heard the cab horn blow. Finally, dropping his arms to his side, he admitted, "This is harder than I thought it would be."

She was looking up at him with those Bambi eyes, and he wanted to scoop her up and take her home with him. Nothing was right about leaving his wife, flying hundreds of miles away, and somehow trying to resume life again.

Nodding, she reached for his hand. "I knew it was going to be difficult, but this is beyond what I expected."

The horn sounded again. Leaning down, he kissed her cheek and hovered there, saying, "Stay inside and stay warm."

"Will you call me when you get home?"

As Mike reached for his bag, he assured, "I will."

Ignoring his instructions, Robin walked with him to the front door and stepped out onto the porch. Mike walked on toward the cab, still obviously feeling ill, and she wondered how he would make the trip. He seemed so weak. With a sudden rush the memory of standing on that very porch watching him leave the summer before came to mind. Then, he was completely broken, and for them both it was a final good-bye. This year, with him looking so very weak, it felt as if she were watching an instant replay. Different from his previous departure, however, she was coming to wonder if there could ever really be a final good-bye.

After he loaded his bag into the trunk, Robin waited as Mike jogged back up to where she was standing. Her heart felt heavy knowing she wouldn't see him again for a very long time. Her heart felt heavy that he was leaving at all. As uncertain as she said she was, she was certain she wanted him to stay. She was certain she loved him. Reminiscent of that day the year before when he came, her heart was once again divided, as if tearing in two. As much as she wanted to be with him, confusion over how to undo all the damage clouded her thinking, maybe even her judgment.

Grabbing her into his arms, Mike whispered into Robin's ear, "You don't have to say anything, but I need you to know how much I love you, how much I'll always love you." He sighed heavily and added, "I promise, after this, we go back to being friends, no more love talk. But I had to say it."

Robin turned her head, pressed her lips firmly on his cheek, and then said, "I love you right back."

The horn blasted again, so Mike turned to leave. Standing by the open car door, he smiled one final time and held his hand out. It wasn't a wave exactly, just his hand extended. She did the same.

17

Emma had been home since the day after New Year's Day, and other than the worst cough she had ever had, Robin was feeling like herself again. All was back to normal at the inn, or what had become the new normal. She talked to Mike most days, and though she was no closer to defining their relationship, for the time being, it didn't seem to matter to either of them as long as they were able to stay in touch. January proceeded this way and then into February. Along with phone conversations, they wrote still, just not as often.

Emma's new normal included Stan, and Robin was sure wedding bells would follow soon. She had never seen Emma as happy as she was with him. He spent most evenings there with them at the inn, always for dinner, and along with his presence, Emma had a new outlook on life and on love.

Having become a part of their evenings, when Stan never arrived one night, Robin became curious. They were sitting at dinner, and Emma's silence on the matter said all that was necessary.

"So, where is Stan?" Robin watched Emma's face and was certain she winced.

"I don't know. I suppose he's home."

"Is everything okay?"

"Sure," Emma said with a smile, "everything is just fine."

Robin knew better. "Did something happen between you?" she probed further.

Emma sat her fork down and shrugged her shoulders. "You know, things like this run their course. We had fun. What else can I say?"

"So it's over?"

"Yes." Emma stood, lifting her plate as she did so. "Don't worry. It's no big deal."

With no more said on the matter, she walked into the kitchen and left Robin there wondering.

Less than an hour later, Stan stood knocking impatiently at the door. Fortunately, Robin was the one to answer, as Emma was upstairs soaking in the tub. Finding out from him that Emma just up and ended things with no real explanation made Robin feel better, at least it wasn't by Stan's choice. It made more sense that it was Emma. Since she had run from love for decades, to see her run from Stan wasn't all that unexpected. Robin was certain; it was something that could be repaired.

Stan left with Robin's assurance that she would try to talk some sense into Emma. Touched by his parting words, that he loved Emma enough to wait, no matter how long it took, Robin was determined to help them find a way through it. Sitting alone beside the fire, she prayed so hard for wisdom. More than anything, she wanted to see Emma love and be loved. It appeared, though, she would fight it to her own detriment.

When Emma never came back downstairs, Robin eventually went up to her room and found her there crying. Entering quietly, she went and sat next to Emma on the bed.

"He loves you very much."

"I know."

"Then why are you doing this? I think you love him, too."

"Sometimes, people are just too different."

"What in the world are you talking about? You have everything in common."

"He's such a good man."

"Yes, he is, and you're such an amazing woman. You belong together."

"There are things…" Emma trailed off, her heart too heavy to finish the thought. Beginning again, she said, "There are just some things that make it impossible. He'll find someone else." Finally, she admitted, "Hummingbird, I really need some time alone."

Robin moved to the door and stopped there. Turning back to Emma, she asked, "What has you so bound?"

Knowing exactly what she meant, Emma looked away. They had discussed it before, but always she refused to tell her. This time, Emma at least admitted, "Choices." Then, looking at Robin, disgrace filling her heart, Emma added, "He deserves better."

"I'm here when you're ready to talk."

"I know and thank you."

Weeks passed and still, Emma refused to speak to Stan. He called Robin often, and she sensed he was at the point of giving up. How could she blame him? With surprising determination he had wooed and pursued Emma without shame: calling, sending letters and flowers, and often stopping by unannounced, but his efforts were in vain. Feeling sorry for him, Robin began to hope, at least for his sake anyway, that Stan would stop the pursuit.

By all appearances winter was winding down. It was April, and though all had not yet thawed, Emma kept herself deep in busyness, preparing guest rooms and planning menus, which Robin knew was all a ruse to keep her mind and heart occupied.

One day, having had enough of the sulking and secrecy, Robin cornered Emma in the kitchen, demanding, "He's about to give up. Don't you care?"

"Of course I care."

Surprised by her honesty, Robin asked, "Why then? Why do you keep pushing him away? He loves you."

Emma walked over to the stool beside the island. Tossing her cookbook onto the countertop, she admitted, "He doesn't know the real me."

"What do you mean?"

"He doesn't know the worst of me, and I'm afraid when he finds out, he won't love me anymore. It just seems easier this way."

Since Emma had accepted the Lord, they often spoke about her past. Robin knew something deep and deceptive had her utterly bound. Although she prayed about it time and time again, asking for insight, none came. Robin had explained the mending of the veil to her, and at times, Emma seemed likely to open up. Whatever it was, it would prevent her happiness and future with Stan if something wasn't resolved.

Robin walked over to her and took her by the hand. "What worst are you talking about?"

Emma patted the stool next to her. "Hummingbird, you don't know the worst of me either."

She sat. By the look on Emma's face, Robin realized for the first time how serious it must be, but still her heart was firm and she assured her, "There's nothing I could find out about you that would change how I feel. I love you."

"Don't be so sure," Emma warned.

"You realize, you'll never be free as long as you keep this inside? You can tell me anything."

Emma looked away and stared out the window. Watching a bird hop along the edge of the flower bed outside the window, she tried to focus on anything but the truth, but no matter how many times she tried to turn away from it, the truth always danced around in her field of vision. It was what she thought of in her final hours each night and her first thought every morning. Finally, weary of the secrecy and lies, Emma blurted out, "After my fiancé died I found out I was pregnant." She looked at Robin, anticipating shock but found only concern.

"I knew I couldn't keep the baby. I was such a mess. For so long after he died, I could hardly get through a day myself, let alone raise a baby. Or at least that was the way I felt then. Now, I know I could have done it. Back then I was weak and a complete emotional wreck. I cried all the time and hardly got of bed most days. After I came here to live with my aunt it took years for me to engage in life again, if that's even what you call this life I've lived."

"Kind of like me?"

"No, sweetie, nothing like you. You're one of the strongest women I've ever known. I was nothing like you."

"What about the baby?"

"I gave her up for adoption."

Robin put her arms around Emma. "You did what was best for your baby at the time. That's selfless. You could have chosen the alternative."

"I was never selfless. I was selfish. All I could think about was what I lost instead of what I could have gained. I regret that decision more than any other thing in my life. If I could go back and do it all differently, I would."

"Now, you're afraid to tell Stan?"

Nodding her head, Emma began to cry.

"He'll love you anyway," Robin assured her.

"What about you?"

"Of course I love you."

Emma sat for a moment, unsure if she should continue on. Finally, she took Robin's hand and gave it a slight squeeze. "I gave my baby girl to my best friend, since she couldn't have children of her own."

Robin sat frozen for a moment, trying to allow Emma's words to sink in. Her mom was Emma's best friend.

"*I* was that baby?"

"Yes." Emma sat, waiting for some sort of reaction, explosive or angry, something.

Though Robin knew she needed to say something, instead, she sat very still and very quiet, trying to process this new information. All of a sudden, when looking back, her life was different…in many ways a lie. For Emma's sake she stammered, "You made sure I had a very good home."

"I knew you would."

Still, Robin was hardly able to wrap her mind around it. Biologically, her mom wasn't her mom and her dad wasn't her dad. All those questions like, "Do I get my eyes from you or my nose from him?" she would ask her parents. How uncomfortable that must have been for them, and all that time she had no idea whatsoever.

"Who was my father? What's his name?"

"Robert."

Connecting the dots, she questioned, "Robin? Is that where my name came from?"

"Yes." Touching her stomach, Emma explained, "When you would move, it felt like the fluttering of little wings. One day I called you Robin, and it just stuck. It was close to Robert, and I felt as if it would honor his memory."

"Hummingbird, where did that come from?"

Emma waved her hand. "Oh, there was no significance to that. You were such a busy little girl; one day I called you that and never stopped. Calling you Robin was the only thing I asked of your mother. Well, that and that she not tell you about me. She hated being dishonest, but I made her swear."

Emma had always felt terribly guilty for the position she put Linda in. "I think you should go and talk to them. They were always willing to be open with you. Please don't blame them."

While the conversation was going better than Emma ever imagined in her head, it was hard nonetheless. Robin was taking it well, and as for her, she felt as if the weight of a truck was lifted from her shoulders. With every word, every admission, the burden became lighter and lighter. Her daughter didn't seem to despise her as she feared she would. Maybe there was freedom in the truth after all.

The rest of the day went by in a blur. Robin talked to Mike but never mentioned anything about the adoption. It was hard enough to sort through in her own mind, let alone try to express her feelings aloud. Her flight was scheduled for the next day, and until she spoke with her parents, she thought it best not to tell him.

Upon her urging Emma told Stan, and just as Robin suspected, he was too relieved to have Emma back in his life to be concerned with such ancient history. He was kind and understanding, a decent and caring man, and would be just what Emma needed. After her admission there was a level of condemnation Emma carried around for decades that was lifted. There was something about bringing secret things out into the light. Once there, she remembered Chris' saying, "you give God something to work with." He had something to work with in Emma's heart, and finally, she would find the freedom she longed for.

As for their relationship, nothing changed as far as Robin was concerned. Emma had done what she thought was right at the time, and Robin could have never asked for better parents to have raised her. If anything, out of this, she gained another mother. That was what Emma already felt like to her. They had become so close over the past few years, and now her strong feelings made a little more sense to her. Refusing to allow this to become some emotional trauma, she instead chose to forgive the secrecy and lies and simply love Emma just as she always had.

Robin spent three days at her parents' home but left feeling more unsettled than when she arrived. Oddly, it had nothing to do with the adoption or the secrets surrounding it. It was more the fact that she realized there was nowhere she belonged anymore. As she had looked around her parents' house, it was unfamiliar to her. With no childhood memories to cause her to think back with fondness, there was no sense of comfort or of being home. It was theirs but not hers. They had a new life there, one that seemed to make them happy and one where she had no place.

Someday, probably sooner rather than later if Stan had his way about it, he and Emma would marry. Where would that leave her? Although certain she would be welcome to stay on at the inn, could she live with the newly married couple and still feel as if she belonged? The thought of it seemed awkward. Newlyweds deserved privacy. Though running an inn allowed little room for privacy, strangers around was one thing, but a daughter who recently found out she was a daughter seemed beyond awkward. Who knew, maybe Emma would decide to give up the inn? So if not the inn and not with her parents, where did she belong?

By her visit, in no way was she looking for answers or explanations, in truth, her motive in visiting her parents was to make them feel secure in her love for them. With that goal accomplished she was on her way back to the airport. Surprisingly, though, the trip unearthed feelings within her she never anticipated. She felt suddenly and terribly alone and without a place to fit in. Not only was she not who she thought she was, she no longer belonged where she thought she belonged.

Insisting that her father drop her off at the departing flights lane rather than going in for a long good-bye, Robin said farewell at the car. After going through a tearful good-bye with her mother at the house, her emotions could handle no more. Once he drove away, she went straight to the airline counter and changed her flight. Instead of flying directly to Concord, she added a layover in Raleigh. Uncertain of how it might help, all she knew was that a familiar face and sympathetic ear was what she felt she needed at the moment. She needed Mike.

During her visit, she had wanted to tell her parents she was talking to him again but could never get up the nerve. How could she? They would be angry about it, and after all the things that happened, could they ever forgive him? What kind of idiot they would think her to be to even allow him back into her life? When trying to envision what the conversation might look like, she felt foolish and pathetic as she made her argument in her head. "He's changed, really. He's not the monster you saw evidence of that terrible, blood soaked night." Would anything she said ever make a difference to them?

Robin sat on a hard plastic chair pondering, at a loss as to how her life could make sense anymore. Nothing made sense. There was a new turmoil stirring within her. She prayed about it all throughout the morning, but peace never came. Since walking again with the Lord, there was a sustained peace she experienced, even when perplexed or uncertain about things, but that peace was gone, and in its place were chaotic thoughts and unsettled feelings. Bewildered by it, she couldn't seem to find her way through the maze of unresolved emotions.

Deliberating between three states and three sources of confusion, she looked at each individually. In New Hampshire there would soon be no room for her at the inn. Grinning at her own play on words, she thought of Emma and Stan, and knew that, out of kindness, they would always welcome her. Still, something about the thought of remaining there caused her to feel unsettled deep within. In Phoenix her parents' new life held no place for her. It was like traveling to a foreign land, one she knew absolutely nothing about. Worst of all options, in North Carolina her face was on a proverbial wanted poster. How pointless to have even considered it in her deliberations. She felt alone, utterly and completely alone.

Disturbed by this lack of peace, she thought of Chris' words, how, when you experience chaos and turmoil, look for a way you may have stepped away from the Lord. Mystified, she prayed, "Lord, I don't feel as if I've moved a step. Tell me what is going on. I feel so suddenly sad, like before." She heard nothing in response.

By late afternoon on Saturday, Robin was driving towards her old hometown. Only the second time since leaving all those years ago, she found herself just as uncomfortable when entering as the last time. Then, she made it a point to go straight to Mike's, the cemetery, and leave town. This day, however, she was daring a stop.

Inside the bakery she was startled to see Mrs. Andrews, whose husband was Mike's football coach all throughout high school. Unsure of how she might be received, Robin stammered, "Hi there, Mrs. Andrews."

"Robin." Ellen's voice was intentionally cool.

Pointing to the case, Robin tried not to make eye contact. "I would like a dozen of the chocolate chip."

Ellen slung the case door aside and reached in with a paper tissue to grab half a dozen cookies. She dropped them in a white paper sack. Repeating the process, she slung the door closed again. Walking to the register, Ellen spat, "That'll be two-fifty."

Handing her a five, Robin noticed with embarrassment how her hand trembled. Why had she come in? She knew better but somehow hoped things might be different after so many years.

Ellen accepted the cash and carelessly dropped the change on the counter. "You have some nerve."

Taking the bag, Robin turned to leave.

"He's rebuilding his life. Last thing he needs is for you to come 'round and mess that up. He's a good man, too good for his own good, I s'pose."

Without turning or responding, Robin walked through the door and inched like a lowly worm to her car. She drove around for a few minutes to clear her head, extremely sad. Making a pass by her childhood home was a huge mistake. It reminded her of her earlier reflections of the morning. Where did she belong? What was certain was that it wasn't there in that town. That fact led to deeper concerns. What was she doing with Mike? He belonged there, nowhere else. Thinking of his letter and what he said about moving on, she realized that as long as they continued on the way they were, he would never begin a new life either. He was still waiting for her. Unintentionally, she was giving him false hope. Their only possibility of being together was for him to leave his home and his job, something she would never ask of him, and even if he did, where would they go? The inn wouldn't always be her home, and New Hampshire had nothing for her besides the inn and brutal cold. Her dilemma was becoming more and more complex and real.

Calling Mike, she was relieved when he answered. She hadn't told him she was coming to town, wanting to surprise him. It crossed her mind more than once that if she was unable to get a hold of him, her trip would be pointless. While the phone rang, it occurred to her that maybe the trip was a mistake.

"Hello."

Mike was glad to see Robin's number come up. Since she had been at her parents', they had only spoken once, and then he could tell she was speaking softly. Imagining she was sneaking off to answer his call, he decided not to call her again, not until he knew she had left there. It was never his intention to make her uncomfortable. Because she still hadn't told her parents about their friendship, his hope of developing their relationship beyond where they currently were faded.

"What are you up to?" More specifically, she needed to find out where he was. Having driven by the house already, she knew he wasn't at home.

"Cleaning up around the church."

Mike took a break and he went out to sit on the steps. No matter how many times they had talked since Christmas, it was still a thrill to him every time. The sound of her voice on the phone made him unbelievably happy. It had been more than four months since that intimate moment on Christmas Eve, and still they never mentioned it. Since then, he had yet to hear her voice that he didn't recall what it felt like with her sitting on his lap, arms circled around his neck, desperately clinging to him. Often, he heard her words again, "I need you."

Clearing his throat, Mike tried to chase the memory from his mind. "What are *you* up to?"

"Oh, just out running some errands. I stopped off and bought some cookies."

"What, not homemade?"

"Not today."

"Don't bother mailing them. Well, you can bother, a cookie is a cookie."

As she pulled into the parking lot, Robin saw Mike sitting on the front steps of the church, and just as he was the last time she came to town, he wore jeans and a white t-shirt. Even at such a distance, the sight of him caused her heart to flutter as if a butterfly was trapped inside, bouncing around, trying to get out. Clearly, he would always have that effect on her.

He still hadn't seen her, so sitting for a moment longer, she studied the white building. It was her church from the time she was born, well, from the time she came to live in the town. It was where she and Mike married. Those very steps he sat on were the same steps they ran down after they were pronounced man and wife, being pelted by birdseed. That memory sent her over an emotional cliff and, uncharacteristically, she began to cry.

Unsure, he asked, "Are you crying?"

His heart sank and he feared the worst. Was she calling to say it was over? At that thought tears formed in his eyes, and his chest felt tight and restricted.

She sat for a moment without answering. Watching him, she could see him rubbing his chin; his head was bowed.

He asked again, "Baby, tell me why you're crying?"

"I'm okay."

She wiped her eyes and sighed. Opening the car door, she grabbed the bag of cookies and began to walk toward the church.

Unmending the Veil

Mike caught sight of her and bounded off the steps. Scooping her up in his arms, he spun her around and around. While grinning from ear to ear, as happy as he could ever recall being, he asked, "What are you doing here?"

"I need to talk."

It felt right to be in his arms, but it wasn't right at all. How had things gotten to this point? When she came to visit him in the fall, she simply wanted things to be settled and over. Then his letter started something that she was beginning to believe was a mistake. No matter how she tried to justify their friendship, when she found herself unable to tell her parents, she knew it was something she was keeping in the darkness. In that case, did that not make it wrong?

He sat her back down and took her hand. "Were you crying just now? You never cry."

Pushing her hair back out of her face, he could see the evidence of it even before she answered. Her lashes were still wet and her eyes red.

"Not all-out crying."

Robin felt silly and knew she couldn't tell him the craziness that was going on in her head. He was clearly excited to see her, so if she did tell him about her reservations, it would be like pulling the rug out from beneath him. That wasn't her intention in the trip at all.

They went back to the steps and sat down. Handing him the bag, she apologized, "Not homemade."

Mike took one from the bag and offered her one.

She declined. "None for me."

The blood rushed to her face in embarrassment when she thought about Mrs. Andrews.

Dropping his cookie back in the bag, he pulled her nearer and asked, "What's wrong, Rob. Talk to me."

Robin leaned her head on his shoulder and sighed heavily. "I just found out I was adopted. That's pretty big news."

Momentarily speechless, he sat there. With his arm wrapped around her shoulder, he gave her a little squeeze. "Wow." What else could you say at such a moment?

"Emma is my biological mother."

"Humph. I didn't see that coming."

"Yeah, me neither."

"How do you feel about it?"

"I'm not angry or anything." Thinking for a minute, she added, "But I feel like I don't know who I am now. Like I'm not who I once thought I was."

"Sure you are. You're no different today than you always were."

"You were there for most of my life. Looking back, did I miss something?"

"No, not at all. There's no way you could have known. I mean, I guess it was unusual how Emma treated you. Think about the elaborate birthday gifts and wedding gifts. She showered you with stuff as long as I knew you."

"True, but I didn't know that was unusual. I thought it was because she never had kids of her own." Seeing the irony of her statement, she added, "Well, besides me."

They had talked for a while when finally he asked, "You seem okay with this. So why were you crying?"

"I've felt very sad today. At my parents, I don't know, they're so far away, and I'm not part of their lives now. Nothing fits anymore."

He thought about how he felt when he was with her during Christmas. He was a visitor in a world where he didn't belong. So he had a sense of what she meant. Mike sighed, admitting, "I get that."

It was getting late and he knew dark would be upon them before long. If she was staying in Raleigh again, it would be best if she started back fairly soon.

"Are you hungry? We can go grab a bite at the diner."

"I better not."

"I'm not talking about a date or anything."

Always fearing he would cross some invisible line of friendship, he constantly felt the need to explain himself in moments like that. Whatever label was appropriate for their relationship, at least he had the comfort of knowing when she needed someone, he was where she came. That meant everything to him.

"I know. I just don't want to go to the diner."

"Does anything else sound good?"

"I don't want to go anywhere or see anyone."

Appreciating that he had no way of understanding her hesitation, Robin explained, "I don't belong here anymore, Mike."

"Of course you do. After so long I know plenty of folks would be happy to see you."

"You're wrong!" Cutting her eyes around at him, she spat, "You can't possibly know what it was like after…"

Robin stopped abruptly. The last thing she wanted was to bring up the past. It was a painful memory for them both.

"What?"

Her tone softened considerably. "Once you were gone, things were different for me, my parents, too. The town became different."

He reached for her, rubbing his hand in circles on her back. "Different how?"

As far as he could tell, the town never, ever changed. It was the same place, the same people he had known all his life. No one came, no one left, well, Robin left.

Realizing he honestly had no idea what happened, she said, "Nothing, it doesn't matter now." She stood. "I think I need to head on back to Raleigh now. Thanks for talking to me, though."

Moving quickly down the steps, in her mind, Robin tried to drown out the cheers of onlookers as they tossed birdseed at her. The memory was so vivid, though, she had to blink repeatedly in order to stop seeing the people there lining the sidewalk. The recollection brought with it such heartbreak, she was uncertain if she could make it to the car without crying again.

Stunned that she was leaving so quickly, Mike jumped to his feet and followed her. She was upset and he wasn't exactly sure why.

"Let me come with you. We can have dinner there and talk some more."

He knew it might be months before he would see her again. If she would let him, his hope was to go back up to the lake in the summer. It was all he could think of since returning from his trip at Christmas.

"I think I need some time alone."

Robin knew Mike couldn't possibly understand what was troubling her. In a sense she wasn't sure either. The past few days had caused her to feel uncertain about most things in her life, including him.

Reminiscent of her departure when she was there before, Mike walked her to the car, and this time without wondering or asking, he put his arms around her and held her close. He wanted to ask her again to stay or if he could follow her back to Raleigh but decided against it. There was something different about her, something distant. When they were together at Christmas, he sensed her fear, in that they were getting closer and it scared her, or maybe she feared what she was feeling. This time, however, it wasn't the same. It was emotional distance, and because of that, it was he who had reason to fear.

As she backed out of the lot, he had a sinking feeling in the pit of his stomach. She was pulling away from him; he could feel it. Deep down in his spirit, he knew it was about to be over. Without the strength of God Himself, Mike was certain he would never make it through life without her.

Tapping on the screen door of his mother's house, Mike yelled, "Mama!"

Opening the door, he let himself in and found her in the back bedroom, vacuuming Trevor's old room.

Smiling at him, she turned the vacuum off. "What are you doing here?"

"I need to talk to you."

"Sure thing."

She set the vacuum back upright and followed him into the kitchen.

Looking around, Mike said, "Looks good in here. Spring cleaning?"

"Sorta. I haven't smoked in three days. I gotta stay busy or I'll blow it."

"Hey, good for you." Reaching out, he grabbed her hand, saying, "I'm so proud of you."

Since Robin had said the things she did in her letters about his mother, he was really making an effort to be more kind and loving toward her. Until recently, he hadn't realized how much he used to distance himself from her. Other than Trevor and him, she had no one, so it was important for them to reconnect.

"I think I might make it this time," she said with hope. "I tried last month but didn't make it past day two."

By the look on his face, she could see something was wrong. "What is it you want to talk about?"

"What was it like for Robin after I went to prison?"

The memory of it made her sad. Robin was a sweet girl and deserved better than she got.

"It was tough on her. Everybody turned on her and her parents, too."

"What do you mean, 'turned on her'?"

"They blamed her for what happened."

"How could they possibly blame her?"

Mike was stunned. Had they not seen what he saw in the photographs? The images flooded his mind, reminding him how crazed he was that night and how he nearly killed her. His sense about her, that she would soon end things between them, could he blame her in the least? Why had she held on as long as she had?

Kathy looked at her son, surprised he was so out of touch. "You were their star, Mike. In their eyes you could do no wrong. When they could think of no way to make sense of what happened, they made things up."

"Like what?"

"Rumors started going around that you caught her cheatin' and you got into it with the man she was sleeping with. Said she shot you to protect him and that you took the blame just to save her from going to jail. They glorified you, as if you were some saint. They had to know you were out drinking several nights a week. If they knew, they sure never spread that around. Folks said all kinds of things but never bad about you. One night, while she was still at her parents' house, someone dumped trash all over the yard and painted nasty things on the garage. She left right after that."

Mike sat there, puzzled, rubbing the stubble on his chin. "I don't know what to say, Mama. I had no idea."

"People like a shooting star, not a falling star. They didn't want to believe you were the problem." Standing to get a cup of coffee, she added, "Some people know the truth, though, 'cause when anyone said anything to me, I set 'em straight." Joining him again, she asked, "Can you believe a town that knows so much about everyone doesn't know the truth about you?"

Hanging his head, he whispered, "It was all me."

"I know." Patting his hand, Kathy admitted, "I should have said something. I suspected – no, I knew what was going on, but I didn't want to butt in. I saw the signs but said nothing. After that night I sure wish I would have." She sat for a moment more before adding, "I blame myself."

"Don't. There's no one to blame but me. I accept that." When his mother never responded, he told her, "Robin was here today."

"She was here? Really, what for?"

"She just wanted to talk. Some things are going on. I tried to get her to go out to eat with me, and she said she didn't want to see anyone. No wonder she feels that way."

Back in her room Robin ate fast food and watched TV. Mike had called twice, and both times, she let it go to voicemail. On the trip back to Raleigh, she thought more about them, specifically, how wrong it was to continue on the way they were. Unsure of where she might end up, she knew it wouldn't be there with him. She had come to a difficult decision. It was time to end things with him, and she would have to make it permanent. He deserved to be set free to find happiness, to have a wife and children in his own hometown, able to live out his dream. When he wrote in his note to her that he wanted her to be free to find happiness, she knew he was sincere in that desire. He wanted it for her. Shouldn't she be willing to offer him the same?

The next morning, Robin's phone rang at six o'clock. Answering it, she softly said, "Hello." She had been up since nearly four, certain he would call.

"I'm here. Can we have breakfast?"

Standing outside of his truck, he looked up at the hotel building, wondering which room she was in. He had been sitting in the parking lot for more than an hour, waiting for it to be late enough to call. The night before had been agonizing, and he hadn't slept even a moment. When he finally decided to drive to Raleigh, by that point he knew what he would encounter there. The anticipation of it was maddening, but if it was what she wanted, to never hear from him again, he would comply with her wishes.

"Yes. I think breakfast would be a good idea."

"I'll meet you across the street. Pancakes okay?"

"Sure."

He sighed in resignation, her tone exactly what he expected.

Sitting across from each other in a booth, they both ordered. He wasn't saying much, and she sensed he knew what was coming. For some time they just sat, looking at each other.

Finally, Mike said, "I talked to my mom last night. I never knew what it was like for you then. I'm so sorry, Rob."

Robin looked away as she said, "That's over now."

"Because of me, you lost everything, your family, your home, everything you've ever known. It was all my doing, and I'm sorrier than I could ever possibly express."

Their food arrived, and for a moment both sat again in silence. Mike mostly picked at his food and noticed she did the same. It was a chilly morning, and she wore the Panthers hoodie he had given her for Christmas. Out of that thought flowed the memory of their kiss, still as fresh on his lips as Christmas Eve. It was a memory he forced from his mind, especially knowing there was no more hope.

Finally, struggling for the right words, she began, "Mike, I'm glad you came this morning. I think we should talk."

Pushing his plate away, unable to eat another bite, he waited for the inevitable. He felt sorry for her as she struggled for the right words, ones that would let him down as easily as possible. She had such a tender heart, and the last thing he wanted was for it to be so difficult for her.

"That note you sent, where you said this might be a mistake…I think maybe you were right."

Mike exhaled loudly, feeling as if he had been punched in the gut. Unable to look at her, he hung his head and rubbed his forehead, reminding himself how grateful he was for the time he had with her and praying for strength to do what he knew was right. While his first inclination was to fight for her, to try and convince her to give them a chance, he wanted her to be happy and clearly she wasn't, so he would have to let her go. Several things popped into his mind, things he wanted to tell her, ways to reassure her she was doing the right thing, but when he tried he was unable to get them out without breaking down. Standing, he leaned down and kissed the top of her head.

"I always said I'll do this however you want. If this is what you want, I'll walk away."

When she looked up at Mike, she found tears in his eyes, and the way his voice broke with each word, she could tell he was barely holding himself together. Still, she assured herself, this was what was best for both of them, so she said nothing.

After tossing a twenty-dollar bill onto the table, Mike turned and walked out of the restaurant. Sitting in his truck, he leaned his head over the steering wheel and began to cry. He recalled the words of Job. "Lord, though you slay me, still I will trust You."

Deciding to skip church, though he had plenty of time to make it, Mike knew he needed to be alone. His heart was heavy, and the one thing he needed was to be alone with the Lord. On his knees in the kitchen, he prayed for Robin and for strength to live another day without her. Once, crying out, he admitted, "I don't even know what to ask. I'm so lost in my grief. Won't You please help me?"

After many hours of this, Mike heard the Lord speak as loudly and as clearly as he ever had. In that moment he caught a glimpse of what his future held, and he had to trust God's grace was sufficient to carry him through.

Taking out several sheets of paper, Mike began to write.

18

When Robin arrived home, she spoke to Emma for a brief moment and then went up to her room. She felt numb, similar to how she used to feel, as if the door to her feelings had closed again. Though she prayed and prayed, the door remained shut. For the next few days, it felt as if every prayer was bouncing off the ceiling and she couldn't feel God's presence as she had come to know over the past year. Isolation and pain were again her unwelcome companions, leaving her to try and face this new separation from Mike all alone.

It was springtime, and her days passed slowly, even while she remained engaged in a flurry of activity. She spent her days cleaning and preparing for the onslaught of guests in the month to come. Intentionally, she kept to herself, trying to find relief. Often, she spent her mornings on the dock, wrapped up in a blanket, pleading for a breakthrough that never came.

By Friday afternoon she was at the point of breaking. Sitting out on the steps, she looked out at the water, too sad even to pray. Simply, she missed Mike. As much as she was certain she had done the right thing in ending things with him, she was just as certain she would never get over missing him. Their last morning together haunted her. When he walked out, she literally felt as if part of her was being torn away, but no matter how painful, she knew if she remained in his life, he would never move on. He deserved a future, and for many reasons she wasn't the one who could share that with him.

Emma came and sat next to her. "Letter for you."

As she handed the envelope to Robin, Emma hoped it was something that would cheer her up. Since her return from her parents', Robin had been different, not with her, but she was sad, the way she used to be. They openly discussed the adoption and more details about her father, and Robin seemed intrigued by their love story, so her sadness wasn't stemming from that. Emma believed it must be because of Mike. As far as she was aware, Mike hadn't called. Sitting there for only a minute more, Emma decided to leave

Robin to read the letter from him, all the while praying, "Please, Lord, let it be something to bring her out of this season of sadness."

Staring at Mike's handwriting on the envelope, she read the name, Robin Jacobs, knowing she would have to tell him the truth about the divorce. She should have already, and for the life of her couldn't figure out why she had yet to. He deserved to know. Opening the letter, she pulled out the paper and waited. It was difficult to unfold the page and read its contents. Before, she was so eager to read every word he wrote. This time, however, she dreaded it. It would be painful, and she was so weary of the pain.

My Sweet Robin,

I'm sorry I was unable say more when we were together. Honestly, I could hardly trust myself to speak and feared if I said anything at all, it would only make the moment more difficult for you. What you said, though it was expected, was still hard to hear. I've stated before, and I meant it with all my heart, I only want your happiness. I want you to find love, and I know now that's not with me. You deserve a chance at a new life. As long as I'm in the picture, that's unlikely to happen.

As for me, I have to make this declaration – no matter what any court says, you are my wife and the mother of my only son. The verse, "husband of but one wife," continually rings in my head. I know that's what God is calling me to be, only yours. Not just now but for life. No one but you. I made that commitment to you all those years ago, and it stands today. No one but you, ever! I'll never be anything other than your husband. I'll always pray for you, seeking your happiness above my own. I love you.

Always,
Mike

Wailing openly, Robin curled into a ball and rolled over onto the grass and wept as hard as she ever had. The past years away from him she had existed in a walking, talking coma state. At least then there was less pain because she had, in a sense, died to her former life. Over the past months, though, allowing him to again be a part of her life, her dormant heart had been resurrected. It was alive and in the deepest anguish she had known since the day they buried their son.

She had to ask herself, was it *for* him? She wasn't so sure anymore. Having read his words, she knew he wanted her above all else, certainly more than his job. His dream of being a cop could only pale in comparison to the love he expressed for her. How could she not acknowledge that based on such a declaration? This was now a matter for God to work out within her. Ending things with him was based on fear not what her heart felt for him. Deep inside her spirit, though she had stated categorically and irrevocably that she would never return to that town, a tiny little seed was growing. Already, she had a sense God would call her back there, and quite simply, she tried her very best to ignore even the hint of it. As a child might stand before a parent with her fingers in her ears, warding off the instructions she didn't want to hear, she ignored her heavenly Father. Over the past weeks there was that still, small voice that whispered, "...and two shall become one." It was a whisper she rebelliously disregarded.

Trying to envision what a return there might look like sent her reeling. The mere thought of it caused her to cringe and become immediately queasy. When she was there before, daring to go into the bakery, all fears were confirmed. Not only was she not wanted there, but she was still despised. If she went back, she would be a prisoner in her home, too fearful to venture out. Such an existence wasn't what she wanted. If she searched her heart, she had to admit she wanted to be with Mike again, but she was absolutely certain she didn't have what it would take to stand against the people of the town.

In the days to follow, Robin lived in complete and utter turmoil. Everything in her rebelled at the thought of going home, but it was the Spirit who churned and groaned. She could find no peace in the thought of remaining in New England, nor could she find relief in the prospect of returning to North Carolina. One afternoon, she sat quietly with the Lord. Sitting in her healing chair, she looked across at the empty chair. Aloud, she admitted, "It's pride, has been all along." Since the early hours of the morning, she had been contending with pride. Admitting it was the hard part, but once she did, narrowing in on the many facets of it was fairly easy. Her truest fear in going back was that the truth was out; they, she and Mike, were not perfect after all.

Year after year, from the time they were in seventh grade, they were the perfect couple. Everyone said so. Somewhere along the way, she began to believe it, too. It was in protecting that lie that she refused to admit something was terribly wrong with Mike when he came home from Afghanistan. When he began to drink, and subsequently to hit her, it was in order to protect the lie that she never told anyone. She could have sought help for them both. Sadly, she had to admit, it crossed her mind on many occasions, but then the fear of what people would think of them stopped her dead in her tracks. The thought was so humiliating, it paralyzed her. Suffering at his hand was a lesser consequence than to make public their failings.

The Lord revealed to her that, though she was in the spotlight all those years because of him, she still felt invisible, and deep down she had always known that. She was somehow absorbed in Mike's glory, a byproduct of his greatness. Being his girlfriend, then his wife, made her feel like somebody. It took all that happened between them to strip her away from him – in order to be torn down completely and be rebuilt. She had to discover who she was and Whose she was. In her new walk with Him, the Lord made clear to her, she was *somebody* to Him. She – or they - didn't have to be perfect, and to strive for such would only lead to destruction. Had that not been well proven?

It was late Tuesday night and Robin was sitting in the parlor reading Chris' Bible. She sat in the very spot where Mike sat at Christmas, where he kissed her, and smiling at the memory of it, she touched her fingertips to her lips. "…and two shall become one," echoed again in her mind.

"Lord, please don't send me back there. I believe if I asked him, he would come here or anywhere, just not there. Please?"

Her mind was distracted from her reading. Having scanned the same words over and over, she could hardly comprehend what she was reading, and while she tried, she was unable to move past them. Finally, beginning again, she allowed the words to drop into her heart as dew would settle onto early morning grass. The words she read, without question, were the very words of God, His assurance, His promise of protection.

"The fear of man bringeth a snare: but whoso putteth his trust in
the LORD shall be safe." Proverbs 29:25

Frozen, Robin sat staring at those words. The Lord was calling her to go home. That explained the turmoil. The chaos in her heart and mind stemmed from her refusal to obey. Since before visiting her parents, she suspected the Lord's leading but ignored it, secretly hoping He would change His mind or somehow forget. That was why He felt so far away. She was running from Him again. Even the fact that she was hiding their relationship from her parents was an act of rebellion. Had she not been convicted for weeks about not telling them? It was she who had moved not Him. A vivid flashback of what life felt like without God near was enough to bring tears to her eyes. She would not, no, she *could not* live life that way ever again. Pulling the fingers from the little girl's ears, Robin said, "Speak, Lord, for your servant is listening."

With her heart blazing within, she rushed to the small desk in the corner, pulled out a sheet of paper, and began what would be her journey home. Afterward, she ran up to her room, rummaged through her boxes until she came to the one she was looking for. Taking the small box from a larger one, she opened it and gazed with tear filled eyes at her wedding band, recalling how one day, soon after she arrived at the lake, she had been tempted to throw it into the water. Thankfully, something prevented her from going through with it. Unsure at the time what caused her hesitation, there was now no doubt. Robin grinned as she whispered, "You always knew."

The next morning, Robin mailed her letter to Mike, deciding not to call him. As they had lived and loved through the written word from teenagers to a newly married couple, and ultimately a separated one, it befitted their love story to reunite in the same manner. His declaration was merely the beginning of the end of life apart. Her plan was to show up and surprise him, and in her mind she tried to imagine his reaction, what the look on his face might be. Many times since they parted that last morning – that was the face she would see when she thought of him. When he pushed his plate away, he was devastated, and his eyes particularly reflected his pain. Soon, that would change. It was all she could think of while packing, wrapping her arms around him, telling him she was home forever. *Forever.* That word brought with it memories of Christmas Eve, of how close they came to making love. He had said, "When it does happen, *if* it does happen, it has to be forever." Robin now had no reservations; it would be forever.

Emma helped her, and between the two of them, they had Robin's things loaded into the car by late Wednesday afternoon. It was Robin's plan to spend the next morning with Emma, leave around mid-day, then stop for the night when she became too tired to drive. She would be waiting for Mike when he returned home from work on Friday.

After lunch the day her daughter was to leave her for good, Emma walked Robin to her car. She was weepy, having been so all morning. Stan would be arriving soon after Robin left. He was a good man, and she was so blessed to have him in her life. Though they had shared it with no one, not even his family or Robin, they were talking about marriage. With Robin gone Emma would be ready to start a new life with him. Stan was truly a gift from God.

"Becky and Tommy will be here soon. Don't worry." Emma assured her, since Robin had been fretting that she was leaving her with no help, "After finals they'll both be here. If things get too hectic, I'll hire someone for mornings to help with breakfast." Taking Robin's face in her hands, Emma told her, "Hummingbird, I've got this. It's time for you to fly again."

"I know. I just worry about you, though. I love you."

"Sweet girl, I know you do, and I love you more."

Emma wrapped her arms around Robin and reveled in the fact that she had a daughter who loved her. All the shame and guilt she had carried over the years was lifted, and she felt freer than she had in over thirty years. The secrecy was finally over, and she could do the things for Robin that she had always wanted to do. After Robin and Mike returned from California, she wanted to buy them a house to give them a fresh start. Of course she insisted that Robin's parents make the arrangements, as if they were paying for it. Emma wanted to give Robin everything she hadn't been able to over the years. Money meant nothing to her, but Robin was everything.

"Listen, when you get there, it may be like starting over. If you need anything for the house, you let me know. I love that kind of thing. You know that. Let me help you."

"I will."

"One more thing."

"What?"

"Someday, I want you to have this place. It could never mean to anyone else what it means to us. It's a special place, a place where you and I were both healed." Again, she put her hands on Robin's face. "Don't get me wrong; I'm not throwing in the towel anytime soon, but when I do, I want it to be yours." She had already discussed it with Stan when they first spoke of marriage. It would be settled legally.

"I would be honored to take over someday."

The thought of Mike and her coming to the inn was a good one. He would retire at some point, and when he did they would have a glorious time together there.

"So get in the car already."

Hugging her again, Robin admitted, "I would've never made it without you." Whispering in her ear, she reminded her, "We're no longer damaged goods."

"No, Hummingbird. We're both free to fly."

As it had become his adversary, most days Mike passed by the mailbox without stopping. Often, by the time he would check the mail, several days' worth had piled up. This day, he passed by again and pulled on up to the house, but when he got out of the truck, he looked back down the gravel drive knowing he needed to check for bills. They were all that came, that and sale papers. So slowly, dreading the feeling of disappointment he would find there, he made the walk down to the road anyway. He knew he wouldn't hear back from her after his letter, and truthfully, he knew it was for the best that he didn't. It was time to let her go, no matter how it hurt and saddened him. Someday, he would find a new normal. As he had done before her visit in September, he would settle into a routine of normal life again. Different, though, after having lived with her in his life for a brief season and subsequently falling so much more deeply in love with her, it could never be as it was. He would live – but just barely.

When Mike opened the door to the mailbox, he found the stack was quite large, and rather than sort through it in route, he held the bundle at his side. He sighed heavily. Checking the mail had become the saddest part of his week.

On the way back to the house, he wondered what she was doing. From what she had once told him, their busy season was about to begin. Was she preparing for that? Every day at random times, he would wonder such things. At breakfast time he would wonder what kind of protein she was eating. He wondered how many cups of coffee she would drink and if she would use the mugs he gave her for Christmas. Each morning he drank milk out of his *Love* mug, regretting having kept it at all. Who needed the reminder, and why did he feel compelled to wash it every night just to have the same reminder the following morning?

Clearly, he admitted to himself and to the Lord, he was losing his mind over her, but it was beyond his ability to control. Robin was his every waking thought, and while thinking of her was painful, not thinking of her caused him to feel an even deeper sense of emptiness, the likes of which he had never known. Even in solitary confinement, kept apart from the other prisoners for his safety, he hadn't felt as alone as he had since he saw her in Raleigh. Every man had a breaking point, and Mike was reaching his. Day after day, he waited for the Lord to give him even the slightest bit of relief, but so far it never came.

Inside the house he tossed the pile onto the kitchen table and went in to change. He was going by his mother's before meeting Tim at the gym that evening. Prior to things ending with Robin, he and Tim met earlier, right after they got off work, but Mike found that nights at home alone drove him even crazier, so they agreed to change the schedule. Often, afterwards, they would eat dinner together or shoot hoops. As a means of avoidance, he was up for any activity that would keep him out of the home his wife made.

After a strenuous workout, one that would leave Tim virtually immobile the next day, Mike and Tim went to the diner. As they ate, Tim asked, "Have things been any different for you?"

"No, not really. These people here must be crazy."

"Maybe they're just forgiving."

"Obviously not."

Mike thought of Coach Andrews' wife and how she practically chased him down the sidewalk to tell him how sorry she was and that she wished she had known the truth before. He wasn't sure what transpired between them the day Robin came to visit, but it must have been significant to them both. Thinking back to that day, when he offered Robin a cookie, there was something unusual about her expression. She seemed embarrassed or self-conscious or maybe a bit of both. With new insight he realized how hurt she must have been over whatever was said. Anything that would bring Robin to tears was a big thing. Tempted to write to her and tell her what Mrs. Andrews said, he knew better. It would be a mistake to try to begin communicating with her again. He simply had to let her go. The truth was, though he would like to try and maintain a friendship, he wasn't able to simply be her friend. He would always be compelled to tell her how much he loved her, to kiss her, and hold her. While with her at Christmas, it was nearly impossible to keep up the pretense. Even then, especially then, he proved he wasn't able.

Tim offered, "I really am sorry about how things turned out. I held out hope, I guess."

Early on, he was concerned for his friend, but after Christmas he had a sense in his spirit that somehow God was up to something extraordinary. Tim was disappointed for him and knew, no matter what he said about his future, Mike was devastated by the prospect of living without his wife. What Tim never doubted, though, was his sincerity about never marrying again. If it were anyone else, he would think, *Oh, give him some time*, but not with Mike. Tim could honestly say, he had never seen a man more devoted.

Mike sighed, admitting, "I don't know that I had *hope* exactly, but I wanted to. You were right about us. Thanks for not saying so."

"You have to know, I didn't want to be right. I was just trying to look out for you."

Tim sat for a moment, hating to see the look on his friend's face. As long as he had known Mike, this was the lowest he had seen him. With as many prayer concerns as he had in the church, Mike seemed to stay at the top of Tim's list, especially lately. Still, he sensed God was up to something. It was a feeling he couldn't shake.

Mike walked into his quiet house and went into the kitchen. Unenthusiastically, he began to sort through the stack of mail, stopping abruptly when he came to a letter from Robin. His hands trembled slightly as he ripped open the envelope, and his mind could hardly conceive that she would write to him again. Maybe she was missing him as badly as he was missing her. Or maybe she just felt sorry for him. Unfolding the page, he read,

Sweet Michael Sr.,

When Mike saw his name written that way he gasped. Suddenly feeling the need to sit down, he pulled out a chair and plopped down heavily. Unable to imagine what the letter could contain, part of him feared reading on, feared hope. For a moment he sat there, until finally, curiosity got the better of him.

> *You had a declaration to make; I have a confession to make. When we first began writing, you asked me a question. I dodged it. You asked again. I said I forgot what I wanted to be back in ninth grade. I lied but only because I wanted to spare you the pain of my answer. The truth is – all I ever wanted was to be your wife. I wanted to be by your side while you pursued your dreams. That was my dream. I wanted to have your children. Michael was my greatest joy. All those things are still true today! Thought you might want to know.*
>
> You have my heart!
Robin

With his breath caught in his chest, Mike considered for a moment that he might drop dead from happiness. Would that not be some irony? His hands were more than trembling by the time he finished the letter, they were shaking outright. Robin wanted to be his wife. She said specifically she wanted to be his wife! He jumped from his chair sending it flying behind him and crashing into the refrigerator. Not caring in the least, he went into his room and began taking clothes out of the closet and piling them onto the bed. There was no way to know what the future held, but finally he had hope, real, genuine hope. As he packed, his intention was to go to New Hampshire and pursue her with all his might. He would woo her and court her. Nothing would stop him. Having her letter as proof that she wanted to be with him again, he would do anything and everything to make that happen.

Deciding not to call her, he instead would write to her and ask her to marry him again. Somehow it seemed fitting that he write. It was how their new story began, through written words. He paused for a moment and tossed around what he would say but never fully came to any conclusion of what he might write. One thing he knew, he would begin by saying, "Oh, me of little faith." Since they began writing, he had prayed for many things, but never had he had the audacity to pray that she be his again. What little faith he had in a gracious Father who loved him well.

"Lord, You always knew."

The next morning Mike went into the Sheriff's office and closed the door. He sat down across from his longtime friend and began, "First of all, I want you to know how much I appreciate the way you fought to get me reinstated. I didn't deserve this second chance. Second, I consider you a great friend, and I'll miss you, but the bottom line is, I have a chance with Robin, and I'm going to take it."

It was settled. He was going after his wife.

19

Finally in sight of her little yellow house, Robin was more excited than she was nervous. In the past weeks since her ponderings on where she belonged, at last, she knew without doubt. It was less about where she was as it was with whom. She belonged with Mike. No matter what had happened in the past, he was her husband. No matter the humiliation that would certainly come, she belonged home, with him. After the journey God had taken her on over the past two years, she found Him to be trustworthy, so if He said to go home, then home was the safest place to be. She had to believe He would deal with all things that came against her.

The morning she left, Robin copied some of Mike's letters, especially the one where he opened up about what things were like when he came home from war, and she mailed them to her parents. Apologizing for having kept their relationship a secret, she tried her best to help them see the new man he had become, not changed, but new. Explaining how God had orchestrated their restoration, she trusted the Lord would soften their hearts toward Mike. It mattered to her that they accept him back as part of the family, but she also knew that if they refused to, it wouldn't change the reality of it. For her this was forever, so somehow they would have to learn to be around him without the bitterness they currently felt toward him.

On the front porch Robin opened the screen door and found the front door to be unlocked, which didn't surprise her since they had never felt the need. When she stepped inside the living room, the house seemed to welcome her, envelope her in. Built in the late twenties, her home had charm that newer homes lacked. The ceilings were high and the moldings were heavy and thick. Painted a crisp white, they framed the bluish grey walls perfectly. Mike had worked for weeks just on the restoration of the woodwork. The room felt warm and comfortable, just the same as when she left.

Straight across from the front entry was a large cased opening leading into her kitchen. From the moment she laid eyes on the old-style farmhouse kitchen, she fell in love with it. It was what made her say yes to the home and where she spent most of her time. Stepping through the doorway, Robin felt herself tumble back to their early days when they were so excited to be in their new home. Then with a flash, the spattering of Mike's blood came to mind. Through prayer, though, she pushed the dreadful memory away. "Forget the former things. See, I do a new thing." It was one of her favorite verses from Isaiah. She sensed she would need that verse often in the days to come, as memories would certainly flood her mind and the accuser would certainly accuse.

To the back and right of the kitchen was a small hallway. To the left of the hallway, the closed door was Michael's room, to the far right, hers and Mike's. In between them was a shared bathroom. When she moved into her bedroom, she found the bed littered with clothes with only a narrow space where Mike must have slept the night before. She smiled at the realization – he was coming for her. Wondering what his plan was, she was most certain he was geared up to fight for her. Little did he know, no fight was necessary.

Robin looked at her watch and noted she had an hour or so before he came home, so she first began putting his clothes away. Afterwards, she began making trips to her car, unloading her belongings. When she lifted the last box from the trunk, she sighed, feeling particularly relieved.

In the hopes of surprising Mike with a home-cooked meal, Robin searched the refrigerator and cabinets but found little to make for dinner. It had been her plan that she could have it waiting for him when he arrived home. After all his belly-aching about having to eat out, she was excited about surprising him with a real sit-down-at-the-table meal. When that plan fell through, she was glad she had stopped and bought a box of donuts. Some traditions should be maintained. Mike would appreciate them, and without question understand their meaning.

It was nearly five o'clock when she heard the familiar sound of his truck grinding to a halt. For the first time in a very long time, she was an object perfectly placed, at home waiting for her husband.

Mike threw his truck into park. Before it was fully stopped, he jumped from the cab and walked over to Robin's car. The trunk was open and empty, so he closed it. Could this be what it seemed? He stood still for a second before looking back up at the house. Was it at all possible he would walk through that door and find his wife had returned to him? Jogging toward the steps, he found her waiting at the screen door. Her smile was sweet and her eyes sparkled with her surprise. At that moment there was no doubt; she was home for good. His heart was pounding at the sight of her standing there, and he could barely catch his breath, let alone speak.

"Honey, I'm home," she whispered.

He nearly pulled the screen door off the hinges he tugged so hard. Grabbing her, he circled his arms around her and lifted her from the floor, and by the way she clung to him, he had no doubt she was his again. As if God had turned back the hands of time, undoing all the damage Mike had done, He brought her home to him. She was his, and in his heart he promised his Lord he wouldn't fail Him again. He would love her and cherish her the way He intended.

Finally, wanting her to know he would give up anything, *everything*, for her, he said, "I was coming there to be with you. I know it's painful for you here. We don't have to stay. As long as you're with me, it doesn't matter where we are."

"Home...I want to be here at home with you. I don't care what anyone thinks. Honestly, that's what kept me away these past months. Deep down I knew I could have no life without you, but I was afraid and too proud, though. None of that matters now. The Lord said to go home. So I'm home."

Carrying her further into the living room, Mike made no move to set her down. In fact, he was unsure he ever would. She had wrapped her legs around him and linked her feet. It reminded him of the day he came home from his second tour, her wrapped around him like a monkey.

Smiling so broadly it hurt, he walked into the kitchen with her, saying, "I quit my job today."

"You did? You might want to call and sort that out. I'm a poor woman with no means to support you."

"I'll call."

He buried his face in her neck. Such tremendous, nearly unbearable emotion washed over him as he whispered, "Baby, I can't believe you're here. I can't believe you would love me again."

With her home and in his arms, after so many years apart, he finally felt whole again, like a missing piece of him was restored. Looking back at her, he felt no shame in the fact that he was crying, and he had to guess these weren't the last tears he would cry.

"I'm here and it's forever." Just before pressing her lips to his, she whispered, "I love you. I never stopped, not one minute; I promise you."

Similar to when he kissed her on Christmas Eve, it was as if an explosion occurred within him. Then, though, he felt the need to maintain some kind of restraint. Today he felt no such need. All he could think of was making love to her. It had been seven long years. He needed her desperately, and just as by the fire that night, she needed him as much. She whispered it again and again as she clung to him, her fingers digging into the skin of his neck.

Then it came, not a whisper but a roar from the past. How could he make love to her for the first time on a bed where he hurt her the way he had? He felt suddenly sick at his stomach at the mere thought of it. Abruptly, he stopped kissing her.

"What?"

She was smiling at him, just as breathless as he was. There was no way to explain his hesitation without dredging up the mire, so he suggested, "Let's pack a bag and head out to the beach. You told me you daydream about being there. Let me take you. We can make it in a couple of hours." He paused then added, "Unless you're tired of traveling."

"No, not at all. The beach, that sounds wonderful."

She giggled gleefully. Honestly, at that moment, she felt like she was thirteen again, as if they had a chance at a brand new beginning. They both were new. All things would be new.

"We never had a real honeymoon. I think we deserve that."

"Me, too," he agreed, smiling so broadly that his face hurt.

They tore through the bedroom like a whirlwind, packing quickly. Stopping suddenly, remembering a not-so-minor detail, Robin grabbed the shoe box and carried it to the bed.

"I have something to show you."

Mike went to where she stood by the dresser to see what she was pulling out, but immediately, just by looking at the folded documents, he knew what was in her hand. Regretting his interest, he held his hand out at the sight of their divorce papers, intending to shut down any mention of that time.

She grabbed for his extended hand and laughed. "Really, you want to see this." Flipping to the back page, she asked, "What don't you see there?"

He saw his name typed out and just above it, his signature. Memories of holding those papers in his hand choked him. It was the single hardest act he had ever performed. At the time his only motive in signing them was to release her from the living hell he had put her through, but it was the last thing he ever wanted. Pleading guilty, even knowing he would serve time in prison, was easier by far than signing those papers. Beside his name her name was typed out, but there was no signature.

Puzzled, Mike studied that blank line for several seconds and finally asked, "What? Are you saying you never filed these?"

"No. When my attorney sent them to me to sign, I tried at least a dozen times, but I couldn't. So finally, I called and let him know I would get back in touch with him. I never did."

Lifting her hand, Mike looked at the ring on her finger. It was the first time he noticed she was wearing it again. He brought it to his lips and kissed it, saying, "Hi, Robin McGarrett."

"Hi, Mike McGarrett."

Robin slid her hands behind his neck and pulled his face to hers. Kissing him tenderly at first, she felt his entire body tremble in response to her. He wanted her, needed her as desperately as she did him.

"I don't want to wait. Make love to me now."

The feel of her lips on his drove him wild. He wanted her more than he ever had but still the roaring sounded.

"Rob..."

He was trying to avoid her lips so that he could even finish a sentence. "You've gotta know how much I want you."

Having trailed her lips to his neck, she mumbled, "And I want you."

Her tone was playful and flirty, and he could tell she wasn't picking up on his hesitation. Finally, grasping her by the arms, he moved her back and said, "Not here. Not now." Mike looked over at the bed. "Somewhere else for the first time. Okay?"

Robin followed his eyes to the bed and whispered, "Oh." Understanding his reluctance, she wrapped her arms around his waist and rested her head on his chest. "I deserve a honeymoon anyway."

"You sure do."

They quickly finished packing, grabbed the box of donuts, and rushed to the car.

After checking into their room, Mike casually carried their luggage into the elevator. Once the doors were closed, however, he grabbed Robin, lifted her off the floor, and pressed her against the wall.

"Still want me?" he asked.

His sudden action caused her heart to pound hard against her chest. She was looking up into his eyes, and the desire she found there caused her breath to catch in her throat.

"I want you," she whispered hoarsely.

He moved his lips to her ear and assured her, "I'll only make love to you when I hear those words."

The roaring began to fade. Truly, he had no fear of ever harming her again, but he needed to reassure her; that man was dead and gone.

When the doors opened, he grabbed the bags, and together, they practically ran for their room. Inside, he threw the bags and lifted her once again from the floor. Laying her gently on the bed, he kissed her face and her neck and her face again. All the while, he told her over and over he loved her and that he would never let her go again.

As he kissed her, Robin was grabbing at the hem of his t-shirt when a sense of unease sprang up within him, and in that moment dread overshadowed his passion for her. He stopped and just looked at her.

As Mike hovered over her, Robin felt him move his hand beneath her shirt and trace his fingers along the skin below her belly button. She realized he was touching her stretch marks from Michael. When he lifted her shirt to look at them, she considered that he hadn't seen such physical evidence of his son in many years, and her heart ached for how they must make him feel. The pained expression in his eyes caused tears to spring to hers.

"If I could take these away, would you allow me?" he asked.

Frowning, she answered, "No, of course not."

She slid her fingers beneath his and felt the small lines that spanned from hipbone to hipbone. Though she thought she had made it through without them, in her final week and a half of pregnancy, they began to appear. No matter how much cream she applied, her skin began to split and tear.

Mike wrapped his hand around her fingers and slid them beneath his t-shirt. Touching his skin with her fingertips, he tried to prepare her.

"I want you to be able to look at me without regret or guilt. This is part of me now." He leaned down and whispered in her ear, "This is when I became a new man, when Jesus came into my life."

Every ounce of passion drained from her. Robin realized, by his preparing her this way, what she was about to see would be difficult. How had she never thought of it? Of course he was scarred. He had to look at them each and every day and was forced to remember that his wife wanted him dead.

Robin watched as Mike moved from the bed and stood before her. She sat up slowly, suddenly apprehensive. As he slipped his t-shirt over his head, she could see three distinct bullet holes and several long surgical scars. Because of the scarring, the hair was patchy, unable to grow on the damaged tissue. It was worse than she could have braced herself for. Pressing her face into his stomach, she began to cry.

He put one hand behind her head and with the other he rubbed her back gently, saying, "Robin..."

There was nothing he could say to make her feel better about what she was seeing. It was a disturbing sight for anyone, but as the one who shot him, he knew it would devastate her. Since he never considered he might be intimate with her this way, he wasn't prepared for what to say.

Unable to do anything but, Robin continued to weep openly. After several minutes more she choked out, "How did we get to that place?"

Mike sat down next to her, bearing the answer to her question squarely on his shoulders. "Because of me. I took us there."

"No. I should have gotten help." She put her arms around him and clung to him. "I'm so sorry."

"Me, too, baby. Me, too." All he knew to do was hold her.

Robin cried for quite some time, and all the while he held to her tightly. At one point she recalled a question Chris once asked her. He wondered why she never cried over Mike. She easily cried about Michael, but he noticed her restraint when it came to Mike. It was true, and she wondered the same thing in the time since Chris had asked her the question. There was something in that very moment that held the answer, as if it was on the tip of her tongue, but it never came.

Eventually, they lay together in silence, Robin's mind whirling with many tangled thoughts. During the drive home, she had tried to brace herself for the many obstacles they would face as they learned to begin again, and already she found she was ill prepared for the anguish of it.

Determined to push through this moment, she propped herself up on her elbow. Tracing her fingers along the letters of Mike's tattoo, she asked, "What is it like to see my name on your arm every day?"

"Before today, a sad reminder of what I lost. Now," he said with a broad grin, "a reminder of how much God loves me, that He would allow you to be mine again."

Gently, she rubbed her hand across his stomach and bent down to kiss each distinct bullet hole. "What is it like to see this?"

"It's my reminder that God loves me so much that He went to great lengths to make me His. I wouldn't give these up any more than you would give up yours."

"Have you ever hated me because of them?"

Mike closed his eyes and whispered, "I could never hate you." Looking back at her, he asked, "You just don't get it do you? Without the scars you very well might be dead right now." He choked up at the thought of what life would be like if that had happened and could hardly go on. Finally, he added, "God used that night to save us both."

His words were true, and she knew it. As brutal and terrifying as that night was, she knew in hindsight, God did save them both.

"Mike?"

"What, baby?"

"You know what verse rings over and over in my head?"

Leaning in, he kissed her nose. "What verse?"

"'And two shall become one.' It's what drew me home to you. So will you please make love to me? I've missed you, and that's what I need right now. I don't ever want to be two again."

He pulled her into his arms. "That, I can do."

Considering the consequences, and with a touch of that old fear burning in her belly, Robin pressed her hand into Mike's chest, saying, "We have no protection, and I'm not ready for that. I'm not scared, not like I was." She reconsidered that. "Okay, I'm scared a little, but I also think we should be alone for a while, just you and me."

"We'll be careful."

Unlike the explosive passion they both experienced at that first kiss in the kitchen earlier, coming together again after so many years was instead tender and gentle. There was no way she could count the number of times Mike whispered he loved her, and she never tired of hearing it. He was clearly overly conscious of his past sins against her, as it showed in his occasional hesitance of perhaps moving too aggressively. At one point she grabbed his face and demanded, "Please, be here with me in the moment. All things are new. You have to believe that."

Mike knew he was holding back, fearing she was remembering who he once was and what he was capable of. At their son's graveside Robin had explained to him how, rather than clinging to her love for Michael, she was clinging to his death. That was exactly what he was currently doing. In the one moment he longed for more than anything in the world, he was clinging to the past, to the man he was, the one who was dead and gone. Choosing to walk in the newness of the life God was giving him, Mike instead latched on to his love for his wife.

From that moment on Robin knew he was present and that his mind was set on nothing but her. He loved her well, and two most assuredly became one again.

The next morning, Robin woke to find Mike gone. Stepping out onto the balcony, she saw him standing before the ocean, pants rolled up, wading in as far as his ankles. With his arms spread wide and his face tilted toward the heavens, he was praying. She had to grin, realizing if anyone else saw him they would consider him crazy, but not her. After the miracle God had given them, they both had reason to praise.

The breeze was blowing in off the ocean and along with it a slight mist sprayed his face. Mike could taste the salty water on his lips, and he reveled in the newness of the morning. Standing in the presence of God Almighty, he worshiped in a way he never had before. After spending the entire night wide awake, even long after his sweet bride went to sleep, he could hardly wait for the morning hours so that he could stand beside the water and pray.

Earlier, as he watched the sun rise, he considered the mighty works of God in his life. At one point, he felt the Lord direct him to consider the ocean waves. After dwelling on them for some time, Mike whispered, "Lord, sometimes You *are* the wave." Had God not swept in and overtaken him, as a wave would a small child?

"I thank You for being the Wave. I thank You for being my Dad. I thank you for saving me. I thank you for another chance at life." Unashamedly, by this point, he was weeping. "I thank you for stopping me that night, and I thank you for my precious wife."

Dropping to his knees, arms still extended, offering all he was, Mike worshiped his God.

They spent the entire week at the beach, much of it hidden away in their room. Finally, on Saturday morning they returned home. Mike had swapped his notice for a week of vacation time, and the sheriff was happy to have him stay on. Since he would have to be at work on Monday, they wanted to have the weekend at home together to get her settled back in.

Though she would never have mentioned it, Robin's trepidation over going to church on Sunday was causing stomach upset. Literally, she was so sick to her stomach on Saturday night that she had to skip dinner. Mike's concern for her was sweet, and he offered to eat her meal in the hopes it would make her feel better to see him eat well. With his attempt at humor, immediately she felt less threatened. She knew he was truly worried about her and was trying to make her laugh to get her mind off the impending day. It would be difficult, no doubt, but he loved her and would be with her. Robin knew Mike would put a stop to anyone or anything that ever tried to hurt her, and greater still, God had assured her He would keep her safe.

Sunday morning, Robin found herself trembling in anticipation of what was ahead, so on the way to the church, she asked, "Can we go in last?"

Aware of how apprehensive she must be, Mike had been praying for her since before sunup. While she slept, he slipped out of bed, went into the living room, knelt and prayed. He knew it was fear upsetting her stomach the night before, so he had tried to keep her mind off the day to come and did his best to make her laugh and keep the atmosphere light. Also, he knew she shouldn't be as worried as she was, and though he wanted to tell her what he had done to end the lies and misconceptions about what happened between them that final night, he feared it would make her even more anxious and self-conscious if she did know. Before the day was out, he would tell her, but first his hope was that she would receive a much warmer reception than she expected. He had talked to Tim during the week, so Tim knew Robin would be with him. There was one thing he was sure of and that was Tim's heart. He would make it a priority that Robin felt welcomed and loved just as when he returned from prison.

When Robin asked if they could go in last, it broke his heart for her that she felt the need to sneak in unnoticed, but he would do whatever made her feel most comfortable.

"Sweetest bride," he said softly, "we can do anything in the whole wide world you want. As a matter of fact, we can park and make out until everyone goes into the church."

Giggling nervously, she asked, "Make out in the church parking lot?"

Mischievously, he reminded her, "Won't be the first time."

"We kissed maybe, but I don't think you could call it making out."

"Let's go for making out this time."

"The Lord is hearing you right now," she teased.

"I know, and He knows I'm completely serious, and I have to believe He's okay with it."

Before she knew it, as Mike had kept her mind occupied with naughtiness for most of the drive, they were pulling into the parking lot of the church. Once parked, when Robin looked around, she found several people were staring at them already. With eyes filled with tears, she turned to look at Mike and said, "I don't think I can do this."

Incredibly anxious, she could barely breathe. Someone, a man she didn't recognize, was walking toward the truck. By his age and build, she presumed him to be Tim, since he was exactly as Mike had described him: short and stocky with light'ish brown hair. As he drew nearer, settling her nerves considerably, Robin found he was smiling broadly, excited to see them both.

Mike took Robin's hand and reminded her, "Baby, I've got this." Pointing up, he added, "He's got this. Trust us."

She only nodded, reached for the door handle, and stepped from the truck, trusting her husband and trusting God.

From that moment until she reached her seat, one person after another came up to her welcoming her home. Many said how much they had missed her or how they had been praying for her. Some seemed to feel awkward, but others were simply happy to see her. It wasn't at all what she expected. *Oh, me of little faith*, she thought.

During the early part of the service, while they were singing, she looked up at Mike. With his right hand he was holding hers, and his left was raised high up toward the heavens. His eyes were closed and large tears rolled down his face. She felt his gratitude and love pouring out as he worshiped just as he had beside the ocean. In seeing such a sight, she was reminded that this wasn't the man she knew before. He was a godly man and would, from that point forward, be a godly husband, and she praised God along with him that he was hers.

Robin's hand held to his tightly and Mike was reminded of the countless hours of prayer offered in the room where they now stood, at the feet of the One he currently praised. How many times had he pleaded with the Lord for her happiness? All the while, He knew she would someday stand beside him in that very same room again. Singing and praising, Mike found God's grace to be more overwhelming in that moment than even at the beach. He was given a second chance he didn't deserve, but isn't that what the grace of God is all about? His love and mercy shown to an undeserving world. As much as he would like to believe he could somehow be the perfect husband going forward, Mike knew better, but he also knew that through the same grace God offered, He would make him to be what she needed.

After the service as Mike was speaking with Miss Allen, Tim took that opportunity to speak with Robin privately. Handing her a piece of paper, he said, "I think you'll want to read this."

Unfolding the paper, she saw that it was a newspaper article. There was a photo of Mike and beside it read: In His Own Words. She scanned the article briefly and realized it was his admission of guilt. Unable to read it in a room full of people, she folded it and quickly tucked it away.

"It was on the front page. Everyone has seen it by now."

"I can't believe he did this," Robin stammered.

"I don't think there's anything he wouldn't do for you, Robin."

She looked at Tim, truly comprehending how much he cared for Mike.

"I believe that, too. Does he know you're giving me this?"

"Not yet, but I'll tell him."

"When did he do this?"

"Right after you left the last time."

Robin scanned the room looking for Mike and found he was still talking with Miss Allen, who had him cornered and was likely recruiting him for whatever event was next at the church. The sight made her grin.

When she turned back to Tim, she told him, "I'm so glad you've been here for him. Thank you for being his friend when he needed one most."

"I'll always be here for him, for you, too."

Mike was walking toward them, so before he was in hearing distance, she wanted Tim to know. "I love him, and I forgive him."

"I can see that, and I can honestly say, I've never seen a man love a woman more."

When Mike came to stand by her, Robin teased, "Are you already jockeying for the caramel apple table?"

Heaving, he grabbed for his stomach, feigning nausea. "Not funny."

The next morning, Robin opened her Bible to the place where she had tucked the newspaper article. Mike was gone to work already, and it was her first moment alone to read his words. She mentioned the article, and Mike asked that she wait until he left before reading it. He seemed self-conscious about her reading it while he was home.

With the page in hand, she looked intently at the photo of Mike, noting the maturity in his eyes. For as long as she had known him, there was a sparkle of mischief in them. In this photo, however, she found wisdom, something gained only through years of walking with God and by experiencing the suffering of loss.

> In His Own Words
>
> I've recently discovered what an injustice has happened in this town. For a town that knows the secrets and flaws of most every person, you have been blind or unwilling to see mine. No wonder you accepted me back after prison with such open arms. As much as I appreciate that, to know it's at the cost of my wife's reputation is something I can't allow to continue. She was an innocent victim, and I want each and every one of you to know that.
>
> Not long after the death of our son, I began drinking. Even prior to that, I was having tremendous problems adjusting after coming home from the Gulf. I was volatile and agitated already, until

eventually, combined with the effects of the alcohol, I became abusive toward my wife. Because she loved me and valued our marriage, she told no one. Over the course of that final year, I hit her dozens of times, leaving her bruised and battered; still she remained silent.

That final night I nearly killed her. What she did was in self-defense, no matter what she thinks, no matter the guilt she has expressed over it. That's the kind of gentle and loving woman she is, one who feels remorse over shooting a man who tried killing her. Though what happened is still lost in a haze of drunken memories, I saw photos of what I did to her. Her nose and ribs were broken, her shoulder dislocated. After the damage I caused, and Lord only knows what more I may have been capable of, only He saved her that night.

Knowing me now, I hope you can believe that I'm a changed man. None of the chaotic thoughts or alcohol-induced rages threatens me or anyone around me. Because of that certainty, I'm able to be open and honest about what happened. I can only imagine how some of you will feel about me after this admission, but defending Robin's character is much more important to me than my own reputation.

Now, discovering how she was treated after I was sent to prison devastates and disappoints me. How could the victim be treated as the criminal? How could a town that knows so much keep so silent on the matter? The police knew; everyone involved in the legal process knew. How then was this kept such a secret?

Now, I want you to get a glimpse of the woman who held me while we waited for an ambulance. In our final moments together, she led me to know the Lord Jesus, assuring me He would forgive me for all that I had done. How is that possible to have such love and compassion for the man who had just beaten you so severely you could hardly open your eyes to see?

The star – that's what someone called me. I was never a star, shooting or falling. I was just a man who made a mess of his life and his marriage, a man who lost everything that ever mattered to him. Now, I'm a man totally devoted to Jesus Christ. I depend on Him daily to help me walk out this life alone, without the woman I love. To Him I'm thankful for the brief, recent time of healing that she and I have come to know, and I've never felt more humbled or undeserving.

So now you know, and I ask if she comes back to town to visit our son's grave or even to see me, that you treat her with all the respect and honor she deserves. She's a godly woman with the highest character. For those of you who were too busy looking at me and never got to know her, you've missed out on the greatest person to have ever touched my life.

Robin sat, stunned by Mike's words. The fact that he had so honestly and openly told the details of their last year together was shocking and even a bit uncomfortable. Looking back on the day before at church, she more easily understood her reception. All those years ago, it wasn't as if she felt condemned by her church family. Many called and tried to see her in the aftermath of what happened. It was at her refusal they were turned away, but still, she had erroneously come to believe everyone hated her, so going to church had been just as terrifying as if she were walking back into the bakery.

She sighed heavily and glanced at the article again. Some of what he said was untrue, even though it was what he genuinely believed. Her secrecy about the abuse, from his viewpoint, was something much nobler than her true motive. In the time to come, when they were settled in and beyond the point of the honeymoon phase, assuming that ever ended, she would share with him her determination that it was pride, rather, that kept her silent. Until that time she would find joy in the things he said about her and find comfort in the fact that that night, God not only saved her, but saved them both.

20

Early afternoon, Robin was in the kitchen cleaning up the lunch dishes. Mike had come home to eat as he usually did. They were easily sliding into a comfortable groove together. It was better than anything they had known before. Even in the early stages of young love, it wasn't like it was now. The transformation was easy to understand. This was the first time that the Lord Jesus lived in the midst of them, a stark contrast to their former life.

They had been home from the beach for just over two weeks, and each day she found something to fill her time. Having been gone so long, and with had a man in charge of the house, she found plenty to keep her busy. Eagerly, happily even, she cleaned baseboards and scrubbed floors. Slowly, it was becoming hers again. After so many years away, she had taken back possession of something she thought she never wanted to see again. Amazing how time could change a heart.

After finishing in the kitchen, she folded laundry and did a few other chores, ran to the market, and put groceries away. By late afternoon she ran out of things to keep her occupied. Her mind had been cluttered all day, and she found it difficult to focus on even the most mindless of tasks. Mike even noticed how distracted she seemed during lunch. He was talking to her, but her mind was elsewhere.

She slid a chair out from the table and sat, looking apprehensively at Mikey's door. Since coming home, she had yet to go inside, but over the past few days felt the Lord drawing her in. Paralyzed by fear, Robin sat for a few minutes more and prayed, "Lord, I don't think I can handle what's on the other side of that door."

"My grace is sufficient for you," was what she heard in her heart.

"I love him so much still. Please make sure he knows."

Empowered by a strength not her own, Robin walked to the door and placed her hand on it then rested her head against the wood and sighed. With unexpected and sudden courage, she reached for the knob and turned it. Swinging the door open wide, she stood in the doorway for a few minutes and found it looked exactly as she had left it seven years before. Not one thing was different.

When she was able to lift her right foot, Robin moved it over the threshold of the doorway. Then she lifted the other, and from there it was a conscious and difficult process to walk over to Michael's crib. Once there, she stood looking at the empty mattress and smiled, remembering what her baby looked like when she would find him awake and waiting for her. When he would see her, he would grin, drool running down the corner of his mouth and onto his pajamas. With her eyes closed she touched the mattress, intentionally appreciating that in those memories of him, she was clinging to love. It was something she had done only in talking about him, but this day she was living out her love for him.

Slowly, lost in the sweetness of her memories of her son, Robin turned and walked to the rocking chair. As she sat, she heard the slight squeak that was once so familiar to her. With each movement there was a tiny little squeak – back and forth creating different tones. Adrift in the motion and familiar little melody, she closed her eyes and held out her arms, peacefully rocking her baby in her heart. In her mind she could see his dark blue eyes peeking up at her as she nursed him and could feel his chubby little hand rubbing her chest. Michael was the sweetest gift, and for ten months she was the happiest mommy in the world. Without question she would rather have those ten months with the pain than to never have known such love.

There, sitting quietly in Michael's room, she heard Chris' words that day they knelt together in his cabin. "The Psalmist said, 'The LORD is close to the brokenhearted and saves those who are crushed in spirit.' He was there, Robin. No matter what it felt like, He was there."

As Chris had suggested, she tried again to see God that day so long ago. With all her heart she knew He was there, no matter what her eyes could see. Suddenly, for the first time it occurred to her, that day she was held in the shadow of His wings. That was why she couldn't see Him. God was wrapped around her tightly, just as she had wrapped herself around Michael. He was so close in fact, that she couldn't see Him at all.

"I will take refuge in the shadow of your wings until the disaster has passed." Psalm 57:1

There was something about that revelation that settled the matter entirely. The one place she had remained so stuck, even after such strides in healing over so many other things, Robin was suddenly and unexpectedly released. Beyond her ability to fully comprehend at the moment, she knew it was something that would be transformative.

Mike stood in the doorway watching his wife. The look on Robin's face was tranquil and tender, her arms extended, cradling emptiness. She was rocking his son, and his heart broke at the sight of her empty arms and brought images of lifting a lifeless baby from them.

He moved quietly and knelt before her in the chair and whispered, "Baby, are you all right?"

Her head was resting on the back of the rocker. Without opening her eyes, she smiled and assured him, "Yes. I'm all right."

"Are you rocking our baby?"

"I sure am."

"Should I give you a few more minutes alone?"

Robin raised her head and smiled at Mike as she quoted, "Many are the plans in a person's heart, but it is the Lord's purpose that prevails."

He wasn't exactly sure of what to say. She had been acting strangely for a few days, and now he was getting a bit more concerned.

"Tell me what's bothering you. I want to help you through this." Drawing her hand to his lips, Mike kissed it, whispering, "Please don't pull away from me, not again."

She reached out and touched his cheek. He was devastatingly handsome and hardly seemed to know it, so when her tummy fluttered at how deeply he affected her, she could only blush as a flash of memory of their first night back together came to mind.

"You weren't quite as careful as you thought."

Shaking his head slightly, he was confused even more, so he asked, "What do you mean?"

Robin guided his hand to her stomach. "I'm a few days late."

Mike lowered his head onto her lap and began to cry. He was muttering what seemed to be prayers and then finally she distinctly heard him whisper, "My baby."

"I haven't taken a test," she warned him, "so maybe you shouldn't get your hopes up yet. But if I'm not, we can begin to try."

Clearly excited, Mike scooped her out of the chair and began to twirl her around the room. Holding on to his neck, Robin allowed him all the happiness he deserved. In all the years of her grief, it was easy to lose sight of the fact that he had lost his son, too. All that time she was holding on to Michael's death, Mike was holding on to his love for him. He wanted to share that love with another child, and she withheld that from him. Never again.

The past few days of pondering and waiting for her cycle to begin, a million feelings and emotions bombarded her. Certain that one time without protection couldn't have gotten her pregnant; she refused to believe it at first. But finally, even without a test, she knew. She felt it deep within her. Instinctively, her immediate reaction was one of paralyzing fear, but the verse she quoted was what ultimately brought her peace. The Lord knew His timing. Just as with Michael, the Lord had determined this baby's time to be conceived. His purpose would prevail.

Mike stopped spinning and suggested, "Let's go get a test right now."

"I knew you'd be excited?"

"More than you could ever know. Are you? Are you scared?"

His unease from the previous days rushed back over him, causing him great concern. The one thing she didn't want since the moment of Mikey's death was another baby. He should've been more careful or waited even.

"You said you weren't ready. I'm sorry."

The look of concern on his face reminded her how much he loved her, so she assured him, "I'm not scared, and I only thought I wasn't ready. I'm ready."

She pointed to the doorway. "I want to paint Michael's name there over the door and put wings beside it. And you know the verse that says, '...and they can no longer die; for they are like the angels.' I want to paint that under his name. This will be *their* room."

While she knew Michael wasn't *an* angel, the thought that he was there in heaven with and like the angels was a tremendous comfort to her. He was waiting there for her, and she would see him again someday.

"I think that's a great idea."

He lowered her to the ground and pulled her close, relieved, excited, and humbled.

"I don't deserve this. I don't deserve any of this."

"You do. You deserve all the happiness you're feeling right now. Please believe that." Robin looked at him and insisted, "Mike McGarrett, you're the kindest, gentlest…"

Resting her head on his chest again, her eyes filled with tears, and she could hardly go on. Overcome by happiness and gratitude, it took her a moment to find her voice again. Finally, she finished. "You are the godliest man I know, and I'm so thankful you're mine."

She thought of Chris for a moment. Mike had become so much like him. Since she had been home, she discovered how much Mike had been pouring himself into others. Not only at the church but with at-risk youth, and who knew what else she might discover about him. As his life without her unfolded, she found herself in awe at the level of transformation in him, and she was determined not to be the reason any of those things ceased. Just as he did, she wanted to reach out to others, and so far, her mind was set on his mother, Kathy. Different than they were before, she wanted to live a life outside of just them.

After dinner they drove to the same pharmacy where her birth control pills were purchased. The irony wasn't lost on either of them, yet neither mentioned it. Their new life together would be filled with such moments, ones that served as a reminder of how lives and a marriage without God at its center would inevitably become unbalanced. Filled with excitement, though, all lingering memories faded. All that mattered to either of them was what the test might reveal.

Back at home they discovered they would once again become parents.

21

Robin stood alone on the dock, looking out at the water she used to consider her escape, when the painting that depicted this exact location came to mind. In the gathering room of the inn, hung over the fireplace, Chris' canvas was displayed as if it were some priceless work of art by one of the masters. That was how they saw it anyway, Emma and her. Painted his first week there, it was what he captured after he saw her dive into the water for the first time. In his final days there, he gave it to her, explaining how he could never draw her into the scene. Having pondered the reason over the course of the summer, he determined it was because she never belonged there to begin with. It was Robin's place to run, never her place to be. Chris' words were the first seeds planted that God would use to eventually draw her home.

When she felt the gentle swaying of the dock, Robin turned to find Mike walking her way. He moved up close behind her and he slid his arms around her and rubbed her swollen belly. At six months pregnant, they knew already they were to have a girl. Never before, while standing in that same exact spot grieving and agonizing over what was lost, could she have dared to believe such happiness would exist for her again. It did, though.

They were at the inn for only a few days and, fortunately, it was in the midst of the season of fall colors. Emma and Stan had chosen the time for their wedding precisely for that reason. The main house was in a flurry of activity, as the wedding and reception would be there the following day. Robin had snuck away from the chaos to step back in time and reflect on how far the Lord had actually brought her. There was a verse that followed her to the dock that day. David once asked, "Who am I, O Sovereign Lord, and what is my family, that you have brought me so far?" That was her question to the Lord that day. What a mess she used to be, but finally she was whole and complete.

"Do you think you'd like to come here to live someday?" she asked.

She had never mentioned that Emma planned to leave the inn to her.

"I'll come now if it's what you want."

She knew that to be true. Without doubt he would move heaven and earth to make her happy.

"No, I mean when you retire. Could you see yourself here?"

"As long as I'm with you, I can see myself anywhere. But, yes, I think I can handle a hard life of boating and fishing."

"The winters are tough, though."

"I'll keep you warm."

She smiled and signed and rubbed his hands resting on her stomach. "I'm content where we are for now."

"Me, too."

It was getting late and Mike knew what that meant, so he asked, "What do you think it'll be like with your parents?"

That's the one place of anxiety that still remained in his heart and mind. It was all he had thought about since getting on the plane.

"I think it'll be okay. Are you nervous?" she asked.

Her parents called her the day after reading her letter. Their tone gave away their true feelings, but they said they supported her decision. Since that time, they only called her on her cell phone, and she suspected they did so to ensure they wouldn't accidently reach Mike if they called her at home. She knew it would take time. With her parents due in that evening, neither of them knew what to expect, so understandably, Mike was anxious about being with them for the first time.

"I'm very nervous."

He wasn't as concerned about her mom, rather her dad. Though taller than Bill since he was sixteen, Mike always felt dwarfed in his presence, as he was such a dominating man. Always strong and confident, godly and good, Bill was everything Mike would want in a father. He respected him more than any man he had known until Tim, and the loss of him from Mike's life had left him with a deep longing to restore what they once had.

"Don't be nervous. I'm with you."

"It'll be fine then."

When Mike turned to go, hoping to be there to greet her dad when he arrived, he asked, "Are you coming back up soon?"

"I'll be up in a while."

When he was gone, she walked to Chris' cabin. Relieved that Emma didn't allow anyone to stay there while she was in town, Robin was glad to be able to go in and spend some time there. With Stan's four kids and their families, plus her parents, Mike's mom, and the two of them, the house and many of the cabins were full. She and Mike were staying in her old room. While it crossed her mind to stay in the cabin during the visit, she decided it wouldn't be fitting. Though it was never spoken, she suspected Chris' feelings ran very deep for her. Actually, she was sure of it. He loved her, and while he never did or said one thing to that effect, she knew still; it was evident in the way he looked at her, especially there at the end.

Robin sat in Chris' chair and recalled the many wise things he had said to her, and the way that, no matter what she felt, he always directed her back to Jesus. Chris was sent for her, and the Lord proved His mercy and loving kindness by that very act. Though never suspecting what was coming; help was on the way in the form of a barefoot, selfless school teacher, who, while facing the end of his own life, poured into hers, giving her the chance to begin again. Her greatest desire was to be more like him.

"Lord," she prayed, "I want to reach out and touch lives and direct them to You. As I've been comforted, I desire to comfort others. I want to have a purpose beyond what I know right now. I'm Mike's wife, and soon I'll be a mom again. Those are the greatest purposes. I know that. Still, there's something deep within, a calling of some sort, and I'm not sure that I fully understand it, but I know You have something for me, and Lord, I sure don't want to miss it."

Mike stood at the door, hesitating. Emma had sent him back out to look for Robin, something about a shoe emergency. When Robin was no longer on the dock, he suspected she was at the cabin, since she once told him that was where she prayed most often. Having reached the cabin, however, Mike froze in his tracks when he read the name on the plaque above it, *Chris' Cabin*. It caused an alarming feeling within his chest, and the hair on the back of his neck stood on end. So now, here he stood, paralyzed at the front door, afraid of what he might find on the other side. Would his wife be grieving over her lost friend? Finally, he tapped on the door and cracked it open to find her sitting in a chair beside the fireplace. Awkwardly, he remained outside and said, "Emma needs you, a shoe emergency."

She nodded and smiled. Most everything that day with Emma was an emergency. Pointing to the chair she usually sat in, she told Mike, "That's where Jesus healed me."

Hesitantly, he walked in and over to the chair, and as expected he felt uncomfortable the moment he crossed over the threshold. As he rubbed the woven tapestry fabric, for the first time he voiced his suspicion aloud, "Chris was in love with you."

Without confirming or denying the truth of Mike's statement, Robin assured him, "He never, ever made that known then. Each and every time we talked, he simply listened and then led me back to God. He was kind and compassionate and helped so many people, including me. You can't imagine the hundreds of people at his funeral."

Her statement startled him, heightening his discomfort. "You went to his funeral?"

"Yes, I did."

"I didn't realize you were *that* close."

"I was with him when he died."

There had never been a reason to mention it before, but she could tell by the expression on Mike's face and the tone of his voice that he was disturbed by it; even the veins in his neck began to bulge. This wasn't the moment to discuss it further. He was upset and that upset her, so she suggested, "I better get back up there."

"I'll be up in a while."

She moved to his side and gently rubbed his arm, asking, "Are you okay?"

"I will be." He smiled half-heartedly.

Standing on tip toes, Robin kissed his cheek. "I love you."

"I love you more."

Once alone, Mike knelt in front of the chair and placed his hands on the seat where his wife would have sat, praying, "Thank You for what You did for her right here in this very spot. Thank you for the man you sent, and I'm sorry I've been so jealous of him. It's just that he knew her in such an intimate way, and I have no doubt he loved her. I suppose that's my fault, though. Had I not left her in the world alone, so broken and vulnerable, she would have had no need of him. I did, though. Lord, I give these feelings to You, knowing You'll take them away. I don't ever doubt her or her feelings for me, but I'm still jealous. I'm so afraid she loved him, too."

Mike reached the back steps of the main house just as it was getting dark out. When he opened the screen door to the porch, he found Robin's dad sitting there in a wicker chair, glaring at him. Approaching him hesitantly, Mike stuck out his hand, saying, "Mr. Jacobs."

Bill stood and took two steps forward. He had dreaded this trip, and even more he dreaded seeing Mike. After what happened Bill swore he would kill him if he ever got the chance, but after reading Mike's letters, and later the article Robin sent, Bill's stony heart began to slowly soften toward him, and he came to regret how he had missed what should have been obvious. Now was an opportunity to somehow build a bridge back toward healing their relationship.

"You could've come to me, son. I would've gotten you some help."

Bill reached for Mike, grabbed his shoulder, and pulled him nearer, embracing him as if he were his own boy. "I would have done anything to have helped you. I'm sorry I missed it."

Standing in that embrace, tears streamed down Mike's cheeks, and he felt the truest sense of freedom he had known in many years. Because he had never had much of a dad in the picture, Bill had always been the closest thing he had known.

"I'd like to think if I had it all to do over again, I would come to you, but I was so confused, and I didn't understand what was happening to me. I'm so sorry. Sorry for everything I did and didn't do."

They spent nearly an hour together talking and sorting through the past few years. For Mike it was one of the final steps he needed to take in the healing process. The things he had done to this man's daughter required confession, and he desperately needed to ask for his forgiveness. Soon, he would have his own little girl, and even with her yet to be born, the thought of any man hurting her the way he had hurt Robin was something that could easily send him into a mind-bending rage. Again, from Bill this time, forgiveness and grace was extended to him, demonstrating God's love in a way he hoped he would always be able to exhibit to others. If there was ever a man whose life could be modeled, it was his father-in-law's.

Later, sitting around the table, Robin scanned the large crowd. Her soon-to-be brother and sisters were all there, her parents plus Emma and Stan, Tommy and Becky, herself, Mike and Kathy; the room was full and lively. How different from exactly one year before when there was only Emma and herself. How much more joy was in their lives! Life was so entirely different, entirely blissful, that it was a testament to the great things God had in mind to do.

Emma was beaming with happiness, a miracle within itself. Becky and Tommy were engaged to be engaged. Situations that had little hope of being just a year before suddenly were. At that thought something began to stir in Robin's spirit, a reminder from the Lord that she had touched their lives. He had used her, even if in the tiniest way, to help them see Him. There was purpose for her in their journeys. Back at home, Robin had been ministering to Kathy and to a youth girl Tim had directed her way.

Had she not just prayed in Chris' Cabin for purpose and to help others? There was already purpose for her. God was gracious enough to open her eyes to understand that she was doing exactly what He had planned for her in that season. As was the mystery of Him, she had no way of knowing what it would look like in the future, but she trusted Him entirely and without fear. For the time being, though, she would simply do what He placed before her.

Earlier on the dock, she thought back to something Chris said on more than one occasion. He reminded her they lived in a fallen world. And sitting around her at that very moment was a group of people who each lived in their own distinct fallen world and experienced pain in differing degrees. Just as each would eventually stand before God as individuals, so, too, the life they had lived was just as individual, uniquely carved out for them. From her own standpoint, she lived in a world where her baby was taken much too early and where the man she loved succumbed to mental illness and alcohol and became abusive. Even prior to those tragedies, she was a young woman, a perfect example of all of fallen humanity, who desperately sought human love to the exclusion of God's love. That was the true basis of her fallen world, one in which she thought she could live and move and breathe without Him.

Mike was hardly even given a chance with a father who abused the entire family, then, and maybe even worse in the long run, left the family defenseless. It's a fallen world indeed when the words, "Our Father who art in heaven," causes you to cringe because it contains the word "Father," a word synonymous with pain and fear. Mike recently shared that with her while talking about the arrival of their new baby. All those years he attended

Unmending the Veil

church with her, he despised the word *father*. In hindsight he said it was what kept him from God in the first place. Once he came to know his heavenly Father, the word became a comfort, something sweet to his ears and to his heart.

Chris' fallen world consisted of losing his father at such a young age then losing his mother to alcohol soon after. He was left with no parents to care for him. As if that beginning were not harsh enough, his end came much too soon and as the result of some aggressive mutation of cancer cells.

Kathy's need for human love tore her from the arms of her children, sending her off in a never-ending pursuit of fallen, human love. Still, even to that very day she reached for what would never satisfy the true longing of her soul.

Becky's need was much the same. The giving of herself to a young man who had no intention of loving her or marrying her was proof that she, too, sought after a love that left her empty. Tommy wouldn't receive a particular gift because of it.

There was Emma. Oh, how she hobbled in her own fallen world for more than three decades, longing for what she lost, then longing even more for what she gave away. Closing herself away in a world where shame and self-loathing bound and gagged her, she forfeited the grace that could have been hers.

Robin's parents not only experienced infertility, but along with the sweetness of an adopted baby girl, they were forced to carry the burden of the secret of her birth, stripping them of the light and joy that could have been theirs had the truth been told.

While each of them inhabited individual worlds of pain and suffering, resulting from consequences of personal choices, their own and those of others, it was the very same Lord who, in His unfathomable mercy stepped into each individual world with the offer of His grace. One Lord, yet to each He offered different elements of His character based on individual need in the initial wooing and pursuing of each of them. To Mike and Chris, they each needed the Father. With that position solidified in their hearts, He then journeyed with them, demonstrating new layers and levels of His nature, cultivating them into sound and godly men.

To her, He was first and clearly most essential in the beginning her Wonderful Counselor, as her need of healing and restoration prohibited further growth. Then eventually and most importantly, after a lifetime of pretending to follow Him, Jesus became her First Love and her God. It was that layer upon layer of intimate knowledge of Him that would ensure she could never again be shaken. He held her firmly. She was His.

For Emma and Becky, He showed Himself as the Lord who hears and forgives, the One who replenishes that which is lost by filling that place of longing with His Spirit and love.

It wasn't lost on her. Almighty God was to each what they needed. As their worlds were unique and individual, He was just as much unique and individual in His dealings with them. In and for all of them, His timing was precise, whether patient or expedient. His touch was as needed, ranging from tender to heavy.

The commonality for all of them in the beginning was that, though He chose to rend the veil and offer direct access to Himself, they each set out on a course to mend it right back. In their pain, shame, and fear, rather than looking toward Him, the One who heals and restores, they began to stitch and mend that veil, or in some cases install a zipper to close Him out. Having pondered for some time as to why, Robin came to the conclusion, at least in her own situation, she wanted to try to maintain some kind of control in a world out of control. Ultimately, she wanted to be her own god, not trusting Him to be, which in turn led to utter devastation and self-imposed separation from the Source of Life Himself. Was that not likely the case for them all, the desire to control and direct their own destiny? As if that were at all possible. Praise God for unraveling the stitches in each and every person sitting around that festive table.

At bedtime Robin and Mike were alone in their room. Since they spoke in the cabin, she was concerned for him and about how he was feeling but knew it was something he needed to work out with the Lord. As much as she hated that it bothered him about Chris, she could never regret Chris' friendship. He was her lifeline back to God.

All evening she had felt conviction in her spirit on a particular matter, so she sat beside Mike on the bed and said, "I need to tell you something." When he nodded, she continued, "Soon after I met Chris, he asked me to dinner, and I said yes. I suppose you could call it nothing less than a date. I'm sorry."

Mike stood and paced for a moment, and her first inclination was to fear his former fits of jealousy. Back and forth he moved, not saying a word. Clearly, he was hurt, maybe even a little angry, but there was no risk of the old Mike resurfacing. She could tell by the look on his face; it was different, his expression more hurt than enraged. Quietly she sat, waiting for some reply. Tempted to try to explain further, she decided instead to let her words sink in and allow him to form whatever questions he might have.

Finally, he stood before her, looked her in the eye, and demanded, "Did you love him as much as he loved you?"

He always had a sense there was more between them. Not as if he had a right to be angry about it, but after seeing how Chris looked at her, Mike knew there was something significant there. In truth, he wished she wouldn't have felt compelled to tell him about the date. He didn't want to know.

"Before the end of the date, I knew my heart was still so full of you that I could never love another man that way." Reaching for Mike's hand, she added, "I never will."

He sat back down on the bed beside her. Elbows resting on his knees, he admitted his true feelings. "I hate that he knew you so much better than I did. Somehow, your relationship with him seems very intimate."

She almost disputed that fact but then considered Chris' remarkable insight into her.

"You know me better now than he ever did." She moved her fingers to stroke the hair above his ear. "I did love him, but it was like family love. Will you believe that?"

"Yes. I know you would never lie to me." How could he look into her eyes and not believe it?

"That's why I had to tell you. We were still married then, so I ask you to forgive me for going."

"At that point, I had no claim on you."

"Yes, you did. You always did."

Mike slid his arm around Robin's shoulder and pulled her to him. With his other hand he scooped her legs up, dragged her into his lap, and buried his face in the curve of her neck, feeling a great sense of relief at hearing her feelings for Chris weren't what he feared they might be.

Robin was snuggled against him, relieved to have told him about the date. Since she had moved home, it crossed her mind several times. Tempted to tell him before, she had decided it was better left unsaid, but once she realized how jealous he was of Chris, she knew it had become a matter of obedience on her part.

"Something he asked me once was why I never cried when I talked about you. I bawled over Michael but not over you. At the time I couldn't figure it out for the life of me. It wasn't until recently that I began to understand."

"Why?"

"After I came here, I thought that if I cried over you, it would somehow give you power over me still. So I bottled everything up and pushed that entire part of my life into the darkness. Now, I realize you can have all the power you want over me, because I trust what you'll do with it. I trust you completely."

He hugged her to him so tightly he felt her sigh, and he promised, "I'll always love you as God loves me. I'll always give myself for you. Looking back, I know my focus was on me; no matter what you say, it was. That's not the husband I want to be from now on. You are second only to Him but always before me."

"I believe that."

She did. Since being back at home, they had the best marriage of anyone she knew. It wasn't the "perfect" pretense marriage, rather a solid, godly marriage, one built upon the foundation of God and supported by the understanding of how precious and rare it was. While as comfortable together as they had been since the early years, they had a new appreciation for one another that can only come by losing and finding again.

Once settled into bed, Mike curled himself around Robin. She was lying with her back to him, and he was gently rubbing his baby girl. Different than when he was with her before, this time he felt as if he belonged. Wherever she was he belonged.

He told her, "Before, when I was here with you, I felt like a visitor. I hated that I wasn't part of your life. I missed so much."

Robin recalled that he mentioned something about being a visitor while still delirious with fever, and now his explanation gave her clearer insight.

"From now on, you'll be a part of every aspect of it," she assured him.

"I know." Kissing her ear, he offered, "I'm sorry I've been so jealous of him. I promise you, I'm working on that. I guess it'll just take time. Believe me, I know how much he helped you, and I'm so thankful he did."

"I've tried to put myself in your position. In some ways I've been jealous of Tim and the role he played in your life. He was there for you when I wasn't. You have a history with him that you don't have with me. Sounds silly, I know."

"No, not at all. That's what I feel, too. It's like, we've always been a part of each other's history, but now there's this gap there."

"I know there's a gap, but just look at what God did inside both of us during that time. He knew He could never be first in either of our lives as long as we put each other first. It's something I've come to terms with. He had to take me away from you in order to allow me to see Him. This may sound crazy, but I don't regret that."

"I don't either." How could he regret a journey that made him the new man he had become?

"We just have to make sure there's never another gap."

"You can *know* that will never happen. I'll never allow anything to come between us again," he promised her.

Mike was silent for a moment, thinking of something else that had been bothering him. The name she picked for the baby was something he vetoed immediately out of jealousy.

"I've been giving it some thought, and I like Christa Grace after all."

"Are you sure?"

Never would she have pressured him into the name. It was important that he love whatever name they picked for their little girl. Up until that day she hadn't understood the depth of his jealousy of Chris, suspected maybe, but not to the extent he demonstrated earlier. Had she known, she never would have suggested Christa.

"I'm certain."

Mike continued rubbing her stomach. It usually helped to put her to sleep. The more he thought about the name, the more he liked it. Christa would remind him of Christ rather than Chris, and Grace would remind him of his new life with his family. Only by God's grace was it even possible.

As Robin began drifting in and out of sleep herself, she listened to Mike's steady breathing. His long frame was wrapped around her; it was how he slept every night, and it gave her the greatest sense of security and comfort. Quite simply, she was content. Contemplating her earliest girlish expectations of some happily-ever-after life, Robin had come to learn, that was a notion of fairy tales, not real life. What the Lord gives is contentment. Even when the world around is difficult or when friends die or illness comes, contentment is still a possibility. A lump formed in her throat at such a thought, but even if Mike were to be killed on the job or her baby girl taken in her sleep, God would still bring peace in spite of the pain.

Looking back, Robin understood that the path to contentment and peace was revealed as a result of unmending the veil. Once every barrier in her heart intended to keep God away was removed, she could see and know and be in His presence as He died to achieve. And in His presence, it was He who began the process of stitching. As if mending by hand, He healed her broken heart and wounded spirit, weaving within her the promise of joy and contentment that could never be stolen away by circumstance. She could never be shaken. In a world where no self-imposed veil remained, a woman could indeed live contentedly-ever-after.

Note from the Author:

Robin thinks, "If there was a possibility of being near to God, it was here."

In the early chapters we discovered Robin had attended church all of her life – still does as the story goes. Sadly, many, if not most Christian women feel similarly. That was exactly how I spent the early years of my Christian walk – or shall I call it my Christian stumble? There seemed to be a distance, a gulf between God and me that I couldn't seem to bridge. Maybe you feel the same. You may work and serve, all in the hopes of drawing nearer, yet you still feel far from Him, at least in your heart.

Walking with Jesus in a close and intimate relationship is what He desires for each and every believer. His presence is our Promised Land here on earth. I invite you to visit www.lisaheatonbooks.com to download the free companion study material to go along with the novel. On the Home Page look for UtV Study Material. The sole purpose of the study is to help lead you into a more intimate relationship with Jesus and learn to love Him with all your heart, soul, and mind.

About the Author

Lisa was born and raised in Nashville, TN and still lives nearby with her husband, Kelly, and their teenage son, Zack. She has one older son, Adam, currently living in South Carolina.

As an author and speaker, her sole passion is to lead believers into a closer relationship with Jesus. Too many in the church settle for less than what Jesus died to attain for them, so through her discipleship teaching and writing, she explains the simplicity of the Christian life: Begin with falling in love with Jesus, and everything else will fall into place. Describing herself as a former "hot-mess," Lisa knows firsthand the powerful effect Christ can have on a life.

Lisa has written ministry material for new believers used by Lifeway, the Tennessee Women's Prison Ministry, and daily devotional material for children.

Having written fiction as a hobby for many years, it wasn't until friends encouraged her to write a companion study to go along with *Unmending the Veil* that she became serious about pursuing publishing, realizing the impact fiction can have when combined with ongoing discipleship.

Watch for other titles by Lisa:
On 4/19 and *Beyond 4/20,* and soon to come, *Deceiver.*

Made in the USA
Middletown, DE
11 May 2015